SACRIFICES

A Novel Of The Vietnam War

by

James Nathan Post

American Honor Books
Albuquerque NM

SACRIFICES

No character or organization in this book is intended to represent any real person or group, and no event described herein is intended to represent any particular real-live incident. Even so, I have elected to use the name "The 17th Assault Helicopter Company" which was for a short time the actual designation of the unit with which I served. This book is dedicated to my comrades in arms, and to the memory of my friend, George S. Cline.

James Nathan Post
17 MAR 85

ONE

How ironic it seemed years later that Kevin Harrey had met Eddie Padilla and Roger Stanton so long ago, and the three of them had never been together again, even though the war, the Vietnam war — and other things they held in common — had interwoven their lives so deeply.

It was in June, 1964, they met. Kevin had run away from his father's home in east Texas and joined the Army two years before, when he was seventeen. He was enjoying his tour of duty as an instructor at the basic training camp at Fort Bliss, in El Paso. The conflict in Vietnam was looking more and more like a war, but he was needed where he was, and could look forward to staying there, war or none. The pay was enough, the climate was great, and there was plenty of amusement across the border in Juarez, Mexico. And there was Carlie.

Eddie and Roger were a couple of years younger, and had just graduated from high school in Las Cruces, New Mexico, about forty miles north of the border. They had grown up together, and had come to the wicked city of Juazoo to officially terminate Eddie's virginity before sending him off to college.

"Jesus Blazing Christ, it's hot," swore Roger Stanton. "Get me to a waterhole." With Eddie at his heel, the big blond youth strode eagerly down the brick-paved slope of the Santa Fe bridge and plunged into the seething and sweating mass of hawkers and tourists on *16 de Septiembre* street in Juarez.

"Me too," agreed Eddie, stuffing his hands into his pockets and trying to appear nonchalant as he skipped and double-stepped on short fat legs to keep up with the long-limbed strides of his friend. Almost a foot shorter than Roger, Eddie was a study in full curves. Beneath an unruly shock of coarse black hair, his dark-olive moon face was dominated by a great hooked Apache nose. His narrow shoulders sloped, and his body flared mid-torso to pear-shape, with a little paunch of late-adolescent fat and a pair of comically-rolling oversize buttocks.

The garish tangle of neon lights flashed crazily, and from the broken windows of a second story dancehall blared the giddy thump and bleat of the Mexican approximation of rock-and-roll music. Roger stuck out his barrel chest and inhaled with gusto, as though the heady reek of sweat, garbage, smoke, booze, and overheated cooking grease were a fresh sea breeze. Roger was a large and unusually strong young man, large not like an athlete, but like a farm boy, with a great solid belly and thick forearms with broad spatulate hands. He stood well over six feet in his socks, and with his cant-heeled riding boots on, the top of his battered straw cowboy hat reached almost seven. Though the hawkers began to press in immediately, Roger easily plowed through them, brushing them aside like stalks of corn.

Clanging and clattering along the street beside them, an electric trolley cruised ponderously amid a pack of dodging cars. On every corner lines of decrepit taxis waited impatiently, their drivers tugging at the sleeves of passers-by, promising delights of all descriptions just a dollar's ride away. The street was lined with shops and bars, windows filled with furniture, leather goods, glass, dentists' sample bridgework done on plaster model teeth, serapes, and blankets. On each block there were two or three kiosk booths, display boxes six feet wide and six feet tall, each painted in bright colors, and all offering the same peculiarly consistent stock: Bowie knives with handles of eagles' heads carved in cowhorn, rings with stones of tiger's eye, onyx, and imitation sapphire, rings cast with the heads of bulls, lions, and devils, switchblade knives with plastic dragons on the handles, in sizes from an inch to a foot long, Indian jewelry made of stamped-out conchos and blue plastic turquoise, tooled leather wallets (the Mayan calendar and "Mexico"), imitation Zippo lighters sporting skulls with red-jewel eyes, plaster savings banks in the shape of pigs and bulls, in sizes up to three feet long, castanets, maracas, and toss-spool yo-yo's, packs of Genuine

Horseshit Cigarettes (they weren't, but might as well have been), feelthy peectures, anemone-glansed French ticklers, and the ubiquitous straw sombreros.

"Hey, come on in here, cowboy," exhorted one oily street hustler scuttling along beside them. "I got it what you want, the best pussy you ever saw for that big pistola you got."

Roger stopped short and pointed a finger at him. "For your information, Pedro, it's a field piece. And the only thing you might have in there it wants is your Mama."

The scuttler seemed delighted to have met a man of such discrimination. "*Si, andale!* She's right inside. Come on."

"I only want her if she's a virgin. If she ain't a virgin, you can fuck her yourself."

"*Si, seguro!* Of course she's a virgin. What you think my mother is some kind of *pinche* old whore? Come on in!"

Roger laughed deep-throated, belly-braying, and he took off his hat and slapped his thigh with it. He ran a hand over the blond bristle of his burrhead haircut, sending a spray of sweat droplets splattering. "Hey, Eddie, what you say we go on in and check out this joint. I want to buy this guy's mother a drink."

"Sure, what you gonna say, *Nalgon*," agreed the eager slick. "Come on in."

Eddie stopped short, insulted. He started to let it pass, then turned on the man and spat words. "Hey, up your ass, *pendejo*. Let's find another place, OK."

"It's all right," laughed Roger, taking his arm. "He's a greasy little jerk with no class. Give him a break."

"*Si,* no hard feelings, OK? It was just *como primos*, eh cousin? Come on, Primo, I fix you up with a very special girl, show you something you never seen before. Come on in."

Inside, upstairs, up a narrow stairwell they climbed to a dark attic-like room. A slink with a flashlight checked them over, took a dollar cover charge from each. The place was almost bare, and was furnished with small wooden tables and metal folding chairs. A few weak bulbs glowed in paper hanging lanterns in faded colors, and a spotlight made from a bulb and a tin can sent fuzzy blobs of light swirling around the room from a twirling mirror ball. It was early in the evening, about nine o'clock, and the place was still almost empty. On the rough board floor, a few couples danced in a rock frenzy to the music of a bored-looking four-piece band. One couple oblivious to the compelling cadence of the drums stood clutching and grinding at each other.

Along the back wall was an enclosed double row of bench booths. It had once been painted in nautical motif, and a ghostly faded neon sign announced it as "The U-Boat". It seemed about the same size as an old sub, a long narrow low-ceilinged tunnel with close-packed booths. The two boys chose one of several empty booths, plopped onto the lumpy and ragged seats. Roger leaned back and sighed with a big grin. "Now ain't this the life?" he asked. A waiter wearing a sweat-stained guayabera shirt appeared immediately to press them for their order.

"What does it cost to get drunk in this joint?" asked Roger.

"Well drinks fifty cents, cocktails one dollar, tequila shots special twenty-five cents."

"Hey, hey, all right! Bring me four shots of that Mexican monster piss. How about you, Eddie?"

"Yeah, me too. Might as well get a head start."

As they waited for the drinks, Eddie slouched in his chair, still piqued by the street hustler's glib use of the nickname he hated. *"Nalgon,"* he bitterly muttered. The Big-Buns. It was a name his family used on him with bantering affection, and he had to conceal his dislike of it, knowing his older brothers and sisters would tease him unmercifully if they saw it irritated him. In school he had suffered extended feuds with other students who had in his earshot used the gringo equivalent, Bubble-butt.

When the drinks arrived, Roger immediately dusted salt onto the back of his hand, licked it, picked up all four shots as fast as he could, and tossed each down in a single gulp, banging the glasses loudly on the table. He heaved a great growling sigh of gusto, and popped two chunks of lime into his mouth. Taking a five from a crumpled wad of bills he carried in the snap-pocket of his western shirt, he tossed it in front of the waiter, who was still standing beside the table, mouth agape. "Four more," he boomed, grinning at the shadowed faces of the other drinkers who peered at him from across the murky room.

"Not me," said Eddie, holding up his hands and indicating the three still-full shots in front of him. "I know better than to try to keep up with this son of a bitch."

As soon as the waiter left the table, two girls detached themselves from the shadows and began to walk insolently toward the table. Both were overweight, and even in the dim light their features appeared coarse beneath layers of pancake makeup, gaudy eyeshadow, and candy-red lipstick. When they bent over the table to display their tightly-bound and uplifted breasts bulging from low necklines, Eddie could see a trickle of sweat running between the nearest pair of quivering globes. Though he was excited by the smell of their over-perfumed and under-washed bodies, he was not yet drunk enough to abandon his virginal inhibitions before these women who made themselves so mockingly available.

"How you like to buy us a drink, Cowboy?" purred one. "Maybe we show you a good time, OK?"

The other tried to insinuate herself onto Eddie's lap, and he balked. "Hey, we just want to have a couple of drinks, OK?"

"*Aie, que chulito*, how cute," giggled the girl.

Laughing heartily, Roger reached around behind the legs of the girl nearest him to draw her closer. He slipped his hand between her calves and tried to reach up under her tight skirt. Startled, she jumped, then laughed.

"*Eeehola, salvajon!*" She swatted playfully at his hand. "Maybe you like to get some of that, anh?"

"How about it, Ed? I'm horny as a ten-peckered toad, and there's no time like the present to take care of that big first time of yours. What you say we jump these two little cows?"

Eddie tossed down his third shot, trying to look bored, and trying not to look at the impudent lumps of the big dark nipples of the girl who was rubbing herself against him. "Hey, it's a little early, you know. I'd kind of like to stretch out the anticipation a bit, see a couple of shows, maybe."

"Whatever you say, Ace. Sorry, *muchachas*, but we need a little more time to get primed. Come back in half an hour — if we're still here, I'll buy the boy a drink and fuck both of you." He handed the girl nearest him a dollar bill, and dismissed her with a meaty-handed squeeze of her ass. "Here, go buy you and your partner a Shirley Temple. Hey, Pedro, where the hell are my drinks?"

Eddie took a look around the little saloon. In the murky light from two bulbs with fly-specked shades, he could see the grimy accumulation of filth on the floor, and he tried to ignore the acrid smell of sweat, vomit, and stale butts. "Yeah, you bet, this is the life," he said, trying to work up a convincingly enthusiastic smile.

"Well, it's better than sitting in old Burwood's history class, isn't it?"

"I can't argue with that."

At the opposite end of the narrow chamber, a couple sat talking quietly in a corner booth, and Eddie found himself watching them absently. Roger had begun to tell a rambling joke about a whorehouse — Eddie had heard it — and the tequila was beginning to run Roger's words together. Eddie giggled, uncertain if the incoherence was due to his own drunken ear or Roger's drunken tongue. If the couple saw Eddie, they gave no indication, and he slumped in the booth and watched them drowsily, nodding when Roger interrupted his joke to laugh.

She appeared to be about the same age as the two friends, and the young man with her could have been a year or two older. He might have been a college student, except that his hair was cut too short on the sides, and his shoes were too well shined. He wore a pair of new slacks, and a short-sleeved solid-color shirt with the sleeves rolled up an inch. He smoked Camel cigarettes, which he ignited with a Zippo he could snap open with two fingers and the thumb of one hand. He was telling his date some apparently adventurous tale, animated with graphic gestures which showed off his slender and well-conditioned body.

Eddie felt a twinge of distaste for him. He was too smooth, too cocksure, too confident his pretty face — or his fast hands — would get him through. He was pretty, Eddie admitted with mixed envy and contempt. He had soft deep brown eyes, delicate features, and red hair — not carrot or copper, but a dark and earthy Sorrel.

The girl seemed to be his counterpart exactly, as though they had both come in the same cellophane-wrapped box. She was blonde and beautiful, dressed for the Prom in a strapless knee-length number with a little jacket and gloves. She was not large, but voluptuous, with soft curves and full lips. As Eddie watched, she slipped one of her spike-heeled shoes off under the table and lifted up her foot to rub at the arch, exposing half her leg. Though the room was poorly lighted, and the table was some four or five yards away, he was impressed.

"Nice clean kids," he said aloud.

"Anh?" queried Roger, breaking off in mid-run-on. "Oh, yeah, nice clean kids! Haw! Yeah, no shit, nice clean kids, that cracks me up. Haw, haw, haw!" Eddie laughed too, though he couldn't make the slightest connection to whatever it was Roger had been telling him.

They were joined in the narrow tunnel of booths by a party of three college boys, about half blasted. All three were big, and they carried themselves like athletes — one of them wore a sweatshirt with the sleeves torn off, a wet-streaked rag with the just-legible declaration: "Property of EPU Physical Education Department".

They ordered drinks, stumbled laughing to the pisser, and pushed each other around. By the time they were all sitting back at the table sucking their drinks and shooting their shit, Eddie noticed that Roger had stopped talking and was watching them with studied cool from beneath the wide brim of his battered summer straw. A familiar chill gripped him somewhere about the prostate, and he took a long pull from his drink.

"Hey, Rog," he said, "what was that one you were telling me about the whore with a cunt in her armpit?"

Roger laughed and began another rambling joke, making a big show of pretending not to keep a suspicious eye on the three goons in the middle booth. Pretty soon they began to grow bored with each other's tales of locker-room intrigue and freshman pussy, and turned their attention on the young couple sitting quietly in the end booth.

"Say," asked one, pointing a thumb at them, "did you ever actually go out there?"

"Out where?" asked another.

"To little killer kiddie camp. You know, Fort Piss."

His companions looked at the pair and nodded. "I see exactly

11

what you mean. If that boy's not on a weekend pass, I'll eat my shorts."

"Got, dang! Don't it just choke you up to think what it must be like to be a real soldier-boy? Dang my doggies, I just can't imagine."

"Yeah, man, I'd be so tough, I'd just go around kicking ass and fucking pussy everywhere I went."

"Hey, no kidding. I might even get me some of that high-class little blonde pussy. What you bet that's the captain's daughter?"

"Whoo-ee, Dawg! I bet you right. What you suppose he'd think if we was to fuck a little of that stuff, too?"

The young soldier was tense, but was maintaining his cool. His date was less tolerant and began to bristle. She turned to him and said something almost audible, and obviously dripping with sarcasm and contempt.

"What was that?" asked one. "Did she say something to us?"

She turned to them with vitriolic arrogance. "What I said was the only thing you jock-strap gorillas are good for fucking is each other's faces."

There was a moment of astounded silence, then one of the three, the country boy in the football jersey, stood up and moved closer to the end booth. "Sugarlips, you may look like a cherry, but nobody gets a mouth that fast without sucking some dick. So unless your boy friend has serious objections, I think before you leave here tonight, I'm gonna fuck your face."

Eddie sat mesmerized watching the drama build toward violent conclusion, and like the three jocks he had completely forgotten that he was a participant in it. Suddenly a deep rumbling voice roared out from across the table, startling him to leap as though burned. "Hey, Fuckface!" blared Roger Stanton.

The three of them whirled around to stare at him slack-jawed. "Who you talking to?" demanded one of them.

"You all turned around," said Roger with a big shrug. "I guess you must be the Fuckface brothers."

"You're gonna get your ass kicked," growled the hog in the sweatshirt, and moved toward Roger, who slid quickly out of his seat and stood to meet him. As the big farmboy rose to his full height and hefted his barrel chest in a show of overwhelming massiveness, the hog hit him a powerful uppercut just below the ribcage.

"Whoof!" grunted Roger, offended he had been interrupted before completing his John-Wayne-getting-into-fighting-stance routine ("All right, Pilgrim."). "All right, asshole!" he bellowed, and charged. The two crashed against the wall and slid to the floor, swinging and clutching. In the same instant, the redheaded soldier came up out of his seat like a cat and threw a kick at the closest of the other two, a dark slug in a muscle shirt. The girl jumped up to stand in the booth, looking wild-eyed and thrilled.

Eddie still sat with his mouth hanging open, marveling at the soldier's kick. It had come up forward and snapped in sidewise, with the toe curled down impossibly to bury itself about two inches below the swarthy burrhead's navel. He looked surprised and dropped to his knees, his face working like he was trying to inhale and throw up at the same time. The soldier threw a short hook at his head, but was stopped by a long jabbing right from the big country boy. It was a strong punch, flush on the cheek, and knocked the smaller man back staggering.

Reluctantly, but resolutely, Eddie hurled himself into the fray and tried to tackle the big football player. He took punches and elbows to the back and caught a knee in the guts, but he hung on grimly.

The soldier came back at once with a flurry of punches and kicks. The flashing foot came up suddenly to snap the big country boy's head back, and then the fighter came in low, sidewise, with an elbow to the bladder. The blow knocked the big athlete into the booth, where the girl surprisingly beaned him with an ashtray.

The management and the bouncers were on them in force, and they pulled Roger from the hog. Seeing the bouncer's big black police billy, Roger held up his hands and backed off quickly. *"Amigos! Amigos! Nos vamanos andale!* Come on, you guys, let's get the hell out of here."

The soldier grabbed his girl friend around the waist to help her down from the table, and they ducked out quickly. One of the bouncers had Eddie by the arm and neck and was dragging him squawking from the booth. The ball player struggled to his feet with blood running into his eyes, and took a swing at the other bouncer. Roger stuffed a wad of bills into the hand of the manager, grabbed Eddie by the back of his shirt, and followed the young couple out the door. He began to laugh uproariously as they burst onto the street.

"Oh, shit," gasped Eddie, "I'm gonna puke."

"Let's go, we gotta get lost," choked Roger between guffaws.

A sharp whistle hailed them half a block away, and they looked up to see the blonde waving at them from the open door of a taxicab. "Come on," she yelled, "move your buns!" They ran to catch up, piled into the back seat with her and the quick-footed soldier, and rode off together, hooting and cheering.

Minutes later they found a booth in a secluded nook against the back wall of the Cavern of Music. "I've got the first round," announced Roger, taking the elbow of the waiter. "We need four shots of your best tequila -- each. *Comprende?*"

"Four shots each. *Si Señor.*" He swished off smoothly, leaving a cool floral scent.

The Cavern was in a basement, and was decorated to look like the interior of a stalactite cave, dark and intimate. An old man in a black suit played Ellington, Chopin, and Gershwin on a roller-rink organ.

"Good golly Miss Molly, that was the greatest!" Roger declared enthusiastically, shaking the soldier around the shoulder. "That was better than cranking the juice to a big Norton Commando Six-fifty. Oh, 'scuse me, I'm Roger Stanton — my friends call me Big Rog. This guy -- hey, Eddie, your mouth is bleeding -- this is Eddie Padilla. We're from New Mexico Southern -- well, starting this fall, anyway. You really from Fort Bliss?"

The soldier laughed and nodded. "Yeah. I'm Kevin Harrey, Spec-Four. This is my, uh, fiancee, Carlie Gold -- well, after tonight, anyway."

"All right! Congratulations! Well, I've got to admit, I was hoping she'd turn out to be your sister."

"Why, thank you, Big Rog," said Carlie. "I've never been more gallantly rescued in my life. Now I know how that damsel felt when Saint George came to kill the dragon." She reached up and kissed him sweetly on the cheek. "You, too, Eddie. You were heroes." Eddie shrugged and blushed when she kissed him too.

"Yeah, thanks, troops," said Kevin. "Things were looking pretty tight for the home team there for a minute. I was sure glad to see you hadn't just come for the show."

"The way you kicked that guy, I think that might have been a pretty good show," said Eddie.

Kevin laughed. "Yeah, it might have. But I guess she wouldn't have been the first girl who went under the table to get out the door of that joint."

"Kevin!" she said, punching his shoulder. "You asshole."

"Come on, don't hit me, we're not married yet. And I'd have died pulling the guts out of those fuckers, you know."

"Hear, hear!" said Roger, pounding the table. "Hey, here come the drinks." Their waiter brought a tray loaded with sixteen shot-glasses of light gold tequila, and another with tall icewater glasses and a bowl of cut limes. Roger handed him a ten, waved off the change, and picked up his first shot. "Let us each propose a toast," he said. "I will begin by toasting the most important four F's in the world: a good friend, a good fuck, a good fight, and a good fantasy." He liberally dosed the back of his thumb with salt, tossed it into his mouth with an exaggerated flip of his wrist, pitched back the shot, and followed it with a chunk of lime.

His new friends laughed and hoisted their first shots. They licked salt from the backs of their hands, knocked down the drinks and gasped as the rich booze grabbed at their throats and guts. Then they winced wryly at the acid bite of tangy lime, breathed great signs of just-barely-endurable gusto, and looked from one to the other expectantly. They nodded, and passed a knowing and conspiratorial smile around the table. Eddie giggled, beginning to look glassy-eyed.

"Hey, look, guys," said Carlie finally, reaching for her second shot. "There's something I have to tell you. You know, back in the U-Boat, you were all just wonderful, and I want you to know I'm just thrilled, but I think I ought to level with you. I know

you all had a good time being heroes, but down inside
somewhere you must think I'm really a space-headed little bitch
to talk like that to those three apes. I mean, let's face it, guys,
that could have got real ugly, real fast." The three young men
looked at her solemnly for a moment, then Kevin sighed
resignedly and nodded with a wry smile. She shook back her
long blonde hair and grinned smugly. "Well, since we're all
friends here, I'd like you to meet my friend Ace." She brought
her hand quickly out of her purse and brandished a pearl-handled
chrome-plated tiny automatic pistol. She set it on the table, spun
it, and picked up her shot. "I propose we drink to this: here's to
being your Ace In The Hole, to cover your back, to back you up,
to hell and back, and that's a fact, Jack!"

"Hear, hear!" cheered Roger. "Lady, you are solid gold!"

"That's my name," she affirmed, quaffing her shot.

"But not for long," added Kevin, quaffing his.

"*Andale pues,*" muttered Eddie. He took a deep breath,
slurped his shot and swallowed, dribbling about half on his shirt.
His eyes popped wide and he gasped as the tequila burned at his
mouth. He inhaled smartly, and almost choked on the fumes in
his mouth.

"You all right, there, Sport?" asked Roger.

"Yeah, you bet. Just got a little down the wrong hole, that's
all. Here, now let me do one, OK. OK." He picked up his third
shot, started to stand, then sat back down. "No. We can do this
one sitting down. OK. Here's to....to us, and to hoping that we
can be friends, and this is the beginning, tonight, and....here, in
the beautiful Cavern of Music...." He paused a moment, giggled.
"...and, we'll never forget...how it all began." He started to take
the shot, then broke out in tears and slumped helplessly in his
chair.

Carlie leaned over to hug and comfort him, and Kevin put a
hand on his shoulder. "Hey, hey, right on, brother," he said.
"Yeah, I'll drink to that." He picked up his own third shot. "To
The Beginning, right, *hermano?*"

"To The Beginning," echoed Roger and Carlie. Eddie
struggled to control himself, and gulped the shot. He sat a
second with his face squeezed shut, then sucked in a huge breath

of air and looked at the others pop-eyed. They hovered at his sides, expressions of such concern on their faces, expressions of such care and affection. He sagged drunkenly and broke into a great beaming moon-faced smile of tearfully ecstatic acceptance, to the applause of his companions.

"All right," said Kevin, standing and holding up his last shot. "I've got a little confession to make, too." He reached across the table and picked up Carlie's little pistol. Then he cocked back the hammer, pointed it at the shot glass in his other hand, and pulled the trigger. To the surprise of his companions and the astonishment of his date, nothing happened. He chuckled, put the pistol back on the table, reached into his pocket, and held up the ammunition clip from the gun. "It's a good idea, but a dumb move. I can handle the goons, but we'd never get out of jail if you killed somebody over here." He hoisted the shotglass. "So here's to a Happy Ending!" he concluded, and quickly tossed back his last shot.

"Why you son of a bitch, you beat me," laughed Roger. "To a Happy Ending."

Carlie got silly drunk. She said a lot of very clever things, and when she giggled she squeezed her shoulders together and leaned over the table to let Kevin and Roger admire and lust for her. She slurped Margaritas and licked her luscious lips.

Eddie got fallout drunk. They propped him up in a corner and nudged him when he began to snore.

Roger got party drunk. He loudly pressed tips on the waiter for running small errands, then hugged him and told him he was a great humanitarian even if he was a homosexual. He ordered a Margarita when Carlie ordered her first one, and swore with bullhorn sincerity that he would never drink another without thinking of her.

Kevin got quiet drunk. He switched to vodka and tonic, and passed every other round. He was enjoying the evening, but maintaining a certain detached tension, smoking cigarettes, letting Roger have the laugh-lines, and insuring that when Carlie finally had enough of amusing herself with the clowns, he would be the one in condition to take her home.

"So what do you do out at Fort Bliss, Harrey? Artillery,

maybe?" asked Roger.

Kevin chuckled and waved a hand. "Naw, I teach classes in AIT — that's advanced infantry training."

"He's a hand-to-hand combat instructor," put in Carlie.

"I'm impressed!" said Roger. "So that's how you rate the best-looking woman in the states of Texas, New Mexico, and Chihuahua. I took some of that stuff once, but I couldn't think fast enough to use it. I've got my own style that seems to come naturally to me though — it's called Ching-Ga-So, also known as Fung Kyu!" He laughed uproariously, and pounded ponderously on his chest. "Big Rog!" he boomed.

"Well, actually, the stuff I teach is mostly basic defense, and quick kill techniques. Guys like me are kind of like Carlie's little pistol," the young soldier affirmed seriously. "If you need to use one to defend yourself, you've got to kill somebody, and the only sure way to survive is to fire the first shot."

"Sounds good to me," said Carlie.

"Me too," agreed Roger. "So how do you feel about going into Special Forces, or something like that?"

The redheaded soldier spread his hands and laughed. "Hey, no, thanks! I've got nothing against action, but I've got nothing to prove, either. I'm studying Spanish, and bucking for a diplomatic job in Central America. I'd be happy doing a whole career in embassy security in some unknown place like Honduras or El Salvador. I retire at 38 on Master Sergeant's pay, buy a couple of sections on a hillside in Costa Rica, and live the life of a plantation owner. Of course, if we ever got into a real war, that's different. God help the son-of-a-bitch who gets himself on the business end of my bayonet!"

"With Carlie by your side all the way, right?"

"Looking just like Scarlet O'Hara, no doubt?" asked Carlie.

"Hey," asked Roger, "are you guys really getting married tonight?"

"Sure," Kevin affirmed quickly. "Why not?"

Carlie patted her hair and cast a patient sidelong look at Kevin. "Welll, I don't know. I'm afraid you're going to have to shoot a lot higher to impress me, Hotshot," she said coolly. "I've been in Central America, in the Canal Zone, and twenty years of life in military housing in the jungle I don't need. And really, Roger, we were just agreeing to become engaged, and I haven't even begun to consider actually getting married yet. But, Kevin, darling, I think the part about the plantation on the hilltop sounds just divine and when you get there, call me."

"I'll do that," he said with a cocky grin that failed to conceal his disappointment.

"What is this I am hearing? The lady is backing out on her gallant knight?" Roger asked with great dramatic gestures of concern.

"No, of course not, Good Sir Roger, she just likes to keep him on his toes. That makes it easier to knock him off his feet." She curled close to Kevin, put her arm around his neck, and kissed him. He tensed, then submitted to the moment and returned her kiss deep and with passion. She writhed against him panting through flared nostrils, then broke away when he began to run his hand up under her skirt. She sat up primly and tossed back her hair so it fell on her shoulders.

"Eee-haw!" hooted Roger, drawing stares from all over the dark and otherwise quiet underground bar. Kevin was flushed and reeling, utterly captivated.

"That's just to let you know what you're up against. Some of us like it hot, Honeypie, and some of us like it fast. I've found myself a little red quarterhorse, and I like him a lot, and now I want him to win some races. So you can forget that shit about laying low in Managua. Get me embassy duty in Paris! And I want a telephone number I can call when I want to use my husband's little executive jet plane to go shopping. Are you listening?"

Roger was gushing tears and guffawing, "I swear it! I swear it on two Bibles and the Book of Urantia, this is the greatest moment of my life! Now that was spoken like the captain's daughter."

"I am the captain's daughter," she said triumphantly.

Roger collapsed in helpless laughter. "It's so magic. It's like suddenly we've met, and it's a different world. You're just such great people, and Harrey, I gotta admit it, I gotta tell you to your face so I can't be accused of keeping it behind your back, brother, I'm in love. I'm just in love, with this beautiful, charming, intelligent, and incredible sexy woman you might just be lucky enough to talk into marrying you....the sweet, delicious, vivacious....Miss Carlie Gold!"

She bowed demurely and smiled as the two applauded her.

"Hey, this is too much. I've gotta wake up Eddie. He's gotta get in on this. Hey, Eddie!" He shook their sleeping friend, who pawed at him, muttering, "I'm listening, I'm listening."

"No, no, let him sleep," said Carlie. "Tell us about you, Roger. What are you going to do now that it's begun?"

Roger giggled, nodded broadly. "All right, I'll tell you. First I'm going to get a degree in Aeronautical Engineering. Yeah, me, haw haw, never know it to look at me would you? And then I'm going into the Air Force. Two years later I'm logging pilot-in-command time, bucking for a shot at test pilot school. Then all I got to do is graduate in the top one percent of my class, and I'm all the way home."

"Where's that?" asked Carlie.

"Sounds like astronaut training," said Kevin. "This boy is downright ambitious."

"Kee-rekt! I've got it all figured out."

"Kevin, that's the sort of thing you'd be good at, don't you think," said Carlie. "Don't you think he looks like an astronaut, Big Rog?"

"Nope. Astronauts will be big guys. Tell me, what's the easiest way to store food for a long trip in space? Dried, frozen? Naw, think about it. How about forty pounds of good solid fat on the body of the pilot? No storage, no cooking, no eating, no waste processing. By the time they figure that out, I'll be first in line."

"That sounds simply wonderful, Roger. And when I see on the television that you've landed up there, I can say, there's Big Rog, mooning the whole world. As for myself, I haven't decided if I want to be an actress or a nurse."

Kevin reminded Carlie that she had a curfew. They all exchanged phone numbers, and Roger carried Eddie up to the street, where he was soon able to stagger along hanging onto his big friend's shoulder. They walked across the bridge in time for

Kevin to drive Carlie back to her father's house on the base by two o'clock. Eddie threw up on the floor of Roger's car on the way home, but Roger didn't mind. He cursed him loudly, and pounded the retching body on the back. "Did you have to wait until you got in the car, you bubble-butt beaner? At least it's good you didn't eat the menudo."

Eddie soon fell asleep against the door of the car, and Roger drove along in silence past the tall smokestacks of the El Paso smelters. He headed north toward his home in the little town of San Manuel, a quiet old Mexican village on the outskirts of Las Cruces. After a while, he turned to his sleeping companion and said, "You know something, sport? That was a fine fantasy, but if I live another day or a hundred years, that Carlie Gold is one woman I intend to see again."

Kevin drove Carlie home in her father Captain Gold's new Impala. She lay back on the seat and let her skirt ride up on her thighs, and she giggled tipsily when his driving jostled her. As they traveled an empty stretch of road along the edge of the city airport, she asked him to pull over to the side by a group of small trees.

"You sick?" he asked.

She snuggled against him. "No. I just wanted to talk. Kevin, if you had somebody who...who mattered to you, you'd want to be somebody for her, wouldn't you?"

He pulled her closer to her and looked into her face. "Of course I would," he said. "Honey, this is the greatest country in the world, and this is a time of opportunity. And I believe in the power of the human mind to overcome obstacles and win. If you believe in anything enough, and you put your whole self into it, an American these days can become anything he wants. I believe that. One thing I know, Carlie, and that is I am a winner. And the other thing I know is I love you. So don't you worry, you hear?"

"Oh, Kevin, I do believe you. It matters so much. Now while we still have time..." She sat up and turned away from him, straightening her back so he could pull the zipper of her dress. "...please fuck me deliciously, then take me home."

TWO

Three days after Christmas, 1967, Warrant Officer Kevin Harrey sat at the head table in the banquet room of the El Paso Great Western Inn, the featured luncheon speaker at the Civic Service Club's weekly meeting. Stiff and self-conscious in his new dress greens emblazoned with Army aviator's silver wings, he only dabbled with his turkey and mashed potatoes. The room was filled with businessmen playing out a familiar ritual they enjoyed, taunting and insulting each other with great gusto. To Kevin, it seemed strange to see men he knew were the financial and political power of the county acting out corny Three-Stooges routines.

When the meeting settled down to business, Kevin walked with them through the motions of the Pledge of Allegiance, the Star Spangled Banner, an Invocation by a Methodist Minister, and a rousing Civic Service Club pep song. Then the President banged on his podium and introduced the Program Chairman, who gave Kevin a pat on the shoulder and took the microphone.

"Gentlemen, Fellow Members, and Guests, we are privileged to have as our guest speaker this noon Warrant Officer Kevin Harrey, who spent two years stationed right here in El Paso at Fort Bliss as an instructor at AIT, and who spent a year in Vietnam as an advisor to the South Vietnamese Army. He has just graduated from the Army's helicopter flight school and will be leaving in a few days to return to Vietnam. We've managed to persuade him to say a few words to us about how he feels. Oh, by the way, he also happens to be the son-in-law of one of our respected brothers from the base, formerly-Captain, as of this month Major Chuck Gold. OK, Kevin, you've got it."

The members and guests set aside their forks and cups and applauded politely as the slender and handsome young man in Army greens stepped up to the podium. He looked at them with sureness in his wide brown eyes, and with his sorrel red hair cut just long enough to lie down on top, he did look professional, in a homey and unthreatening way. He smiled softly and took hold of the podium with both hands.

"In three days I'll be leaving for a year of combat in Vietnam. When I tell people that, I have been getting a pretty discouraging reaction. They tell me they're sorry. When I tell them that I didn't have to go, and that I volunteered, and I'm looking forward to going, they are really surprised. They tell me I must be a very unusual young man. And that is what I find so discouraging — that people seem to think that our country is represented more accurately by the oddball groups, all yelling Ban the Bomb, or Bomb the Ban, or Let's All Get Bombed." He got a good polite round of laughter on that one, and continued. "You can blame some of that on the media. When an educated young man stands in the street and defies his country's laws in the name of one thing or another, it's dramatic, and the dramatic sells newsprint. But that makes a big impression on the reader, and he might get to think that dissident represents the youth of America. Well, I'm here to tell you that it's not true! It's not true.

"All Army aviators are volunteers. We are told when we enter the program not that we might go to Vietnam, but that we WILL. There are about fifteen thousand rated aviators, and we're one of the smaller volunteer groups. All service pilots are volunteers, and so are the Special Forces, the Navy's Seals, and the so-called Junk Fleet. I would bet a pile of chips that all those men and women alone account for more people, by warm-body count, than there are real practicing public dissenters in the country." He got some genuine applause on that.

"The training we undergo is about ten months long. It's difficult, and they demand the next thing to perfection. You have to get the most out of yourself and your equipment, because anything less will get you killed. Being an airplane driver is only part of being an aviator. We study military history, tradition, leadership, courtesy, the rules and techniques of handling men and developing teamwork. We study political science, and are acquainted with communist doctrine, techniques, and history.

We know who the enemy is, and we are trained to resist brainwashing. And in addition to all that, we must keep in top physical shape.

"Some of us, selected for gunships — that is, armed helicopters — learn air-to-ground gunnery and rocketry. We learn low-level cross-country navigation. By low-level, we mean with your skids trimming the top leaves from trees. Things go by fast, so you have to keep your head up. The training we get is very thorough, so when we actually get into combat, we are better prepared for it than any other group of pilots have ever been.

"The war in Vietnam is a guerrilla insurgency, so we have developed a technique to beat the guerrilla — the Army calls it the Airmobile Concept. The use of helicopters provides never before matched reaction time, surprise, and maneuverability. First an aircraft with some sophisticated detection device, like radar, infra-red, even a new one that actually smells the enemy is used to locate the guerrilla without his even being aware of it. Then a strike force of helicopters loaded with a company or a battalion of men flies to the area. While the gunships provide covering fire and attack the enemy's fortifications, the slicks — troop carrying helicopters — land in small clearings and offload fresh combat-ready troops to destroy the enemy in his own backyard. That's how it works, bam, a whole strike force.

"So the next time you hear someone say that the youth of America are being forced against their will to fight a war they do not believe in for a government they do not trust and a people they no longer care about, and that they are sent to war with inferior weapons and outdated tactics, then remember this, and you can believe it: America's youth is far more accurately represented by the volunteer units of our armed services than by the overpublicized minority of dissenters. We are armed with the finest weapons our nation's technology has produced, using tactics developed specifically for this type of war. Though many of us don't always agree with the way the war is being conducted, we leave our homes and our families willingly, because we believe it is right to defend and uphold the decisions of the government which we, our families, and our countrymen have elected. Thank you, Gentlemen, may I entertain your questions?"

There were no questions, and his audience stood and applauded. There were tears in more than a few eyes, and Major Gold could have walked on water. They blessed him, they praised him, and they said he was a shining champion of the Right, a Saint, and a true American.

Kevin happily accepted their congratulations. It did feel good. He had graduated first in his class in Warrant Officer flight school, and he was confident that he could come home from the upcoming tour with a direct commission as a First Lieutenant. What a speech he would make to the Civic Service Club then. For a moment, he felt a strange detached sense of history, of destiny, as though he were somewhere apart from time, watching a great officer's career unfold.

A few days later, he stood in the airport and kissed Carlie goodbye, and he kissed their baby son George. Then, feeling more than a little awed by the weight of responsibility his countrymen were placing upon him, but girded with the armor of their trust, and armed with the cleansing sword of American righteousness, Kevin strode out to the airplane with his head held high, prepared to travel halfway around the world to drive the Devil out of Paradise.

Warrant Officer Eddie Padilla had an aisle seat on the flight from Hawaii to Saigon, so he didn't get to see much of the Vietnamese countryside before landing. They made a wide turn just after crossing the coast, and all he could see looking out through the little plexiglass window two seats away was a succession of jungle-covered hillsides, lush green except for several peculiar bands of brown. They were still quite high, and Eddie's pilot training enabled him to judge the size of the bands — a surprising thousand feet wide by a mile long. His impression was that of a Walt Disney nature adventure animation gimmick — a big paintbrush wipes over a jungle in springtime, and leaves behind a swipe of autumn.

Suddenly he was on the ground, putting one foot in front of the other, stepping into the blast of heat and glare and sound, riding in a bus with steel-mesh on the windows, trying to appear cool and relaxed, trying not to appear self-conscious, trying to take in the mad rush of people and businesses and fortifications and hovels and animals all at once, trying not to look like a rubberneck bumpkin, and trying not to notice that the driver was Vietnamese, and apparently laughing at him.

Inprocessing was routine. He was passed from one waiting line to another, and began to chafe a bit as the day wore on, until he noticed the much longer lines of enlisted troops waiting their turns. He smiled and relaxed, recognizing for the first time that he was no longer the kowtowing officer candidate, but an officer who could expect preferential treatment. He walked easily through the moves. The officer who was to finally certify his papers and dispatch him to his assignment was a fat, balding First Lieutenant about forty. The man wore impeccably starched fatigues, and he sipped beer from a large flagon bearing his name, "CURT" to match Curtis on his name tag.

"OK, Mr. Padila, looks like you're going out to The Scabbard." The big man smiled genially.

"Padilla, Sir. What's The Scabbard?"

"That's what they call the airfield at Bao Trang, in the highlands about a hundred and fifty miles north of here. It's home for the Black Sabres, your new outfit. You've been assigned to the 17th Assault Helicopter Company."

"Sounds good."

"They're new in-country. Got here about four months ago. They spent some time training south of here with the Ninth Division at Bearcat, and we shipped the whole unit north to Bao Trang last month. They ought to just about have things set up for you. Your shit seems to be in order. Questions?"

"Uh, how do I get there?"

"No problem. You want to get anywhere in this country, you just take a copy of your orders to the nearest airfield, and you get on the manifest for a flight to where you want to go. The Air Force flies C-130's into Bao Trang at least once a day. The other way, since you're a pilot, would be to catch a ride over to the helipad at Hotel-3 and hitch up with one of the helicopters from your outfit."

"That sounds like the way to go."

"Great. There'll be a truck going over there in an hour or so. Give 'em hell, Padila, and we can all go home."

"Yessir! And thanks."

"Don't thank me, sucker," the Lieutenant said to Eddie's departing back. "Who's next?"

The helipad, one of the most active in Saigon, was a tangle of motion. Eddie stood where he had been dropped off and looked around in a circle, jaw hanging open in genuine awe. The area was well inside the built-up part of the city and there were buildings and structures on all sides. One end of the short, rutted, and uneven area used for a runway was blocked by a two-story wall of timbers covered with corrugated metal. There were tall buildings, water towers, antennas, and poles sticking up into every logical approach pattern Eddie could envision, and everywhere he looked he saw wires, a hazard guaranteed to strike every rotor pilot's heart with fibrillating horror. By any of the standards he had been taught in flight school, this should not be a major traffic terminal, but a confined area off limits except in emergency.

As he watched, a pair of gunships swooped down to land and moved at a brisk hover to the rearming pits, where they plumped to the ground and sat with rotors muttering at idle. The four members of each crew leaped quickly from their birds and ran toward the racks of rockets readied for them, leaving their helmets in their seats. Their fatigues were streaked with sweat, and by their heavy but dogged double-time gait, Eddie could tell they were tired but determined. "They must be into a hot one somewhere," he thought with a delicious excitement.

The gunship crews ran back and forth again and again carrying thirty-pound four-foot air-to-ground rockets to fill the big round cannister pods slung from the sides of the ships. Then moving as fast as they were able, they loaded what seemed to Eddie an endless belt of machine-gun ammunition into trays in the cabins of the helicopters. After what seemed only a minute or two, they hovered over to the fuel pit and shut down their turbines. While one troop carried a hose to refuel each helicopter, the others in the crews began to inspect them closely, opening and peering into access panels, and crawling beneath and on top of the squat tadpole-shaped machines. They passed a canteen around briefly, then cranked up their warbirds again and strapped their battle helmets back on their heads. In seconds, they brought the rotors to flying RPM, checked to see that each bird would hover in place, then dipped their noses and accelerated three feet off the ground toward the corrugated wall at the end of the strip. The hair rose on the back of Eddie's neck as they waited and waited, and then tipped their rotor discs back and swooped up sharply over the fence, one after the other, like whirling balls of fire shot from a Roman candle.

"Wow!" yelled Eddie, clapping his arms together. "Wow! Outstanding!"

For the better part of an hour, he sat and watched the ships come and go. Most of them were UH-1 Hueys, either the short weapon-hung UH-1C "Charlie-model" gunships, or the longer UH-1D "Delta-model" troop-carrying ships, called "slicks". Once a huge twin-rotored CH-47 Chinook came in, hovering down almost vertically the last two hundred feet of its approach, and creating such a cloud of dust that Eddie had to take shelter.

Each flight brought a new bustle of activity, as boxes, bundles, and people were loaded or unloaded. Some of the troops were mud-encrusted and battle weary, and some were in crisp tailored fatigues. From one sleek and shiny Delta model command ship, an officer in pressed fatigues led two very pretty Vietnamese women to a waiting jeep, their brightly-colored satin pajama-skirts fluttering in the rotorwash.

"I wonder if there are any women at Bao Trang," he mused. "I wonder what they'll really be like." All through flight school he had heard the stories about the live-in housemaids, the professional whores trained in all the Oriental secrets, and the dark-eyed nubile little girls who will do it for the candy in your C-rations. Though the intimate companionship of a woman was something Eddie had still never known, he found himself beginning to feel already the soldier's urgent loneliness.

He decided to walk through the revetments where transient aircraft were parked, and in a few minutes he spotted a Delta-model slick bearing on its nose the emblem he had been instructed to look for: a large black spade, with a black sabre piercing it from side to side. Hoping the crew had not planned to remain the night in Saigon, Eddie looked around for a place to sit. The revetment was made of sandbags, and except for a few oily patches, was covered with a layer of fine chalky dust. He propped his duffle bag into a corner in the shade, started to sit down, then hesitated, reluctant to get his clean new first-time-worn jungle fatigues dusty. He looked around for something to sit on, and finally found a cardboard circle which he identified by the tomato stains on one side as a pizza plate. It was a bit small, but he decided it was sufficient, and he sat down on it, leaned against his duffle bag, and tried to catch a nap.

The crew returned shortly, a captain and a warrant officer, followed by two enlisted men, the crew chief and gunner. They were chatting easily, and seemed to be in no great hurry. Carrying a dufflebag behind them was another warrant, one who struck Eddie as strangely familiar. He jumped to his feet and snapped the captain a salute.

"Good afternoon, Sir, I'm Padilla, Eddie. Are you with the 17th Assault?"

The captain flashed back a salute, then stuck out his hand. "Right. You just get in country? Yeah? Joining the Sabres?"

"Yessir."

"Glad to have you. I'm Jack Miller. This is Mr. Kretzer."

"Billy," said Kretzer. "The two buttholes in the back are Pullen and Moon."

"Hey, yer Mama's butthole, Mr. Kretzer....Sir," said Moon, a tall weasel with a New York accent.

"Call me Eddie," the young warrant said, extending his hand awkwardly. Billy Kretzer shook it, and the two crewmen nodded noncommittally and busied themselves with a preflight check of the ship.

"This is Mr. Harrey," said the captain, indicating the third warrant. "He's just been assigned to the Sabres too."

"Name's Kevin," said the slender young pilot. They shook hands and looked at each other quizzically. "You sure do look familiar to me. Where you from?"

"New Mexico."

Kevin's face lit up with a grin of recognition. "Yeah, I got you. You were with Roger Stanton the night we met, that crazy night in Juarez. And now you're a fling-winger too."

"I'll be damned, you're right. I remember too, sort of. I was pretty bombed that night. You were the guy with Carlie. I sure remember her. I saw some really foxy pictures Roger took of her later. Did you ever see her again?"

"Yeah, I married her, and we've got a little boy going on two years old. What kind of pictures?"

"Oh. Uh, just party pictures, I guess. She just -- really looked nice, that's all. So, what class did you graduate with? I don't think I ever saw you in flight school."

"67-17," said Kevin.

"I was a few months ahead of you," said Eddie, "but I got held up at Fort Rucker waiting for some kind of mixup with my orders to get straightened out."

They stood uncertainly a moment, then Captain Miller called back to them from the pilot's chair, "Pitch your gear in the back there, you two, and let's get some air under this bitch so we can get home before dark."

"Yessir!" Eddie jumped smartly to pick up his duffle bag, and heard somebody chuckle.

"Hey, boy," he heard the captain say, "it's bad enough you present a target that big to the enemy, but did you have to paint a bullseye on it?"

"What?" He turned around, confused. From behind him, Billy Kretzer laughed. Eddie turned again, and saw that Billy was looking at the seat of his pants. He looked down and could see that he had collected a big round patch of the chalky dust on the wide shirttail of his fatigue jacket, and that right in the middle of it was a perfectly clean round spot exactly the size of the pizza plate on which he had been sitting. The effect was an almost perfect ring of white, a band some six inches wide centered exactly on the green-clad bubble of Eddie's great protuberant gleuts.

Eddie's face flashed red. "Hey," he replied, mustering his bravado, "that's just so I can flip the old Viet Cong the moon."

He jumped up into the bird and fumbled among the seat belts

for a pair that matched. By the time he and Kevin were strapped in, the rotor was at flying RPM, and Captain Miller turned around and yelled at Eddie over the throb and whine, "Ready to go, Bullseye?" Eddie grinned rather sickly, and gave the thumbs-up.

In seconds, Saigon was slipping by under them, a dirty, bustling tangle of streets and alleys choked with people, cars, and trucks. Ancient pagodas and modern office buildings shared an incongruous proximity, as different times and cultures were shoved shoulder to shoulder. Every few blocks he saw the rubble of broken buildings, and vacant lots bristling with barbed wire and sandbagged gun positions.

As they moved north they overflew groves of rubber trees, broad patches of gray-green rows which exuded a peculiar musky smell recognizable even as they flew two hundred feet above it. Kretzer was flying the helicopter, staying low, sightseeing, while Captain Miller stared out the window, smoking a cigarette, lost in thought. They crossed a river, broad, greasy-brown, with clusters of thatched hooches along the sides and sampans occasionally drawn up on mud flats along the banks. The jungle below was green, every possible shade of green, lush, and tangled with feather-like waving fronds of bamboo, pale paddle-blade banana leaves, and tall silver-barked trees that raised their dark green crests of leaves twelve stories above the vine-tangled jungle floor. Narrow cart tracks led to tiny clearings where trees had been cut and laid out in sections, their inside ochre-red in contrast to the surrounding green. Along the edges of the clearings lay strange mound shapes, some of them broken open to reveal blackened interiors. Eddie nudged the crew chief sitting next to him. "What are those?" he shouted, pointing.

The troop cast a bored glance at the the clearing to which Eddie was pointing. "Charcoal pits." Eddie nodded, feeling a little foolish.

An hour later they flew through a narrow valley, crowned on both sides by high, rugged peaks with jungle clinging to near-vertical sides. In places the rock was bare and streaked with black, and on the very top of one great peak a single monolith of steel-grey stone five hundred feet high thrust itself like a ziggurat above the matted green. Just where the jungle met the rock Kevin could see a bit of masonry, a wall, a row of steps, perhaps some kind of shrine. Just below it in a jagged ravine a patch of rock sparkled with the reflection of the sun in a tumbling waterfall that showed itself for only a second. For a moment, Kevin was arrested by the flash, and he felt as though he were sitting on the side of the mountain, looking out into the reddening haze of evening, and watching as the helicopter made its steady, unhurried progress up the valley, rotor muttering softly, like an old man muttering to himself, walking home in the sunset of his time.

Kretzer made an adjustment in his power setting, and Kevin looked forward. The valley ahead narrowed, and ended in a ridge. A paved road wound up the valley and climbed the ridge in switchbacks. He glanced forward at the instruments and saw that the ship was climbing with almost full power. "Gee," he thought, "if an empty slick has to pull this kind of torque to get through here, I'll bet it takes everything a loaded gunship can put out to clear that ridge." As they swept past the ridge only a few feet above the trees, he could see that they had flown through a low point in the irregular lip of a natural bowl about thirty miles across.

In the center of the bowl below, they could see a village with a few modern buildings and a good-sized airfield with a steel-planked runway. The military complex lay on the opposite side of the runway from the village, and the first impression Kevin and Eddie had of their new home was DUST. The entire area had been scraped clean of vegetation, leaving an ugly khaki-colored scar in the middle of the little green valley. "That's The Scab," yelled Billy Kretzer. "That's home."

Miller took control of the helicopter and settled to a hover at the approach end of the runway. At their left was a pile of boxes, paper tubes, and metal ammunition cans, and a crude rack with a stack of long green rockets. They recognized them as the 2.75-inch high explosive rockets they had trained with in school. Beside this rearming pit were the gunships' revetments, L-shaped walls of sandbags, sagging at the corners.

Two Charlie-model gunships sat waiting for a scramble call,

tubes loaded with rockets, and T-shirted gunners lying asleep under a poncho lean-to nearby.

Halfway down the strip beyond the gunships' stand-by area, a few low shacks had been built by the Air Force around a steel-planked area on which sat a four-engined C-130 Hercules.

On the far end of the strip sat a cluster of drab, ugly GP-medium army tents, some of which had low walls of sandbags around them. It was a temporary-looking encampment, completely devoid of the clean straight lines which mark a secured and squared-away company area. It looked like a boot camp bivouac pitched in a dusty parking lot.

Captain Miller eased the helicopter into the slick's narrow revetment and shut down the turbine. Eddie waited until the rotor had stopped swinging, then stepped out of the ship into a puddle of sticky black tar.

"What the hell?"

"Pcneprime." Kretzer grinned, stepping around the puddle. "They spray this shit all over the place to keep the dust down. The result is black, sticky dust....and puddles. You'll love it once you get used to it."

"Lovely," said Eddie, wondering what it would take to put a parade shine on his boots again.

Kevin dragged his duffle bag out of the ship and hefted it to his shoulder, then stepped around the helicopter, watching where he put his feet. "OK, so this is it. Where do we live?"

Kretzer paused a moment for drama, then pointed down the runway. "See that bunch of tents just off the end of the runway? That's ours."

Kevin spent that first night at Bao Trang sleeping on an empty cot in the waiting-room of the Flight Surgeon's medical tent. He had spent most of 1966 in the Saigon area with Military Assistance Command, Vietnam, known as Mac-V, as a troop-handling sergeant, an instructor to the cadre of the ARVN's basic training command. It had been an easy tour — hotel quarters, starched fatigues, and drill-field duty, and he had slipped through without being in a hot firefight. Though he worked with them, he had avoided becoming personally involved with the Vietnamese. There was no rush of newness in his arrival at Bao Trang, but rather a return to the familiar, a sense of inevitability. He pulled the stiff army blanket up around his neck, shrugged his shoulder under the uncased lumpy pillow, and sighed deeply. "This time it's different," he thought. "This time I'm kicking ass and taking names, and coming home with some prizes." He smiled, and slept.

Eddie Padilla found an empty cot in the operations tent. It was a quiet night, but he spent most of it awake listening to the night sounds and wishing the jungle were not so near. The jetlag had his circadian rhythms scrambled. Though he was terribly tired from the long trip, and it was dark and surprisingly cool outside, his body clock was telling him it was the middle of the afternoon.

Sometime late in the night, the stand-by gunship team was called out to assist someone in hot contact somewhere. When the call came in from Battalion, Eddie jumped out of bed and stood in his stockings watching excitedly as the duty officer ran to scramble the pilots. They had been sitting awake in their tents, playing cards and waiting. Two of them, a warrant and a lieutenant, came to the ops tent to quickly jot down coordinates and call signs, and then they piled their equipment into a waiting three-quarter-ton truck and jumped aboard after it. Eddie marveled at the amount of stuff they carried. Each pilot carried a pistol, and each wore a net vest with numerous pockets and pouches loaded with survival equipment. Each carried a heavy curved plate shaped like the silhouette targets on a rifle range. Fitted with long velcro belts to strap them against the chest, these bullet shields had been displayed to Eddie in flight school, and he and his classmates had been told by the old veteran sergeant teaching the class that they would stop anything up to a fifty-caliber....sometimes. In addition, each carried an M-16 automatic rifle, and of course, his visored "brain-bucket".

In what seemed only seconds after they departed jouncing through the chuckholes and the dust, Eddie could hear the reluctant whine of a cold turbine being urged to life, and then a minor third behind, another. Then the rotors began to whip the air. They had hardly reached full RPM when Eddie could tell by their deep whopping throb that the pilots had pulled full pitch on the great rotating wings to leap off into the night at a sprint. He heard them rumble toward him, then pull up sharply right over the tent, making the rotors WAP! WAP! WAP! like bursting fireworks.

"Fucking gunnies," the duty officer muttered as the helicopters grumbled away into the moist foreign darkness.

Eddie returned to the cot sat with his heart pounding. This was it, the stuff of heroics. Steel-eyed champions on sabre-winged steeds charging forth into the night to do deadly battle with...what? He lay back and reflected on the circumstances that had brought him to the brink of riding with them into the fray.

To at least one person, Eddie was already a hero. That was his little sister, Cecilia, and when she first saw him stepping out of the big 707 airliner at the El Paso airport wearing his new officer's dress greens to spend Christmas leave at home, she rushed to him and leaped up to hang on his neck yelling, "My Hero!" at the top of her lungs. It was delightfully embarrassing to Eddie, and he really did feel like a hero, even if she was only twelve years old. He hugged her and laughed, and swung her around twice.

He had arrived early in the evening, and his family met him at the airport and took him to a fancy steakhouse across the border in Juarez. It was a giddy party. Reymundo Padilla got drunk very quickly toasting the courage and success of his son, and though Dolores Padilla had loudly declared her displeasure at Eddie's dropping out of college after two years to enter the Army's flight school program, she was wet-eyed and sniveling with sentimental pride.

Popping the cork from the first bottle of Champagne, Reymundo raised his hands for quiet. "In the War, in the Big One, in World War Two, I was in the Army, in Italy, and when I was promoted to the rank of Corporal, I thought I had really accomplished something. And maybe I had, because I didn't get my American citizenship until after the war — not bad for a little *mojado* wetback, huh? But now, now look how far the Padillas have come. My son is an Officer! I want to be the first one to say, Congratulations, Warrant Officer Padilla, Sir!" He stood to a straight and proud if potbellied approximation of a position of attention and snapped his son a great exaggerated salute.

Little Ceci hung on Eddie's arm and mushed and gushed and squeezed and squealed, "Oh, I love you, Eddie. My hero!"

Reymundo Padilla had come a long way. His construction company had development projects covering blocks, and his home was one of the first in town with a swimming pool. Mundo had invested in some large plots of cheap undeveloped land along the road to the Army's rocket testing base twenty miles away at White Sands. When the space industry began in the late 1940's with the testing of Der Fuhrer's captured V-2's there, the little town of Las Cruces was the first to feel the effect. The demand for lowcost housing on the east side of town made "Adobe Mundo" Padilla a rich man with a respected name. His wife could go every year to pick her new car, and most important, he could afford to send his children to any university in the United States of America.

There had been an unpleasant moment when Eddie came home at the end of his Sophomore year to inform his parents that he had decided to drop out of college and enter an Army program to become an officer and a pilot. Reymundo had been furious at first, but Eddie had convinced him it was just an important part of his technical education, and an opportunity to build a strong background of experience. The Army would send him to the best schools after the war, in whatever technical specialty he wanted. And more, it was a good time to be supporting the President of the United States. Reymundo bought it, but with reservations.

The first weekend Eddie was home, Dolores convened a big family fiesta. She and the other women — brother Johnnie's wife Amandita, sisters Luci and Ceci — created a huge commotion in the kitchen to turn out a tableful of *enchiladas,* roast pork, *frijoles,* fresh *tortillas*, shredded slaw with vinegar and pickled *jalapeños*, and *empanadas* of mincemeat, apricot, and cherry. It was an easy part of the family-affair experience for Eddie. His mother wished only to gorge him at the chile-flowing *masa*-mound breast of Mother Mexico, and Eddie did love to eat. For two solid hours, he was able to detach himself from the familiar ceremony which characterized his parents' big family dinners, and devote himself to the delights of the Mesilla

Valley's little secret treasure, the most delicious chile dishes found anywhere on earth, as no one could render them better than his mother.

After dinner they poured snifters of rich Mexican brandy, and the men retired to the living room. "So, little Lunchie has grown up to be a pilot," mused Reymundo. "Who would have thought of that?"

"Lunchie," laughed Eddie's big brother Johnnie. "I haven't heard that in a long time. Ceci, we used to call your brother Lunchie because he always carried his lunch around in his pants."

That drew a big laugh from Reymundo, as usual. "He still looks like he carries his lunch around in his pants," Mundo hooted. "How do they let such a *Nalgon* fly a helicopter?"

"That's why they picked me," Eddie shrugged. "They needed somebody who was built to sit around in a chair all day long."

After dinner everyone wanted to hear about flight school, and Eddie spent two hours telling them about the disciplinary horrors of pre-flight training, Grundy day, leadership drill ("Sergeant, put up that flagpole."), and the baffling task of actually controlling a helicopter.

"It's a little like trying to make love standing on your head in a hammock," he informed the family.

"Eddie!" gasped his mother.

"It's because they're unstable," he continued. "If you let go of the controls, a helicopter will roll over and die."

The thought upset Dolores, and she had to get up and leave the room. The party quickly began to break up. Johnnie took his family home early, Ceci went to bed, and Mundo came in and told Eddie that his mother was resting and would like to see him.

The Padillas lived in a modern house, but the Spanish influence was strong in its decoration, particularly in the big master bedroom. The furniture was dark and heavy, and a large picture of Jesus with a burning heart gazed down with infinite compassion from a gaudy frame. With her weathered Spanish Catholic Bible beside her, Dolores lay on her bed, clutching a rosary in one hand and a kleenex in the other. Dolores was small in stature, but rounded in shape, and in the soft light of a bedside lamp and several candles in a niche in the wall, she looked like a little stuffed doll propped up on the pillows. From the niche, the blue-cowled face of Our Lady of Guadalupe wept for Dolores in the candlelight of her sorrow. Eddie sat down beside her without speaking and waited.

"I believe," she said finally, "that The Lord is going to be merciful to me. I always hoped that one of my sons would become a priest. And now my Eduardo is going away from me, into the fires of hell itself. And if anything were to happen....oh, Eddie *mi hijito*, I just couldn't stand it if anything happened to you. The Lord would not do that to me. He knows I could never stand so much grief. He would never ask me to suffer so much, I know it. Oh, Eddie, I will pray for you, every day. I pray He will bring you home safely to me."

"It will be all right, Mom," Eddie said, taking her hand and feeling like an idiot. "He will take care of me, you'll see." He hugged her, and she wept a while, then finally let him go.

After a while the fire team returned, and Eddie was able to get a few hours sleep.

THREE

They let Eddie sleep late in the morning, and when he sat up suddenly in bed remembering where he was, he was surprised to discover it was after nine. Most of the crews were already out on their missions, and the company area was quiet. He could see a couple of men outside throwing a ball back and forth. The duty officer directed him to the nearest latrine, and instructed him to get some breakfast in the mess tent, then report to the Commanding Officer, Major Csynes.

In the mess tent he found Kevin Harrey finishing off a cereal bowl of apple pie. "Morning," said Kevin. "Get yourself some pie and coffee, and we'll go meet the CO."

Meeting Jacob Csynes was a jolt. He was lean and tall, and he wore tightly tailored fatigues, glass-shined boots laced with clean white parachute riser cord, and skin-tight leather flight gloves. His features were sharply defined, angular, and he was completely hairless. His neck and jaw, and all of his skull which could not be protected by hands over the face were covered with burn scars. The ears were gone, and the effect was unmistakably reptilian.

Kevin and Eddie stepped up smartly in front of the desk and saluted. The major uncoiled his long legs, stood to full height, and rolled them a sinuous salute, his arm snapping the wrist up to pop just over the eyebrow, then falling at his side like a whip.

"Sit down, men. Welcome to The 17th Assault Helicopter Company, or as we call our little fraternity, The Black Sabres." His voice was as surprising as his appearance, high and reedy, but rounded and full, like an English Horn in its upper register.

Though the company's facilities were makeshift and temporary, the little office had been decorated with meticulous care. It occupied the back ten feet of the single quonset building in the Sabres' tent city. Behind Csynes the American and Vietnamese flags were draped to flank an artist's rendition of the company's heraldic shield, bearing crossed black sabres and a row of daggers. President Lyndon B. Johnson gazed benevolently from a portrait frame to one side, and a group of pictures and framed documents balanced the set on the other side. "Since you're the first new pilots we've received since we got in country, I'm going to take this opportunity to try out my new welcome-aboard speech. Smoke if you like. I don't — got too close to the fire once, as you can see."

The Major draped himself over his straight-backed chair, and waved Kevin and Eddie to others. "Our mission is to locate and control the channels being used by the Viet Cong and the North Vietnamese to move men and supplies through these highlands into the Saigon area south of here."

"You mean the Ho Chi Minh Trail, Sir?" asked Kevin.

"Exactly. Across the ridge to the west of here is the A Lan Valley. The borders of Cambodia and Laos lie on the west side of that valley, and a lot of stuff gets moved into Vietnam from both of those countries. Except for the B-52 bombing missions, we don't control the valley. By the end of this year, we will.

"To accomplish that, we have three platoons of slicks, flying UH-1D's, and one platoon of gunships, the Daggers. We've got plenty of missions, so you'll be able to get all the flying time you want. You can spend today getting processed and settled, and we'll get you on tomorrow's flight roster. You'll be flying co-pilot for a while, of course, before making A/C — aircraft commander. I'll tell operations to schedule you for some of the logistic supply runs so you can check out the area."

"That sounds great, Sir, but may I make a request?" asked Kevin. The major nodded. "Well, Sir, I know it has been the general practice that pilots have at least six months in-country before flying guns, but I would like to request immediate assignment to the gunship platoon."

Csynes turned a second-look glance on Kevin, raising his hairless eyebrows in surprise. "Why should I put you in Dagger platoon?"

The young officer took a deep breath and sat up a bit

straighter. "To begin with, Sir, I'm one of the first students who got gunship weapons indoctrination in flight school. My class got to practice insertion-fire-cover racetrack patterns, we got more low-level maneuvering and navigation work, and we got to fire live rockets and miniguns. I think the Army will probably want to get feedback on how well that training is working as fast as possible. The other reason is attitude, Sir."

"Attitude?"

"Yessir. If you don't mind my expressing an opinion, Sir. It seems to me there's a difference in attitude that goes with flying guns. It's not braver, or even bolder — everybody's heard about how far guys like the Medevac pilots will hang it out — it's just a feeling that you ought to be out front, Sir."

"How about you, Padilla?" asked Csynes.

Eddie gulped, and then nodded. "Yes, Sir, I think I know what Mr. Harrey is talking about. It's like when you encounter enemy fire, the slick's job is to get away from it to protect the troops on board, and the gunship's job is to go where the enemy is and take him on."

"There's something to that," said Csynes. "Do you feel that way, too?"

Eddie looked over at Kevin, who grinned back at him. "Well, Sir," he said to the Major, "I think I'd feel better about being the one to go over and kick his ass, if you'll pardon me, Sir. If I had wanted to stay out of his way, I'd have stayed in school. I guess I belong in gunships, too."

"You've got me convinced," the Major affirmed. "We'll find out how the training command is doing their job these days. Your asses now belongs to Captain Duke Randall, Commander, Fourth Platoon, Daggers. You keep up that attitude. I like it. Some other things I like are cleanliness, order, and a high sense of professionalism. I don't like chicken shit any better than any other soldier, but I do like spit-and-polish, and I do like an atmosphere of respect. I think the way to survive here, and succeed here is to act like we thought of ourselves less like soldiers doing a job, and more like warriors serving a cause."

"That's exactly how I feel, Sir," said Kevin.

"Me too," said Eddie.

"Good. I think you'll be right at home with the Daggers. Welcome aboard." The Major stood, and the two warrants rose and stood before him at attention. "Dismissed."

"Yes, Sir," they said, saluting and turning on their heels to leave.

"Oh, one more thing." Jacob Csynes stopped them at the door. "Just to start the record off straight, there's a nickname you're likely to hear used around. I suppose it's good for the company's reputation in a way, but I don't like it, and I don't like to hear my people use it. You understand me?"

Eddie turned to look solemnly at the Commanding Officer. "I know exactly how you feel, Sir," he said.

As they were leaving the Command shack, they encountered Captain Jack Miller, the pilot who had flown them up from Saigon, commander of Second Platoon, the White Hilt slick team. He was a thin and beaky fellow with a bristly shock of straw-colored hair, and his motions were quick and nervous. He looked up from the clipboard he was carrying at the last instant to avoid colliding with Eddie.

"Ah, the new men. You met our Commanding Officer, no doubt?"

"Yes, Sir. I was very impressed," said Kevin. "He sure seems like he knows his business."

"He means business, too, let me tell you. One of the best." The captain nodded conspiratorially. "The very best. So which platoon did you get assigned to?"

"Gunships," said Eddie with satisfaction. "We're assigned to the Daggers."

Miller looked stricken. "He put you in the guns? Hell, you're brand new in-country. Did you try to talk him out of it?"

"Oh, no, Sir. We requested it."

That stopped Miller cold. "I thought you looked like you had some sense," he said with disgust. "Good luck, Bullseye. You're gonna need it." He buried his face in his clipboard again and continued toward the Operations tent, hopping and scuttling, muttering to himself.

Eddie stood and watched him, congratulating himself on his decision and his boldness. The throb of rotors caught his attention, and he watched a single Delta-model slick rise into the glaring blue of the midday sky, followed shortly by a light fire team of two gunships.

The Daggers' tent was closest to the end of the runway. Though the day was quite warm, the sides of the tent were rolled down, and when they stepped into the dark interior, they felt a wave of hot fetid air. The space was cluttered, crowded with folding cots in two rows. From the light of a single bulb hanging from a wire near one end of the tent, Eddie could see that some of the cots had dusty bug nets stretched over them, and most had a duffle bag, box, or zipper bag of some kind stuffed beneath the foot. Each box and bag bulged with clothes, flight gear, and an assortment of personal items. A man in jungle fatigue trousers and undershirt sprawled on the cot nearest the light.

Eddie started to walk into the tent, and tripped over a root sticking up from the dirt floor. He dropped his duffle bag and grabbed the nearest tent pole, shaking the entire tent. The soldier on the cot lowered his copy of Poonboy Magazine and eyed him silently.

"You, ah, got a place I can park my ass for about a year?" Eddie asked, reciting the entrance line he had been rehearsing.

The man on the cot screwed his face into an expression of intense concentration. "Hm?" he said.

"Is this....is this the Daggers' tent?"

The man sat bolt upright on the bed, pointed an emphatic finger at Eddie, and grinned wickedly. "Yeeees, it is! Fact, truth, and deed, worthy of all men to be received. Sure you're not in the wrong place?"

"I've just been assigned to the gunship platoon," Eddie informed him. "Is one of these cots empty?"

"Make that two," added Kevin, stepping inside behind him.

"Two? No." The stocky warrant officer spread wide stubby hands and shrugged, staring at them with eyes that seemed a little too blue for his dark face and frizzled black hair. "You'll have to sleep together until somebody gets killed."

Seeing their blank stares, he chuckled and stuck out his hand toward Eddie. "I'm Skip Gilman, and you can take the two cots on the end. You been flight checked yet?"

"No. Just got here last night."

"Too bad. If you'd been checked out, you'd have gone on counter-mortar stand-by tonight, and I could get some sleep."

"Wow, that soon?" asked Eddie.

"Naw, not really. You'll probably get a few jack-off missions to get acquainted with the area before going out on the hot night stuff — a couple of days or so anyhow. We've only been up here ourselves for a month, you know."

"And they went ahead and started the war without us, huh?" asked Kevin with a grin.

"That's about the size of it. Might as well jump right in. For openers, I'll sell you a genuine American name-brand beer. You might as well get used to spending that monopoly money they gave you for your greenbacks.'"

"Sounds great to me," said Eddie. "Can I buy the house a round?"

"Delighted." As Eddie dug into his pocket and looked through his bankroll of the unfamiliar little military payment certificates — MPC — Skip pulled the top from his styrofoam ice chest and produced three cans of beer.

"I take it you've met the Old Man," said Skip, as they punched holes in the tops of their cans with a church key hanging on the tent pole by a string. "What did you think of him?"

Kevin shrugged. "Good soldier. Gung-ho. Got something to prove maybe, and it looks like he's got what it takes to prove it. Could be raving nuts, too."

"That's about right," Eddie agreed. "We could have done a lot worse."

"Yeah," said Skip, raising his beer, "I can drink to that. Here's to Jake the Snake."

The two new Dagger pilots looked at each other in surprise, then nodded solemnly. "To Jake the Snake," they toasted.

They finished their beers and unpacked their duffle bags, and Skip suggested they get to the mess tent early for lunch.

"I'm for that," said Eddie. "How's the food here?"

"You'll puke," said Skip. "Actually," he confided as they set off toward the mess tent, "it's pretty good. It's all pre-packaged stuff, but Sergeant Porter and guys in the kitchen really do try to make it the best they can. One thing you'll find about living in a combat zone that's different from a Stateside base is that over here the support troops are part of the club too. You'd be surprised how much difference it could make in your life to have a friend in the mess hall, or in supply. It works the other way, too. If some guy just has to be an asshole, and pisses off the wrong cook's helper, he could end up with cyanide in his thermos bottle."

"Oh, yeah? That sort of thing really happens?" asked Eddie.

"Oh, probably not very often. But it sure doesn't pay to screw with the troops. Let's face it anyway, a warrant pilot is just a spec-5 with an Officer's Club card. In an outfit like this, we are the troops. Slop chute, next stop."

The food was good as Skip had promised, canned, bland, and prepared to the specifications of an unimaginative regulation menu, but prepared with care and rationed generously. Eddie dug happily into a full tray of meatloaf, mashed potatoes and gravy, peas and corn, cole slaw, more apple pie, and fresh-baked bread.

"Say, this is pretty good," he commented. "Is there any, uh...." He looked down the long folding mess table.

"Chile?" asked Kevin, with a grin.

"Yeah. I guess not, huh?"

"The closest thing you'll find here is Tabasco," said Skip. "The Vietnamese have some hot peppers too, but they're different."

"I can see now I'm going to have to straighten my Mamacita out about what to put in the care packages," Eddie said. "But how about the Vietnamese chile? Can we go into town?"

"Sure," Skip affirmed. "But it's off-limits at night. You gotta go in some afternoon when you're off-duty. Things will probably lighten up after the Vietnamese holiday, though. It's their new year -- they call it Tet, and we're going to have a three-day cease-fire, or something like that. Everybody will party and get shitfaced, and we'll be able to go into town. Then some chiselbeak will get bored and we'll all go back to kicking ass and taking names." Skip chuckled and dumped ketchup on his potatoes. "Hey, look who's coming," he said, pointing to four pilots walking into the mess tent.

Their fatigues were dark with sweat, and their faces still bore the scrunkular press-marks of the rubber earphone guards in their helmets.

"Some of the Brethren," said Kevin.

"That's some of the Cistern," said Skip loudly. "Not a Real Helicopter Pilot in the lot of 'em."

"That's right," called back one of them, a pudgy fellow with a cherubic face. "Gilman's the only Real Helicopter Pilot here."

"Hey, Gilman," called another, a scrawny rodent-faced 2nd Lieutenant, "you know the only difference between gook pussy and a flight helmet full of shit? Nah? Well, you can stick your head in either one, but in an emergency, you can eat the flight helmet."

"And you tried both, didn't you, Petch?" replied Skip.

"He did, I saw it," said the third pilot, a gangly youth with a skimpy new moustache and longer-than-usual hair.

The fourth, a large, square-jawed captain, came over to the table and pointed to Eddie. "These our new men, Mr. Gilman?"

"Yessir," Skip replied, standing. "Warrant Officers Eddie Padilla, and Kevin Harrey, Sir. Our Platoon Commander, Captain Duke Randall."

"Pleased to meet you. Major Csynes told me you looked to him like a couple of fireballs."

"Well, that's, uh, very flattering, Sir," said Kevin. "I guess I'd have to say the feeling was mutual."

Duke Randall nodded. "You got that right. Major Jake is definitely a fireball. Sit down, please, eat your lunch. We'll grab a tray and join you."

The captain was an Oklahoma football player, tall, rangy, deep-chested, and sandy-haired. Older than most of the pilots, he had come up through the ranks. He was soft-spoken and easy-going, but friendly and eager like a Great Dane.

The four pilots filled their mess trays, then returned to the table to join Kevin and Eddie. The gangly young pilot punched Kevin lightly on the shoulder. "Peter Hawking," he said, extending a hand to Eddie. He indicated the round-faced pilot. "This is Round John Bergin, our resident capitalist, who thinks too highly of office furniture and is rumored to be very rich."

"It's only a very small bank, really," protested Round John. He toasted Eddie with a loaded forkful of meatloaf and happily began packing his cherubic face.

"I'm Petch, Wilbur D.," said the rodent-faced lieutenant. "My friends call me Bud. You're in my section, so you won't be sitting around. We'll get you an orientation flight this afternoon, and you'll be on the duty roster tomorrow."

"Great! Any chance I'll get a hot one?" asked Kevin eagerly.

"There's a chance you'll get a hot one every time," said the captain.

Over the next three weeks, they got to know the other men in the unit, and quickly settled into the routine of missions and life in the company area. There were two sections of pilots in the gunship platoon, and each section had its own tent. Petch was the section leader by virtue of his being a commissioned officer rather than a warrant, which fact he owed to a college degree in drama. The other section leader was 1st Lieutenant Rudy Bakersmith, a former member of the Army's Golden Knights demonstration parachute team.

The Blade and Spade, the company's club, was a tent set up with a TV set, two refrigerators, and some tables. The TV set received one channel, the Armed Forces Radio and Television program — whitewashed news, and reruns of I Love Lucy. A tape deck, some board games, a set of darts, and a stack of Poonhouse Magazines rounded out the unit's recreational facilities. Often as not, the main activity in the Blade and Spade Club was turning the TV picture on with the sound off, putting some country music on the tape deck, and shooting the shit.

"I'd just like to know the purpose of all this," said Peter Hawking one night to the others in the Club. "We're putting a lot of energy into this game, for a bunch of people who don't know what we're trying to do."

"Where the hell did you grow up, Henry Hawk — some pool hall?" asked Lt. Bakersmith. "The purpose of war is to defend people's freedom, to protect our political beliefs."

"Right," said Hawking. "We fly an Army halfway around the world and put in the middle of somebody else's country to defend itself."

"Americans sometimes defend other people's countries, too," the lieutenant said loftily.

"Because our hearts are pure and generous," said Skip.

Hawking flipped him a bird. "We are on our side, therefore everything we do is good...by definition, right? I'd just like to know why we should divide ourselves up into little nationalist clubs we have to promote by wholesale slaughter of each other. What for? Care and feeding? Some kind of moral thing? What?"

Kevin waved a hand. "Sure, it would be great if we didn't have nations, or races, or different religions, and everybody could speak English. We'd all be one big happy family. But that's not the way things are, old buck. Nations exist, and they fight a lot, no matter how you happen to feel about it. And no matter what side wins, the losers are gonna get treated like shit, so it pays to win."

Round John Bergin searched for the church key and popped open another can of beer. "All that idealistic stuff seems pointless to me. I don't like war. A few people get rich off wars, but I think in the long run they are not economical. But my society demands that I spend a year over here fighting a war it has decided for some reason to fight. If I'm going to be accepted, I have to do that, just like brushing my teeth."

"Some choice we've got, Herr Oberleutnant," Hawking said to Bakersmith. "Come over here and kill people and die in a pile of burning scrap metal defending The American Way, or let the bad guys line me up against a wall and blow my brains out? Are those really the only alternatives available? Sounds like the Great American Experiment has already failed."

"Bravo," said Round John. "The battle's lost, but our mad leaders drag us on and on. So how come you're over here stuffing undesirables into the ovens with the rest of us?"

"Why am I here?" The tall pilot shrugged. "Circumstances. Stupid. Gullible. Curiosity, maybe. I don't know."

"I know why I'm here," said Kevin. "Far as I can see, right or not, moral or not, logical or not, almost every major conflict of ideas in man's past has been resolved by force of arms. I believe

American democracy is worth defending, and this has been my profession since I left home. I'm here because I believe my minigun carries more real voting power in the world than your weeping for a just world."

"History will tell you anything you want it to, Babycakes. You seem to have nice pat answers to all your questions, and that's great. More power to you. But I don't have all the answers I need yet, and when I do get it all together, I hope the hell it doesn't leave me needing to blow up somebody's house every couple of days. It's just not neighborly."

"Smartest thing I've heard you say, Henry Hawk," said Kevin. "When you get it figured out, you tell me, OK? In the meanwhile, I plan to be on the winning side. So what about you, Eddie? You haven't said a word in two hours."

Eddie blushed. "Well, I believe in all those things too, but I think the truth is that I just want to be here so I can look good to my family — and my friends — when I go back home."

For a moment the Club was silent, and everyone turned to look at him. "Right on," said Peter Hawking softly.

Eddie said that on impulse, and about half facetiously, but it kept coming back to haunt him. It was a fantasy he had indulged before: he was sitting up on the back seat deck of a convertible, riding down the main street of Las Cruces to the cheers of thousands. He was going to meet the President, who had flown in from DC to award him the Congressional Medal of Honor. His mother sat in the seat at his knee, weeping in sanctified joy and tenderly stroking the folded and pinned leg of his dress uniform, empty from the knee down. At the other knee sat The Girl. She was a variable factor in the dream, usually borrowed from among his classmates in school. He looked down at her, and he felt his body thrill to the promise in her eyes, and the ripe swelling breasts she presented to him.

Then, too, there was Roger. If it hadn't been for Roger, he would never have been likely to quit college to be a combat pilot. He lay back on his cot in the tent and remembered his last visit to Roger's home in San Manuel, a few days before leaving for Vietnam.

That afternoon he drove his two-tone blue '56 Bel Air south

through the big pecan orchards and cotton fields of the Mesilla Valley. It was a cold, clear day with a high overcast, so colors were washed out, and line detail heightened. To the west, the crumbling solid-surf escarpment of the Black Mesa lava flow rose to obscure the distant horizon. The Organ Mountains a few miles to the east seemed to just support the clouds, as though the valley were a tunnel with sides only a short distance away.

He was both dreading and looking forward to seeing Roger Stanton again. Since graduation from high school in 1964, they had seen each other only occasionally, though they had spoken by phone several times. The New Mexico Technical Institute where Eddie had gone was in the northern part of the State, and though Eddie had his own car, his visits home had been rare. Roger had stayed in San Manuel, and had attended classes in engineering at New Mexico Southern.

After a single year of college, Roger had begun to complain to Eddie that he felt he was wasting his time. "I've either got to get myself into a top school of aerospace technology, or into flying corporate jets, or something like that, if I'm going to get ahead of the pack trying to get into astronaut training."

The next time Eddie saw Roger was briefly during the following spring break, at which time Roger announced that he had been selected for Marine Corps pilot training. "It's all set," he declared proudly. "I finish two years here at Southern, and report to Pensacola, Florida as a Marine Aviation Cadet. It's a perfect plan. I get my wings, rack up some good career points cleaning the Commies out of Vietnam, then come back to the States and let the Corps put me through the schools they want me to have to get into test pilot school. I'm on my way, Eddie."

Eddie had been impressed, and he also was dissatisfied with his experiences at college. Roger's plan began to look more and more attractive to him, so he took steps to investigate. Though he was unable to get into the MARCAD program with Roger, he was welcomed with enthusiasm by the Army, and after his sophomore year at Tech, he too went to win the wings which set pilots apart from all others in masculine mystique. Now, a year later, he had come home with the prize, a slim silver emblem of a winged shield, pinned to the otherwise bare breast of his new uniform.

Roger was not home on leave. Eddie knew that he had completed four months of pre-flight training, had soloed in the little Beechcraft T-34 trainers, and had gone on to jet training at Meridian, Mississippi. Then, after a few weeks there, he had been suddenly dropped from the program, discharged from the Marine Corps, and sent home.

As he drove into the little town, Eddie could see on the mesa a half mile west the clump of trees and the tall red-tiled front of the home which Roger's father Otto Stanton had built when Roger was a child. Designed in Southern-California neo-Spanish, but with a peculiar Norman turret over the front door, the lime-green-stuccoed mansion had always been known as the Green Castle. He smiled, recalling many good times he had spent there, then turned away toward the plaza, and the little saloon where he knew he would find his friend.

"Bar CHATO'S Coors", read the ancient neon sign over the door to the old adobe building. The building had once been a small hotel, and like many of the old saloons in the valley, was reputed to have been one of the hangouts of Billy the Kid in the 1870's. It was probably true. Eddie stepped inside and peered around in the darkness, trying to adjust his eyes.

"Hey, did anybody here call Roto-rooter?" boomed a gravely voice from the far side of the room. Recognizing the big jelly-belly guffaw of his friend, Eddie groped his way into the cool and cluttered little saloon. As his eyes adjusted, he walked past the long curved bar and joined Roger at a table in the back beside the little gas-log fireplace.

"How you doing, Big Rog?" he asked, grasping Roger's hand.

Roger stood and wrapped his arms around Eddie in a big bear hug. "All right, look at you! Peter Pilot, rotorhead first class. Well, congratulations! Here, let me buy you a drink. Hey, Felix, two more of the same."

Eddie pulled up a chair and sat down, and old Chato's son Felix brought a tray around the end of the bar and set two draft beers and two shots of tequila on the table. "Here's to good old times, good old broads, and good old booze," said Roger, holding aloft his shot.

"Andale pues," affirmed Eddie, and they tossed back the shots and followed them with chunks of lime. They growled with gusto and laughed.

Roger had been home six months, and had not shaved. His close-cropped Marine haircut was growing in at the same rate as his beard, and he was beginning to look shaggy like a mountain man in blue jeans, plaid shirt, and huge engineer boots.

"So what the hell, Big Rog, what happened?" Eddie asked.

"Anh. I had a little disagreement with the Corps, and they decided I was just too loose to be flying their hot little toys."

"I thought the MARCAD contract required you finish out two years of service if you didn't complete the program."

"That's right," Roger agreed, "but I wasn't about to spend a year of my life packing an M-14 as a grunt. So I arranged to get thrown all the way out."

"How'd you pull that off?"

Roger held up his beer glass. "My old friend Demon Rum came to my aid. I started drinking everything I could get my hands on, hair tonic, cough syrup, anything, and getting into fights — punched out some dipshit major I ran into in a bar downtown. They sent me to the base shrink, and he decided I was too unstable for duty, so they gave me a General Discharge and sent my young virgin ass home. And before they let me back in there, they're going to call up the old ladies and the cripples. So I've got my military service behind me, a guarantee I won't get called back up, and I learned how to fly airplanes in the process. Sounds to me like beating the fucking game."

"That's really....all right," Eddie tried gamely to agree. "Yeah. Those jets must have been great."

"Fact, truth, and deed. Flying jets is really one of the greatest thrills of human life. But let's face it, that astronaut business was never anything but a crazy dream. If everything had gone right, I'd have spent the next ten years training for one glorious moment, then retired to be a public relations jerk for the rest of my life. I can do without that shit. Now I'm going to make some money, fuck a platoon of hot pussy, and get down to living the good life. By the time you finish your tour of duty and get back here, I'll have it all set up, and you can make up for some lost time."

"Sounds great. So, what now, Big Rog?" Eddie asked his friend.

Roger stared into his beer. "Oh, I've got some plans. I walked off with over fifty hours of flight training, including ten hours in the jets. Getting a private license will be a piece of cake."

"That sounds great, Roger," said Eddie. "When I get back from Nam, you can teach me to fly fixed-wing. I've still never been in one."

"You've got a deal. I think in the meanwhile I think I'll take advantage of Dad's machine shop and do some custom car work. I'm going to buy a couple of neat old cars of some kind and turn them into showroom stuff, get off them and make some bucks. Maybe I'll travel some, see some car shows, party a lot. Oh, yeah, and let me show you what else I've got going." He reached into the pocket of his sheepskin coat and brought out a package of color photographs. "Check these out," he said, spreading them on the table.

The pictures were of two different girls, both of whom appeared to be about nineteen. Both were attractive, but not exceptionally so. Both were nude, or mostly nude, and were shot standing in one artsy pose or other against the backdrop of the Black Mesa. The posing was clumsy, the framing of the pictures crude, and several were incorrectly exposed, but the effect was pretty sexy nonetheless.

Roger laughed gleefully. "Parlor tricks," he said. "It's just like magic. I got a 35-millimeter camera, a couple of photo flood lamps, and printed up an official-looking model release, and went to work. You would be blown away how many girls will peel their clothes off and show you everything they've got the minute you start waving a camera around."

After a couple more drinks, both men were getting pretty sloppy, and the sun had long since gone down. They left the little saloon and went up to the Green Castle, where they continued to drink on into the night. Roger showed Eddie more pictures of the girls he had photographed, and just before the sun came up, he spoke again of his brief encounter with the Marine

Corps. In retrospect, Eddie was never sure he had the details straight, never sure how much of what he remembered had actually been said, but he knew that for all his usual bravado and glib dismissal of his adolescent dreams, Roger was deeply shaken by his failure, and Eddie never mentioned it to him again.

They enjoyed a few more days of family holiday celebration, and then Eddie rode with his mother, his little sister Ceci, and Roger Stanton to the airport in El Paso, where he hugged them all, and left them behind him.

A letter from home.

My Darling Kevin,

Here I am missing you again. I guess it's because I love you so much. And of course, because you're gone so much. Sometimes it seems like you were never here and I'm still missing you from last time. Then whenever I think of you, it's like you just left an hour ago, and I start missing you all over again.

Especially I miss you whenever I look at Baby George. He is such a big baby, and so healthy looking. I know he misses his Daddy, too. He needs you so much now that he is learning to talk and do so many things. I will get some pictures taken of him soon and send them to you, so you can bore the other pilots with them. His second birthday is coming up (you haven't forgotten, have you) and Mom wants to have a party. Maybe I will send you some snapshots of me too.

I moved out of my parents place and got an apartment of my own. It keeps me very busy taking care of one baby — it is impossible to take care of one baby, plus one doting grandfather who is afraid Booboo is going to drool on his dress tans, and one mother who thinks her little girl just got a new pee-pee doll and wants to recite her personal operating manual on it twenty-four hours a day. She just wants to spoil him silly and feed him everything, and change his clothes about six times a day. I can't get him to do anything, because he just yells and she runs over and picks him up and tells him what a nasty old mother he has. She was always bothering me about where I was all the time, too, which is crazy because I haven't gone anywhere, and what does she think I'm going to do?

Actually, I'm still spending most of my time with the same people we did before you went to Flight School. Of course, we're all old married grumps now, and it's coffee and television and early to bed, instead of tequila and rock and roll. Daddy still likes to take me to the Officer's Club for dinner every few days, and it's a great feeling that I can go there now because I'm an officer's wife, instead of an officer's kid. I still get goose bumps when I remember how you looked when we were here on leave and we all put on "full dress" and went there together — you with your new Warrant Officer bars, and Daddy with his new Major leaves. I felt like solid Gold, but I was happy and proud that my name is now Mrs. Harrey. Other than that, though, I haven't been down to the Club. I just can't stand sitting around with the Waiting Wives drinking martinis and clucking about the bulge in some soldier's pants. (Just kidding, I haven't been looking.) Daddy bought me a little television set at the Commissary. The stuff they broadcast in El Paso hasn't improved any, but it gives me a choice from reading myself to sleep. I like to go to the movies on-post, too. You're missing a lot of good flicks — we'll have to go out a lot together when you get back to catch up on lost time. (We'll have to stay home a lot to catch up, too.) I saw one last night about Elizabeth Taylor playing the wife of a Major on an Army base in the South. He was played by Marlon Brando, and he turned out to be queer, or something like that. But the place was very romantic and picturesque, not just a bunch of old green buildings like Fort Rucker. I think I would just love to live on one of those really old Southern bases, and spend my afternoons on the veranda with some other Colonel's wife, sipping cocktails and showing off my new hairdo.

Have you submitted a request for your next assignment yet? I have been looking at travel brochures for a month trying to decide where I would like to go most. How do you feel about someplace kind of exotic, like Iran, maybe? Daddy says if you're hot you can get a direct commission to Lieutenant, and they'll just about let you pick your next duty station. Have you ever stopped to think if you get a commission, you could retire on a Major's pension in 1982, and you won't even be forty yet? Daddy thinks they will offer him Lt.Col. if he stays in instead of retiring when his twenty comes up. So either way, you would come out a winner, if you did that too.

Well, how is the war coming? Is it much different than last time? I hope you can stay out of the worst places. Daddy says gunships look more dangerous, but really aren't because you can shoot back. Is that right? I've got better sense than to sit around worrying about how much danger you're in, but the news reports are like a horror show. Half of the news is American troops all shot up in some field hospital, and the other half is these "hippy" people running around waving flowers and burning things and saying it's immoral to fight for your country. Don't they know they're just making the war longer by giving the enemy the hope that we'll quit? It makes me so mad because we are the ones who have to suffer, we who have to sit home alone afraid to answer the telephone or open official mail, and who have to go away to terrible places to face brainwashed Communists. The hippies think a free country means free food, free education, and free love. They forget that somebody has to make the sacrifices.

Oh, well, no matter what the rest of the country does — they can make Martin Luther King the People's Chairman, for all I care — I just know that I love you, and I can't wait for you to get home again to me and your son George. You had better get some rest on the way home, because I am going to give you a boner that won't quit for two weeks, and I am going to ride around on it everywhere you go. Until then, keep it in your footlocker, and take it out and oil it once in a while. And think of me when you do. I can feel it all the way over here.

> Love, sex, love,
> love, sex, SEX,
> Carlie and George

PS: When is your R & R? Daddy says if you can get sent to Hawaii, he will buy me a ticket, and I can meet you in Honolulu! But all I will want to see is a lot of beautiful ceilings.

FOUR

One evening shortly after Kevin and Eddie arrived, Major Csynes called a full-company briefing in the mess-hall tent. Everybody was there early, and the morale was high. The Sabres had suffered no casualties, though several helicopters had come back from missions with bullet holes. The pilots were all well acquainted with the local operating area, and they were beginning to feel at home. That old familiar ballteam spirit had begun to raise its proud and predatory head, and the boys were spoiling for a fight.

The briefing was brought to order precisely at 19:00 hours by Captain Neil Koontz, the Company Executive Officer. "Cmpny, uTenh-Huht! Gentlemen, the Commanding Officer."

The Major wore fresh starched fatigues, and a cologne which gave him an air of coolness, as though he had just stepped from another planet into the fetid and funky tent full of sweaty soldiers.

"At ease, men, sit down," he said. He looked from one eager expectant face to another. "Like General George Patton, I believe that a certain sense of the drama of combat helps the warrior to be more effective in his job. That sense of drama is the power behind Medieval chivalry and Japanese bushido. In the ring it makes the difference between a bum who can fight and a champion. Here in Bao Trang, it makes the difference between a bunch of GI's who blow up things and schlepp troops around and a unified fighting machine with a reputation that keeps the Cong on the other side of the mountain.

"Men, when people see us coming, I want them to know who it is. I want them wondering how our area can look like it was laid out by an architect, when everything else around here looks like it grew out of fungus. I want them to see that we are in control of the environment, so they will understand that we are going to control them too, or protect them, as the case may be.

"The Viet Cong make a practice of putting a price on the heads of the American troops they fear most and would most like to see dead. I want a price on the head of every pilot in this unit. I want them so upset when they hear the name Black Sabre or Dagger, they sell the shithouse and put baby sister on the street just to find a way to pay somebody to save them from us."

That got a hearty round of applause from the company. In spite of a certain salty and cynical reluctance to succumb to such locker-room coaching, the Daggers in particular found Jake Csynes' rationale to strike a familiar chord within themselves, and their excitement began to rise.

It was music to Eddie's ears — a rousing march by a prancing band. Here was someone who understood. This cool, dapper, and towering reptile of a man had been sent from Heaven just to lead him to the moment of glory he had come for.

"Tomorrow morning we are going to show the people in this valley what a full-scale company assault is supposed to look like," Jake Csynes continued. "Let's make up our minds right now that we are going to look sharp, and fly sharp, and make this a showcase mission. We are going to insert three platoons of Infantry in two ten-ship lifts onto a hilltop on the ridge west of here, and over the next few weeks we are going to turn it into a secure firebase from which we can conduct operations in the A Lan Valley. We do not expect the LZ to be hot, but we will permit the Daggers to provide one fire team for a pre-insertion rocket strike, and the other two teams will provide full suppressive fire on the first insertion. I want to make sure we get the attention of every Vietnamese in the area, the good guys and the bad guys."

"All right!", and "Hey-hey!" from the Dagger pilots.

"Captain Koontz will brief you on the coordinates, the tactical frequencies, and the crew schedule. He will be flying lead slick, by the way. I will be in C-and-C, which also makes me the primary rescue ship if anybody goes down. We will pull pitch at zero-seven-hundred, so I recommend that all of you get some sleep and I'll see you on the line. Your show, Neil."

"Cmpny, uTenh-Huht!" The men snapped-to as The Major

stepped down from the low speaking platform and strode from the tent with a scar-twisting smile and a wave of comraderie.

The briefing was routine thereafter, and Eddie and Kevin learned that they would be flying in one of the teams escorting the slicks. Rudy Bakersmith and pilots from his section would fly the pre-insertion rocket strike.

After the briefing was over, several of the pilots and other crew members went to the Blade and Spade to have a few beers, but Eddie decided he preferred to stay sober. He stepped out of the mess tent into the relative cool of the evening and strolled off by himself. The sky was clear, and a waning moon cast a soft light by which he could see the hills to the west. It was strangely quiet. Eddie stood for a moment listening to the night. It seemed the first time he could remember not hearing the muted muttering of rotor blades anywhere in the valley. He looked up, and smiled softly observing that the sky was clear, but the moist tropical atmosphere dulled the stars to a mottled pattern of warm little blobs, instead of the myriad needle-points of icy crystal which he was accustomed to seeing in the stark desert skies of New Mexico.

He wandered down to the flight line, waved to a sentry, who recognized him, and walked beside the aircraft, reaching out occasionally to touch the cool dark surfaces of olive-painted aluminum and tinted plexiglass, and the blued-steel barrels of the stubby Gatling-style miniguns.

In the moonlit darkness the waiting gunships looked to him like great clumsy goggle-eyed bugs crouching with wings furled in nooks of piled-up blobs of mud. "The Locusts of Armageddon," he thought, "and here I am one of them. If Mama could see me now." In fact, he did wish she could see him. He wished he could take her on his walk among the resting chariots. He wished he could strap her into the co-pilot's seat and take her for a thrilling night ride across the Vietnamese countryside, and then for a low-level sweep around the family house in Las Cruces, and then down to San Manuel, where he would rock the bird from side to side to hail Roger Stanton as he stood waving excitedly on the broad patio of the Green Castle.

He laughed softly to think how after all the years he had been

Roger's sidekick and listened to him tell how he would be a great pilot, and one day an astronaut, it was he instead who was the pilot, and the warrior.

Eddie rolled out of his sleeping bag at 04:30, spent the better part of an hour in the mess tent eating breakfast, then walked to the flight line early and was waiting there when the rest of the crews arrived in the three-quarter-ton truck. With Skip, for whom he was flying co-pilot, he conducted a thorough pre-flight inspection of the aircraft and its weapons. At 06:40, he watched the Major's Command-and-Control helicopter, "C-and-C", crank up and lift off in a cloud of dust. On that signal, the rotors of all the birds began to swing, and the whine of the turbines cut through the morning stillness.

At 06:45 the helicopters began to rise one after another from the narrow sandbag revetments. In a ponderous ballet of plump floating creatures, they moved to the runway, where they lined up according to the order given in the briefing. As Eddie watched, the two gunships assigned to the pre-strike team moved past the ten slicks and took the position at the front of the column. Then Skip called, "Coming up!", and began to pull up on the collective lever beside his seat. "Clear right!" came from the gunner, followed by, "Clear to port."

The helicopter rose smoothly straight up about eight feet to clear the sides of the revetment, then began to hover toward the runway with the three other gunships of the escort teams. As soon as they were clear of the sandbags and over the runway area, Skip let the ship settle to a low three-foot hover, smoothly took his position at the tail end of the formation, and plunked to the ground.

The infantry company had been assembled in squads along the side of the runway, and they turned their backs and grimly endured the wall of churning dust raised by the powerful rotors. As soon as the helicopters touched down and the pilots rolled the throttles back to idle, the infantry squad leaders urged their troops forward. Crouching low to avoid the rotors swooshing five feet above their heads, they scurried to the waiting open side doors, and in a few seconds the flight was loaded.

On the VHF radio channel used by the slicks, the ten troop-carrying helicopters checked in. "Sabre chalk one, up." "Chalk two, up." The practice of referring to one's position in the lineup as a "chalk" had not made sense to Eddie until the first time he had seen the infantrymen with whom the 17th worked standing in lines with their position numbers written on their helmets in big white chalk numbers. "Chalk ten, up."

Then on the FM tactical freq used by the gunships, Eddie heard Captain Randall call for his pilots to check in. "Dagger two-six, up," came from Lt. Rudy Bakersmith, fireteam leader of the pre-strike team, followed closely by, "Two-four, up," from his wingman, Warrant Officer Arlo Jeter. Though the slicks used their positions in the flight as callsigns, the gunship pilots used their own call numbers. "Dagger one-seven, up," called Kevin, fireteam leader of the second escort team. "Dagger lucky one-three, up," said Skip, his wingman. "One-six, up," called Bud Petch. Then Duke Randall came up on the VHF freq and reported to C-and-C, "Sabre Six, Dagger Six, you have three light fire teams up." For some reason known only to some admin planner somewhere, the commander of any unit was always given the number Six. Major Csynes was Black Sabre Six; Captain Randall was Dagger Six.

"Roger that," came the Major's reedy voice. "I have 07:00. Sabre lead, you have the flight."

"Roger, Sabre Six. Sabre flight, Papa-five," came the deep and calm voice of Captain Neil Koontz, using the pilots' jargon which meant "pull pitch — that is, take off — in five seconds." The dust swirled out to the sides as the pilots smoothly applied power to the whirling rotor wings, and like a single beast the flight rose from the runway and began to move forward. The two lead gunships of the pre-strike team quickly pulled out ahead of the slick column and hurtled down the runway, staying about three feet above the ground to gather speed. Then they suddenly swept up in a steep climb into the morning blue.

The four gunships of the escort teams stayed close beside the column until the flight passed through five hundred feet altitude, then made wide turns to the outside to fall in about a quarter of a mile behind and slightly above the slicks. A few hundred feet above the formation and out to the right cruised the Delta-model

C-and-C ship. "Sabres and Daggers, you're looking great!" called Jake Csynes heartily.

Eddie was feeling great. From his position in the left front seat of the last aircraft in the flight, he could see the whole formation. He was on the right side of the column of slicks, and about a hundred yards to his left was the wing ship of the other escort team, flown by Bud Petch and John Burgin. Like his own, the gunship was armed with a powerful array of weapons. Both had an open door on each side of the aircraft where the door gunners crouched behind 7.62mm M-60 machineguns fed with belts of ammunition. The pilot in command, the A/C, sat in the right seat, and was given a weapon in keeping with his job as primary pilot in combat situations. From his right seat, Skip Gilman grinned at Eddie and reached up to pat the rocket sight mounted in front of him. It was a heavy assembly bearing a glass plate with a lightbeam reticle. Skip's rockets were mounted in two pods of seven cach on the sides of the helicopter, and they were aimed by pointing the helicopter at the target.

Eddie's favorite weapon was the co-pilot's, the snarling miniguns. Mounted on a folding arm like an office lamp beside him was a pistol-grip fastened to a box-shaped tube he could peer though. When he looked through the tube, he would see a tiny circle of light which appeared to be floating in space a long way away. When he moved the pistol-sight around, it appeared that he could put the circle of light onto things on the ground. On short hydraulic-operated pylons on the sides of the gunship were the two six-barrel miniguns. They were slaved to the pistol-grip-sight so that both of them pointed directly at whatever Eddie put that little ring of light on. When he squeezed the trigger on the pistol, the little Gatling guns were driven at high speed by electric motors, and fed with belts of the same 7.62mm rounds as the door gunners' M-60's and the infantrymen's M-14 rifles. Because the helicopters could carry only limited amounts of the heavy ammunition, the Daggers' miniguns were geared down so they only fired forty bullets per second per gun.

Four of the six Dagger gunships were armed with miniguns and seven-round rocket pods, and were primarily used as anti-personnel weapons. The other two were specialized for harder targets, and for some unexplainable reason were called Frogs. A quarter of a mile ahead of Eddie flew his fireteam leader, Kevin Harrey, in one of the platoon's Frogs. As A/C, Kevin's weapon was the rocket, but instead of pods of seven rockets, he carried two pods of nineteen each. Flying as his co-pilot, Peter Hawking was armed with a belt-fed, turret-mounted grenade launcher. Looking like an oversize beachball mounted on the nose of the helicopter, it fired the same round as the infantryman's M-79 single-shot grenade launcher, but at the rate of two per second. It was a difficult weapon to master, but a man who was good with a "blooper" could walk a line of explosions up a ditch, or plunk them one after another into a hootch, sighting through a swing-down double-handled reticle sight.

Eddie's mind raced as he mentally took inventory of the firepower his company represented. The steady jog of the Huey and the flickering of the rotor hypnotized him a moment, and he stared down to watch the quilted paddies and Nipa-palm breaks change to tangled jungle with tall puff-crowned trunks. Ten slicks, each with four crew, plus six more people in C-and-C. Each slick armed with two M-60 door guns, with 1000 rounds apiece. Six gunships, with crews of four. Seventeen helicopters, seventy men, thirty-four M-60 machineguns, eight miniguns, two grenade launchers with 150 grenades each, 132 artillery rockets, and a total of 58,000 rounds of 7.62mm bullets — not to mention that each helicopter carried two M-16 rifles as survival equipment, and each crew member carried his personal sidearm. The function of this behemoth, Eddie marveled, was to put sixty infantrymen on the ground, no matter who didn't want them there.

The voice of Lt. Rudy Bakersmith cut through on the radio. "Sabre Six and Sabre Lead, this is Dagger Two-six. I have the LZ in sight, and I'm going to make a low pass to drop smoke for positive identification, over."

"Roger, Dagger, this is Sabre Six. I have the LZ in sight also. You are cleared to mark. Sabre Lead, you are four minutes out, and you should be able to see the LZ on the slope at your ten-o'clock position. Commence a wide orbit to the right and stand clear for pre-strike."

"Sabre Six, Lead. Roger that."

Kevin had the LZ spotted also. It was an obvious location, a bare shoulder on the slope of a ridge, a flat little island in a sea of wave-like ridges covered with the green foam of jungle vegetation. As he watched, the sun glinted off the flashing rotor of Bakersmith's helicopter on its low pass over the LZ. Behind him rose a plume of bright purple smoke.

Major Csynes' quickly called to confirm the drop. "I have grape smoke in the LZ, Dagger. You are cleared to strike."

Bakersmith was just climbing back for another run, and his wingman Warrant Officer Arlo Jeter was set up for his run in the Frog ship. "Roger, cleared," called the Lieutenant. "Go ahead and make the first pass, Two-four."

"My pleasure, Sir," replied the deep-south former Special Forces team leader as he rolled in to make a firing pass. He fired four carefully placed pairs of rockets along the treeline at the back of the LZ, then rolled off. As soon as Jeter was clear of the target area, Bakersmith fired two pairs of rockets, then made a slow pass so his co-pilot Jerry Malins could work both sides of the LZ with minigun fire. Jeter rolled the Frog in again, fired a few pairs of rockets, then made a high slow pass so his co-pilot Lorenzo Ferranti could walk a ring of the egg-sized grenades around the remote little clearing in the jungle.

From five clicks away, Kevin and the other Sabre troops could see the columns of dirt thrown up by the small artillery warheads on the rockets, and the rows of marching fat little balls of dark smoke from the blooper. Four pairs of the rockets on the Frog were Willie Pete — white phosphorus — which made huge white puffs, like elephant-sized popcorn, and which left fires burning.

"Sabre Six, Dagger Two-six. Strike fire team is clean and clear of the LZ. Received negative fire, over."

"Roger, Dagger. Nice shooting, Gentlemen. They know where we are now, so now let's show them what we've got. Sabre Lead, you are cleared direct to the LZ for the insertion, over."

"Roger that, Sabre Six," came Neil Koontz's reply. "Sabre flight, make your final checks and advise your troops we're going in. Stay loose — we've got plenty of room. But don't get sloppy! Dagger Six, you are clear to provide full suppressive fire on the insertion — one pass only, please."

"Dagger Six. Roger, Lead. Daggers, keep your rockets well outside of the LZ, and use outside minigun only. That's right, only one gun," came Duke Randall's Oklahoma twang.

As the flight of slicks lined up for their landing approach, the lead gunships hung poised a quarter of a mile behind, and as the slicks descended slowly, the gunships dived down with weapons blazing. Randall was flying the lead gunship on the left side. He put two pairs of rockets into the jungle, then let Ray Swomney, his new warrant co-pilot from second section, shoot up the trees with his minigun. Likewise on the right, Kevin fired two pairs of rockets into the woods, then let Henry Hawk poop off a few rounds with the blooper.

Seconds before the slicks made their touchdown, the lead gunships pulled up and to the outside in a steep zoom climb, so as the slicks settled to a light-on-the-skids landing, the wingman gunships were just rolling in for their firing runs. Knowing he was only going to get one run, Petch tried to get off all seven pairs of his rockets. He kept them aimed wide of the flight, but one still careened wildly over the slicks into the trees beyond. Since the rocket firing switch was rigged to interrupt the miniguns (so they wouldn't shoot the rockets as they were fired), Round John was unable to get off a shot. Skip fired only one pair, and then let Eddie shoot his minigun. Eddie laughed with delight at the abrupt and vicious snarl of the little gun. GAKKK!! Then he could see the troops spilling from the slicks and running toward the perimeter of the LZ, so he held his fire. As he flew past the slicks, he saw them rise together, and then Skip rolled to the right and he lost sight of the flight. At the same instant, he heard another ripping burst of minigun fire, then screaming confusion on the radio.

"Cease fire! Cease fire!"

"We're hit!"

"Swomney, you shithead!"

"Sir, I thought it was...."

"Check intercom, shithead."

"This is Sabre Six. Who's hit? Are you receiving fire?"

"Dagger One-six, Sir. Negative fire, Six. I think it was....my door gunner's hit. Says he's OK.....bleeding is, uh, under control. The aircraft....everything's working, I think."

"Dagger Six, break off and escort One-six back to The Scabbard," ordered Csynes. "I want a report as soon as I get there. Dagger Two-six, get your fire team rearmed and stand by to escort the second lift. Who is the leader of the remaining team, over?"

"Sabre Six, this is Dagger One-seven," called Kevin Harrey. "I have one light with a Frog. Over."

"What's your ammo load, One-seven?"

"Seventeen pairs and about eighty percent on the blooper, Six. One-three, what's your status, over?"

"Six pairs and full cans around," reported Skip.

"Roger that, Daggers. We've had a call for a fire team from a unit in contact in the valley between here and The Scabbard. Break off from the flight and proceed on a heading of one-one-five degrees, and stand by for coordinates and call sign."

"Roger, one-one-five and stand by. One-seven, out." Kevin broke away from the flight of slicks, and Skip fell in behind.

"Whoo-eee!" hooted Skip over the intercom. "Looks like we're going to run off with all the action."   "What the hell happened?" asked Eddie over the air.

"Go Jack Benny, down two, over," came Kevin's cryptic reply.

"Two back of Jack, Rog." Eddie reached to the radios and set the frequency Kevin had told him to tune in: Jack Benny, that is FM frequency 39.00, and down two, to 37.00, which was likely to be an unused channel, and so one they could chatter on without the rest of the company monitoring. "One-seven, up," came Kevin's call.

"Hey, Babycakes, did you see what happened?"

"Yeh, I did. One-six kept shooting rockets all the way down, and he was just breaking off when Randall rolled in to pick up the flight. Swomney squeezed off a burst of minigun right on top of Petch. I could see tracers hitting the tail boom. Damn near shot Bud The Dud right down."

"Whoo-ee! Babies and doggies, I'll bet Randall's ready to shit a bucket of bricks," said Skip.

"Randall?" Kevin scoffed. "Randall's gonna be pissed all right — but Jake the Snake is gonna eat somebody's whole ass."

Over the intercom, Skip asked Eddie, "You've never seen Csynes get pissed off, have you? All those scars turn purple and he gets rigid and hisses. The guy's a little weird, you know."

They got a call from C-and-C giving them the coordinates and the call sign of the infantry unit which had requested them, so they returned to their company tactical frequency and settled down to the business at hand.

"Blue Ribbon Six, Dagger One-seven, over."

The infantry unit quickly replied, "Dagger One-seven, Blue. We've got you coming up on us about two clicks out. We're straight ahead of you, and we'll pop smoke when you get here. How long can you remain on station, over?"

"Blue Ribbon, Dagger, we're good for about half an hour."

"Roger. Request you set up an orbit and observe ahead of our troops. Smoke is out. We're in the APC at your one o'clock. If we flush anything, we'll call you down, over."

The two gunships set up a wide wagonwheel pattern about six hundred feet above the paddies and scattered hooches of the area. From their mobile vantage points, the Daggers could see the GI's moving from paddy to paddy, treeline to treeline, hootch to hootch, and they could easily spot anyone trying to get out of the area ahead of them.

"Too bad you didn't get in-country training, Eddie. It was very instructive," said Skip over the intercom. "They told us anybody running is fair game. Our dinks don't run — only enemy gooks run. That's because the dinks are too lazy, and the gooks run because they're scared of helicopters."

"What if it's just some dink civilian in a hurry?"

"Tough shit. And anybody with a gun is game. An ARVN troop doesn't carry his weapon when he's off by himself, because the VC would take it away from him, or he'd sell it to them."

Eddie scanned the ground below him, watching the troops move along the dikes between the paddies, and expecting at any second to see a wave of coolie-hats and black pajamas dashing in full retreat ahead of the advancing friendlies. The area was quite open, with wide flat paddies separated by narrow dikes and ditches. Some of these were lined with bamboo, nipa palm, or trees.

The nearest village was only a cluster of ten or twelve hooches, and there were a few scattered hooches at corner-points in the patchwork paddies.

As Eddie watched, a single person stepped from one of the lone hooches and began to walk across a paddy toward two other hooches surrounded by trees. From the chopper, Eddie could see he was an old man, with bandy knees sticking out of short pajama pants, and white hair sticking out from under his conical coolie hat. He clutched some kind of long package under one arm, and walked coolly and purposefully out across the open space. When the gunship passed over him, Eddie looked back to watch, and saw him begin to shuffle quickly, walking as fast as he could without running.

"Hey, Skip. There's a guy down here acting kind of strange," he said.

"Yeah? Let's have a look." Skip squeezed his transmitter switch and called Kevin. "One-seven, Lucky. Checking one out back here." He pulled the helicopter around in a tight turn, and Eddie pointed the man out to him.

"He came out of that lone hootch over there. He was trying to look cool until we overflew him, then he started hauling ass."

Skip chuckled. "Let's see if he spooks easy." He nosed the gunship over as though beginning a gun run. The man stopped, looked back toward the hootch, started to continue slowly again, then stopped and raised his arms as the ship bore down on him.

"Hey! He had a package — a long thing," said Eddie. "He must have ditched it when he saw us coming back."

"That ties it." Skip broke off the run and pulled back up to make another. He called Kevin, "Got a hot one, Babycakes. Headed away from that lone hootch I just overflew. Call for clearance?"

"Go ahead."

On the ground commander's freq, Skip called, "Blue Ribbon, we've got one in the open who started to run for some hooches when we overflew him. Had a package he dumped somewhere. Request your clearance to fire, over."

"Dagger, this is Blue Six. You have mine to pork him," came the infantry commander's rather bored-sounding reply.

"Roger that!" Skip acknowledged. "Scratch one gook!" As Skip set up for his run, Kevin fell in behind him to follow up.

As though the old man could hear what had taken place in the helicopters, he had turned and was trying to get back to his hootch. Eddie lowered his minigun sight and flipped the arming switch. "On HOT," he said.

"He's all yours," said Skip.

Eddie looked through the pistol-grip gunsight and placed the little ring of light around the man in the rice paddy. He was walking quickly, with the stiff-legged gait of one fighting the urge to break and run. As the helicopter dived down he seemed to Eddie to grow huge in the sight, and it seemed impossible to miss. With a kind of detached self-consciousness Eddie watched himself squeeze the little red plastic trigger. The guns snarled abruptly, deep-throated, roaring, vicious, and a stream of tracers ripped up the ground twenty feet behind the old man. He leaped, and for a second Eddie thought, impossibly, he had heard him cry out. His cone hat flew off and his stringy white hair flopped as he tried to run, high-stepping and awkward, with his knees turned out, trying to force a last heroic effort in the futile hope of outrunning the stream of ripping bullets. He was six seconds, five seconds away from the hootch and the hiding place it was sure to contain when Eddie fired a second burst. The steam of red tracers crawled up around him, and at the door to the hootch he jerked and flailed, clawing up into the air, then fell to his back sprawling. Eddie shouted once, "Yah!" and held the gun on the hootch and the body before it, kicking up the dust, the blood and straw.

"Wow! Outstanding!" Skip hooted as he broke off the run and pulled the gunship into a steep climbing turn. "Did you see that old bastard jump when you opened up? Man, he knew he was about to meet his ancestors. Great shooting!"

As the ship swung around, the door gunner began to fire his M-60 into the hootch. Eddie could feel the blood pounding in his head, and his legs tingled as he stared down at the tiny thatched house and the crumpled body beside it. He was startled when an explosion half the size of the building burst nearby. He looked up and saw Kevin Harrey's Frog ship in a steep dive. Two streaks of smoke squirted out from the rocket pods. One hit short, and the second ripped through the side of the hootch and exploded, blowing a hole in the roof and setting thatch on fire.

"How about that shit?" crowed Kevin. As he broke off his run, he kept his helicopter low and made a sweeping pass over some of the other nearby hooches, rolling from side to side so his crew could peer into ditches and back yards looking for bunkers or people hiding in corners.

"Dagger, this is Blue Ribbon," came the call from the ground unit. "We just drew a burst of automatic weapons fire from that large house you just flew over — the one with the tile roof. Can you check it out?"

Kevin lay his ship on its side and swung back to the house. "I've got the house."

"Roger, Dagger, request you put some fire on it. We'll mark our forward position with a smoke, and you can work the ditch from there to the house."

As Kevin set up for his first firing pass, he instructed his crew. "Door guns, hold your fire until we pass the friendlies' smoke. Hawk, I'll fire four pairs, then you switch to blooper and work the ditch." He squeezed the mike switch to transmit and called Skip. "One-three, put a couple of rockets down there, and don't use too much minigun unless you see something alive."

"Roger that."

In the field below them, the ground troops advancing on the house tossed a smoke grenade out to mark their position so the gunships would not fire too close. As the grenade blossomed on the ground, Kevin set up a long, high firing pass. He waited a second to stabilize his run, then very deliberately pickled off four pairs of rockets. The door guns began to chatter, kicking up dust in the courtyard of the building. Hawking's blooper spat a stream of explosive rounds which walked neatly up the ditch leading from the friendlies' position to the house, then Kevin broke off high and made a slow turn to see if they were going to draw any fire. The crew chief spotted a pig running wildly around the yard and hosed him down with a stream of fire. The animal was still struggling, still trying to run with shattered legs when Eddie's miniguns finished him off.

Hawking's voice came up on the radio, apparently intended for intercom, "Hold it. There about two hooches beyond the one we hit — four people moving out."

Kevin's voice cut him off. "One-three, carry your fire into those two hooches past the tile roof. Looks like four troops on the run."

Skip fired two rockets into the hooches, and Eddie held the trigger on his miniguns, releasing fingers of fire to probe the straw huts and bamboo clumps for the soft bodies of human beings.

Kevin fired another four-pair barrage, and dropped a water buffalo in the yard of the second hootch. Hawk's blooper jammed for a second, and he quickly recycled the arming switch to clear it. In the pause, he saw a figure in black pants and blue shirt dart from a clump of weeds and dash for one of the hooches. The crew chief saw it too and swung his door gun to spray tracerfire. Hawking squeezed his triggers again and as the first rounds chugged out of his turret, he saw the figure fall struggling to the ground. Then the blooper rounds began to explode around the Vietnamese, obscuring the body with smoke.

"I think that was a woman," said the gunner. "I got a pretty good look just before the grenades hit her."

"It was," said Hawk. "My fucking blooper has jammed again."

"Blue Six, Dagger One-seven, we just zapped one of those four in the open," Kevin called. "I think it was a woman, over."

"Dagger, Blue. Right on. They took over a whorehouse here last week and killed a couple of our guys. Request you hold ammunition if you have it and let us move up to that first house."

"Blue Ribbon, we've only got about fifteen minutes and twenty percent, but we'll hold as long as we can. By the way, be advised we drew negative fire, over."

"Roger that, and be advised our flank element has confirmed your kill at the other site. Confirmed two dead — and they found the package in the ditch — a homemade bangalore about four feet long, definitely VC. Nice work, Daggers."

"Roger two confirmed," replied Kevin happily. "That's what your friendly Daggers are here for — you got somebody who needs to be zapped, you know who to call."

"Andale, pues!" agreed Eddie enthusiastically.

A letter from home.

Dear Ed,

Hey, you crazy fuck, so you're in Vietnam!! I hope you're scared shitless and you get the clap too. Serve you right for getting to fly gunships. So is it really the greatest game on earth, or just another standard GI FUBAR? Things are A-OK for The Original "Big Rog". I'm staying busy doing what I like, making a pile of money, and getting laid a lot. You won't believe it. My Dad decided to retire, and he sold the business — yeah, the whole enchilada. He got a bundle for it, which he's putting into stock, securities, that kind of shit. Also a ton into fixing up the house — would you believe a new coat of stucco? Guess what color? Yeah, green again. Of course, he won't let me touch a dime of it, as usual. He'll probably live to be ninety and croak the day before the market crashes again. Doesn't matter, though. The shop here at Castle is outfitted for anything, and I do mean anything, and I can use it for whatever I want to. I've got a lot of ideas for ways I can make some bucks in the shop, without having to go take a job somewhere.

He's in there too a lot, working on his projects, but we don't get in each other's way. In fact, it's really pretty good. We don't talk a lot, but it's good being there together. I guess I did a lot of things trying to please him — learning to make things, and know about how things work. But it was like he was Mr. Stanton to me too, like to you and everybody else. It's still hard to think of him as "Dad", like a kid has a dad, but I am enjoying getting to know him as Otto. Some things are the same as ever, though. He's one fussy blockhead — he'll spend two hours doing a job, then two days more making sure the nuts are all polished on the hidden side. He has decided to build a museum, and to fill it with his latest hobby: perfectly restored nineteenth century farm machinery.

Me, I'm building cars. Yeah, I decided to go for it. I buy a trade-in off Bill Greede's back line, steam and detail, tune her up, bang the dings out and shoot it two-tone blue. Then I take it to Juazoo on Friday for a custom genuwine leather interior, which they put in while I'm downtown hitting the old familiar waterholes. Saturday night I drive up to Southern to hang out with the bunnies and make the boys wish they had my car, and I put up a 4-Sale sign at the Canteen. Takes me about a week, and I can make about five C's a shot — not a fortune, but it keeps me in beer nuts. So Carlie's husband is in your unit. How is that little red-headed peckerwood? I thought you knew they got married. She is still living in El Paso, with her folks. They both came up here to San Manuel, right after he got back from his first tour in Nam. We went to a game, then hit a couple of joints for a cocktail or two. My date — the little blonde nymph with the big pink nipples, you remember — kept trying to get Kevin off to a dark corner, but he wouldn't get ten feet away from Carlie. I guess he was just glad to get home.

I thought about going back to college. I've got bennies coming, and it would be easy to go here, since I can live at home. But the truth, Ed, I just don't think there's anything there for me. I could get back into the space program by getting the right technical degree and going in through NASA, but the fire isn't there. I still believe in Heinlein's basic ship-captain-crew social values, but let's face it, you've got to be happy standing in straight lines to make it in the space game these days. They gave me a rough time in the Crotch about being too big for jets, too, but that's just because I got pretty fat running on all that high-octane bootleg booze I was getting at Meridian. You know they call that cracker-piss Moonshine because it'll make you howl like a dog even if there's no moon out. I'm drinking Scotch these days, like Otto. He's been hitting it pretty good, for an old geezer.

So school isn't it. All it's good for is getting a job, and I don't want one. Instead of working forty years and spending twenty keeping busy while you grow old, I'm going to get rich raising hell for forty years, then spend twenty more drinking up the profits as Chairman of the Board. I can make a lot of bucks with these crazy cars. When you get home, we can get a surplus C-119 Flying Boxcar to ship the cars around in. You'll pick up your fixed-wing rating in no time, and we can do some serious flying and partying. I've been thinking about making a rail, or a funny car, and taking a shot at big-time racing, or maybe getting into carshow street rods. Either that or professional photography — I'll probably take a few classes in that whether or not I go back full time. And my little 35mm thigh-spreader is still better than a poontang credit card. $2.75 buys a roll of film, which is good for a free photo session at her house, which is good for a naked aspiring actress trying to get in the mood to look horny on film, which is good for a hot piece of pussy, which is good for a shower and dinner, and a back-up kit with candy and champagne is usually good for breakfast.

So how are those Saigon sweeties? Is that stuff horizontal, or does that only apply to Zipponese? The pictures I've seen look a lot like squinty-eyed little Mexicans, so I guess you ought to feel at home, right? How about sending me a couple of pictures of your hootch girls — one polishing your boots and one polishing your knob. Do you have a camera? You ought to get yourself a good system at the PX — you can really beat the prices over there. Maybe I'll have you buy me some lenses and stuff and ship it to me. I'm sending you a box with about half a pound of Mesilla Valley red chile. Don't that give you a duodenal orgasm? Well, that's about it for now. Keep a tight asshole, and bring your Mexican burrito home in one piece.

Yer old pal,
CS1 Roger Stanton

*CS1 = Civilian Stud, First Class, sucker.

FIVE

Kevin eased the cyclic control back to slow his gunship, and lowered the collective pitch lever slightly so that the helicopter would descend smoothly. He scanned the now-familiar landing strip as the aircraft settled toward it, and he picked a well-tarred spot where dust wouldn't blow up to obscure his vision.

Ahead of him Skip Gilman's ship was turning smoothly to set down near the re-arming pits. Jockeying the controls lightly, he hovered his ship over to the pad and held steady for a second, then allowed it to settle gently to the ground. The whine of the turbine dropped and the grumbling throb of the rotor began to fall off. Kevin jerked at the catch on his lap belt, flipped the boom mike away from his mouth, and pulled his olive-drab helmet from his head. He sat for a moment and rubbed slowly at his face, trying to massage away the numbness. The beginning of a headache was gnawing at his temples, and the muscles of his neck were knotted and sore. "Every day here is Monday," he muttered, wiping sweat from the stubble of moustache he was growing.

"What time you got, Sir?" asked the crew chief.

"About 17:00. We'll be done in a few minutes, then we're secured for the day." They went over every inch of the ship's metal skin looking for the tiny bullet holes which could indicate damage done to the vital parts inside.

Skip finished first and walked over to Kevin's ship carrying his helmet and chicken-plate. "I hope we got a few of those fucking gooks," he said wearily. "We wasted enough time shooting at them."

Kevin nodded and spat into the sticky dust at his feet. "Left gun jammed. Malins got off about three seconds and it quit. I hate losing my weapons up there, even when there's nothing to shoot at."

"Yeah, I know just what you mean. Makes me feel like a man

with no dick."

A three-quarter truck came from operations to pick them up, and the two crews loaded their flight gear into it and jumped in, then leaned against the slat sides and settled back, beginning to relax for the evening.

"Think I'll go into the village for some boom-boom and some Bamuoiba," Skip mused.

"You can't go tonight," said Round John. "The Major put the town off-limits."

"How come?" demanded Skip.

"Vietnamese New Year, or something. Csynes said he doesn't trust Charlie to be cool and stick to partying."

"Well, damn, that's right. Tonight's the beginning of Tet," said Kevin.

"Kiss my mother dawg! New Year night in the cathouse, and everybody is gonna be there except us." Skip Gilman shook his head in disgust. "I can't figure that guy Csynes — he's like a tiger on one end, and a pussy on the other. Shit. I was going to get some nuoc mam and take it over to the boom-boom parlor."

"Oh, yeah? What for?" asked Round John.

"I was going to pour it in old zipper-eyes's snatch."

"To improve the smell?"

"There it is. You know something, I actually tried to eat that stuff once — the nuoc mam, I mean. I puked before I got it past my tonsils."

"You know how they make that shit?" asked Kevin.

"I found out too late. They pack whole fish and salt in a barrel, then bury it in a shitheap until it all ferments to scales and slime. Then they let it age. Ecch!"

"That's it. The name means something like 'Elixir of Life'. I had a Vietnamese Captain tell me he loved the taste of nuoc mam so much it brought tears to his eyes when he thought of it."

"Did you guys get any action out there," asked Captain Randall when they pulled up to the operations tent.

"Nah. We got a little light small arms fire right at first, but that's about all. Just another ratfuck."

"OK," Duke grumbled sourly. "I'd sure like to see some confirmed kills. This division is getting pretty stingy about giving kill credit to the gunships."

"I heard a rumor the General rates his commanders by body count," said Kevin. "You want eagles, boy, you get those kills. You lie, pad your reports, steal from the gunships, whatever."

Lieutenant Rudy Bakersmith stepped into their tent with a roster sheet. "Padilla in here? Oh, there you are. You're going to fly counter-mortar standby with my section tonight, Ed. I'm the fire team leader, with Ferranti, and you're the aircraft commander of the wing ship, with Swomney."

Tired, and wishing he could take the evening off, but excited about the chance to fly a night mission as A/C, Eddie picked up his flight gear and left with Bakersmith.

The runway at The Scabbard ran almost north-south, about a kilometer west of the village of Bao Trang. The perimeter of the base camp was guarded by sentry posts, which ranged in size from two-man pillboxes to the battle-bunkers at the main gate and at the MACV compound, right on the road along the edge of the village. The camp was divided roughly in half, the north half being the Black Sabres' company area. The south half was a large open area, bulldozed clean, with a bermed section in the middle. Inside the berm were the neatly spaced cement and sandbag revetments of the main ammunition dump.

Just outside the wire on the south side was a little cluster of Vietnamese shacks called Cheap Charlie's, built specifically to offer concession services to the soldiers of the camp. The main business was the Washington Laundry, which kept a good-sized staff working round the clock. Next door at Figaro's the endless lines of men in green kept three barber chairs and a shoeshine bench constantly filled. The rest of the establishments were junk shops, and a little canteen which served Bamuoiba beer and a crude approximation of the basic American hamburger.

Almost exactly in the center of The Scabbard, beside the runway between the fuel pit and the gunships' revetments, sat the counter-mortar stand-by fireteam's ready-shack, an old mobile home. The eight men of the fireteam's crews sat or lay in the bare interior, waiting for — but not expecting — the scramble call which would send them out as the first response force to an attacking enemy. By late evening, several of the men had found blankets and crawled onto the bare mattresses of the bunks, and a group of others had begun a card game of some kind.

The field telephone on the drainboard beside them chittered jarringly. Everyone turned and looked at it in disbelief a moment, then Bakersmith picked it up. "Dagger Two-six, stand-by, go ahead." His eyes widened as he listened, then he nodded. "Roger. We'll be up in two minutes."

The crews grabbed their helmets and pistols and ran out of the building toward the birds. "Go ahead and crank this bitch," Eddie yelled to Ray Swomney as the other warrant jumped into the seat behind the minigun sight. He tossed his chicken plate into his lap and twisted behind his shoulders to reach the safety straps. He draped them across his shoulders and stuck the tongue of the lap belt into the loops, then fastened the catch. By that time, Swomney had snapped on the battery, had flipped the fuel switch forward, and was cranking the throttle around to the starting setting.

"Clear!" he called.

"Clear and untied!" came the reply from the crew chief.

"Coming hot!" He squeezed the trigger on the collective lever and the starter whined into life. The igniters began to tick and the sibilant whistle of the turbine began to climb. Swomney watched his instruments, eyes scanning the RPM gauges, the exhaust gas temperature, the voltmeter. The broad blade of the rotor swung slowly by in front of them, followed by the next and the next as the engine drove it around faster and faster. Eddie stuffed his helmet on his head, sticking his fingers under it to set his ears straight in the tight earphones. As he plugged the phones into the fitting hanging beside his seat, Swomney reached overhead and hit the inverter switch, and Eddie heard the electrical equipment begin to hum and whine. As he pulled his clammy flying gloves over his hands, he saw Swomney turn on the radios. The rotor was turning at idle, throbbing deeply and shaking the ship from side to side.

"I've got it," Eddie yelled. He grasped the controls, twisting the throttle on to bring the rotor to flying RPM. Swomney nodded and reached for his own lap belt and helmet.

Bakersmith's voice came over the radio. "Dagger One-five,

Two-six. You up?"

Eddie squeezed the mike switch. "Roger that. Hear you Lima Charlie."

"You too, loud and clear. Break. Bao Trang, Dagger counter-mortar team scramble from Dagger pad, over."

"Dagger Two-six, light fire team, cleared immediate takeoff, wind two-two-zero at six knots, altimeter two-niner-niner-six."

"Roger, on the go!"

Bakersmith's aircraft had already risen to a hover and was moving onto the runway with its nose low and in a turn to parallel the strip. It settled and almost touched the ground with the skids, then abruptly swooped upward as it gathered speed. Eddie lifted off behind him. He swung in a wide low turn to fall in behind the lead, and the two gunships stayed close to the ground, headed toward the tent area.

In the section tent below, Kevin, Skip, and the others had been sopping up beer and enjoying the fact that they did not have the counter-mortar duty and could take the evening off and get sloppy. As they sat talking, they had heard the familiar whine of the turbine engines starting, and the throbbing whoosh of rotors being brought rapidly to operating RPM.

"It's the counter-mortar team," Kevin declared. "They've been called out. I think I'll wander down to operations and check it out." Kevin stepped out into the night and made his way carefully toward the Ops tent, stepping around the stakes and ropes that anchored the quarters tents. Each tent had a low wall of sandbags stacked between it and its neighbor, and he picked his way along the walls to avoid having to walk all the way around the tent complex. The tents were well-lighted, and he could see the men in them doing their evening things, paying no attention at all to the sounds of the fire team being scrambled.

The night was hazy and moonless, and only a few stars gleamed dully in the murky sky. As Kevin watched, the gunship team zoom-climbed over the tents, their rotors wapping like cannonfire. He stood and watched them swing north and climb out, rotors muttering as they grabbed air. A few miles away a parachute flare winked to light, revealing hills along the side of the valley in its wavering red-orange glow.

Suddenly the lights in the tents around him began to go out. He saw Lt. Bud Petch run from one tent to another, and heard him tell someone to turn off the lights. "Blackout — the Major wants complete blackout. Yeah, the TV set, too. Shut 'em out."

"What's up, Petch," he heard Duke Randall ask.

"It's Fort Selden, Sir. They're being hit."

"Jesus!" said Randall, then he yelled out loud, "Daggers, listen up! Everybody's on stand-by, as of now. Get ready to move out, and assemble in the bunkers! Do it now!" He took off on the double toward the Operations tent.

There was a sudden flash... WHRAAAMMPH! Then quickly, two more. WHRAAMPH-AAMPH! For all of four seconds, Kevin stood rooted in unreason and urgent uncertainty as his mind accepted what he already knew....rockets! All around him was instant turmoil, voices shouting, crying, "Incoming! We're being hit! Oh, shit!" Men ran, scrabbled across the ground, tripped over ropes and furniture, cursed and cried.

Kevin's body flashed with fear, but his mind was cool, detached. He was surprised at his reaction — he looked around slowly, paralyzed by the realization that he could not see in the sudden darkness, and he didn't know the way to the nearest bunker. "My God," he thought, "I'm going to get it standing in the open ten feet from a bunker." Over the noise he could hear clearly, as though someone in his mind somewhere were doing nothing except listening to it, the soft crackling hiss of the next one falling in. WHRAAMPH! Close! A shock, and somebody screamed. Something buzzed past him, an abrupt gnarled sound with the vicious suddenness of a mantis's attack. A new fear grabbed him — he was going to panic. He would panic and run screaming and be hit and they'd find him broken and gutted, poor damned fool lost it and ran and got hit, got his brains blown out, and please, don't let his family find out he got it and nobody else was even hurt. The thought jarred him loose, and he dived to the ground and rolled against the nearest wall of sandbags, with his head buried in his arms.

Somebody yelled something, a command. Somebody started a siren, and on the perimeter someone fired a burst of tracerfire. Someone nearby was whining softly, "Why don't they do something? Huh? Why the fuck don't they do something?" The small arms fire on the west perimeter began to increase. Kevin lay trembling, wanting with all his being to get up and run to a bunker, but madly fearing if he moved his special bullet would find him.

There was a silence — a little rifle fire — and a longer silence. Then somebody moved and Kevin heard footsteps in a nearby tent. "If they fire any more," said a disembodied voice, "it'll be in about ten minutes. That's their favorite trick." Kevin took a long breath, then jumped to his feet and ran at a crouch back to the section tent. He ducked into the dark bunker, tripped over someone's feet, and fell to his knees.

"Welcome to the party, Babycakes," said Skip's voice. A cigarette glowed, and Kevin could see the forms of four other men crouched against the walls.

"Wow," he said, breathing heavily to calm his racing heart and trembling muscles. Then he sniffed and looked up surprised. "Pot? You guys are smoking pot in here? Jesus, aren't you a little...."

"Paranoid?" Henry Hawk giggled nervously. "I'm scared shitless, just like everybody else, but not about getting busted."

"What are they going to do?" asked Skip. "Send us to Vietnam?" He held out the joint to Kevin.

Kevin looked at the glowing cigarette, then sat down beside Skip. "Fuck it," he said, and took the joint. He took a short toke, coughed once, then took a long one. He handed the dope to Hawking and sat holding his breath. He exhaled slowly, then spit into the dirt between his knees. "I'm really not happy here at all," he said.

They had passed the joint around twice when the bunker suddenly lit up with bright orange light. They had time to see each other's startled expressions before the shock wave struck them. The ground and the walls of the bunker were slammed hard enough to knock the men sprawling, and the sound was a deep and extended roar. It was not one explosion, but a chain of them, a shuddering barrage of bursts which began to rain small debris on the roof of the bunker.

"Holy shit, they've hit the ammo dump," said Hawking.

Over the continuous grumbling and cracking of the exploding piles of artillery shells, the men could clearly hear the chattering popcorn of M-16 fire, and the staccato insistent woodpecker bursts of the M-60 machineguns on the perimeter.

"That's the perimeter," said Kevin. "They're trying to hit the whole camp!"

Duke Randall stuck his head into the bunker. "We're under attack, and it looks like some of them are inside. You men get your flight gear and get down to Operations. We're going to get the other four gunships in the air before something blowing out of that ammo dump disables them, and we're going to kick some virgin ass on that perimeter. Let's move."

Eddie stared through the windshield of his gunship, transfixed by the image before him. Ahead of him a quarter of a mile, Rudy Bakersmith's helicopter hung in the thick black of the moist tropical night, a silhouette of some sleek and stubby-taloned predatory bug, with lights that fluttered, ghostly. Beyond, still five miles away, a lighted arena hung suspended in the darkness. A huge inverted bowl of light in pink and peach colors centered upon the bald-topped hill where artillery firebase Fort Selden had dug itself in. In the top of the bowl shone a half-dozen ruddy-glowing little suns, artillery flares being shot in from another base. As Eddie watched, one burst to light high above the base, and began to descend on its parachute through the tangled smoke-streamers left by its predecessors.

As he followed Bakersmith into the circle of light, Eddie was surprised to experience a rush of vertigo. From within the bowl, the night outside appeared as an impenetrable void, and the high vaulted black ceiling gave the scene a sense of height and volume he had never before experienced. For a second impossibly he thought he could hear the roar of cheering crowds.

The hills close to the base and the main slope of the ridge behind it could be seen clearly. From just outside the ring of light, a burst of tracerfire stabbed into the little cluster of sandbagged revetments and foxholes. It was returned by several guns along the perimeter, and judging from the crisp little explosions in the treeline below the fort, by someone armed with an M-79 grenade launcher.

"....about eight of them," the radio cut into the ground commander's communication. "Made contact with us, then deedeed up the ridge. We're holding our position. Over."

"Break. Muddy Viper Six, Dagger Two-six. We're a light fire team coming up on your area now. Can we play?"

"Dagger, I have two platoons deployed in the jungle on the ridge to the west, each of 'em out about four hundred meters. One of them is in contact with a small group that just moved back upslope, and there's somebody up higher on the ridge putting mortarfire on us. I think the troops we contacted are just to slow us up so the ones above can keep firing. With your cover, I'm going to advance my Charlie unit. Over."

"Roger that, Viper. Do your platoon commanders have a flare pistol?"

"That's affirm."

"Rog. Just tell them when they need us, to fire a flare from their forward position toward the intended target. We'll take it from there," said Bakersmith.

Over the intercom, Swomney called Eddie. "Got to be damned careful working around moving troops like this," he said with an edge of bitterness. "Some shithead takes a bullet while the gunships are working, and I hear they'll try to burn the pilot."

Then on the hillside above the base a flurry of tracers erupted, and Eddie could hear the popcorn crackle even over the noise of his helicopter. The radio began to babble as the platoon leader, the ground commander, and Lt. Bakersmith set up the action. He judged his distance behind Rudy and rolled in to cover him as the lead gunship positioned himself for his first run. On the ground, a red comet pointed like an arrow directly upslope from a darkened hollow. Rudy pounced on the flare like a cat. He rolled his ship around steeply and nosed over to deliver two pairs of rockets. Since the solid-fuel rockets were not much different from common fireworks, but much larger, they rode huge streams of showering sparks to burst below. The miniguns fired a short burst, and the doorgunners probed the trees with their fingers of fire. Eddie was relieved to see that the lead ship took no fire at all.

He rolled in for his run as Bakersmith broke off, and following his example, put two pairs of rockets into the woods just upslope of his. Swomney sprayed the area with the miniguns, and Eddie held the attack in close so the doorgunners could fire a few rounds also. He had just tightened his grip to pull up and away from the trees, when the world erupted. From below came the unmistakable chatter of automatic weapons fire. The little crimson streaks of tracers whipped past in front of the aircraft. His body knotted and surged as his glands dosed him with their powerful stimulant, and he felt suddenly charged, as though he had grabbed a high-tension line.

"Receiving fire! Receiving fire!" he yelled into his mike. He heard the thick whop of a smoke grenade being popped in the back of the ship as the crew chief marked the spot. In his fear, everything seemed to be in slow motion, like the nightmares he had suffered as a child, being chased by a monster through syrup, thick and clinging. He pulled on the collective and nosed into a left turn, diving down the slope of the hill away from the murderous hail of fire. His mind was racing, counting the weapons firing at him, "Three...four...my God, there's dozens!" His eyes raced over the instrument panel, and he refused to believe what he saw. His engine was putting out more power than he had believed it could, and his airspeed was over one hundred twenty knots as he hurtled down the slope. "Good God, I can't be going that fast...it's taking forever...will I never get off those guns?"

"Smoke is out, Sir. I think we got it right on top of them," called his crew chief.

"Roger," replied Eddie, suddenly aware that they were free of the fire zone. "Did we take any hits?"

"Gauges are OK," said Swomney. "No warning lights."

"I think we took a couple, Sir. There's one right by your head there." Eddie turned and saw the tiny hole, flower-petalled and about half the size of a dime in the door post only inches from his head. The bare aluminum edges of the petals reflected the red of the instrument lights, and for a second Eddie had a premonition of funeral flowers.

Rudy had seen the tracers coming up at Eddie as he rolled in to cover him. He saw the smoke grenade Eddie's crew chief had thrown, and he had a pretty good idea where the enemy were. He quickly set up his firing run and started blasting the ridge above the infantry positions. The radio had gone wild. As the VC opened up on Eddie's ship, they also hit the two platoons of infantry which had been chasing the enemy squad up the hill. The squad was a lure, and a company of hardcorps Vietcong were waiting to ambush the advancing Americans. The sudden barrage of fire the enemy had loosed at the gunship had caught the infantry by surprise, so they were still a bit off balance when Charlie opened up on them. The two elements both tried to move back, and the enemy tried to drive a wedge between them.

On the ground, Viper Six, the infantry commander, was monitoring three radios when all of them started screaming at once. He heard the gunship call receiving fire, and from his position on top of a bunker in the firebase, he could see the tracers stab upward to strike the helicopter. As he watched, excitement gripping him, the helicopter tipped on its side to an impossible angle and begin to dive down the hill. Then the other gunship spat smoke and he heard the sibilant Whoooosssh-Khrak! of the rockets. With a long flatulent roar, a glowing stream of minigun rounds sprayed down onto the hillside as though squirted from a hose.

"Taking fire!" screamed someone over the radio. "Oh, shit, we're being hit! There's too..."

"Viper Six, One-six. Two-six is taking heavy fire — sounds like a whole platoon. We're moving....Jesus Christ!" The sound of gunfire tore through the headset.

"We're trying to move back....ambush. I've got three men shot and..."

"Receiving fire," from the lead gunship. "Estimate fifteen or twenty automatic...."

Panic started to wrap itself around the guts of Viper Six, a young infantry captain. "Not an ambush....my troops moving...gunships are hitting my men....they're moving....gunnies don't know where they are!" A sudden clear picture flashed in his mind of his men being chewed to pieces by the devastating fire from the gunships. He squeezed the switch on his mike. "Daggers, Viper Six," he shouted. "Hold your fire. Hold your fire!"

Eddie had just begun his run. "I'll have to carry this one in close to cover Rudy," he thought, and the realization that he was about to fly again into that raging hail of bullets chilled him. For an instant he felt a detached awareness — he could hear his mother many years later telling someone how she had been jarred awake from her nap to share her son's fear, and his vision as he challenged the hellish guns. He concentrated on his rocket sight, picking the exact spot in the trees he wanted the missiles to hit. His thumb tightened on the firing button.

"Hold your fire, gunships! You're hitting my men!" The frantic voice of Viper Six grated metallically through the headphones.

Eddie's heart wrenched with sudden new dread. "Oh, God, what a time to....I'm in too close! They'll chew my ass to pieces!" The fingers of tracerfire began to find the ship. Smoke began to gush from the radio compartment beside him, and two jagged holes spanged cracks across the plexiglass windshield. Eddie pulled power until the warning horn cut stridently through to him. "John Wayne. It's just like John Wayne," he thought, clearly, horribly aware that someone was shooting at him, trying quite deliberately to kill him, and any second might succeed.

Just as he made it out of range of the small automatic weapons, the enemy brought out their big gun. It was the first time Eddie had seen fifty-caliber fire at night, and his first reaction was awe. From a position on his right, almost level with him on the ridge above the base came a stream of crimson flaming golf balls. They floated out toward him, and it seemed impossible that they could miss him, and that they were falling just below and behind the gunship. He turned and looked to his left, where his lead ship was holding off high, and he saw that the glowing comets of fire were streaking in flat trajectories clear across the bowl of light, and were still climbing when they burned out in the darkness high above them. "We're fish in a barrel," he thought. "We can't get out of range of that gun, and he can't keep missing forever."

He looked below and could see exactly where the heavy

machine gun was situated. It looked like just the right place from which to fire mortars at the base also. And he was exactly set up for a long, flat firing run at the position. "I'm taking it out!" he yelled into the microphone, and pulled the gunship into a tight right turn, facing renewed small tracerfire.

Something clattered, spanged in the cockpit. "Carbajal's hit, Sir! Oh, Jesus, he's had it! I..." The gunner turned inside to reach for the sagging body of the crew chief.

"Stay on your gun!" yelled Eddie. Swomney was firing both miniguns, spraying the bullets like streams of molten lead on the hillside. The flaming golf balls made trails of ghastly fire as they streaked beneath the ship. He tried to remember everything, hold steady, stabilize the run, wait....wait...now! He squeezed the thumbswitch on his cyclic, and the first pair of rockets flashed forward, sparkler plumes of gold and silver flame showering behind them. He squeezed again, and then again. Still the golf balls kept coming, and he was more afraid of breaking off his attack than continuing it. He bored in closer, and fired another pair of rockets.

The high explosive warheads burst with a yellow flash, then suddenly a dozen more bursts ripped the hillside beside them. Some of them were flung up into the air and burst aloft. Eddie broke off and climbed back into the sky along the edge of the lighted area, with his door gunner firing back to cover the turn.

"Bullseye!!" yelled Rudy Bakersmith over the radio. "You got boocoo secondaries on that last pair. I think that's the last we'll see of that mortar position. I'm going to unload mine in there too, and we can break off and reload back at Scab."

"Roger that. Wow!"

"Viper Six, Dagger lead. I've got five pairs and some minigun. My wingman is about empty, and we have maybe fifteen minutes time on station left. Recommend we unload on that position, then return to refuel."

"Roger, Dagger. Go ahead and dump what you've got, then get back to Bao Trang to reload. And fellows...thanks."

"Roger that, Viper. You set up, One-five?"

"Uh, Dagger lead, be advised my crew chief has been hit. Gunner confirms he's dead. Over."

"Roger. Sorry about that. Let's dump it all in one pass, and we can get the hell out of here. By the way, that was some pretty fancy shootin', Bullseye."

"Just got lucky," Eddie replied. He followed Rudy through his firing pass, unloaded his last rounds, and he wished he could capture the glory and the fulfillment he felt at that moment, and take it back to Las Cruces that very night and hang it on the wall of his father's home.

Major Jacob Csynes spent most of the night in his own office sitting behind his desk with his topographic maps of the valley, conducting the company's operations by field telephone. Soon after the ammunition dump blew, he had made a walk-around inspection of the company area, telling the slick pilots to remain in their bunkers, and making a point of remaining standing when others dived for the ground at the sound of the incoming mortars. Captain Neil Koontz, the XO, was on duty as Operations Officer in the Ops tent, and Captain Duke Randall led the gunship action from his office in the right seat of his Frog ship.

The action dropped off during the early hours of morning, and Eddie and Swomney were sent out to keep one fireteam in the air flying a cap over the base. Eddie flew round and round the camp as the sky lightened, amazed to see the fires he watched at night revealed by the dawn to be the hooches and shacks of the familiar little communities which surrounded the base.

Takeoffs were scheduled for 07:00, and every helicopter available was to fly. Most of the crewmen were already awake, but it still came as a surprise when Csynes called for a full company formation at 06:00. Captain Koontz called the company to attention, and presented his report to Csynes. "The 17th Assault Helicopter Company is present or accounted for, Sir!"

"Thank you, Captain," replied Csynes, returning the XO's salute with his peculiar whiplike snap of the wrist. "At ease, men. I would like to begin by saying, I told you so. And I would like to conclude by saying, I am pleased in general with the way this company behaved under attack. I would particularly like to commend Captain Randall and the Daggers for their outstanding performance during the night. Now, it is my special pleasure to recognize an act of conspicuous gallantry which took place last night, and which very likely saved the lives of dozens of men at Fort Selden. Not only was this act reported to me by the fire team leader, it was reported by the commanding officer at Fort Selden to Division Headquarters, and Colonel Meola, our Aviation Battalion Commander, called me less than one hour ago to tell me about it, and to authorize the following on-the-spot decoration. Company, Atten-Huht! Warrant Officer Padilla, front and center."

Eddie had just landed from flying cap, and he was rumpled, sweaty, and stiff. His head was ringing and his vision glassy from having not slept, and he felt awkward like some kind of stuffed toy as he stepped off a square-cornered zig-zag path to stand before the Commanding Officer. He listened in astonishment as Major Csynes read the official version of his act. "....he did, at great personal risk and without regard for his own safety, attack and destroy the heavily defended command position of an enemy force attacking Firebase Fort Selden. Though his aircraft had been struck many times by enemy fire, and his crew chief killed leaving one side undefended, he turned without hesitation into the face of heavy fire from a fifty-caliber heavy anti-aircraft machinegun, and with exceptionally accurate rocket fire, succeeded in completely knocking out the position, which broke the back of the attack, and saved the lives of the American troops at the firebase. This act of conspicuous bravery and heroism under fire in aerial flight in the Republic of Vietnam is herewith acknowledged by the award of The Distinguished Flying Cross. Congratulations, Mr. Padilla."

Eddie stood astonished as Csynes pinned the medal to his chest. The DFC — the Blue Max of Vietnam! He saluted with all the enthusiasm he could muster, and tried not to goose-step back to his place in the ranks.

"Now, there is another matter," continued the Major. "I know some of you have thought my concern for the condition of our company area was something to joke about. Well, now I hope you are convinced. Last night the perimeter of this camp was breached in two places, and at both of them, the sentry was found with his throat cut. Whoever cut those throats were Vietnamese with a reason to be inside the compound, and those sentries got their throats cut because they were asleep. Other sentries reported being approached on duty by prostitutes. The sappers who blew the ammunition dump came through a tunnel dug from the Washington Laundry, where no doubt some of you lost your uniforms last night. About two hours ago, the body of Figaro the barber was found hanging on the wire outside the MACV compound, bearing papers identifying him as Captain Nguyen Van Xe, of the North Vietnamese Army. One of our pilots was killed by mortarfire while he was sitting on top of his bunker taking pictures of the firefight going on around him. He had neither his helmet nor his weapon with him! I am sorry to say it, but that man was killed by his own lack of professionalism, by a case of terminal tourist mentality. And that, men, is what I am talking about. This is not a jolly foxhunt where the foxes can shoot back — this is a goddamned war! And if we are going to survive here, and win here, we have got to think like warriors. An outfit that looks like slobs will think like slobs, and they will fight like slobs too. When I see this place looking like a refugee camp, it makes my blood run cold with fear!

"Now I want this clearly understood: I will not put up with it. I will not sit back complacently and let this company get blown to hell one piece at a time because we refuse to think and behave like professional soldiers and Army officers. There is just too much at stake! And I am warning you right now, that I will do whatever I have to....anything I have to....to obtain the level of professional performance I demand! I will not take less, Gentlemen, I promise you! I hate chicken-shit command as much as any of you, but I will have a high degree of order and security in my company area, and I will see a professional attitude displayed by every swinging richard in this Assault Helicopter Company, if I have to harelip half of you. That's all. Company, Atten-Huht! We've got a big day, men. Let's get to work. Captain Koontz, dismiss the Company for duty."

The men stood a bit numbed a moment, then fell out to quickly depart for their stations. The pilots crowded around to congratulate Eddie. One of the first to get to him was Captain Jack Miller. "Congratulations, Bullseye. Sure glad to have you flying on my wing."

As the pilots headed for their tent to get their flight gear, Skip Gilman shook his head. "That man Csynes worries me, bro's. I can't tell if he's a bad-ass because he wants to be a hero or because he's scared shitless. Let me ask you. If he was one of us, and not the CO, would you say he's got a personal problem, or not?"

"You've got a point," said John Bergin.

"He's got a couple of personal problems. But they don't seem to keep him from doing his job," said Kevin Harrey. "You want to hear the best-kept secret of the war? Just within the brotherhood, you understand? I got the word from a guy I ran into over in MACV, a guy I used to know in Saigon two years ago. He said Csynes was a Ranger, and had done a couple of years here already with MACV. He went back and got the aviation specialty because he was one of the first guys involved in developing the airmobile concept. But apparently he had made some enemies when he was here back in the late fifties doing sneaky-pete stuff as an advisor. One night his hootch girl got out of his bed, dumped a can of lighter fluid on his head, and set him on fire."

"No shit?"

"Documented fact, apparently. The Army grounded him, sent him off to some VA hospital, and tried to give him a medical discharge. So he went to Air America, and got a letter from them saying they would hire him if the Army gave him the door. The Army got the picture, and here he is."

"Who's Air America?" asked Eddie Padilla.

"You'll see them. Helicopters and Heliocouriers in Uncle Sam civilian colors. It functions like a little airline, flying diplomatic missions all over Vietnam — and the rest of Southeast Asia. It's operated by the Central Intelligence Agency."

"The CIA?" squawked Peter Hawking. "You know that means he could be working for them now. Those shifty fuckers don't pass up an asset."

"Fellows, I lived with the Vietnamese enough when I was here before to get a pretty good idea how they think," said Kevin, "and I've been waiting two years for them to decide they've had enough of us, and to go on the offensive. When that happens, the only thing that can prevent the local population from throwing us out of the country is if we can keep the North Vietnamese from arming them. So if I read the situation right, that puts us exactly on the spearhead."

"How do you figure that?" asked Skip.

"I think the reason we're here is because Jake the Snake used to live in that valley over the ridge west."

"You mean, The Graveyard?" asked Malins.

"That's right, A Lan airfield. When the Special Forces camp there was overrun in '63, Csynes got his first Silver Star for holding that command post until they could get a chopper in to pull them out — an H-21 in those days. That valley is a VC artery that feeds the heart of South Vietnam, from North Vietnam, and from Laos and Cambodia. Csynes was the last guy out, and I've got a feeling he might just have some personal stake in being the first guy back in."

"You mean, he made a deal with the Army to get this command?" asked Hawking.

"Suppose he did," said Kevin. "If they wanted to jerk your wings and send you back to Kansas just because you're ugly, and put you driving a truck, what would you tell them? You'd tell them to put you on the line, and you'd prove your shit or die, wouldn't you."

Skip fixed a beady eye on Kevin. "Are you telling me Csynes is freaked-out because he's not sure we can cover his bet?"

"What's he, a shrink?" asked Hawking. "Csynes just knows his job. You keep the troops busy with bullshit they can bitch about so they won't have time to think. And he's obviously loony as a striped-ass baboon — but how crazy can you get and still do the job over here? When you've reached the point of invading a country to defend it from its own people in the name of democracy, it helps to be crazy."

SIX

In the weeks following the three-day struggle which was from its beginning called the Tet Offensive, the Daggers' combat action picked up, and their off-duty life became practically cloistered. The village of Bao Trang was off-limits after 19:00, and much to the satisfaction of Jake Csynes, most Vietnamese civilians were not permitted inside the camp at all. The GI laundry was expanded, and everyone had to shine his own boots. Csynes found projects to keep everyone busy as much of the time as possible. The walkways became drawn with straight lines of whitewashed rocks between the wood-sided wabtoc tents, and down the center of each walkway a neat row of used shipping pallets made a path elevated from the dust, or the mud. The Ops tent was hardened by making the walls of telephone poles, and the roof of two-by-twelves and a layer of sandbags. The Blade and Spade had become a comfortable little club, with padded benches, a well-stocked wet bar, a pool table, a record player, and a TV set. Someone had even found a neon beer-ad sign.

During the day, one group of Vietnamese were allowed to come on-post. The company's area lay roughly halfway between the market in the village of Bao Trang and the tiny Montaignard village northwest of the airfield. The road between them ran through the center of the Scabbard, from the main gate to the north gate, right past the tents of the Dagger platoon. If they were denied the use of the road, the "Mountain Yards" would have to walk an extra three miles to go around the post. It was rumored that the headman of the village told the post commander they would all become VC if they couldn't use the road during the day. The rumor was never confirmed, but the Yards were permitted to pass through.

Kevin had made a trip into the larger base at Bien Hoa, bought a 35mm camera with a long telephoto lens, and set out to spend his free time snooping around behind the tents and along the road taking pictures of the grotesque little people. Though he could speak and understand quite a bit of Vietnamese, Kevin seldom engaged villagers in conversation, and he preferred that the other pilots did not know he spoke more than the handful of words which made up the pidgin used by GI's with hootchgirls and hawkers. Some of the other men had expressed their interest in knowing what the Yards thought about the war, and their regret they did not have a good interpreter, but Kevin found himself growing more and more certain that he did not want to know. He had shot two rolls of film and sent it home to Carlie, then stashed the camera in his footlocker.

"Weird, the way they can walk with those loads like that," said Hawking to some of the other Dagger pilots one hot spring afternoon as they sat on the wall of sandbags in front of their tent watching the Montaignard tribesmen pass. They watched a gnarled and scrawny old man walking with a heavy load of four burlap bags on a choggy stick. A few paces behind the man of the house walked his wife, with a similar load. They passed unhurried, refusing to notice the disorder around them, walking with steady, quick and resolute steps. Using the long bamboo choggy sticks bent over their backs with a sack on each end, they shouldered their loads in silence. "I've been trying to figure out that step," said Hawking. "I've decided it can't be done without one of those loads. Watch. When the load goes down, both feet hit the ground, and when the load bobs up, they take their step. See, that's how such little people can carry so much weight." Bob, bobble, bob, bob — steady steps and huge loads, muscular cordwood legs naked and walnut brown, bare feet gnarled with crusty soles padding up the ochre talc dust.

Kevin shook his head and picked up the letter he had received that morning from Carlie. She wrote of familiar things, of their home and life together, and yet the more he watched these strange people ("the real Vietnamese", he kept hearing his inner voice say), the more his life with her seemed alien, and superficial. With no war in their country, would these people be living simple, happy, primitive lives — or would they be suffering the grinding poverty and ignorance of the utterly undeveloped? In their eyes, was he a Promethean avenging angel on a rescue mission into Hell, or was he the Devil in Paradise? He knew he was confused...and that was very unsettling to think about. He tossed the letter onto the cot beside him and lay back listening to the other men talking. Hawking had got into a rap with John Bergin about Americans not caring about anything as long as our side wins.

"My family won't say two words about their experiences in Korea and World War II, except what a great man MacArthur was, or Eisenhower," mused Hawking ruefully. "'Trust the government, and over the top' is about as far as they can think, I'm afraid."

"My father talks about his war experience a lot," said Eddie Padilla, "but it's like hearing about a movie he saw — the same few things over and over: hitting the beach at Anzio, getting promoted to Corporal, and marching into a city someplace with George Patton. Nothing about feeling, or thinking."

"My people have always had plenty to say about it — all feeling," said John Bergin. "They run on for hours about how good we've got it, and how gas was rationed, and the prices of everything you could get were controlled, and the refugees, and the horror, and blah, blah, blah. And if I ask them what all that has to do with this war, they tell me if I'd watched Hitler kill all my relatives, I wouldn't ask questions about war."

"Sheeit," said Hawking in disgust. "If I have to hear again about how because Hitler killed six million Jews, it's all right for us to kill a million Vietnamese, I think I'll puke. So big deal anyhow — how come six million Jews is the biggest news since we lynched that heretic from Nazareth, but we don't hear a word about the twelve million Russians who died fighting while we stood in lines waiting for the showers?"

"Hey," said Skip, "you commie pinko Nazi rat. What have you got against Jews?"

"Aw, moon you, Gilman," said Hawking, tossing a boot at him.

"Yeah, Hawk," said Round John, "what's with you? You don't like the government, but you volunteer for a war, and now you tell me you're an anti-Semitic Jew."

"So just because I belong to the club, I've got to believe

everything it does is right? No way. I believe feeling that way about any religion or political institution on Earth is social disease."

Kevin began to find Hawking's rhetorical sidestepping irritating, though it usually just slid off him. "All in one box, eh, Hawk?" he said. "No such thing as good guys and bad guys, huh? Look, you just try communism, or fascism, or a dictatorship under anybody. Try a police state. Try one of those little social diseases."

"Oh, you mean if you're not paying tithes to the Cult of Washington, you're sick?" asked Hawking. "And we're just here to deliver the medicine, right? Is that what you're telling me, Babycakes?"

"You can call it a joke if you like, but it is the truth. What we're doing here is...a kind of social surgery."

"Right," said Skip. "And when we make the whole world well, everybody will have TV and a wife who looks like Doris Day."

"You could have a wife who looks like that," Kevin said, pointing toward the passing wife of one of the Vietnamese.

They watched the woman follow her husband, a tiny creature with scraggly gray hair and flesh which looked like old dusty jerky. Her load hung from one side of her body, and in a cloth on the other side slept an infant.

"Where the hell are all these good-looking bare-titted Yard chicks we kept hearing about in flight school?" complained Skip.

"Come on, Skip," said Kevin. "Didn't you see that one came strolling through here this morning? Oooee!"

"A real sweetheart," added Hawking. "Looked like a monkey with a pair of douche-bags slung around her neck."

One of the women who walked by was taking a serious interest in the Army tents. She had two ragged kids with her, and was carrying a baby. "Uh-oh, here comes one," warned Hawking. She came flapping up to the tent with a great big black grin and an outstretched palm. "Pretty smart, letting the old lady and the kids do the panhandling," he said.

The beady eyes flashed over the beds and the footlockers, quick to search out a loose B-3 unit left from someone's C-ration lunch or a pack of cigarettes not quite finished. "Chop-chop? Cigget?" she crooned. A little genuflection, show the baby, pat the belly, fingers to the mouth.

Leaning forward in perplexed interest, Skip put his hand behind his ear. "What? You what?" he asked, repeating her gestures and teasing. "Chop-chop? Who, me chop-chop?" He pointed to himself. The old woman shook her head. "Oh, you chop-chop!" When she nodded in eager agreement, he bowed deeply. "Chao ba, Chop-chop. How do you do?"

She shook her head in exasperation and started over. Point to the smokes, pick up the baby and show it to them. She danced before them, grinning and cooing, shaking her head from side to side like an old bird.

"What? Cigarettes for baby-san? Oh, no, no. Not cigett for baby-san?!"

She hung her head to one side and bobbed back and forth, cooing a hurt lament, "Oohm, ooh." Suddenly Skip's face lit up with delighted understanding. "Oh! Chop-chop! Why you no say so first place?" He stepped into the tent and began to rummage around in his locker.

"What the hell you giving her?" asked Jerry Malins, coming out of the tent.

Skip held up two C-ration cans. "One White Bread, sour and delicately flavored with Victory yeast. Anybody rather eat it himself? No? And one Ham, with Water Added, and Lima Beans."

Malins nodded. "Yeah, I guess that shit's all right. Nobody can eat that ham and lima beans."

"Nobody but Petch," said Kevin. "He eats it."

"Yeah, Petch eats it, that's for sure," said Skip.

Seeing the old woman leave the tent with her booty, three little kids headed over chattering excitedly, looking like street kids anywhere in the world — grubby kids, with scruffy hair chopped short, bright eyes, and huge toothy grins. The eyes were wide and sorrowful, not wide and innocent like American kids, but bright just the same.

On a sudden mad impulse, Kevin leaped up, grabbed Malins' big Marine bayonet and yelled at the top of his lungs, "Deedee mau, dinky dau! Get the fuck out of here, you zipper-eyed little bastards!" The kids jumped back looking startled, then they decided it was all a big joke. They moved forward again, but not as close as before. Kevin pounded on his chest and roared like a lion — well, actually like a bantam rooster roaring like a lion. The kids began to giggle.

"Show 'em your peter, Babycakes," said Skip.

"I hate every slope-headed dink in this country!" Kevin growled. "Curse the dirt, damn the state, to hell with the people! This place sucks, do you little dinks understand that?" Then he fished in his fatigue jacket pocket for his pack of smokes and solemnly offered each of them one, bowing and speaking to them softly in formal Vietnamese. A bit awed, they stood while he used his lighter to light each of their smokes, polite and looking quite dignified in spite of their costumes of cast-off GI underwear and parachute-nylon sarongs.

Malins watched as the kids moved away from the tent, then pointed at them when they picked up their sandbag booty sacks, which they had left a way off from the tent. "You know," he said, "I'm tempted to go apprehend a couple of those little apes and inventory those sacks. No telling what they've picked up."

"Come on, Malins, even a little slope kid has some kind of rights," protested Hawking.

"Sure, Hawk, you fucking commie. Next week your watch will end up in one of those sacks."

John Bergin lay on his cot staring at the kids. Finally he said solemnly, "You know, fellas, I'll bet those kids rake in a small fortune with those sacks of theirs."

"Oh, yeah," said Skip. "There's more rich dink kids around here than you can wag your weenie at. If they do make anything with their garbage trade, it all goes home to papa-san. You ever watch one old man and a pack of kids come around? The old bastard will eat up anything you give the kids while they stand there and watch."

"There ought to be something we could give them the old farts can't take away," mused Bergin.

"How about a bath," asked Kevin.

That drew some chuckles, but Round John stood up looking

quite serious. "You know, Harrey, you might have something there. Maybe it's not the way to clean up on the war market and go home rich, it might be a cool way to spend the afternoon. We could take some pictures and get one of the guys from division PIO to do a story on it for Army Times. That kind of shit goes over real big — and it would keep the old man in good spirits."

Duke Randall had been lying quietly on Skip's cot, reading one of his skin magazines. Shaking his head in amazement at the notions bored men will decide to act on, he stepped to the refrigerator for a beer. Round John and Skip headed for the mess tent to get one of their big cooking kettles, figuring that was the only thing around large enough to be used as a kids' bathtub. Hawking left and stole a box of laundry soap from one of the slicks' tent, and returned about the same time as the others got back with the huge double-handled pot. They filled the kettle with water from the two-wheeled "buffalo" trailer, dumped in half the box of soap Hawking had stolen, and set the kettle in the open area in front of the tent.

Kevin located one of the boys who came through along the road with a shoe-shine kit, and had a few words in Vietnamese with him. He took off running and a few minutes later came back with a half-dozen friends. They stood around watching solemnly, willing as always to get in on something good, but not at all sure that this bath idea was a good enough thing to warrant one of them's being the first to step up and claim one.

Skip stood up, peeled off his shirt, dropped his pants and splashed his hands in the water. He rubbed his hands over his chest and armpits, grinning like a monkey mugging for the rubes at the carnival, and singing at the top of his lungs. "Nothing could be finah than to be in her vaginah in the moooorning..." The kids laughed and jumped, but not one of them made a move toward the tub.

Duke Randall stood laughing in the tent, scratching an armpit and shaking his massive square head back and forth. Hitching his bulk as though shouldering an enormous load, he marched toward the little cluster of kids. He grabbed the first one he reached, picked him up by his bony shoulders and plunked him into the kettle, clothes and all. The kid squawked once and Duke dunked him, then fished him out and peeled off his clothes. He took a huge washrag made of half a GI towel and tied into the kid. The rest of them squealed and laughed and pointed when Duke took the rag, slung it between the skinny legs and scrubbed it back and forth over the hairless balls, sing-songing, "Ah, numbah one shine, twennyfi' P."

Then they all wanted in on the act, and they came charging over, jostling each other like wives at a bargain sale, laughing and shouting for all the world like there wasn't a war going on at all. Pretty soon Duke got into it and was laughing and carrying on like an enormous kid himself, and nobody else got a chance to wash one solitary zipper-eyed little dink.

In the middle of it all, a jeep pulled up and dropped off a big dark curly-haired spec-4. He was festooned with little black leather boxes on straps around his neck, and looked peculiarly out-of-place in his crisp starched fatigues, like a civilian wearing an Army costume. "I'm Buddy Nichols, from Division PIO. We got a call about you." He began to shoot pictures, bought a beer from the refrigerator, and got into the swing of the fun. He left swearing that Duke Randall would be famous, and promising that he would be back. "I've heard you guys kick ass. If you can take the weight, I'd sure like to bring my camera along on a hot Dagger mission sometime." They promised him he could go along anytime, and laughed as he departed in his jeep, grinning sappily with bright-eyed enthusiasm.

"I wouldn't have believed it if I hadn't seen it with my very own eyes, boys and girls," said Skip. "Yes, that's what I'll tell my grandchildren about their old grand-daddy's exploits in the war. I'll tell them about how I stood right there, not ten feet from the great Duke Randall — course, he was only a lowly captain then — right there next to him, the biggest, roughest, hard-ass war hero of them all, and watched him singlehandedly clean up a whole village of Yards."

SEVEN

As the unit encountered more and more action in the weeks following Tet, the CO's exhortations to discipline and fearless gallantry became longer and louder. The company area continued to change as he made his influence felt. The tents all had wooden sides, painted pale green. The sandbag walls around them were built to a uniform height and whitewashed. Everything was raked clean, and neat wooden walkways led from place to place. In the tangle of tents, ruts, and make-do structures of the camp at Bao Trang, a little patch of square-cornered regularity began to emerge.

One of the outside walls of the new mess hall was painted with a mural designed by Csynes. In a bold and romantic style like a Marvel Comics adventure, three warriors stood together, a Knight and a Samurai behind, and an Army pilot in front, wearing helmet and visor. The morning it was officially unveiled, Buddy Nichols, the Armed Forces News photographer, came to take pictures and to interview the major.

Two primary missions were scheduled for the day, a battalion-sized insertion and a recon flight. Nichols had also been given permission to ride on the recon ship, which was to be flown by Csynes himself.

"This mural represents our attitude," Csynes told him. "For some people, being a soldier is just a dirty job they have to do. For others, the call to arms is a sacred trust. For them, danger is just an opportunity to test their courage, and seeking out the most dangerous and the most devastating missions is their greatest honor. For the Knight and the Samurai, taking the sword is an act of piety. The true warrior is more than just a fighter, he is in a sense....a priest of war."

"And the mission we are going on this morning, Major, is it such a mission?" asked Nichols, speaking into the microphone of his little portable tape recorder.

"Yes, it is. The A Lan Valley is the major artery for enemy supply and troop movement into South Vietnam. It has been Charlie country for five years, and if we had taken it back before now, we could probably have avoided the Tet Offensive. Now the Cong think they can get away with murder, that valley will look like a superhighway for supply from the Communists. Beginning today, we are going to start flying recon missions into that valley, to locate enemy concentrations so the artillery from Fort Selden, Fort Thorn, and Fort Craig can put some effective harassing fire on them. Taking that valley may be the most important objective in the conflict at this time, and the task could not be in better hands than the Black Sabres and the Daggers."

Several pilots and crewmen stood in a group by the mural to pose for a shot, and the men were enjoying the hoopla even though they had to make formation half an hour earlier than usual for the occasion. Suddenly Csynes called for a halt to the activity.

"Just a second there, Buddy. Mr. Hawking, would you mind stepping out of that picture, please. That's right, just step over there to the side."

"Sir?"

"That's right, Hawking, I don't want you in the picture. And I'd like you to do something about your appearance."

Hawking moved over to the side, then spoke up. "Sir, if the Major wouldn't mind, could you be a bit more specific?"

"Your hair, Soldier."

"It's within regulations."

"I'm aware of that, Mr. Hawking. If it were not within regulations, I would order you to correct that. It is within regulations, but it is not what I want printed in Army Times as an example of what a Dagger pilot looks like. You look like a slob, Mr. Hawking, a slob."

"I think I do a pretty good job of looking like a Dagger pilot when the shooting starts, Sir."

"That's right, you do. And for that you can expect to be decorated — but not displayed. You don't seem to understand that reputation is a very important tactical consideration. It is not enough to be good at fighting — you have to look like a warrior, and that means trimmed, polished, and on the bounce!"

After the photo session, most of the crews departed to fly the troop insertion mission, and those selected for the recon flight met in the mess hall for a final briefing.

"Here's the drill," said Csynes, posing beside an unrelated map for pictures. "We will use two slicks and one light fire team. The guns will be led by Lt. Bakersmith, with Mr. Padilla commanding the wing ship. Mr. Stapleton, from White Hilt platoon, will fly the chase ship, and I am flying the People Sniffer myself. Specialist Nichols will be riding with me to get the story, and of course, so will Captain Todsen from the Chem Corps. The instrument he is bringing is one of the most amazing devices in the inventory — it actually smells the enemy. Now, I am not at liberty to reveal how it works, but it can detect the smallest traces of certain chemicals released by the human body. These occur in a concentration matched only by chimpanzees, and since there are no chimps in Vietnam, we don't make any mistakes. To fly the mission, I will be on the treetops, where the readings are the best. Stapleton will fly about a thousand feet above and behind me, with the map. His copilot — that's Foley — will follow every move I make on the topographic map, and whenever Captain Todsen gets a reading on his Sniffer, he calls it out and Foley marks it on the map. The Daggers will fly on either side of Stapleton, so if anybody takes a shot at me, I can call in immediate fire. When we get an area with lots of hot spots, we call artillery, and they pound the place every few minutes for a couple of nights."

The flight got airborne and climbed to altitude to clear the ridge to the west. As they passed over firebase Fort Selden, they set up their positions for the run — Stapleton a thousand feet above and behind Csynes, and the two gunships behind and just below the chase ship. Csynes crossed the ridge at treetop level and dived steeply down the back side, following a small canyon.

Farthest back, Eddie Padilla lowered his collective lever and nosed over slightly to descend with the Sniffer. In the seat left of him, John Bergin fiddled nervously with his minigun sight, peering thorough the prism, recycling the arming switch, and checking that the pylons were correctly pointing the weapons.

The door gunners crouched at the ready behind their M-60's. Eddie squirmed in his seat as a trickle of sweat tickled beneath his helmet. In order to provide fast cover for the Sniffer flying so close to the treetops, the guns stayed up about five hundred feet. For a man with a rifle in the jungle, a helicopter on the treetops went by too fast to hit easily, and a helicopter above one thousand feet was just about out of range. But one cruising along at five hundred was a big fat juicy target. The position was fondly known as the Suicide Slot.

Csynes's voice came up on the tac channel. "Dagger flight, Sabre Six. Prepare to fire a test burst with all door guns and the miniguns, on my command. We're going to let people know we're here — maybe sucker somebody into revealing position. Ready test: FIRE."

With the morning sun glaring behind them, the flight swept down the side of the jungle-covered ridge toward the waving plain of buffalo grass on the valley floor below, and their eight M-60's and four miniguns snarled their challenge. Pointing his weapons down and to the left away from the Sniffer slick, Bergin fired a neat burst about three seconds long. The door gunners pecked away at the treeline below, and Eddie found himself laughing. From the guns of the helicopters in front of him, streams of brass shell casings tumbled to catch the sun, and he found it funny that they looked like handfuls of gold coins twinkling in showers.

"Sniffer, Sabre Six," came Csynes peculiar reedy voice. "Heads up, now, we're beginning our test run. Doorgunners may return fire. Daggers, hold miniguns unless we need them, and break position for attack only on my command. Check?"

"Roger that," said Bakersmith. "We're cool."

"Dagger One-five, cool, uh, Roger."

The Major knew exactly where he was going, and he kept up a running monologue like a tour guide as he traced a path along the edge of the valley, following treelines and convoluted little waterways. "They use these channels to run sampans loaded with Chinese mortar rounds and small arms ammunition out of Laos. The north end of the valley — those hills you can see in the distance north — that's in Laos. South of here, the other side of the valley is in Cambodia."

"Hot spot," interrupted Captain Todsen.

"Roger, spot," replied Foley from the chase ship.

Csynes led the flight up a ravine choked with trees and banana plants.

"Six, Sabre Two-two, there appears to be a well-used trail running about one hundred meters to your right," reported Foley.

"Hot spot! Another. Hot spot! Wow!"

Suddenly Eddie could hear popcorn, and a stream of tracers lashed out at him from the hillside across from him. "Receiving fire!" he called. His right-side doorgunner opened up and spat tracers back. A second position began to fire down toward the Sniffer.

"Hot spot!"

"No shit!" yelled someone.

"Hold your positions," called Csynes calmly. "Break left, now." He pulled up and to the left rapidly, and hurtled over the crest of the ravine. As his gunship cleared the ravine behind the Sniffer, Eddie glanced back to see his left-side gunner leaning out of the door on a monkey-strap to point his machinegun back and down to answer the last tracers streaking after them.

"That's A Lan hill, there at eleven o'clock," said Csynes, indicating a little wooded peak which rose up about two hundred feet from the valley floor a couple of miles ahead of them. "The old A Lan airfield is just this side of it." As they passed the site of the Special Forces camp where Jacob Csynes had held his ground until rescued five years earlier, the major called out, "There it is, men: The Graveyard."

Eddie looked down on the bomb-pocked scar. There were no structures, but a few concrete slab floors still remained. The tattered ruins of sandbagged revetments protruded from the shattered red soil like fossil teeth. The earth had been cleared for some distance around the little camp, and it was still barren and open, and apparently unvisited. In the clearing eerily lay the corpses of several helicopters. To one side the hulk of an old H-21 "flying banana" sat upright, gutted and scorched. There were two or three clearly recognizable as Hueys, and one mangled pile of scrap and ashes displayed the characteristic stinger-tail of a

"Loach", the fast little egg-shaped LOH — light observation helicopter — which had been introduced to replace the old bubble-nosed "whirlybird" of Korean War vintage.

"Daggers, set up a wagonwheel and keep your heads up for anything that moves. I'm going down to have a look."

To Eddie's amazement, Csynes circled back to the camp and landed on one of the old concrete slabs. Then he and Buddy Nichols jumped out of the helicopter and trotted a few steps away from it. Still wearing his flight helmet, Major Csynes planted his boots wide and raised both of his fists to the sky. The pilots cheered and hooted over the radio as Buddy Nichols took the picture which would appear the following week on the front page of Army Times.

Then without warning a fountain of red dirt erupted fifty yards from the helicopter — a mortar. Csynes and Nichols dashed to their bird, and as they took off, a second mortar splashed twenty yards closer.

"Congratulations, Major," called Rudy Bakersmith. "I guess they've been expecting you."

"They're in for a hell of a surprise, right, Rudy?"

"Roger that!"

They flew the rest of the circular route they had planned, and located several more concentrations of "hot spots", but drew no more fire. As they headed back toward the ridge to return to Bao Trang, Csynes called for a change of plans.

"Daggers, Six. How'd you like to go back and unload your ordnance on those gooks that shot at us?"

"Now you're talking, Six," replied Bakersmith.

"Roger that," added Eddie. "Let's get 'em!"

Csynes made a zoom climb to about a thousand feet and turned toward the ravine they had flown through half an hour earlier. "Dagger Two-six, we'll back you up with doorgun fire, but from here on in it's your show, Rudy," he called.

"Roger that, Sabre Six! OK, Bullseye, we go down in hunter/ killer formation. I'll be on the deck where Ferranti can work the mini's. You hang in the Slot, and if I can flush something, you waste it, over."

"That's a big rog, Lead!" Eddie called back, his voice pitched high with excitement. He checked his rocket arming switches again, then looked up surprised to see Major Csynes's big Delta-model slick rising up close alongside him. Buddy Nichols was hanging on a gunner's monkey strap, leaning out of the helicopter to take pictures of the gunships in action.

The chase slick set up a high orbit to wait until the gunships had delivered their ordnance, and to provide a rescue ship in case somebody went down. Bakersmith leveled off at a high speed about a hundred feet above the trees and began working up the ravine. He flew the terrain with the spontaneous fluidity of a ski racer, spotting possible target sites and the corresponding positions of advantage, and smoothly stemming from one advantage to the next, setting up his gunners to cover the widest possible field. Eddie jinked and slalomed above him, flying S-turns and yo-yo's to stay in a position to deliver fire below the lead gunship.

They got fire almost immediately. Several bursts of tracerfire spat up from the hillside, from scattered locations. John Bergin answered them with the lead-spitting twin gatling guns, and the doorgunners of all four ships pumped tracers into the dark places among the trees. One of Bakersmith's gunners tossed a smoke grenade to mark fire beneath him. "Put a couple of rockets down there, Bullseye. I'll go around to cover you." The lieutenant pulled his ship up and around to zoom climb and turn back behind Eddie.

Eddie rolled in smoothly and lined his helicopter up in a steep dive. He set his rocket sight about a hundred feet short of the smoke plume, checked that his run was stable, then carefully pickled off a single pair of rockets. "Put some minigun down there, Round John," he said. When Eddie completed his run and pulled up and around the racetrack pattern, Bakersmith rolled in and placed another pair of rockets. Then instead of coming back around again, he resumed his low-level prowl, with Eddie back up behind him at five hundred feet.

"Nice work, beautiful pattern, Daggers!" cheered Jake Csynes. "Wup! Taking...taking hits! Somebody put some fire on that son of a bitch." Csynes had swung low and wide to get pictures, and had taken a burst of fire from the trees beyond the smoking rocket craters. "We took a couple — seem to be OK."

The lead gunship rounded a curve and came upon a little protected hollow on the side of the ridge. From above, Eddie saw a complex of some kind of earthworks — little trenches, patches of straw mats, holes in the hillside, tiny cultivated spots. As though a single command had been given, a dozen weapons opened up on them. "Holy shit, coming out!" yelled Bakersmith, and he pulled up in a tight turn, with Ferranti spraying the treeline below with the inside minigun to cover them in their vulnerable position. Two little crystal stars appeared in the windshield in front of Eddie, and something spanged off the armor plate at his shoulder.

He fired one pair, then a second, and held his descent to let the guns work. He could hear the crackle of groundfire, and he could see tracers coming from several directions. His attention was arrested by one burst which came from above and behind him. He quickly glanced back and even in the heat of battle was surprised. Csynes was following him down on his firing pass, hanging just above and behind the gunship, but close in. His co-pilot was flying the ship, and Csynes was firing his pistol out the window. As Eddie watched — a second or two perhaps — two tracers punched through the tail of Csynes ship.

"It's all small-arms stuff," announced Csynes. "I think we've got an infantry base camp. Let's unload and get the hell out of here!" He broke off to one side and started to climb up toward the ridge to return home. Rudy Bakersmith fell in to cover Eddie's roll-out, and put two pairs of rockets into a little patch of mats and mudworks. A stuttering burst of secondary explosions announced his discovery of a cache of mortar rounds.

"That's what I like," crowed Csynes. "Get in close and kick some ass. You might get killed, but you won't get hurt."

Then from the chase ship which was orbiting at fifteen hundred feet overhead came Warrant Officer Stapleton's horrified cry, "Receiving fire! Oh, God, it's flak! We're....oh, shit!"

"Break off, Daggers, get the hell out of there!" ordered Major Csynes immediately. "The chase is hit. We've got a 37-millimeter in here somewhere."

As he broke off his attack and zoom climbed to cross the edge of the ravine, Eddie looked up to see the chase ship high above. To one side and behind it were four dark, greasy puffballs. As he watched, two more burst closer, and a thin scumline of smoke came from the helicopter. Stapleton chopped power and dived for the trees. Though relatively safe from small-arms fire, he had been a prime target for the 37mm Chicom anti-aircraft cannon, a weapon designed to shoot down low-flying jets, and supplied through Laos.

"We've got severe vibration, and warning lights on....there goes the turbine RPM....we're going in. Tail rotor sticking....hang on!" Eddie turned to follow Bakersmith as he set up a pass to cover the spot where it appeared the chase ship was going down. The slick was settling steeply and was turned several degrees sideways. Stapleton tried to stop it at the bottom, but the tail swung around and struck a tree about fifteen feet above ground. The helicopter snapped over sharply and the rotor splintered and scattered itself.

Rudy pounced on the spot at once, and made a long, slow firing pass, letting Ferranti and the doorguns spray the trees to keep the enemy's heads down as long as possible. He broke off only a few feet above the downed ship, and reported that he could see movement. Eddie followed with a similar pass, and saw two men jump out of the wreck, then another.

"Cover me, Daggers," called Jake Csynes. "I'm going down to pick them up."

"What you got left, Bullseye?" asked Bakersmith.

"Four pair, and about twenty percent on the guns."

"I've only got two pair — I'll use both of them on the way in. You hold high until they get loaded, then put all of them in there to cover the pickup."

"Roger that."

With Bakersmith close behind him, Csynes dropped into the little clearing where Stapleton had crashed, and came to a high hover. The three men had dragged the fourth from the wreck, and were carrying him toward the slick. Some tracerfire fell on them from somewhere high on the hillside, but there was no close fire. Csynes put his bird down and the crew of the chase ship tumbled in. Eddie readied himself for his firing run to cover Csynes, but there was a moment's delay.

"Make sure Foley's got that map," yelled Csynes, accidentally squeezing his mike switch past intercom position to broadcast. "Good boy! Coming out!" As Csynes lifted off, Eddie chopped the treeline with four neatly-placed pairs of rockets. The flight turned to follow the line of the ridge to gain altitude without getting up into the range of the 37mm cannon, and they crested the ridge only a few feet above the trees.

"Sabre flight, Sabre Six. My congratulations, Sabres and Daggers, that was a monumental mission. In the next few months we're going to turn that valley into a place you could bring your kids. Daggers, you're released to return to The Scabbard, and stand by. I've got to get Stapleton to the hospital pad — seems he broke his leg climbing out of his helicopter. Good work, men. Sabre Six, out."

Then the voice of Buddy Nichols came up on the radio. "I'm just proud to be here to see this — you guys are what the word heroic is all about, and I'm going to tell the world. This is Buddy Nichols, Armed Forces News, with former Golden Knight Rudy Bakersmith, Warrant Officer Bullseye Padilla, and Major Jake The Snake Csynes, the one man the Viet Cong fear the most, in the A Lan Valley, Republic of Vietnam."

In order to make Major Csynes's mural-dedication formation, the Dagger crews had gone down to the flight line with their flashlights in the pre-dawn chill to complete the meticulous ritual of pre-flight inspection of their aircraft. A few of them had risen early enough to go to the chow hall for breakfast, but most had just passed through the kitchen and picked up what they could carry to eat later. The maintenance crews had been up all night working so that every gunship would be ready to fly. The four crewmembers of each ship had rubbed tubing to discover the first signs of leakage, twisted and shaken the push-pull rods of the control system to spot slack or binding, and checked the rotor system from Jesus-nut to servos. They had noted cables, tail rotor, engine, transmission, hydraulics, fuel systems, electrical equipment, antennas, and flight controls. They had ascertained that survival kits, first aid gear, jugs of cold fresh water, and boxes of C-rations were aboard. The weapons systems required a complete inspection also, and the crews had carefully checked pistols and M-16's, the gunners' M-60's, the miniguns, bloopers, rocket pods, sights, and arming systems — and each had chambers, switches, chutes, trays, delinkers, cams, electrical contacts, safety pins, and a long list of other things which had to be exactly correct. All over the aircraft, the nuts and bolts which held the machines together were meticulously checked for safetywire bindings. All of them....and every time.

The flight assignment for the day had brought groans from the crews at the briefing. It was simple enough: put a battalion of ARVN troops into a big open field outside of a bombed-out village in the flatlands south of the Bao Trang valley.

"So we all gets to fly for little Marvin the ARVN," said Skip Gilman. "Ten bucks MPC says it's a ratfuck." There were no takers.

"Here are the crew assignments," announced Captain Duke Randall. "I'm flying first team lead, with Mr. Jeter. My wing ship is Mr. Harrey, with Malins. Lt. Petch will lead the second team, with Hawking, and Gilman will fly his wing, with Swomney. And gentlemen, we can look forward to a very long day."

"How come?" asked Kevin Harrey. "It shouldn't take more than a few hours to move a battalion — and it's sure not likely to be very hot."

"We've been ordered to provide a cap over them all day. We've got to keep a fire team in the air orbiting at all times." Randall tried to make it matter-of-fact, but it was hard not to sound apologetic.

"Did they give us a release time?" somebody asked.

"As soon as they feel they don't need us any longer. Look, it's their war, remember."

The crews departed for the flight line as soon as the Major's formation was dismissed. In minutes, the eleven Black Sabre slicks began to whine into action. The gunship crews ran through their starting checklists, and settled down resolved to spend the day flying idiot circles around the sky of Southeast Asia.

Captain Neil Koontz was flying the C-and-C ship, and the Red Hilt platoon leader Captain Jim Mitchell was flying the lead slick. The ARVN compound was about thirty miles away, in what had once been an ancient walled town. What remained was a flat area of several acres enclosed by an eight-foot zig-zag stone wall with a fighting parapet, surrounded by a few long pools which had once been a moat. As the flight came over the old fortification, the pilots could see the tangle of tents and makeshift buildings which had grown up along one end of what had been a formal garden. An old stone temple building standing at the other end had been converted to an official headquarters, with the attendant flags and long black cars.

The C-and-C stayed high, the gunships set up a wide circular orbit around the place, and the ten slicks went in to pick up the first load of troops. A few minutes after they touched down, Sabre lead called the C-and-C.

"Charlie Charlie, there's nobody here. I can see a few over by the bunkers, but the only people out here on the strip are the Pathfinders who popped smoke, over."

"Roger, One-six, sit tight and I'll try to give them a call. Break. Marker Six, Sabre Charlie Charlie, over."

There was a moment's hesitation, then the Pathfinder began to transmit. "Ah, Black Sabre Charlie Charlie, this is Marker Six. Go ahead, over."

"What seems to be the holdup, Marker Six? My lead advises there's nobody there but you Pathfinders. What's going on?"

"Sabre, it appears one of the ARVN commanders decided he wasn't needed on this mission, so he sent his people home. We're trying to round them up. Over."

"What? Understand he just sent a company of men home?"

"That's affirmative, Sabre. My counterpart doesn't seem too upset about it, but he won't go without them. I'm afraid there's not too much we can do. Suggest you shut down on the runway and wait until we can get things straightened out here. Over."

"How long do you expect that might be?"

"Ah...that'd be a little hard to say, Sabre."

There was a long silence, then Koontz replied coldly from C-and-C, "Roger, we're shutting down. Dagger Six, you come on in and shut down behind the slicks."

The four gunships slid in behind the slicks and shut down their turbines. The C-and-C landed behind them and hovered to the head of the column of helicopters. As the other pilots and crewmen watched, Captain Koontz got out of his ship, threw his helmet angrily to the ground, and stalked off toward the old stone temple.

After a few minutes, a half dozen ARVN troops began to wander toward the helicopters. With smooth boyish faces and long black hair hanging in their eyes, they appeared to be no older than about sixteen. Each wore a new set of camouflage fatigues and combat boots, and each was carrying a new American weapon. They stood a few yards away, chattering excitedly among themselves and pointing toward the gunships. Then, putting on enormous grins, they began to move toward Kevin's ship.

"Du ma, didimau! Muon soc mau, khong?" he yelled. The Vietnamese soldiers halted, looking at him with uncertainty. He turned his back on them and continued to eat his C-rations.

Ray Swomney stood beside his ship, a little embarrassed by Kevin's quick and harsh reaction to the troops' approach. In the few months he had been in-country, he had picked up enough Vietnamese to catch the insult that had accompanied Kevin's admonition to stay away from the helicopter. He started to turn away also, hoping that Kevin's warning would keep them away from his aircraft as well. He miscalculated by a second. One of the ARVN troops saw him looking at them, grinned happily, and saluted. Swomney, honor-bound in spite of himself to obey the military custom, reluctantly returned the salute.

The result was like flapping a steak at six puppies. The soldiers promptly trooped over to the gunship. Completely ignoring Swomney's feeble objections, they began to examine the gun system, wide-eyed and eager. "Ah, numbah one!" they chattered, jostling one another like a pack of kids. Swomney stood and watched them, not wanting to get involved at all, but reluctant to make a show to drive them off. One of them motioned to get his attention. "Sah? Sah?" He pointed to the minigun and made a motion like shooting a machinegun. "Shoo'

VC?" he asked.

Ray Swomney smiled self-consciously and moved a step toward the helicopter, eager in spite of his discomfort to try out the few words of Vietnamese he had learned. "Da duoc," he said. Their eyes flashed with delight. "Sung may sat nhieu VC. Machinegun kill many VC, you bet." They all laughed uproariously, then began to make sweeping machinegun passes at each other. They took turns being the cringing VC being blown to pieces by the snarling guns. One pounded Swomney's shoulder with enthusiasm, and another pumped his hand. He found himself laughing with them and joining in their pantomime.

"Numbah one! Tot lam!" they laughed, nodding and repeating his gestures. A few minutes later somebody over near the bunkers shouted something in Vietnamese, and the six troops waved and saluted, then moved off smiling happily to join the growing body of soldiers near the tents and bunkers.

As they left, Swomney looked up and saw Kevin watching him quietly. A quick flush of embarrassment reddened his face, and he shrugged his shoulders and smiled.

"Yeah, you go on and fuck around with those slopes," Kevin called to him. "You just be sure you look your ship over real close before you take off. There'll be something missing — or something added."

It was two hours and twenty minutes after the scheduled lift time that the ARVN commander finally decided to put his men on the helicopters and start the assault. It took ten minutes to get the first load of troops aboard their proper aircraft. Captain Koontz called up just before they finally got airborne to advise everyone that he was already composing the words he would use in his "unsatisfactory mission" report to Division Headquarters.

The flight had just cleared the stone walls of the compound when Skip Gilman's crew chief called him on the intercom. "Mr. Gilman, didn't we check the first aid kit when we ran the pre-flight this morning?"

"Yeah. What's wrong?"

"It's gone."

"Yes, Sir, and so are our C-rations," added the gunner.

Skip gave his co-pilot a long eyeball askance. "You know anything about that, Swomney?" Looking disgusted, the young warrant said nothing, but he nodded wryly. "Well, we can probably get some extra C's from the slicks," said Gilman, then added, "that is, if you ask them real nice."

The lead slick was flown by Captain Jim Mitchell, with Warrant Mike Ramsey. Both of them were old soldiers, and had spent a previous tour of duty in Vietnam. Both recognized the complex nature of the influences motivating the Vietnamese, and so maintained an alert and highly professional attitude toward them. As the allied troops climbed into their helicopter, the two pilots watched them closely, looking for any sign of a suspicious action, or an unnecessary bundle.

They loaded seven ARVN soldiers into the ship, and each one found himself a place to sit in the seats or on the floor. The crewmen eyed them all closely, making a quick inventory of those things aboard which could be easily picked up. If one of the troops grabbed something on his way out at the LZ, there would be no time to go after him to get it back. One young Vietnamese who by his appearance could not have been over sixteen settled himself on the floor behind the left seat where Jim Mitchell was checking his flight systems for takeoff. The boy pulled up the sleeves of his fatigues, which were several sizes too large for him, folded his arms across his chest, and grinned at the crew chief. The crewman nodded perfunctorily and began to check his M-60 door gun.

The flight lifted off the dirt strip in formation, each pilot jockeying his ship to get into a good tight position. Jim Mitchell made a wide turn, acknowledged the trail ship's call that the flight was in formation, and headed toward the LZ. There was some light haze, but the pilots could clearly see the smoke from the artillery shelling that had been pounding the LZ for several minutes.

Captain Koontz called from the C-and-C. "Sabre lead, Charlie Charlie, the artillery is lifting at this time. The guns will make one firing pass, then drop smoke for you on the next. Your outside door gunners can use full suppressive fire, and you'll have gunships firing on both sides of you when you go in.

Over."

In the pre-strike gunship team, Lt. Bud Petch acknowledged the C-and-C's call on the FM tactical channel to inform him that the last rounds from the artillery had impacted. "Roger, Charlie Charlie, understand Redleg is complete." He lowered his rocket sight, checked it for the reticle — the pattern of light pips he used to sight — and broke out of the wagonwheel pattern to set up for his first run. He gave Skip a call, then snapped the weapons arming switch to HOT. In the seat next to him, Hawking scratched his long nose and reached overhead for the sight to his 40mm grenade launcher.

As Petch set up his run, Hawking and the two gunners scanned the dikes and lines of nipa palm for any sign of trenches or bunkers. Then the lieutenant rolled the nose of his ship over and began to fire his rockets. He pickled off the pairs quickly while still high, scattering them rather indiscriminately around the LZ. Hawking counted three, then threw the switches to the blooper and squeezed the triggers. The turret moved and the egg-sized gold projectiles began to pop out of the short barrel, making a noise like someone pounding on the nose of the ship with a rubber hammer, Bok! Bok! Bok! Bok! The rounds lobbed out toward the target and he watched them fall, judging where they would hit.

Petch broke off the run and pulled the helicopter around hard. "Did we draw any fire?" he asked anxiously.

"Naw," replied Hawking.

"Negative fire on that pass," called Petch over the radio.

"Roger that," replied Skip from the second gunship. He pulled his ship up sharply until it was almost hanging in the air, then tipped the nose over and began a long, slow pass. He fired six rockets one at a time, carefully spacing them along the far end of the LZ, the area which would be hardest to hit when they were escorting the flight of slicks into the field. He carried his attack low and close in, letting Swomney work the treeline and the clumps of nipa palm thoroughly with his miniguns. The door gunners worked their rounds to cover any spot in the LZ which conceal a man with a rifle. Skip broke off almost at treetop level, pulled in all his ship's power, then zoom-climbed four hundred feet to pick up Petch, who was getting ready for his second pass.

Jim Mitchell watched the gunships work, and he timed his turn for Petch to make one more pass to drop a smoke marker. The lead gunship was easily recognizable by the round ball turret on its nose. He watched it pitch down ahead of him, fire another pair of the streaking rockets, then pull up and fly over the LZ. A streamer of purple smoke plummeted from the gunship toward the ground.

As the flight settled slowly toward the rice paddy, Mitchell concentrated on his flying, carefully picking his landing spot to give the rest of the flight room to set down safely. He tried to consider how quickly the troops could get to cover, and though he tried to put the fear of being shot out of his mind, he scanned the trees on all sides of the LZ to try to guess just where the enemy fire was most likely to come from. He was a career professional pilot, and he took pride in trying to make every lift as near perfect as he was able. Though it left him exposed in the air a few seconds longer, he made his approach slowly and smoothly, so his flight would have no trouble following him. As he neared the touchdown, he called for his gunners to open up. The door gunners on the outside of the staggered-trail formation in each ship began firing, chopping into the lines of palm and bamboo with their machineguns.

Skip on one side and Kevin Harrey on the other began pounding the sides of the LZ with minigun and doorgun fire, and the men in the slicks could hear the ripping WHOOOSSSHHH-KARUMPF! KARUMPF! of the gunships' rockets as they flashed past the formation and exploded. Out of the corners of his eyes, Mitchell saw the gunships peel off, guns blazing as he touched down. He shouted for the gunners to cease fire, and the ARVN troops began to leap out of the helicopters and run crouching toward the dikes along the sides of the LZ. At that instant, when the door guns were silenced and the troops exposed, the enemy opened fire. "Receiving fire!" several voices shouted or screamed over the air.

Jim Mitchell squeezed his mike switch and yelled, "Coming out!" He pulled up firmly on the collective lever and nosed the ship over to get out of the vulnerable clearing.

"Got 'em spotted," somebody broadcast. "Clump of palm on the left. Tracers."

As the flight cleared the ground and began to move forward, Jim Mitchell began a shallow turn to the right, away from the LZ. Then he heard several sharp metallic thunks, and he knew he was hit. His crew chief immediately confirmed it. "Taking hits!" His eyes snapped to his instrument panel as the big red FIRE warning light flashed on.

In his mind he saw clearly the inside of the back of his helicopter, where the tail boom was held on by four bolts fastened through metal which would burn easily if heated enough, and over the radio he heard the four most horrifying words anyone had ever spoken to him: "You are on fire!"

"I'm going to set her down," he said, trying to stay calm. Sabre Two, you have the flight." He turned toward a wide rice paddy near the LZ, trying to squeeze all the time and power he could from the crippled engine, risking explosion. He scanned the instruments quickly, trying not to think about what would happen if the engine exploded, or the tail rotor drive shaft burned through, or the control systems failed, or...

"Put some fire down there," he called to his gunners. The crew chief and gunner sprayed the area with tracerfire as he set the ship down gently in the middle of the rice paddy. He twisted the throttle off, shut off the fuel and engine master switches and threw off his seat belts, noting as he did that one of the gunships was already covering him, chopping into the treeline beyond him with tracerfire.

The instant the ship touched down, the crew chief leaped out, opened the cockpit door, slammed back the armor plate so the captain could get out, grabbed the fire extinguisher and ran back to the burning engine. Jim leaped out and dropped to the ground, scanning the treeline for any sign of the enemy. Nothing moved, and he heard no fire except the sporadic chattering of riflefire from the LZ a short way off.

In a minute or two, things seemed to be in pretty good shape. The C-and-C was orbiting overhead, the gunships were making low passes over the treeline nearest him, the crew chief had put out the fire in the engine compartment, and they had made no contact with the enemy. While Mike Ramsey pulled the radios from the nose compartment of the ship, Jim helped the crew set up their M-60's at either end of the bird. None of them had been wounded, and they knew that the slicks would quickly bring in a party of infantry to secure the ship until a heavy twin-rotored Chinook helicopter could be flown in to sling-load the Huey out.

Ramsey stepped to the back of the aircraft to remove all their flight gear and the emergency kit with the morphine and methedrine in it. He had to personally sign for the kit because of the "controlled substances" included. He glanced under the seat to see if he had missed anything, and cried out in surprise. "Hey, Cap'n Mitchell, there's a grenade in here under your seat."

Mitchell ran around to the side of the ship and looked where Mike was pointing. "Don't touch it," he said. The grenade was an American fragmentation type, wedged under the lever which adjusted the position of the seat. Mike started to reach for it. "No, hold it a minute," said Mitchell, blocking his arm. "It could be a booby trap." He leaned down and examined the little bomb closely. It had been firmly wedged in, with the safety lever against the floor. Any attempt to move the adjusting lever, or any strong vibration, could have shaken it loose and set off the fuse. The pin had been pulled.

"Those fucking gooks. Those rotten, stinking, treacherous little dink bastards." Mitchell stared at the grenade in disgusted rage. "If I had anything to say about it, somebody else could lift the whole pack of them out of there — or they could walk back."

Ramsey spit. "It's good we did get shot down, or we'd probably have been blown right out of the sky when that thing finally shook itself loose. I'd sure like to catch up with the little slope sucker who put it there. I'd feed him his balls."

"OK, you three guys get yourselves some cover," said the captain, reaching under the seat. "I'm going to get rid of this thing." Ramsey and the crewmen moved a few feet off and lay down in the rice paddy. Mitchell carefully grasped the grenade, holding down the safety lever with his fingers. When he was sure he had it securely, he drew it out slowly. "Keep your heads down. I'm going to toss this into that shell crater in front of the ship." Jim had been a baseball player, and he knew he could easily hurl the grenade forty meters. Planting his feet, he drew back his long arm and threw.

The saboteur in ARVN uniform who had left the grenade had replaced the five-second delay fuse with an instant detonator. The weapon exploded ten inches from his fingertips. The shock slammed Mike Ramsey against the ground, and he felt the sting of tiny pieces of shrapnel biting into his legs. In sudden horror he looked up and saw the shuddering remains of Captain Jim Mitchell sliding down the riddled side of the aircraft, a one-armed faceless pulp.

EIGHT

Duke Randall popped open a can of beer, wrapped his big square hand around it, and held it up before him. "Here's to Major Jake," he toasted. He sucked the can empty in a few swallows, then crushed it as he held it to his mouth. "So how about that, men?" he asked, tossing a magazine in front of the group of Dagger pilots. "'Jake Csynes Returns To A Lan', on the cover of US Newsday."

Kevin, Eddie, and some of the others stared in amazement at the arresting picture. Csynes stood on the shattered red earth of A Lan airfield, arms held aloft, his face a moving portrait of heroic determination. Behind him, made much closer by the long lens Buddy Nichols had used to take the shot, rose a fountain of red dirt thrown up by the first of the mortar rounds fired at them on the people-sniffer mission.

"I don't know how that makes you men feel," said Duke, "but it really gives me a sense of...of being somebody, to know that all over America, our CO, and the Sabres and Daggers are the living proof that we're winning this war. Your name is in the story too, Eddie. Yeah, it says, 'DFC-winner Eduardo Bullseye Padilla, of Las Cruces, New Mexico'. Gee, what an honor, huh?"

"And you wanted to be a local hero," laughed John Bergin.

"I wish it was true...that we're winning the war, I mean," said Jerry Malins. "We're showing America a picture of a recon mission into a Communist-controlled area, and calling that some kind of victory. And the only reason we aren't in there yet is because the Vietnamese have got their shit so scrambled it would be easier to win this war if they weren't here at all. The government is full of crooks and jetset scumbags, and the ARVN...the fucking Arvin is so full of fucking VC they can climb right in our fucking helicopters! Goddamnit, I'm sorry, Cap'n Duke, but if they'd just let us fight this war...."

Kevin Harrey lay on his bunk staring out through the open end of the tent. The loss of Captain Mitchell to a saboteur in ARVN uniform kept pressing upon his mind, not because another of the company had been killed, nor because the captain had been someone special to him, but because of what the enemy had done. "Lighten up, Malins," he said. "A nice piece of work, if you ask me. If you had sneaked on a gook supply junk and blew it up, they'd give you a "V" for your Bronze Star. I can't help thinking that sneaky little zipper-eyed bastard was a hero too."

Malins came up off his bunk ready to fight. "Just one minute, you son of a bitch. Jim Mitchell had two kids and happened to be one hell of a nice guy, and you can call the little commie fucker that murdered him a hero? I think somebody ought to..."

"You better zip your lip, Malins," said Kevin very calmly, "or I'm going to surprise you like Santa Claus never could. I liked Captain Mitchell too, so quit waving your flag over his grave. He wasn't murdered, he was killed in action."

"Yeh, nobody's getting murdered over here," put in Hawking. "Both sides have leaders who say it's all right for us to kill each other."

"What I want to know," Kevin said, "is why the ARVN can't find their asses using both of their hands and ours too, and the VC have troops like that one who will sit with a big smile in a helicopter with ten of the enemy and rig a bomb that might go off in his hands."

"The crew chief said he remembered the slope sitting there was just a kid. I wish I had that kind of balls," said Eddie Padilla.

"You guys give me headaches," growled Duke Randall. "Nobody is the enemy — communism is the enemy. These people have become communists, and that means we have to fight them. We didn't plan it that way, they did. If you screws could shoot as well as you can talk, we'd have won this war a long time ago, and I could be back in Oklahoma raising hogs and studying Scripture."

"Right on, Captain," said Malins. "That's exactly right on. And the sooner we press to a final confrontation, the sooner we can wipe them out and go home and live in peace. Kill them all and let God sort them out, that's what I say."

"Well, one thing is for sure," said Duke Randall. "With the Major getting this kind of publicity, we can expect to get a shot at all the best missions. At the rate we're going, we're going to make 'Dagger' the generic word for helicopter gunships, and when the history books get written, it will be the battles we fight that go in them. That's what it means, Gentlemen, to serve with a man like Jacob Csynes."

As the men talked, the three-quarter truck from the flight line arrived, and dropped Skip Gilman, Rudy Bakersmith, and Ray Swomney at Operations. When, they came into the tent, the conversation quickly dropped off. The three pilots sagged onto their bunks and sat silently with dazed expressions.

"What happened?" asked Round John.

Skip shook his head. "Jesus. Where do you start?"

"I thought you guys had a routine one today," said Eddie.

"We lost a full slick," said Rudy Bakersmith. "Just shot right fucking down."

"Who was it?" asked Kevin.

"Linc Olson, the maintenance check pilot, and Mike Wills. They took a B-40 rocket right in the cockpit, and the whole thing blew when they hit. Crew and six troops didn't have a chance."

"We lost Ferranti," said Skip quietly.

"Dead?" asked John Bergin.

"Yep. The whole thing just took seconds. We started receiving fire and he was plugging away with the blooper. I broke left — the slicks were all over the place — and we took a burst of small arms fire, just a couple of hits. I looked over at the Wop and he was just sitting there looking surprised with a hole about the size of a silver dollar in his neck. He was dead a long time before we got home."

Hawking dropped his hat to the floor. "Awww. What a bummer."

"Jesus, Skip," said Kevin.

"No shit, man," said Skip. "It really set me back. He knew. He was just sitting there with his hands in his lap, looking surprised. He was alive maybe a minute or two — long enough to think about it."

"Too bad," said Duke. "He was a nice kid."

"They kill a lot of those over here," said Hawking.

Bud Petch had been sitting apart from the others in a corner of the open-sided tent-roofed building. He was scribbling away in a spiral notebook, having informed the other Dagger pilots he was compiling notes for a book. He also was keeping the PRC-25, the portable FM radio unit used by troops in the field, with which he was monitoring the communication between Black Sabre operations office and the unit for whom his fire team was on stand-by.

"Sabre Control, Bengal Tiger Six Yankee, over."

Petch jumped to the radio set and raised the volume. "Hey, that's our people," he called to the others.

"Sabre, we've encountered some hostiles in this village and we've pulled back our recon teams. We're going to run a sweep through with our dusters, and we'd like the gunships on hand to wipe up anybody who tries to run. How soon can they get to our location? Over."

"We can scramble the gun team and be over you in fifteen minutes," affirmed Petch.

"Roger! We'd appreciate that, over."

"They're on their way, Bengal Tiger!"

"Yeah," said Eddie, "lets see if we can go out there and even up the score a little bit."

The team was airborne in minutes and humping it towards the village they were working some ten miles away. The mission was routine, and they had drawn no fire inserting the troops earlier during the day, but the Daggers were keyed up to fight.

"There's our village," called Petch on the FM tactical freq as the little cluster of thatched and tile-roofed buildings came into view before them. "Looks like they're ready to sweep." The village was set off by itself in the center of a little flat plain cultivated in rice paddies. Two long lines of nipa palm led along the ditchbanks toward the less cultivated area to the east, but to the west a single broad paddy half a mile across separated the target village from the larger complex of the next little community.

The American troops were clearly visible, in position to begin their advance. On the north side of the village a platoon of troops lay in the dusty paddy, spread out a few yards apart. Behind them sat two squat "dusters" — tanks, each armed with a pair of forty-millimeter cannons.

The Daggers set up a wide wagonwheel pattern, watching for any sign of activity, or for defensive earthworks, as Petch talked with the ground commander. "OK, Daggers, we're going to start moving through. If we flush something, give us a call and we'll mark our forward position with a smoke. Then you can work the targets while we move in the tanks to mop up."

"Roger that, Bengal Tiger. We'll maintain orbit."

The tanks moved forward, firing rounds in flat trajectories into the hooches ahead of them. The explosive rounds ripped the walls outward from the shacks, and the roofs collapsed into the bursts of smoke and flame. Then the line of troops advanced past the tanks, moving cautiously through the rubble they had created.

Daring shrapnel from the 40mm armor fire, Kevin let his helicopter slip down another hundred feet closer to the rooftops. His excitement mounted as he maneuvered to see into each courtyard and behind each clump of palm and bamboo. He jumped in his seat when Petch's voice squawked in his earphones, "Tiger, Dagger lead. I've got a haystack down here that looks like a camouflaged bunker. It's got an open space at ground level — facing north — about forty meters ahead of your troop positions. How about I dump a couple of rockets on it before your people get there?"

"Roger that, Dagger. I'll have my lead element pop smoke."

"That dildo Petch just wants to shoot some rockets," said Eddie over the intercom to Kevin.

"Me too," said Kevin, "but I'd rather have meat in my sights." He swung the bird in behind Petch to cover him as he tipped the nose of his ship down and neatly pickled off two single rockets. The first was wide by ten meters, but the second nailed the haystack precisely, setting it on fire and revealing the earthworks beneath it.

"Dagger lead, Bengal Tiger. We've got it spotted. Nice shooting. Request you hold your ammunition and let us move the dusters in there. G-2 says we've got an NVA basic training cadre in here somewhere, and I want to make sure we get them, and not just their VC recruits."

Ten minutes, then twenty minutes, the tanks moved forward firing, shattering the hooches and starting fires in the rubble piles. Then Kevin heard the unmistakable crackling of small-arms fire. Quickly he spotted the tracers at the northeast corner of the village. "There!" shouted somebody over the air. "Two of them, trying to move down that palm line."

"Got 'em!" called Petch, his voice high and squeaky with excitement. Kevin watched the lead ship tip steeply as Petch dived to get his guns to bear on the running men, tracers already flashing from the doorguns. Then a stream of tracerfire stabbed upward toward the plunging gunship, from a line of palm to the left of the ground troops position. A row of hooches cut off the dusters line of fire to the enemy position, but some of the troops chopped into the palms with their rifles. Kevin lined his ship up for a firing pass behind Petch.

"Hold your rockets, One-seven," called Petch. "Use some minigun, but hold the rockets for hard targets."

"Rog," he replied, feeling disappointment even in the heat of the action. He made a flat gun run, diving low and driving in close to let Eddie work the line of palm with the snarling miniguns. Then he broke off and turned steeply over the target, tipping his rotor almost vertical and deliberately placing himself in a vulnerable position to let his door gunner fire straight down on the line of covering vegetation.

"I see two bodies down there," said the gunner as they rolled off from the pass. "I don't think we took any fire at all."

"Great!" said Eddie. "Looks like we got them."

As they climbed up and began again to fly a wide circle around the village, Kevin's crew chief called on the intercom, a strange note in his voice, "Mr. Harrey, look over there, about two o'clock. There in the rice paddy."

Kevin looked to his right toward the paddy and was surprised to see a group of people and water buffalo moving calmly out of the southwest side of the village into the open, walking at a leisurely pace toward the next village half a mile away. "Let's check this out," he said. He widened his orbit and flew over the party. Without looking up, they continued to move slowly into the open. Kevin counted four riding on the buffalo and five walking, all apparently young men wearing white peasant garb and carrying no weapons.

"What do you think, Sir?" asked the gunner. "Do we pork 'em?"

"I dunno. It looks pretty strange to me. We'd better check with the ground unit first." He squeezed the transmit switch to call. "Tiger, we've got a group of people down here moving out toward the village to the south. Nine of them, with about six water buffalo."

"They carrying weapons?"

"Negative. They're in the open, moving slowly."

"Keep an eye on them. I'll check with my ARVN counterpart."

"Roger that." The gunships made two complete orbits, watching as the little cluster of people moved out into the middle of the rice paddy.

"Dagger lead, Bengal Tiger. Understand they're all men? No women or kids?"

"That's affirm, Tiger. All men in pajamas."

"Roger, Dagger. My counterpart advises me there's not a village this size for twenty miles with that many fighting-age men working as field labor. He thinks that's the VC recruit corps trying to sneak out of the area. It looks like we got to them before their ammunition supplies could be infiltrated to them. You are cleared to waste them, cleared to fire, over."

"Roger that!" crowed Petch. "OK, One-seven, let's eat 'em up!"

"Give them credit for balls, anyhow," said Kevin to Eddie as he watched Petch make a climbing turn to set up for a long rocket run on the people in the middle of the paddy. Seeing the gunships' intention, the Vietnamese leaped from the buffalo and tried to scatter themselves over the flat surface of the field. Petch fired three pairs of rockets, blasting men and animals apart. The miniguns belched for a second and the doorguns spewed tracers at the running troops. "Goddamnit, my guns have jammed!" yelled Hawking over the air as the gunship broke low to give Kevin a clear field of fire. Kevin pickled off his rockets, striking one buffalo squarely and dropping two of the men. The two gunships stayed low and close, all of the men in them eager to keep their guns on target. With Hawk's miniguns out of action, the lead ship was quickly down to the doorguns in firepower. Kevin fired the last of his rockets on his second pass, and by the time Eddie had expended his minigun rounds, the helicopters were both making low and slow circles around the shattered bodies, almost at a high hover to permit the doorguns to make certain of each kill.

"Sir, there's one still alive," said Kevin's crew chief. "He's hiding between those two dead buffalo there in the center."

Kevin pulled back gently on his cyclic, bringing the ship to a hover about forty feet above the bodies. "All right, now pork him," he said.

The gunner fired a burst, then began to fumble with the belt feed on his M-60. "I think I hit him, but..."

"Jesus shit," muttered Kevin, dropping the bird almost to ground level. "Eddie, hold this pig here at a hover. Chief, hand me that M-16 back there."

"Sir?"

"The M-16, goddammit!"

"Yessir." The crewman took the rifle from its rack on the side of the cabin and handed it forward to Kevin, who unbuckled his lap belt and held the cabin door open with his foot.

"It's not that hard to kill one lousy gook," he said, pulling back the arming lever to charge the weapon. He looked out and hesitated for an instant. Twenty feet away he could see the Vietnamese, his face contorted with terror as he tried to work his skinny body under the dead buffalo. He looked up and his eyes met Kevin's and he froze.

"What the hell is going on down there?" called Petch.

Kevin raised the rifle. The VC troop crouched behind the buffalo shaking his head, the rotorwash whipping his hair into his face. On an impulse, Kevin motioned with the weapon for the man to stand up, then he pointed with his thumb at the back of the helicopter. Understanding that he was to be captured instead of killed, the young troop stood.

"One-seven, what the hell are you doing?" demanded Petch.

"Shall we pick one up?" asked Eddie over the air.

"What? Are you crazy? Get the hell out of there!"

"Uh, Roger," replied Eddie, hesitating.

Kevin took a long breath, and a frustration rose in him, a fury without root. Feeling a delicious and appalling visceral surge of groin, gut, heart, and throat, he emptied the magazine of the rifle into the body of the young man in front of him, watching the rounds tear chunks from the flesh.

"Let's go home," he said, his voice husky.

NINE

The sun had just set, and the day's stifling heat still hung thick and clinging in the musty tent. A fan pumped the hot, damp air from one side of the place to the other, but did nothing to lower the temperature. The Dagger pilots sat quietly on their cots, letting their evening meal settle and waiting for something to happen. Hawking had bought an expensive tape recorder and a set of speakers at the PX, and had discovered that Special Services made available long tapes of selected music. By sending each of the pilots to get a tape, they had accumulated a good collection. The system was playing soft country music, and from the clubroom built between the two gunship tents came the nagging babble of an old sitcom broadcast by the Armed Forces TV.

Kevin Harrey lay on his cot with his eyes closed, listening to the music and letting the heat soak into him, trying to imagine he was back in El Paso with Carlie. He rolled to his stomach and pounded his knuckles slowly on the floor. Then he sat up on the edge of his cot and stared out through the door. The whitewashed walls of sandbags blocked his view of the rest of the company area. The sluggish evening breeze brought him the unmistakable odor of burning diesel oil and shit.

"The Eternal Flame of Vietnam," he said aloud. The split fifty-five-gallon drums were the standard sewage disposal system, burning almost everywhere, almost all the time.

He glanced through the back door of the tent and saw the dark gaping entrance to the bunker. For a moment he saw himself crouching there, shaking, terrified, clawing blindly at the dank earth in the deepest corner of the hole, listening to the sibilant whisper of the rounds coming in. "It's not real," he mumbled to himself, trying to relax.

"You're right," said Hawking, interrupting his thought. "The present is just a three-dimensional snapshot of a four-dimensional situation. The past is absolute unchangeable order; the future is absolute unpredictable chaos. Here, you need an attitude adjuster." The tall, slender pilot fished in the pocket of his jacket and brought out what appeared to be a pack of American cigarettes. He opened the bottom of the pack and pulled out a lumpy smoke with one end twirled shut. He tossed it to Kevin, who took it and stepped outside the tent.

It was becoming dark, and a cooler breeze began to blow. Far to the south the sky was lighted with glowing flares which blinked to light and descended slowly, leaving long ghostly columns of smoke hanging in the sky. The ever-present throb of rotor blades drifted through the evening sounds, made more distant by the growing darkness. Kevin leaned against the sandbag wall, looking toward the dark mountains to the west. "Right over there in those hills, and beyond them, are hundreds, maybe thousands of the enemy," he thought. "Every one of them is out to keep me from getting home." He sighed and reached into his pocket for his lighter. "One man, one gun, one bullet....and I never see home, or Carlie, or Baby George again. That simple."

He put the marijuana-repacked cigarette to his mouth and touched the flame to the twirled end. It popped once as a seed caught fire, then began to burn smoothly. He drew the sweet heavy smoke into his lungs and locked it down with a swallow. Wary, he looked around and noted the direction the smoke was blown by the evening breeze. He exhaled half his breath, then took another drag on the glowing joint.

Peter Hawking stepped out of the tent to join him. He handed Hawk the smoke and watched him repeat the process. They stood a few minutes, passing the joint back and forth in silence. "So it's an escape from reality," Hawking had once argued. "So what? Over here any escape from anxiety that doesn't impair your ability to fight is a good escape."

After a few minutes, Eddie stepped out also and stood with them. "What the fuck is going to happen if they catch you with that stuff?" he asked.

"What are they going to do — send us to Vietnam?" asked Hawking. He reached into his pocket and gave Kevin a fresh joint. "I'm going for a little walk," he said, taking the one they had been smoking with him.

The two men sat down on the sandbag wall and watched the flares descend. After a while, Eddie said, "Never could get into smoking that stuff. Hell, I might even quit drinking. That's what got to Roger Stanton — the booze, I mean. But then, I guess he was a boozer as long as I've known him — which is a pretty long time."

"How far do you and Roger go back?" asked Kevin.

"Junior high school. We got together because we were both in the science club. I think I was interested because I wanted to impress my father, and well, his father was the guy making the rockets — you know Otto, don't you?"

"I met him. Not somebody I could talk to."

"Me neither. But I always had a lot of respect for him, with his machine shop, and his telescope, and pieces of rocket engines and stuff lying all over the house. Did you ever see his telescope?"

"No, I don't think so."

"Otto made it in his shop, and when I first met Roger, he used to ride me on the back of his Cushman scooter down to San Manuel to look through it. I can still remember the first time I saw the craters on the moon, and the rings of Saturn. And when I was about fourteen, I got to meet Dr. Clyde Tombaugh there at the Green Castle one night — he's the astronomer who discovered the planet Pluto. He lives there in the Mesilla Valley."

"I didn't know that," said Kevin.

"Yeah. We'll have to go there together sometime when we get back, and you can look through it."

"I'd like that. It's only a half hour drive up there from El Paso, and I can bring Carlie and George. They're living in El Paso now, you knew, didn't you?"

"Yeah, that's what you said. How old is your kid now?"

"He just turned two in February — on Valentine's Day."

"So you guys got married right after we saw you in Juarez."

"No, not really, not until about a year later. I knew I was headed for a tour over here, and Carlie didn't know what the hell she wanted to do. And then of course, she got pregnant. She was pretty upset about it, and came to me crying about how she'd messed everything up, and suicide, and a bunch of crazy shit. Hell, I was delighted. So we got married, and I did my first tour as a drill sergeant advisor with MACV. So what about Roger and the booze?"

"Oh, yeah." Eddie paused a moment, fished a Camel from the pack in his pocket. "That's what happened to his thing with the Marine Corps. He had all those dreams about wanting to be an astronaut. He told me a lot, Kevin, the night I went down to see him before I came over here. We got really drunk, and he told me all his secrets — girls he laid, things he did to get even with some asshole — and he told me about what happened in Marine flight school.

"It's kind of strange, because I don't think it would ever have occurred to me to quit college and join the service if Roger hadn't done it. And I don't think Roger would have done it if he hadn't been hitting the sauce so hard. He was partying pretty steady, had his own apartment just off-campus, a nice car, and getting laid a lot. Me, I was up at Socorro taking geophysics because I thought the word was neat — five hundred men and six women on campus. Well, he told me he wished he had been able to finish out his degree before going into the Corps, but he was starting to have trouble keeping himself interested enough in his subjects to keep his grades up. You know college parties — everybody gets drunk as shit, and the last guy on his feet gets to fuck the chick."

"So that's why he went into the Cadet program?"

"Yep. It was the only jet program he could get into with only two years college. He had to have jets to get into the astronaut program."

Kevin nodded in understanding. "He'd have had a lot better chance of getting space training in the Navy or the Air Force, but the Marines would take him two years earlier, and he was afraid he might not be able to hold out two more years without bombing out of school for being drunk all the time, is that right?"

"Exactly what he said. He didn't have any trouble whizzing through their entrance screening tests, and signed up to go in as soon as he had completed his Sophomore year. I guess I'd been following him around for so long it had just got to be a habit, so I applied too. I didn't have the grades, or the desire to do the long hitch for jets, so I took this route.

"Well, anyway, he got down to Pensacola and made it through the four months of pre-flight training without too much trouble. They ran his ass ragged and got him dried out and tightened up, and he apparently did pretty well. Then he went to primary flight training and got through solo in T-34's."

"Right, then to Meridian, Mississippi for basic jet."

"You got it. And that's where the trouble began."

"Hitting the booze."

"Yeah. He said for a dry state, Mississippi is the wettest place he ever saw, and he discovered moonshine. You know, to tell you the truth, Kevin, I think he liked the adventure of buying and drinking moonshine as much as he liked the alcohol. But he got to slugging it pretty hard, thinking he could get away with flying like that if he went down to the flight line an hour early in the morning to sit in the cockpit breathing oxygen to sober up for his flight."

"Doesn't work," affirmed Kevin flatly.

"No shit. Well, he was out one morning on an early flight in a T-2A. He'd been out all night screwing some chickie from Meridian, and he was pretty shitfaced. They did some aerobatics, pulled a bunch of G's, and then came back to the base to shoot some landings — him and his instructor in the back seat. So he came into the landing pattern fast, the instructor was screaming at him, and he was about ready to puke anyway, and his head was pounding, and he had all this shit coming at him from all sides — those things have checklists a foot long for everything — and he missed a step."

"What did he forget?"

"Well, you know, jets have speed brakes — they call them 'boards'. You're supposed to land with your boards out, so you can carry a higher power setting on the final approach, because the power response of those jet engines is so slow." Eddie took a last drag on his Camel and flipped it in a glowing arc. "So he forgot to put his boards out. He just kept pulling back the power trying to get the speed down. He was high too, so he tried to slip the airplane down by putting in a bunch of rudder. I don't know what that instructor was thinking. He should have called for a go-around a long time sooner. About that time, Roger figured out what he had done wrong, so he corrected the mistake — he put his boards out. The airplane stalled and started to roll, so the instructor fired both of the ejection seats. Roger broke a few ribs, and got cut up pretty bad by the berry vines he landed in. The instructor's seat fired when the plane was almost upside down, and he sort of grabbed a tree."

"Killed him?"

"Sure did. They put him on a medical suspension and began investigation. Apparently it looked to Roger like they were going to wash him out for the crash, and he'd have to finish out a two year hitch as a grunt, so he went for the whole thing. He broke into the base hospital's medical grain alcohol, got bombed and went AWOL, and got picked up by the local Sheriff in a dice joint full of blacks over in Lauderdale."

"Jesus, that could be more dangerous than crashing."

"He said he had a blast. Every time he won a toss, he'd buy another jar of the moonshine they were pushing and pass it around. He didn't remember why the MP's came to bust up the party, or how they got him into bed, but they had his ass on the carpet the next day. So blam, there it is — and his whole plan goes down the tube. And then I end up over here."

Kevin chuckled. "Life's full of surprises, isn't it. I've been turned around about three times getting here, myself. I figured when I got back after my first tour I'd seen the last of this place. I was going to stay home and live it up with Carlie. I remembered what she looked like when I left, wearing those long golden prom-curls down to her shoulders, her tits getting bigger and harder, and her belly just starting to show. She was something, I'll tell you. But when I came home, I found this different woman. She was skinny, and she moved around all the time, and talked different....right down to business, you know. Baby business. Like a machine, like a junkie — baby, baby, and baby-baby-baby. And she had cut her hair off. She got a nice stylish little shag, and she spent her time running to the Club with her mother. They figured this all out for me, and had our whole life planned and locked in when I got back."

"This was part of their plans?"

"I'm afraid so. After all, the lady was the Captain's only daughter, and none of them was very happy about my being a shitbird sergeant. Chuck — Captain Gold, her dad — had already run down all the necessary information, and all I had to do was sign the papers. I was in flight school after thirty days leave. So here I am, and I guess the truth is that I'm over here so Carlie can be an officer's wife. Now they're pushing me to go for a direct commission."

"Second lieutenant?"

"I put in for first lieutenant."

"Already? Then you're going career, for sure?"

"Yeah, I guess so. There's a lot about it I don't like. I'm having more trouble accepting the reasons they give me for the things they order me to do. Regardless of how they feel about each other, I'm beginning to understand why all of the Vietnamese, on both sides, are learning to hate us. And the more I see that, Eddie, the more I have to face the fact that my reasons for being here have nothing to do with how I feel about Vietnam's politics, or America's politics either, and that bothers me....a lot. I'm killing people, and risking my own life, for reasons that have nothing to do with the issues at hand. In fact, if I start looking at those issues, it becomes more difficult for me to do my job. And that bothers me a lot, too. You don't have to tell me that's one hell of an attitude to start a career with. And it doesn't make it any easier to keep hanging my ass out day after day when I don't have to."

"*Seguro, Amigo,*" Eddie said, nodding solemnly. "I remember Rudy told me one time it's not too good to be too good at this job. I'm beginning to understand what he was talking about."

Kevin nodded. "You know, I like being a little gung-ho, especially in combat. I think it helps to keep me from cracking up. But the longer this goes on, the harder it gets to psych myself up. I'm not here for what I can do to the enemy — I might have thought so once, but no more. I'm here for what I can have if I survive. I've got to go out there and bang heads with Victor

Charlie, and in this game only one of us gets to go home. I'm afraid it boils down to a simple case of 'him or me'. I don't like having to kill some ignorant farmer just because he got swept up in this crazy thing, but I'm sorry, Charlie, you are standing between me and what matters most to me in the world, and I am going home."

"I hear that," said Eddie, in almost a whisper.

They strolled down to the orderly room to pick up the new issue of Stars and Stripes and overheard bad news as it was reported to Major Csynes. They returned to the gunship pilots' tent looking grim.

"Skip around?" Kevin asked.

Hawking sat staring dreamily at the TV screen. "Not come in yet," he said.

"Did you know he had a brother over here?"

"I didn't know the miscegenated son of a bitch had a brother at all," said Hawking genially.

"He just got his Purple Heart — the hard way," said Eddie.

The tent was quiet for a moment, then Hawking got up and moved over to Kevin's bunk. "How'd it happen?" he asked.

"I don't know." Kevin shrugged. "I guess he was a grunt down in the delta somewhere — I heard them tell the Major he was hit by a mortar round."

"Funny Skip never talked about him," said Eddie.

Hawking smiled ruefully. "Skip's a funny guy. None of us know much about him except what we see."

Kevin sat staring at the floor between his feet, jaw muscles working slowly. "I hate this fucking place," he said quietly. "I really hate this fucking place."

Duke Randall came into the tent, followed by Arlo Jeter and Rudy Bakersmith. They were in the middle of an enthusiastically angry discussion, confirming each others' opinions that America ought to pursue victory even if the whole population turned VC. Someone had sent Bakersmith a BB gun, a rifle with a big ring on the cocking lever like the one Chuck Connors on TV used, one which could be cocked by twirling the whole weapon. He swaggered in behind Jeter, and as the stocky, leather-faced older pilot opened three beers, Rudy twirled his rifle and pooted off a shot which pinged against Kevin's metal wall locker, then twirled again and pooted and pinged another locker. Kevin eyed him malevolently, but decided not to say anything.

"It aggravates me," said Duke. "It really troubles my mind when I hear people say that we're only over here to spread some kind of Yankee Imperialist Pig philosophy. Why is it so hard to recognize we are only over here trying to help some people who don't want to be commies?"

Hawking jumped right into it. "Oh Jesus," he groaned. "I can't stand it. Who says they don't want to be communists?"

"They do have elections here, you know," said Duke dryly.

"Oh, sure. The dinks can vote for anybody they like, as long as the candidates are all approved by Saigon and Washington.

"Don't play dumb, Hawking," said the captain. "You know as well as I do if they wanted to be communists, they wouldn't be asking for free elections. The two don't mix."

Poot! Plang! Bakersmith's BB rang on a fan blade. Kevin clenched his jaw, certain if he told Rudy to quit shooting in the tent, he would likely keep it up.

"That's right," said Arlo Jeter, "and we're having the same kind of trouble here that the police back in the World are having trying to protect people." Jeter was a former Green Beret from Arkansas. He was older than most of the other pilots, and usually much quieter, but he had spent the day off-duty drinking beer, and was letting off steam. "When the bad guy comes along, people can't defeat him alone, but you can't get them to stand up and point out who the bad guy is, because they're afraid."

"Damn right they're afraid," said Hawking. "If somebody came at me with a rigged ballot box and a machine gun and said he was there to protect me from people who don't vote the right way, I'd be afraid too."

"Hey, let me tell you something, there, Hippie Hawking. Let me tell you just how old Charlie goes about setting up a village. This is Charlie's answer to the ballot box, OK."

"By the way, Hawking, didn't the Major tell you to get a haircut?" interrupted Duke.

"Yessir. And I did."

"Well, get yourself another one."

Hawking burned, but kept his cool. "Yessir, Captain, Sir. Don't want to have some dink thinking I let my grooming slip — he might stop respecting us, and we'd lose the war."

"Right," put in Rudy Bakersmith. He spun his BB gun and pooted a shot at Hawking's feet.

"Hey! Lighten up on that, will you?" Hawking complained.

"So what about these VC political *movidas*, Arlo?" asked Eddie.

"You tell Malcolm X here to keep his shirt on, and I'll tell you. All right, easy there, Hawk. Easy, boy. Now here's what happens. One day Victor Charlie and a few of his boys come into a village to visit a piece, and they round up all the people. You all picturing this, now? Old Charlie can talk faster than a Pentecostal preacher selling vacuum cleaners, and he gets up there and tells them that he can prove just how badly they're enslaved by the Americans. They tell some old boy if he'll cooperate, they'll make him the village commander instead of the Yankee puppet running things now. If this old boy agrees, they get on with it, and if he doesn't, they don't waste a lot of time trying to educate him." Jeter pointed his finger at Hawking like a pistol. "Bang," he said, eyes wide and solemn.

"Then Charlie asks the next guy in line. 'Brother Gook,' he tells him, 'you can be respected village commander in the people's freedom forces, or you can be dead Yankee puppet.' He might have to go through two or three candidates, but sooner or later he'll find one who'd prefer being a live goat to a dead sheep."

"So much for elections," commented Bakersmith, pooting his BB gun at the flight helmet on the foot of Eddie's bunk.

"That's just the beginning," said Jeter. "They give this peckerwood a rifle, and they tell him to announce that he is going to lead the fight for freedom, and to take a shot at the next helicopter that flies by. Now you all tell me what happens when some Sabre slick carrying a load of beer and ice cream draws a bunch of fire from some little village. Right, a couple of old boys from the Daggers come over there and kick some ass. And when the shooting is all over, old Charlie comes back and rounds them all up again. He says, 'Is this what the round-eye babyrapers mean by helping you? Ho Chi is a gook like you, not a piss-blood big-nose. Ho Chi freed you from the French in 1954, and he'll free you from the Americans in 1969! That's a promise, and the sooner you start killing Americans, the sooner he can keep it.'"

Eddie got up from his bunk and went over to John Bergin's. He pulled a cardboard box from beneath it and began to paw through the contents. He found what he wanted — a large round tin of homemade fudge — and bent over to pluck up a choice piece. Poot! Whak! Bakersmith popped a BB off the tightly-stretched fatigues covering Eddie's exposed Bullseye butt.

"Yipe!" yelped Eddie, leaping up and grabbing at his cheek. Rudy thought it was very funny, and twirled the rifle to rearm it. Kevin reddened and tensed, and looked to see if Captain Randall was going to rebuke the cocky lieutenant. He didn't, but Arlo Jeter pointed an admonishing finger and said with a chuckle and a big country grin, "You point that little nigger-shooter at me, and I'll tie a knot in your weenie, boy."

"I almost forgot," laughed Rudy. "You're one of those bad-ass Green Beret guys. So tell these shitbirds what's wrong with the way we're running the war."

"We must be doing something right," said Eddie, rubbing at the sore spot on his butt. "How do we get the people to support the government?"

"What the hell do gooks know about government?" demanded Hawking. "All they've ever known is a little place that has belonged to the ancestral landlord for generations where they could raise some rice and fuck their wives and go on living. We come along and say we're going to give them constitutional republicratic elections with a bicameral legislature and gibble-gabble babble-babble shredded-baloney and they're all going to be free. Free from what, f'Christ sake? No matter who is running the shop in Saigon — or Hanoi — the dink is just going to have a plot of land to grub and taxes to pay to somebody. Economic development, medicine, education — both sides promise them that kind of thing, so we're not saying anything meaningful to them."

"If you mean they don't know enough about freedom to

recognize it when somebody brings it to them, I agree with you," said Duke Randall.

"That's about right, Hawking," said Arlo. "That's why communist propaganda can get to them so easy. Charlie comes along and says he's going to get rid of the landlords, and the land will belong to a worker's state, and they can grow rice for themselves. Well, those are things they can understand. Course, in the meantime, they've got to pay some taxes and kill some Americans. Some old boy doesn't like the idea, he's accused of standing in the way of his neighbor's progress, and....bang! Now, those are terms they can damn well understand. We're just not as willing to use the high-pressure techniques as the VC."

"I'm afraid I'd have to call the US Army pretty high-pressure arm-twisting," said Hawking, "especially in the name of self-determination."

"Self-determination? It's too bad," said Duke, "but the truth is that if Ho Chi wins, the Vietnamese get one way, and if we win, he gets another way. This war is bigger than just the Vietnamese now."

"Now that is one hell of a tragedy," said Hawking.

Randall shook his head in disgust. "Shit, Hawk, you ought to be a social worker. Tragedy is a matter of whose bull is being gored. It's a tragedy this war is still going on when we could have won it years ago."

"Captain, if you've got it all figured out, you're wasting your time telling a bunch of lowly warrants," said Hawking.

"You're a wise guy, but I'll have to admit you're the ugliest wise guy I ever met," Randall said patiently.

Poot! Whak! Rudy put another BB between Hawking's feet.

"So far nobody has figured out how to tell the wet-noses the way to handle a war is get in there and win," Randall declared.

"So you want to quit screwing around and bring in the nukes?"

"I'm not that stupid. Nuking Hanoi might solve one problem, but it would cause a bunch of others. But there are lots of ways we could get this job done a hell of a lot more efficiently."

"We're not lacking in mass killing techniques," said Hawking. "But aren't all those convenient devices inhumane, against the rules of civilized war?"

"Just a minute there, Young Christian, before you go accusing me of being inhumane and immoral. I ask you, how much is one American life worth in VC blood? How many gook lives do you have to save before it's humane and moral to sacrifice a single American to save them? Morality is a matter of whose side you are on, and if you don't have the moral fiber to fight for the right side, then you don't deserve to be on the right side. I think a lot of people back in America have got the idea that it's immoral to win. When they start sacrificing Americans to take the pressure off the enemy so they don't have to see him beat, they're cutting their own sons' throats. And if you don't think that's inhumane and immoral, you're dead from the neck up."

"What about using food as a weapon? Or medicine?" asked Arlo. "China and Russia may be able to supply Ho Chi with guns, but they can't supply him with food and medicine. It would be no problem to spread some rice blight that would wipe out the crop. Ho Chi would have only one place to come for enough food to keep his people alive. That's pretty good leverage. Or, we could innoculate Saigon for every disease known to man for the cost of one B-52. Spread a few diseases around, and they either come to us for life, or die. We beat them without having to kill them."

"Not exactly what I had in mind," said Hawking. "Those are not much less violent than burning towns, but I mean real non-violence, like converting them all to the Mormon religion, or industrializing Ho Chi's country if he'll put American television in all the homes. Brain warfare."

Kevin shook his head in disgust and picked up his newspaper. "That's bullshit, just fucking bullshit. Load their water with LSD, or defoliate the whole country. We've got lots of bullshit options, and we are going to continue to bullshit until somebody blows our heads off!"

"You're bullshit, Babycakes," said Rudy, swinging the gun to cover Kevin. Poot! Whak! The BB snapped against the paper in Kevin's hands.

Fast like reflex, Kevin spun to a crouch, whipped his .38 from its shoulder holster, and cocked back the hammer. There was a moment of breathless silence as Kevin held his bead between Bakersmith's wide-popped eyes. "You shoot that BB gun at me again, I'll blow that cute little smirk right off your face."

Bakersmith's jaw flopped up and down as he tried to think of something commanding, or clever, or courageous to say.

"Harrey, are you out of our mind?" yelled Duke Randall. "Put that piece away!"

"The BB gun!"

"All right, all right! Now put it down."

"What the hell is going on in here?" They all turned to see Skip Gilman enter the tent. Having just returned from a long escort mission, he was sweaty and rumpled, and his face sagged with weariness. They stood frozen in tabloid, like lovers caught inflagrante, each waiting for someone else to begin trying to explain. Skip was astonished a moment, then a twinkle came to his eye and he grinned. In the same instant, they all remembered, and they recognized that Skip had not yet been told.

Kevin dropped his pistol to his side, and stood unspeaking. Skip looked from one to the other. "What is it? What's wrong?"

"Mr. Gilman, Major Csynes wishes to speak with you," said Duke Randall, regaining control of the situation. "I think you should report to his office directly."

Skip hesitated a moment, as though to ask a question, then nodded. "Yessir." He turned and departed quickly toward the new CQ building.

"And the Major is going to want to talk to you two screws also," Duke growled, indicating Kevin and Rudy. He shook his head in resignation. "Dumb. Very dumb."

Major Jacob Csynes sat behind his desk trying to keep his mind busy, but it kept returning to Skip Gilman. He was not unaccustomed to the peculiar emotional ambivalence of bearing devastating personal news to strangers. In fact, he entertained a certain poignance about the notion of being remembered for giving one's life in combat, and had sometimes become very moved when writing a letter to a wife or parent describing their beloved's heroic sacrifice. He dismissed as a cynical character flaw — and at the same time indulged — that part of himself which took a certain satisfaction from knowing with those letters he was creating family heirlooms which would bring tears to the eyes for years to come.

He could picture the family going to their church in gabardine and crinoline, to receive the treasured flag and Purple Heart. It was so easy for them to picture their soldier dying a clean death, falling with his weapon in his hand, a painless and merciful bullet through the heart — so easy to picture him lying as though asleep in dress uniform inside the sealed casket. "But what do I say to the man who knows?" he thought. "How do I tell a man who has seen the rubber bags full of rotting meat that his brother died an easy death?" Another thought intruded, one he would rather have dismissed unacknowledged: "How can I send him back out there tomorrow?" He accepted his own answer with a long-practiced resignation to the tragedy of his profession: "It comes with the territory. Cry if you've got to, but when the balloon goes up, it's 'Over The Top'."

Csynes leaned back in his chair and ran a weary hand over the back of his neck. He grimaced with distaste at the rolls of greasy caked dust that came off on his fingers. Though he broke out fresh fatigues at least once a day, he felt he could never quite maintain the crisp image he wanted. His uniform felt damp and heavy, and stuck to the middle of his back. From the orderly room in the front of the CQ building he heard Skip enter and ask the First Sergeant, "What's up, Top?"

"Major's expecting you, Mr. Gilman. Go on in."

Gilman stepped into the office trying to rake his hair into some kind of order with his fingers. The young officer's fatigues were dark with sweat, and though his rubber-featured round face lacked its usual lopsided mischievous grin, his walk was still cocky and confident. Csynes drew himself up in his chair and tried to look properly sympathetic. Suddenly it struck him with self-conscious surprise that he really was sympathetic — this was not some civilian stranger, but one of his own. He wanted to put his arm around the man's shoulders like a son and ease his grief.

Gilman reported at attention. "Good evening, Sir. I was told you wanted to see me."

"At ease, Mr. Gilman. Sit down, please."

Skip slid back the chair beside the Major's desk and sat down uncomfortably.

"I have some bad news for you, Skip. I wish....I wish I knew a way to make this easy for you, but...well, you know of course the risks we take in our....our duty." He hesitated, for an instant afraid that he would just blurt it out clumsily, crudely. "I received a message a short while ago, and I felt I should be the first to tell you. Your brother was killed in action last night." Afraid of leaving it hanging, he rushed on. "He was hit by a mortar round while defending the perimeter at Dak Son. His commanding officer said he left his bunker to aid a friend."

The two men sat in silence for a long moment, then Skip dug into the pocket of his fatigue jacket for a cigarette. He fumbled for his lighter, and too quickly, awkwardly, Jake Csynes reached across with his own crest-emblazoned desk lighter, which he kept though he did not smoke.

"Thank you, Sir," said Skip.

"I'm sure you would be proud to know he has been recommended for decoration. His commanding officer said he was a fine soldier, held in high esteem by the other men of his company." Csynes struggled for words, hating himself for what had suddenly become inane cliches. "He was someone to be proud of, Skip, and you can be proud he didn't die in vain, he... he..."

"I know what he died for, Sir," Skip interrupted stiffly. "I've seen what he died for, every day for six stinking months." The bitterness, the anger, the helplessness, the grief welled hot and thick in the back of his throat, and for a second he feared he would spew it all out, a reeking mess on the Major's polished desk. Then he took hold of himself and dragged slowly on the cigarette. For a moment they sat silent again, then Skip asked, "Major, could I ask you a personal question?"

"Sure. Fire away."

"You've been in this business a while. Do you believe we're really fighting this war to defend the free world? Do you really think if we don't stop the North Vietnamese, we'll be fighting commies in California in ten years?"

Csynes gave Skip a long cool gaze, then nodded. "Well, I don't know about fighting in California, but I certainly believe that Communism is the major threat to the freedom of the western world."

"How come nobody else seems to think so? If the whole free world is so worried about creeping Communism, how come they're not over here getting their guts blown out?"

Csynes hesitated, picked his words carefully. "Mr. Gilman, it is very easy to create political violence — armed fighting — in a small country, around a small issue, or a few emotionally-loaded words. And it is easy to say those little skirmishes are the war, because they are visible, and they're local. But the real war is happening all over the world, and it is being fought in many different ways, and it is being fought all the time.

"Let me try to explain something to you. That war — that continuous world war — is my personal lifetime pursuit. It's what I do. To do that, I've got some resources, and I've got some limitations. One of the limitations I have to remember is that for most of you young soldiers, the war is one year long, and when you get back, you're going to do something else. You see, I am never going to do anything else. I'll just do it in different ways and different places, so in a sense, I don't have a future, not like you do. I have already arrived. This is my personal place in the endless war for the freedom of mankind — right here, and right now. You men talk about going back to the Real World — well, for me, this is the real world, and what matters to me....is winning."

Skip stared at the Major in a kind of awe, his brother for a moment forgotten as he marveled that the man suddenly exposed behind the martial mask was so much more deeply committed than he felt he could reveal to his troops. "Well. I'm sorry for the digression, Mr. Gilman," the Major continued briskly. "I've already arranged for you to leave here on the first courier flight in the morning. You'll be able to leave out of Cam Ranh Bay to take your brother home."

Skip nodded woodenly. "All right, Sir."

"I think it would be possible — that is, if you wanted it — I think we could arrange a compassionate reassignment. I saw in your record that you signed a waiver of the sole-surviving-son provision to get here. There's a very good chance that you just wouldn't have to come back. You let me know what you want, and I'll do everything I can to help you."

Skip gazed at the floor, and to Jake Csynes he looked very old and tired. "I don't know, Sir. I guess it would be easier on my family. I'll think about it, Sir. I don't know what's right just now." He got up a little uncertainly, and carefully replaced the chair beside the Major's desk. "Thank you, Sir," he said, and saluted. The CO started to speak, then just nodded.

Skip got as far as the door, hesitated in the doorway, then turned around abruptly. "No. I don't have to think about it. I just want to go to my brother's funeral, then I'm coming back."

Csynes looked at him surprised. "Well, all right, Skip, if that's what you..."

Skip interrupted him. "I'll tell you something, Sir. I don't know about your world war, or your CIA connections, or if you know something nobody else does. As far as I can see, what we're doing here is a crock of shit. If commies takeover the US, it won't be by overrunning Vietnam, or California — it'll happen in Washington. Most Americans don't give a shit about Vietnam anyway, as long as they've got beer and television. Well, I don't give a damn about Vietnam either. Fuck the Vietnamese government — if they had a right to be in office, they wouldn't need us to keep them there. And fuck the Americans and their jack-off riots and their rip-off politicians. Fuck all of them. The only ones this war matters to is us poor fuckers who have to fight it, and if somebody had cared a little more about that, maybe my brother would still be alive. So I'm going to stay over here and fight for the only people in the world who really give a damn about this phony little war, and every time I see one of them go home alive, I'll know I've done my job!"

Without waiting for the Major's reply, Skip turned and walked quickly out of the office, wiping at his eyes with the back of one arm.

Chines sat staring after him for a long moment, then nodded slowly. "Good boy," he said. Then he reached over and knocked on the wall separating his office from the orderly room. "Top," he called, "send those other two shitbirds in here."

Warrant Officer Harrey and First Lieutenant Bakersmith

snapped to attention and reported before Major Csynes' desk. He glared at them coldly. "I understand you drew your sidearm and threatened the lieutenant with it, Mr. Harrey. Would you mind explaining to me just why you did that?"

"I was preparing to return fire, Sir," Kevin answered.

Csynes leaned back in his chair. "Oh, is that right? Well, Lieutenant?"

"Sir, I'm sorry Mr. Harrey took offense. I didn't expect anybody to get upset at a little harmless fun, and nobody else seemed to be bothered. I mean, it's just a toy."

"I beg to differ with the lieutenant, Sir," Kevin interrupted. "And that is exactly the point I was making. That weapon was being treated like a toy, but it is not a toy. It is a low-power small-caliber rifle which fires a real projectile with enough velocity to put out a person's eye. That weapon was fired in the direction of my face, and hit the paper I was reading. The lieutenant's idea of harmless fun could have ended my career as an Army pilot. I don't believe anybody has the right to subject me to that kind of risk just because I don't have the rank to tell him to stop."

"Did you ask him to stop?"

"Mr. Hawking objected, and asked him to stop, and Mr. Jeter threatened to, uh, do violence to him, but that didn't stop him from shooting Mr. Padilla in the backside."

"You did that, Lieutenant? You intentionally shot Mr. Padilla with your BB gun?" The Major drew back his head and fixed Bakersmith with a cold eye like a sidewinder.

"I'm sorry, Sir, I...yessir. It just didn't seem like such a big thing, Sir. It won't happen again, I promise."

Jake Csynes leaned back in his chair and stared past them for a long time. "It's too bad," he said finally. "It's just very disappointing, when some men are doing their jobs like Mr. Padilla, and like Mr. Gilman, to have two men of your caliber become so bored, and so unconcerned for what we are doing here, that they can do the kind of stupid shit that you two have done today. Lieutenant Bakersmith, Mr. Harrey's point is exactly correct, and you will dispose of that...toy of yours at once. And you, Mr. Harrey, I am particularly worried about. The fact that your point is correct does not excuse your inexcusable behavior. I could have you submitted to psychiatric examination and court martialed for assaulting a senior officer with a deadly weapon. That leads me to wonder if I didn't make a mistake last month when I recommended that you be commissioned a first lieutenant."

"Sir, if I had been the lieutenant this afternoon, that BB gun would have been fired in the tent once, and no more."

"I see. That's very reassuring. But let me tell you something. If you two shitbirds were enlisted troops, I would pull every stripe you have. Unfortunately, the Army won't let me do that with its officers, so I have to be more resourceful in dealing with you. Your concern for safety details impresses me, Harrey, and I intend to make good use of that. And Bakersmith, you obviously don't have enough outlet for your feelings of aggression. Therefore, gentlemen, I am going to give you the honor of being the first gunship pilots on my new Official Shitbird List. Now here's what that means: first, one pilot from the Shitbird List will be assigned to the counter-mortar stand-by team every night. Since there are only two of you, that means you each are on duty every other night. And second, you get the missions nobody else wants. Assignment to the Shitbird List is indefinite, and you get off when I'm impressed enough with your performance and your attitude to let you off. Are there any questions?"

"No, Sir," both answered without hesitation.

"That's all, then. Clear out."

The two officers saluted and scuttled for the door. Csynes called after them. "Lieutenant, there's one more thing."

"Sir?"

"You will report to Mr. Padilla at once, and you will apologize for shooting him with your BB gun. Then you will tend to his wound."

"I beg your pardon, Sir?"

"You will kiss it, Lieutenant, and make it well."

"Yessir," muttered Rudy Bakersmith, closing the Major's door behind him.

A letter from home.

My Dearest Eduardo,

You cannot imagine how much I miss you, and how much I wish you could be home again with me. I pray always to the Blessed Virgin to return my son to me, to spare me from suffering as she suffered. God knows I am not strong enough, so I know He will bring you home safe to me.

Everyone here is so proud of you, Eddie. Your Father tells me that people stop him on the street every day when he goes to the County offices to ask him how you are doing. And every week Father Sambrano makes a special mention of you in prayer at the church. Cecilia, of course, just worships you. She has your picture on her dresser, and every day she sits down beside it to say a Rosary for you. She loves you so much. She is doing so well at school. The Sisters told me she works hard and makes very good grades.

Your Father just got a new contract for a new city building, a Post Office, I think. Those men at the County offices are trying to get him to run for County Commissioner. Do you know what he said? "I am an American. I have a good business. My son is an Officer. Why shouldn't I run for office?" Johnnie told him he was crazy and he should stay with the company and take care of his own business. I told him Johnnie can run the business, and he can become Governor of New Mexico.

Celinda's husband Robert is due for a promotion, that's what she said, in the Air Force. He is going to Vietnam too, but they are going to live in Guam, which is by Hawaii, I think. Couldn't you live in Guam, too? I looked in the atlas for Bad Trang, but I couldn't find it. It said, French Indochina. Is that where you are?

Oh, yes, did you know when you were here that Celinda is going to have another baby? Gracias a Dios, what a blessing that she has such a beautiful family. I pray every day when her husband Robert goes up in his airplane that he will come back safe to Celinda. It would be such a burden to lose one of our beloved sons or husbands, valgame Dios! Sometimes I wish all of you had become priests, or maybe that everybody would become priests. Then there would be peace. Perhaps that is how things will be when Our Dear Lord returns. Then to grow old will mean more than just to increase in sorrows. God help us to bear our sorrows, and God help you to do what you must do. I hope you don't have to kill anyone. You were always such a gentleman.

Oh, I have to tell you that your brother Hector got into a wreck in your car, the Chevrolet. But it's not too bad, and Hector said he took it to San Manuel to show it to Roger, and Roger said he can fix it. They were going to just have it all fixed when you got back, but I thought I better tell you so you wouldn't be angry with Hector.

Roger is the same as ever. I never know if that boy is just fooling or if he is the Devil himself. He and Hector have been running around together, and I hope he doesn't get Hector into trouble. I think he is drinking an awful lot.

You be good, and please take time to pray. I know it must be very difficult to find time to seek the Sweet Lord when you have a war all around you, but I hope you will find a way to pray to Him every day. It is so important when there is so much evil all around you. I will pray to the Blessed Virgin every day to spare me her sorrow, because her son Jesus died for our sake, and so she should bring you home safe to the Mother who loves you so much. God bless you, mi hijito.

Love,
Mother

TEN

The matter of the missing speed pills was first reported to
Major Csynes by the Flight Surgeon, Captain Dave Comer, M.D.
It was part of Comer's duty to periodically inspect the first aid
survival kits carried on the aircraft. It was redundant work — if
the occasion to open a kit came about, the unused parts would
likely be abandoned in the field. It was easier to requisition a
replacement kit than a particular component. The inspection
surely would have been unnecessary had not the kits contained a
packet of ten tablets of methedrine, a "controlled substance"
intended, no doubt, to keep the survivor awake in times of high
stress. Dr. Comer had discovered that several of the kits had
only eight tablets, and one kit had only six.

Jacob Csynes glared grimly at the violated survival kit which
lay on his desk before him, and he put down the Flight Surgeon's
report beside it. "It could be worse, Dave," he said. "Hell, I've
got into the stay-awake stores myself once in a while when the
shit got deep. If it were up to me, I'd issue them for any night
mission. Unfortunately that isn't the point. This is a systematic
abuse, and I can't afford to have that."

At 06:30 the following morning Csynes stood before a full-
company formation, with the red glow of dawn blazing from his
silvered sunglasses as though his eyesockets opened into a
flaming furnace. "We have a small problem, men," he said, "a
problem which can spread through a fighting unit like a disease.
I am speaking of abuse of drugs and alcohol. Now, I appreciate a
couple of cold ones in the club, and getting about half lit and
blowing off some steam once in a while is all right too. But I
have been getting reports concerning some of our flight crews
taking beer on missions, and I have been getting reports about
drinking and card playing going on long after the club has been
closed. That means to me that some of you have been going on
combat missions without sleep, and under the influence of

alcohol. That frightens me.

"It is no secret I have a special interest in the A Lan valley, and I consider it my privilege to have been given the mission of supporting the long range recon patrols which will make retaking the valley possible — our mission, men. It is not a job for people with weekend-warrior mentality, not even a job for the ordinary combat helicopter pilot, good as that may be. It calls for a special kind of soldier, the kind who will find the hottest action because that's where he can do the most good. I know I may not expect you to be that kind of soldiers — some of you certainly are — but I am going to accomplish that mission nonetheless, with whatever resources I am given. That means that I must conserve those resources, and protect them. For that reason I am now imposing the following restriction: there will be no more private holding of alcoholic drinks, including beer. All alcoholic beverages will be brought to the club, with a label on the bottle identifying the owner, and drinks will be served from them by the bartender. The bottles will be kept in a secure cabinet, locked between the hours of 23:30 and 17:30. This policy will begin as of today, and it will continue indefinitely."

There was some grumbling in the ranks, and he stood and waited for it to subside.

"I said we have a little problem. I expect to handle it as a little problem....but I will handle it. As you are no doubt aware, your survival kits contain a small number of stimulant tablets. They are there to assist you if you get shot down and have to walk out. The Flight Surgeon has reported that someone — and probably just one person — has been opening these kits, and taking some of these stimulant tablets. Someone in this unit is developing a growing dependence on drugs, and that frightens me very much. That man is going to get some of you killed — starting with himself — if somebody doesn't find him, and stop him. The person who is responsible for the shortage of the stimulant tablets will report to me in my office at his earliest convenience. Until that time, all personnel assigned or attached to this company are confined to the company area except for duty. All liberty, and all R-and-R is canceled. The Blade and Spade is closed.

"As Army Aviators, we are all members of a very elite group. I am calling upon you to be the elite of the elite, and to be that, we must be able to trust each other with our lives. I believe I have a right to expect that of each of you, and I believe you have a right to expect that of each other. If our discipline fails here, then our mission will fail here, and more of us will die here. Men, I do not intend to permit that to happen. I will be waiting for your response."

Reactions covered the spectrum, and few took it quietly, but everybody took it. One particularly vocal group were the regular boozers, who had bitter maledictions for the self-serving speed freak who was standing between them and their fix'n'soda. Suspecting the culprit was probably one of their own number who had grown unfaithful to the Real Soldier's Social Sacrament and had gone whoring after the strange gods of the pharmacopoeia, they initiated a petition calling for the most extreme detection measures, and for the apprehended degenerate to be dishonorably discharged, disemboweled, dismembered, and fed to the POW's. They circulated this among those known to be juicers, and anyone who refused to sign it was immediately suspected.

Duke Randall enjoyed his beer, and spent a lot of time at the Blade and Spade, but he would have no part of the witchhunt. "I don't believe we are going to find that man in the gunship platoon," he told them. "If one of those slugs started looking half-conscious when he could be racked out like the rest of them, he'd stand out like a nigger trombone player at a Mormon funeral. Besides, I'm not about to go on record for trying to tell Major Jacob Csynes how I think he ought to be doing his job."

"I wouldn't mind telling him how to do his job," complained Hawking. "I think he'd have made a great Nazi. Somebody cops a dozen popcorn-fart no-doze pills, and he declares martial law. I think the son of a bitch is dangerous, myself."

At 06:00 the following morning, WO Billy Kretzer let himself into the Major's office. He was rumpled and red-eyed, and his hands shook when he lighted one menthol cigarette with the butt of the last. Taking a deep drag, he sat down quietly in the chair beside the desk to wait for Csynes. The Major had heard him come in. Though the CQ building had been considerably improved, Csynes still preferred to live in a small hex-tent attached to his office. When he stepped into the office, Kretzer jumped clumsily to his feet and stood at attention before the desk. He stood there a moment looking miserable, then remembered to salute. "Good mornem...morning, Sir," he garbled.

Csynes stood staring at him silently, then rolled his arm up in his peculiar sinuous salute. "At ease, Mr. Kretzer," he said gently. "Sit down, please."

"Yessir." Billy sat down meekly, head bowed, spine not touching the back of the chair.

"You look like shit. How long has it been since you got any sleep?"

Kretzer shrugged. "Couple of weeks, I guess. That's why I.... It was because I couldn't sleep. I started having these nightmares."

"So you started drinking to get to sleep?"

"Yessir. But it didn't work. I just got drunk and still had nightmares. I took the pills because I didn't want to go out on a mission all fucked up. I just let the other pilot fly the helicopter, and I don't think anybody ever thought I wasn't all right, Sir. Actually, the pills work pretty good. I don't start having trouble until I try to get to sleep at night. If I don't drink enough to knock me out, I get the nightmares. Sir, I know I'll be all right if I can just get through another two weeks."

"What happens in two weeks?" Csynes already knew. He had seen it before. He watched Kretzer squirm, embarrassed and repelled that he could see so clearly the man's terrible need, and how terribly ashamed he was of the need, and how terribly frightened it might not be fulfilled.

"I'm supposed to meet...that is, I was going to....Sir, please. I've told you I took the pills, and I'll take whatever I have coming for that, only please...you can't....you just can't cancel my R-and-R, Sir. I just couldn't stand it!"

"Get ahold of yourself, Mr. Kretzer."

"My wife had to schedule her vacation three months ago, and her airplane tickets to Hawaii cost all of our savings because we just had to pay for the baby, and..."

"That's enough, Kretzer. Now pull yourself together."
Csynes watched silently a moment while the man composed
himself by lighting another cigarette. "I'm glad you came in here
so soon. I don't like imposing hardships on men who do not
deserve it. So. Experience and instinct tell me that I ought to
cancel your R-and-R, jerk your wings for flying drunk, throw the
book at you for stealing drugs, and get you the hell out of my
outfit. But I'm not happy with that. It's not enough for me,
Billy. I don't want my men doing their duty only because I can
destroy their lives if they don't. I want it to come from them — I
want it to come from you.

"So I am going out on a limb for you. I am going to cover
your tracks....once. Captain Comer will make an entry in your
medical records prescribing some stimulants to be used for sleep
irregularity, and the medications will be used to replace those you
took from the survival kits. You are relieved of duty for the next
seventy-two hours, and confined to a bed in the medical tent,
which you will leave only to eat and move your bowels — and
you will do both. When you return to duty, you will be on the
top of my Shitbird List, and God help you if you ever fuck up
again. But I don't expect you to fuck up. What I expect you to
do is to get your balls screwed on good and tight, go tell your
wife in Honolulu that you've volunteered for the toughest
mission in Vietnam, and that you're coming home in honor, or in
a rubber bag. And then I expect you to come back here and
prove it.

"Now get your crybaby maggot-eaten candy ass out of my
sight before I change my mind and have an accident cleaning my
sidearm. We have a formation to make in ten minutes.
Dismissed."

The Major's address at the formation was brief. He said,
"Men, the Blade and Spade will be open today at 17:30. You
have your briefings. Let's fly!"

Billy Kretzer spent three days on sick call, then returned to the
line. True to his word, Csynes put him on the top of the Shitbird
List. For Kretzer, that meant flying the shitty little one-aircraft
missions left over after the main resources of the company were
allotted to the primary missions. That could be as boring as

flying toilet paper out to Ft. Selden, as tedious as ferrying some Vietnamese Lieutenant around from one ARVN camp to another, or as dangerous as an emergency call for medical evacuation in bad weather. In any case, it would be unlikely gunship escort would be available.

The weather socked in shortly after Billy started flying again. It was bad weather. The problem was that it wasn't bad enough to be good weather — that is, bad enough that helicopters could not be flown. It was just good enough they could still fly, which is as bad as weather can get for a helicopter pilot. The ceilings and the visibility were low, and the hollow spaces beneath the ceilings were occluded by tattered scud. The rain was irregular — scattered showers, and occasional deluges. Figuring that the company might be out of operation for a few days if the weather became worse, Major Csynes decided to send supply missions out to as many of the forward recon outposts as he could reach.

The last fireteam to return to The Scabbard that evening was led by Arlo Jeter, who was sporting his new Chief Warrant Officer bars. In the wing ship, Kevin Harrey amused himself by flying in very close formation behind and above Jeter. Next to him John Bergin sat comfortably, staring off into space, and whistling softly to himself. Kevin listened absently to Jeter as he contacted company operations before hovering to the fuel pits. He was looking forward to getting to bed early, having got only a few hours of sleep in the counter-mortar team's ready shack the previous night.

As the two gunships hovered across the black-tarred surface of fuel pits, swirls of fog streamers spun like cotton candy from the rotor tips, making the ships look like great bugs, creeping through the fog on writhing translucent tentacles. "Sabre, Dagger Two-four. We're the last ship out, aren't we?" Kevin heard Arlo ask.

"That's a negative, Dagger," came the reply. "There's one aircraft still out." Kevin recognized the voice of Captain Jack Miller, who was on duty in the operations office. "It's a medevac we got called in from Battalion about an hour ago."

"Without gunships?" Jeter demanded.

"Uh, that's affirmative, Dagger Two-four. The stand-by

team's aircraft have still not been signed off by Maintenance, and he was the only aircraft available."

"Where is he, Sabre Control?"

"Platoon-size outpost on this side of the ridge, up north of here just past firebase Ft. Craig. Is there a problem?"

"If I were flying that slick, I'd say there was a problem. I have one light fire team with full fuel and armament load. Request immediate permission to depart in support of that medevac flight. Over."

"Uh, understand you request....wait one, Dagger." There was a pause, then he came back up again. "Dagger Two-four, I don't, uh....look, Dagger, recommend you come up to Operations and we'll put in a mission request for you, over."

"Control, request you get Sabre Six on this freq."

"That won't be necessary, Dagger," replied Captain Miller curtly. "You have Sabre Control clearance for immediate departure to intercept Sabre Two-seven. Coordinates to follow."

"Thank you, Sabre Control. Break: Dagger, One-seven, you all up back there?"

"That's affirmative," replied Kevin wearily.

"Bao Trang, Dagger Two-four, light fire team to scramble from the pits."

"Roger, Dagger, cleared immediate takeoff, altimeter two-niner-seven-seven, wind two-two-zero at less than five knots, last reported ceilings eight-hundred broken, visibility three-to-five miles in low scattered clouds, and rain showers. Over."

"Roger, Bao Trang. That's about how it looks to me too. Break. Black Sabre Two-seven, do you copy?"

There was no reply. Arlo flew at treetop level along the road which led from Bao Trang to the villages north, then turned and followed the new trail which the Army had carved through the jungle to reach firebase Ft. Craig. He tried several radio frequencies, but was unable to make contact with Sabre Two-seven or with the supported unit, call sign Sugar Bandit. The weather was deteriorating as the fire team headed up a narrowing valley north of the firebase. The cloud base was quite stratified, and formed a ceiling above them which lay against the sides of the valley and created a long low tunnel through which they could fly. It was the kind of hazy passageway into the rugged mountains which fog could close in a few minutes.

Kevin flew in grim silence, knowing Jeter would hang it out to the max, having been a recon troop himself. The fact it was starting to get dark didn't make him feel any more comfortable. "Who is Sabre Two-seven?" he asked Bergin.

"That's Kretzer, I think."

Kevin shook his head in disgust. "I might have known. So this was Jake's idea of a Shitbird mission. The boy steps in a little do-do and he's expected to make 'honorabur aporogy' by flying suicide missions. I'm getting a very bad feeling about that man's ideas of motivating the troops, Round John."

"Aw, relax. It probably turned out to be a ratfuck, and he's up in the soup somewhere trying to figure out how to get back to The Scab without running into a mountain."

"So how come we can't raise him on the radios?"

"I don't know. Maybe he ran into a mountain."

The tunnel valley ahead of them narrowed to a little saddle, a little pass into the darkening hollow beyond. The open space was narrow — less than half a mile — and from the treetops at the lowest point to the gray deck of clouds above was only about two hundred feet. They flew into a little cul-de-sac, an almost circular bowl-shaped depression in the hills. On all sides the green jungle-caped hills rose up to disappear into the cloudbank, except for the saddle through which they had flown. The helicopters were just able to make a wide circle in the tiny hollow. As they passed through the saddle, Jeter was able to make contact with the ground unit, who were clearly relieved to get the call.

"Dagger Two-four, this is Sugar Bandit. We're sure glad you finally made it here, over."

"Roger that, Bandit. Have you been in contact with Black Sabre Two-seven, over?" asked Jeter.

"That's a negative, Dagger. We've been waiting for you guys an hour and a half."

"Bandit, we're a light fire team of gunships. We were sent out to support the slick who was supposed to pickup your wounded. Have you been in contact in the last hour?"

"Negative, Dagger. We've been getting a little some general harassing fire from the hillsides around us all afternoon. They don't want to take us on, but they don't mind pecking at us."

"Roger that, Bandit. We're not really equipped for pickup operation, you know. Can your wounded stay the night, over?"

"Uh...that's hard to say, Dagger. I'd sure like to see them pulled out of here before this weather cuts us off for a week."

After a moment Jeter said with finality, "All right, Bandit, here's what I'm going to do. I've got to unload my armament to be able to carry those two men on this gunship. Do you have a flare pistol?"

"That's affirmative."

"OK. Now you fire a flare in the direction you think the enemy might be, then you all get your heads down, cause I've got about three dozen rockets to get rid of. Break: Babycakes, you hold your fire so you can cover me if we flush anything. I'm going to unload, drop into that hole they're hiding in, and pick up those two wounded. Then we can get the hell out of here." He released the mike trigger a notch and spoke to his copilot on intercom. "You hold your blooper fire, too, Jerry, in case it gets hot."

Kevin saw the pistol flare arc out and watched Arlo quickly set up a firing run which would enable him to drop into the hole without having to go around the circle again. As though anticipating him, a burst of tracerfire stabbed upward from the hillside toward the gunships. Jeter answered the fire by carefully placing his first salvo of rockets into the trees only fifty meters beyond the troops' small perimeter. He had set his armament switches to fire four pairs at a time, and the result was quite spectacular. He fired four salvos from the Frog ship's big rocket pods, adjusting his aiming point each time. As he finished his run, he came to a high hover, and dropped vertically into the hole in the jungle. One of the infantry troops held a flashing hand-strobe, and Jeter landed the ship almost on top of the piercing blue-white tweak of light. He was on the ground less than twenty seconds, then made a max-performance takeoff through the treetops.

The saddle was still open, but it was only a lenticular spot of light, like a balefully-staring cataracted eye into which they had to fly. At slow speed only a few feet above the trees, the two gunships felt their way through, then dropped into the long narrow valley below. The visibility was poor, but it was enough. It was dark by the time they got back to Bao Trang, but they were able to land without difficulty, deliver their wounded to the medics, and shut down for the night.

Sabre Two-seven never returned.

The weather broke in a couple of days, but search missions found nothing. It was quietly acknowledged that the jungle had swallowed up the four men of the crew, and they were officially listed as missing in action.

Their personal effects were gathered up and brought to the operations shack to be inventoried. Early that same evening, a runner from Operations came to the Daggers' tent and told Eddie Padilla to report to the mess hall. Eddie set his unfinished beer on the bar and departed promptly. He arrived at the building to find a small group of other officers and NCO's assembling. The only other gunship pilot he saw was Arlo Jeter. Major Jake Csynes soon joined them and got to the point.

"Sit down, men, and don't make a big show of this. We have a rather special job to do tonight. While Mr. Kretzer's personal effects were being inventoried this afternoon, something was found among them which may well explain why he is no longer with us." Csynes held up a small plastic box, one of the three-by-four-inch cases used to mail small reels of recording tape which the men used with battery-powered recorders for a popular new form of correspondence. He snapped the case open and allowed the contents to fall onto the table before him. It was a small cellophane bag containing about a tablespoon of crumbled green leaves. "This is marijuana," he said, "and it proves to me that I made a very critical mistake in dealing with Mr. Kretzer, a mistake which could have serious repercussions on my career in the Army. If I had taken the hard line, and handled the situation by the book, Kretzer would no longer be flying helicopters, but he would not be missing in action, and neither would the three other men who went down with him. I will tell you the same thing I am going to put in my report to the General. I chose to let him off with a reprimand instead of reporting him for stealing stimulant pills from the survival kits. I chose to consider his motivation to be a stress problem, and not a drug problem. But now I see I was tragically mistaken. Apparently, he has been receiving this loco-weed in the mail from his wife, and if he doesn't get home, well, she has herself to thank. A man who flies with booze under his belt is a damned fool, but the man who thinks he can fly a combat helicopter under the influence of a reality-distorting drug like marijuana is a suicidal maniac, an irresponsible and unforgivable threat to the lives of every man who flies with him or near him. He is likely as not to step out of the helicopter to stand back and admire himself flying it, or to land it upside down so he can look at the flowers.

"Well, I am going to make certain I do not repeat the mistake which may have cost the lives of four men. If there is any other pilot, crewmember, or anybody else in this company who is risking our lives by going out on dangerous missions with a load of goofy-smoke between his ears, I am going to do him and the rest of us a favor by getting him the hell out of this unit.

"You men have been selected to be here tonight because you are men I believe I can trust. Having said that, I trust that none of you will be offended when I ask you to stand and empty the contents of your pockets onto the tables in front of you. Do that now, please."

Looking a bit embarrassed, the men stood to empty their pockets. A few attempts at jokes fell very flat, and they quickly moved to comply, then stood waiting silently. Captain Neil Koontz walked around the tables and looked perfunctorily at the little piles of stuff.

"Thank you, gentlemen," continued Csynes. "Now we are going to make an unannounced inspection of the quarters tents. Each of you will return to your tent, and under the supervision of the platoon commanders, you will make a complete examination of everyone's personal effects. We will not, I say again, we will not be defeated in our critical mission by moral weakness when we are so close to our goal. In ancient times, the Knight and the Samurai would conduct rituals to purify themselves before going into battle. That is what we are going to do now. So let's go clean house!" Then he added, "Mr. Padilla, I am going with you."

As the Major stepped into the Daggers' tent, Eddie called for attention. Surprised, the pilots jumped to their feet. With some obvious relish, Csynes announced the reason for his visit. "I have come here," he concluded, "because I would like to commence this inspection personally with Mr. Hairy Hawking here."

Hawking looked stricken for a moment, then he pulled himself up to a straighter position of attention, and sang out loud and clear like a flight-school boot. "Sir, Warrant Officer Hawking, I respectfully protest this unfair treatment. You have no grounds on which to single me out for this invasion of my privacy, Sir."

The Major was genuinely surprised. "Hawking, you dumb cluck, where the hell do you think you are? In some college dormitory? Everything you have is subject to inspection any time, soldier, including all the places where the sun never shines."

Trying his best to look like a righteous acolyte being led to the lions, Hawking plunged on. "Sir, to be singled out without provocation is personal persecution, and I don't believe I have to take that. I respectfully request the right to take this matter to the IG."

"The Inspector General? You do that. And you take the matter straight to the Chaplain, too. But you will do it after this inspection. Now empty your pockets. Mr. Padilla, you will go through all of this pile of trash, and you will look for unauthorized materials."

Hawking emptied his pockets onto his bunk, then quickly picked up his toiletries kit and dumped it onto the bunk also, so the pack of filter cigarettes he carried wouldn't be conspicuous. Eddie immediately recognized them. He knew Vietnamese black-marketers emptied the tobacco and repacked them with the high-powered local dope. He could see that the pack had been slipped out of its cellophane wrapper, opened at the bottom, then slipped back into the wrapper and opened at the top. Csynes watched with a patient little smile as Eddie picked up the pack. Feeling the same kind of sinking in the pit of the stomach he experienced being shot at, Eddie opened the top of the pack and tapped out one of the long filter cigarettes. It was smooth, and the end was flat. He sniffed it. "Tobacco," he said, and set the pack down among the other items.

Csynes was clearly disappointed that a search of Hawking's belongings did not turn up the bag of reefer he had expected. "Well, Mr. Hawking," he said when Eddie had finished, "I am glad my suspicions were apparently wrong, but your wise-ass jailhouse-lawyer attitude I find very offensive. As of tonight, you may consider yourself officially on my Shitbird List."

"Thank you, Sir," snapped Hawking. "At least I don't have to worry about being sent out without gunship cover."

The Major glared at him coldly in the moment of breathless silence that followed in the tent, and the gnarled scar tissue on his neck and the earless sides of his head flushed red-and-white. "You had better be very careful, Mister," Csynes said softly in his strange round oboe-tone. "I do not have the time or the margin of safety to screw around with the spreading of discord through this company. You had better get your head screwed on straight, or you are going to find your ass in a very tight jam."

The inspection took a couple of hours. Most of the shakedown searches were perfunctory glances through lockers and bags. A great show was made around Jake Csynes, and a few hapless selectees endured having their socks unrolled, their soap dishes snooped, and their dirty laundry exposed as the posse of inspectors tried to impress the Major with their diligence and cleverness in identifying potential hiding places. A small ornate box found in one crew chief's footlocker was pounced upon and presented to Csynes with the knowing smiles of a pack of cartoon weasels about to open the basket with the baby in it. When it proved to contain only three locks of hair — from his wife and children — the spell was broken, and the necessaries remaining were accomplished quickly. The raid resulted in no disciplinary action — no pot was found, and the three bottles of illicit whiskey discovered were placed with the others in the Blade and Spade, with a stern but unofficial reprimand given to their owners.

After the inspection, Hawking rode down to the counter-mortar ready shack with Kevin, who had the duty again. They walked around behind one of the revetments, and Hawking took out the pack of smokes Eddie had examined. He opened the bottom and drew out a lumpy smoke with a twirled end. "I'm sure glad I started putting a few straights in the front of the pack," he told Kevin.

"Poor old Bullseye," Kevin laughed. "He thought you'd had the pork and there was nothing he could do about it."

"I thought I'd had it too," said Hawking, not amused. "You know what I'm thinking, Babycakes? With a guy like Jake the Snake on our side, we don't need any enemies."

ELEVEN

Kevin and Eddie sat in the cockpit of the trail ship of a three-gunship heavy fire team. It was early evening, and the objective of the flight was to insert a recon team of Green Berets and Vietnamese Rangers into the A Lan valley. The rationale was they could fly in at dusk, make the insertion at last light, and then return by climbing to altitude under the cover of darkness. The alternative to the night insertion, it was pointed out, was to alert the enemy of their presence on the way in, and then to run the gauntlet line at treetop level to get out, since the helicopters could not climb to high altitude quickly enough to be safe from heavy 12.5mm anti-aircraft guns of the North Vietnamese Army. The two slicks involved were powerful old Sikorski S-58's which belonged to the Vietnamese Air Force. The pilots, it was pointed out at the briefing, had been flying in the area almost seven years, and did not even bother to take maps on their missions.

Kevin dreaded the dusk insertion. It would probably work, he reasoned, but it set the stage for a much more dangerous job to follow. If the team got dropped off into deeper shit than they could handle, the Rangers would likely decide to go for a night extraction. That would call for the gunships to fly around in a circle at 500 feet drawing and returning the enemy's fire while the slick hovered at treetop level to a hand-held strobe light, and pulled the team up on a sling hoist. It did not comfort him to think that those dink Ranger pilots had seen a lot of babyfaced round-eye gunship drivers come and go, and had brought along three gunships so they had one to waste if they needed extra time.

In the left seat, Eddie sat as though hypnotized, staring at the space between his plexiglass windshield and the darkening jungle below. He found himself listening to the changeless whine of the turbine and the steady jogging of the rotor, and he rubbed at his face, suddenly frightened by a strange sense of unreality, something like the sudden awareness that one is dreaming. He shook his head to try to clear it, and the jungle slid by silently below him. In the hollows the cooler air collected and began to generate vaporous tendrils of fog that probed the dark spaces between the trees and the broad-leafed undergrowth. Eddie looked over at Kevin and watched his comrade-in-arms as he flew. He was relaxed, with his left hand cradled in his lap away from the collective lever. "He seems to be at ease," thought Eddie. "I guess I should be too."

Kevin reached over to the switches on his radio control panel and made an adjustment which isolated the intercom between himself and Eddie. He could switch it back, if he needed to address the crew chief and gunner, but until then only Eddie could hear him. "Hey, Eddie, do you ever think about what we were saying — this being 'him or me', and the name of the game is to get home alive — you ever think about that?"

Eddie nodded, looking at him expectantly.

"Yeah, me too, and it keeps coming out ugly. At best we're killing one group of strangers so another group can get rich doing business with America. As far as I can see, that's no reason to justify taking any risk I can avoid. So I take the risks I can't avoid, and kill the enemy because if I don't, I don't get home. OK?"

"Yeah, I guess that makes sense," said Eddie, "if you've got no real cause to fight for."

"Right. So here's what's bothering me: that gook I have to kill to get home — if I've got no moral cause, then he doesn't deserve it, does he?"

"Well, maybe not, but it's still you or him, isn't it?"

"That's what I figure. We didn't either of us make this war, and he's in the same boat as me. So what if somebody else who doesn't deserve it should happen to be in a position like that gook to be the cause of my death? Is it still 'him or me'?"

"What are you talking about?"

"Let me point something out to you. I'm on Jake's Shitbird List. That means I have a higher risk of getting into a hot night firefight. Anybody who drew that medevac mission might have been killed, but Kretzer got it because he was on the List. Now look at you. You're on Jake's Hotshot List — your shit doesn't stink. So does that mean you get reduced combat risk?"

"You kidding? It means I get to be first in line to hang it out past the point of no return."

"How about that. The risk goes up if he hates you, and it goes up if he likes you. It's probably worse for you, because he likes to hang it out so far. You know what I think? I think he keeps his ass hung out over the line because he's afraid he'd crack if he ever let up. He fast-talked his way into this job because he couldn't stand being back in the Real World. Think about it. If you were that ugly, and all you knew was killing, would you be in a big hurry to get back to Kansas? Csynes may be a real American hero — no, I mean it. He may be a schmuck, but he's a real pro. But— he is going to keep his ass hung out past the edge until somebody kills him. Until then, he is going to get a lot of guys killed trying to keep up with him. Like us, for instance."

Eddie shrugged. "We're the Daggers, remember? When the kitchen gets too hot for the Devil, you send in Babycakes and the Bullseye, and they cook somebody's goose, right?"

"Yeah, I remember. I just keep wondering if somebody wouldn't be doing a lot of good old boys a favor by putting that loony lizard out of his misery."

"You mean like 'it's him or us'? Come on, that's crazy. I mean, it may make sense, but that kind of sense is....just not sensible. It's like shooting yourself so they'll send you home so you won't get shot."

Kevin nodded. "Well, that's a paradox, all right," he said. They rode along in silence a minute or two. Ahead the A Lan ridge was cleanly silhouetted against the slate-gray western sky, and the two big droop-nosed Sikorskis looked like great hump-backed locusts, accompanied by the fat dragonfly Hueys.

"Hey, Ed."

"Yeah."

"Did you ever get anything like a premonition? A feeling, like, that something was going to happen?"

"Yeah, I guess. Why?"

"Well, you know, I was just sitting here, and suddenly I got this really strange feeling, like I was kind of detached from things, and I started thinking about Carlie, and little George. I just felt like....like I wasn't ever going to see them again, after tonight. And I just realized for the first time that they are the only reason I'm here, and they are all I have to lose."

Eddie stared at him in silence.

"You know, Eddie, it sure seems to me I just heard some kind of really peculiar vibration, like from the tail rotor, maybe. I mean, an intermittent vibration, you know, sometimes it's there, and sometimes it's not."

Eddie looked searchingly at Kevin, who flew looking straight ahead. Finally he nodded. "Yeah, I think I heard something like that too. Like something was coming loose and vibrating, then falling back, and you don't know when it's going to come loose again."

Kevin reached down to his radio control panel and flipped the tiny switch which put the crew chief and gunner back onto his intercom. "Hey, fellows, this is Harrey. For the last few minutes, Mr. Padilla and I have been feeling some really strange vibrations up here, like something was coming loose in the tail rotor."

"We haven't felt anything, Mr. Harrey. I checked that rotor completely last night," said the crew chief.

"That's right, Bailey, I know you did, and I checked it myself before we took off, and I saw you did a good job. But you know, sometimes things that don't show just come loose, and it's nobody's fault, but you just have to abort the mission and go back and try to figure out what it was that went wrong. Isn't that right?"

"Abort? Uh...yessir, I guess it is. Tail rotor vibration is nothing to fool around with, Sir."

"That's exactly what I thought." Kevin squeezed the mike trigger to transmit, and called Bakersmith. "Dagger Lead, we seem to have a little problem back here. We're getting some strange vibration in the tail section. It's intermittent, like something back there was coming loose and shaking around, then popping back into place for a while. I get a little pedal load when it happens, too. Request your recommendation, over."

"One-seven, did you say you were getting some binding in your pedal controls?"

"Uh, only when the vibration is happening, Lead. It's not doing it right now. If it doesn't happen again, maybe we should just go ahead and stretch it on in with the flight, do you think?"

There was a pause, then Bakersmith came up on the radio again. "Negative, One-seven. We can continue the mission with a light fire team. I recommend you abort, contact Sabre Control, and return to The Scab by the most direct route. Over." On the separate channel he used to communicate with the Vietnamese slicks, Bakersmith called to advise the ARVN captain in command of the mission that they were going to proceed with only a light fireteam.

The captain's reply was immediate and emphatic. There was no way he was going to fly the mission with only two gunships. If the entire flight was not going over the ridge, then nobody would go over the ridge. When Rudy confirmed apologetically that one of his helicopters had a mechanical problem, and could not be counted on to complete the mission, the mission commander's decision was prompt. He turned his helicopter around, released the gunships to return to Bao Trang, and departed into the night.

They rode back to the Scabbard in silence and shut down the aircraft. Eddie was confused. He wanted to apologize to somebody for the way the mission had been scrubbed, but he suffered the nagging feeling that everyone else had been happy to have an excuse to forget the whole thing. He knew he would be questioned, and his answers would sound as ludicrous and contrived as the others. He knew the mechanics would find nothing wrong. He also knew the answers would be accepted, the rotor rebuilt, and the incident permitted to pass. He was frightened by his confusion, and more frightened by the nebulous gut superstition that Kevin had been right about the premonition.

Kevin stepped wearily into the Dagger tent, lay down on his bunk, and let the tension drain from him. After a little while, he laughed softly, wryly acknowledging his recognition that he had never felt more completely alone in his life, nor more personally secure.

Eight days later, at 03:41, according to the logbook of the Officer of the Day, the company was awakened by a large explosion in the company area. The rocket attack siren wailed, the counter-mortar gunship crews sprinted to their helicopters, and the rest of the men leaped for their holes. After about fifty seconds, two more explosions burst nearby.

Eddie huddled against the cool sandbag wall of the bunker, frightened, but still interested in knowing what was going on. He tried to identify the unfamiliar fat THOOMF of the explosions. Somehow they did not sound to him like the sharp-edged KRUMPF of incoming mortars, or the ground-thumping WHRAMP of rockets. After a few minutes, a runner from Operations came around and said they had taken one of the rockets in the company area, but that everything was under control, and everyone should return to bed. A few minutes later the word spread through the unit that Major Jacob Csynes was dead. The first of the three rockets had struck his tent, and had exploded almost directly under his bed.

The major was gathered up, put into a rubber bag, and sent away. Buddy Nichols came around from the news service, took pictures, and conducted emotional interviews. The Colonel came down from Battalion and announced that Neil Koontz would take over as CO, and that his promotion to major had been advanced by three months. Major Koontz vowed that he would fulfill Csynes' dream to lead the Sabres into the promised A Lan, and he announced that he was going to recommend Csynes be posthumously awarded the Legion of Merit.

Eddie went to look at the impact site, and became quietly distressed. Kevin joined him and stood watching as he walked around the place where the major's hex-tent had stood, a perplexed expression on his face.

"What's up?" asked Kevin.

"Just doesn't feel right, you know. Take a look around. Find me one piece of shrapnel from the rocket that killed Jake Csynes."

Kevin shrugged. "Maybe it wasn't a rocket."

"Dammit, Harrey, the only thing I know that would blow a hole like that is a sapper with a satchel charge." He glared at Kevin pointedly, challenging him to reply.

Kevin held the gaze, then nodded slowly. "There was a good

price on his head. Maybe somebody sneaked in and collected. So what do you want, Eddie? The FBI in here?"

Eddie shook his head sadly. "Oh, God," he said very softly, "what have we become?"

The change of command in practice had little effect on the company's missions, or on life at Bao Trang. The Shitbird List was abolished; restrictions on drinking hours were maintained. Some of the men missed the magic of Jake the Snake's esprit; some of them were glad to be done with the play-acting. Word came down through the company grapevine that a particular LRRP mission — or a series of missions — was due to be scheduled soon. The invasion of the A Lan valley was imminent. The only thing which yet needed to be known was the strength of the enemy waiting just across the borders of Laos and Cambodia. The only way to know that was to go count them.

Duke Randall came into the Daggers' tent shortly after supper one evening to announce crew assignments for a LRRP mission to be flown the following morning. "One fire team, with a 05:30 takeoff. We're using three of our slicks, and we're putting a small team of Special Forces troops in the valley. I've got the lead on this one myself, with Skip on my wing. Hawking, you're with Skip on the blooper, and the lucky boy who gets to ride with me is the Bullseye. This one should be lots of fun, boys, so get some sleep."

"You sound way too happy about it, Cap'n Duke," complained Skip. "Going out to the flats to shoot up some gook boot camp is one thing, but screwing around that border is something else."

Duke eyed him suspiciously. "Who said anything about the border? We don't get our assignment until the briefing at the Special Forces camp in the morning."

"Who you bullshitting, Captain? It's even in the newspapers we get from home — they've got a couple divisions of NVA over there ready to jump the minute we put troops on the ground. We're the guys flying that area, so how does that add up to you?"

"I'd say you're a pretty smart little guy, Skip. So we might be going across the border. That bothers you?"

"You mean because it's out of bounds? Nah. Those NVA

over there are enjoying the hospitality of the neutral governments of Laos and Cambodia. If I were going to start objecting to our saying one thing and doing something else, it wouldn't be to complain about driving a few tactical spies into countries who think neutrality means playing both sides against the middle."

"So what's the bitch?"

"I can answer that question in one word," put in Kevin. "Heat, pure and simple. This die-for-your-country shit gets all too damned real out there."

"Well, sure, it's dangerous. That's the difference between this and the movies. But, hell, staying in bed is dangerous. I'll take the action, myself, and trust The Lord to decide when my time is up."

"It seems men will do all kinds of strange things for six hundred bucks a month these days," said Kevin.

"Excuse me, gents." They turned to see one of the troops wearing a steel helmet and the brassard of the Sergeant of the Guard. "Mr. Padilla in here?"

"Yo," said Eddie, standing up and stepping into the lighted area in the center of the tent. *"Que pues?"*

"Sir, you're on the roster to inspect the guardposts. When you're ready, I'll be in the Orderly Room."

"Oh, that's right. This is the eleventh. Just hold on, Sergeant, and I'll get my steel pot. We can take care of that now while there's still a little light." Eddie pulled his helmet and his pistol from his footlocker, swung his arm through the strap of his shoulder-holster, and departed quickly with the sergeant.

Eddie rode in silence in the right front seat of the Operations jeep as the Sergeant of the Guard drove out to the perimeter of the camp. The Black Sabres were responsible for manning four of the twenty-seven two-man sentry posts which surrounded the camp, and though the perimeter had not been hit since Tet, the posts were inspected sometime after sunset every night. As Eddie and the sergeant walked from the jeep to the first post, the sun had just officially set, and the sky was still light. Like most of the others, the little pillbox was made of concrete and sandbags, with a bed in a closed-in bunker below, and a parapet with a machinegun mount above. One soldier was lying on the bunk listening to a letter from home on a small tape recorder, and the other had propped his feet up on the parapet and sat staring off into the haze. When he heard the team arriving, he swung his feet down and turned around. "Halt who goes there," he said conversationally.

"Sardna Guard, Whammo," said the sergeant, "and the OD's inspector."

"Oh. Good evening, Sir," said the sentry, saluting.

"Good evening," said Eddie, returning the salute. "So, uh, has there been anything to report?"

"No, Sir, just the usual shit."

"Just what is the usual shit?"

"Well, Sir, the generals didn't like the fact that no matter how deep we bury our garbage, the dinks will dig it up and take off with it as soon as we're gone. So they decided the thing to do is bury it in the berm where we can guard it." He pointed out to the cleared area which surrounded the perimeter to a distance of about one hundred yards. "As soon as it gets dark, the kids come out and root for garbage in the berm. We used to pop flares when we heard them out there, and at first they took off running, but after a couple of times they'd just stand there in the light and moon us. Somebody popped an M-79 grenade round out there one night and killed a couple of them, and the village made such a stink about it the generals just ordered us to leave them alone."

Eddie stared at him, hoping he had misunderstood. "You mean you have people moving around in the berm area all night, and you're supposed to ignore them? What if a bunch of VC just walk out there with them some night?"

The sentry grinned. "Aw, I don't think they'd fool me much. When they stop calling me a dinky-dau doo-ma-fucker and hooking for their boom-boom baby sister, that's when I pop a flare."

"Right. I guess this post seems to have its shit together, Sarge. Anything you want to ask?"

"Nope."

At the next post, Eddie asked the sentry where the nearest field telephone was located.

"We're supposed to have them in the sentry post, Sir, but

there haven't been any since the wiring went out in that last rain we had." The sentry pointed to the bottom of the bunker, where the phone and power lines disappeared into a puddle of slowly-drying mud.

"Well, if you need to contact the Sergeant of the Guard, how do you expect to do that?"

"No sweat, Mr. Padilla. If it's something that isn't real urgent, I can run back to Operations in about two minutes. If I don't have time for that, I just squeeze off a few rounds, and everybody in Bao Trang comes out to see what's going on."

"I guess that seems sensible enough."

"It might not be in the Drill Manual, Sir, but if it works well enough cover my ass five more months, that's enough for me."

By the time they had visited and inspected all four posts, it was fully dark, and the sergeant had brought out a small flashlight from his pocket to assist them in picking their way along bulldozer ridges, potholes, and piles of sandbags to return to the jeep. Puffing a bit for breath, Eddie stood a moment at the edge of a bulldozer tailing which dropped off about six feet below him.

He was troubled inside, more troubled than he had been at any other time since he had decided to become a soldier. He was troubled about the way he felt toward the mission he was to fly in the morning. It would be hot, no question about it, but that had never before really disturbed him. He had taken pride in the fact that he went out of his way to get the hottest missions, and found them so exciting. But suddenly, suddenly things were different. "Here I am," he thought, "in the name of everything I've ever been taught to respect — my family, community, government, and church — going out daily and risking my life to hunt down and kill people for no greater crime than preferring commie rice to yankee hamburgers. And God forgive me, I have been enjoying it!" Then he thought of Jake Csynes, and he gave a deep shuddering sigh. "It is possible one of us may have murdered a fine officer, and might have saved my life by doing it. If I had known, would I have stopped him?" For the first time since he arrived in Vietnam, Eddie was afraid he was not going to get home.

He turned slightly toward the sergeant, who stood a few yards away holding the flashlight. He took a step forward, and as he put his foot down, he felt the edge of the tailing give away beneath it. It was an almost-premeditated impulse which made him stumble, which made him let the edge of his boot slip sideways, and which made him let his ankle fold forward. Letting out a yelp of pain and surprise, Eddie fell down the side of the tailing and lay in a thick puddle of mud. "Oh, shit, this is ridiculous," he said, trying to extricate himself. He put his weight on the ankle and yelped again, and it was only with the assistance of the Sergeant of the Guard that he was able to climb the tailing and return to the jeep.

The sergeant returned him limping to the Dagger tent, looking bedraggled and embarrassed. He accepted Kevin's help in limping to his bunk, where he sat and removed his boot. He rubbed the twisted ankle, wishing it were as red on the outside as it was painful on the inside. After a few minutes, Duke Randall came from Operations to see him.

"Hey, Bullseye, I heard you fell on your ass. You all right?" he asked, pounding Eddie on the shoulder.

"Yeah, I think so, Cap'n Duke," said Eddie with a grimace. "I just twisted the hell out of my ankle."

"Oh yeah? Well, I guess that scrubs you for tomorrow."

"Oh, maybe it'll be all right by morning. I wouldn't want to flake out on a mission if I didn't have to."

"You want to walk twenty miles on it tomorrow morning if you get shot down?" demanded the captain. "Come on, Padilla, you can't have all the good ones. You're off the roster."

"I guess it probably wouldn't be such a good idea," said Eddie, laughing weakly. "A bubble-butt with a busted ass would slow everybody up for sure."

"Right. And report to the flight surgeon first thing in the morning. So who's the relief pilot tonight?"

"Why do they call it relief pilot?" asked Kevin. "I've got it, and I sure don't feel relieved."

"Harrey, huh. OK, young Christian, I hope you're feeling hotheaded tomorrow morning, because I've got a feeling we're going to run into a bunch of boys with some big BB guns."

Kevin and Eddie both went to bed early. Kevin lay awake for a short time thinking about the fearful mission he would have to fly in the morning, then he put it out of his mind and went to sleep.

TWELVE

Kevin lay in his bedroll, surprised he had awakened before being shaken by the duty runner from Operations, and feeling the peculiar sensation that he had been dreaming about something very significant, something which faded from his mind like fog when he tried to look at it. Without opening his eyes, he listened, moving his attention out to locate himself in place and time. He expected maintenance would be test-flying the last of the aircraft for the mission, and the mess hall would already be bustling with greetings and wisecracks, and the jangle of metal tableware. Something was wrong. There were no helicopters, no jangle of trays, but an echoing of soft voices. Even before he blinked his eyes open, he could see it was already daylight, and when he opened them, nothing would come into focus.

"The mission!" he said, trying to sit up. A wave of pain and nausea engulfed him. In panic, he tried to move again, and felt fires flash along his limbs. He froze, rigid. "The mission!" he cried out, suddenly horribly frightened he had forgotten something very important.

There was someone beside him, touching his face with something cool. "It's all right. Lie still," she said. Astonished, Kevin turned his head slowly and brought his eyes into focus. She was short, chubby, big-nosed and curly-haired, twice his age, and certainly the most radiant and beautiful woman he had ever seen. Then he noticed that she was wearing the uniform of a nurse, emblazoned with the gold leaves of a major.

"I've got a mission," he told her.

"It's all right, Kevin," she said gently. "You went on the mission. You're safe now. You're in the hospital."

"Hospital? Where?"

"In Hawaii. This is Tripler Army Hospital, and I am Nurse Frances. Now, don't try to move. You've had a lot of stitches, and you need to rest."

He looked around groggily after she left, and saw beds, and other men, cool green walls, and Venetian blinds. "How did I get here?" he wondered, and close upon that another question, the most horrifying question, "How badly am I hurt?" His body was numbed, and felt very remote from him, but when he moved, the keen edges of sharp pain cut through very close to him. Lying very still, and finally aware only of his weight in the bed and the echoing murmur of the ward, he tried to remember.

Last night, he had been in the tent, in the Daggers' tent at Bao Trang. He was with his poor little buddy Jake, earnest, frightened little Jake, the lizard who came down the chimney to be one of the gang, and with that crazy Roger Stanton, the big-mouthed son of a bitch who thought it was funny to send him on this mission to China. And Carlie kept telling him to be careful, because she was afraid she couldn't keep him up there long enough to get back to her. But, he thought, that had to be a dream he was remembering, because that was the place he always kept waking up. He would think about it again in the morning.

Three weeks later he was released from the hospital ward and assigned a room in transient officers quarters some distance from the main hospital complex, up on the high slope overlooking Honolulu. As soon as he had become really aware of where he was, he had asked that Carlie not be notified of his condition, and that he be permitted to contact her when he was ready. He had not called her. He wanted to know more about his situation. If he were to be given a medical discharge and sent home soon, there would be no point in Carlie's spending the money to fly to Hawaii, but if he were going to spend several weeks in recovery, then returned to duty, nothing in the world could please him more than to have her with him.

For the time being, though, her visit would be no erotic holiday. Over one hundred sutures had been used to repair Kevin's skin, which appeared to have been peeled from his body in long tatters. Rows of the little knots ran along the right side of his torso, shoulder, and neck, across his belly, and along the inside of his left thigh. The right side of his face was raw, as though he had been attacked with a sandblaster, and the crown of his head was bald, with a crust of scab as though something had jerked every hair out of its follicle. Several of his ribs had been cracked, and bruises the colors of pansies mottled his body. There were a dozen places where bits of metal had been cut out of the flesh. He had terrible cramps in his forearms, and little strength in his hands. The doctors told him that he had suffered a brain concussion, and had been unconscious six days before awakening in the ward.

Hawaii was obviously a dreamland, and he was looking forward to going down into the city which sprawled so comfortably on the green shelf before him — just as soon as he felt like moving. In the meanwhile he nodded daydreaming about the Vietnamese, and how the guys had given the little kids a bath, and what a great bunch of guys they had been.

Periodically, he was visited by an attendant with a wheelchair, who took him by shuttle van to the main hospital for examinations or tests. The doctors who saw him were busy, friendly, and matter-of-fact.

"I don't think you're going to have any problem with these skin wounds, Mr. Harrey," said one eager young physician, examining the livid octopus of fast-healing scars which wrapped itself around his body. "These explosion wounds are very strange sometimes, like lightning. Sometimes a close explosion won't leave a mark on a man, but his insides are a pulp, and sometimes one will peel the skin off like a tomato and not even break the eardrums, like you. You're very lucky. If you don't have complications from the concussion, you could probably take some Christmas leave and be flying again the first of the year."

"Then just between you and me, Doctor, you don't see a medical disability discharge here?" Kevin asked.

Wrinkling up his nose, the doctor replied, "Not likely. Not because of this, anyway. If something shows up that indicates you have a problem with changing pressure or motion, you could lose your flight status, and being a Warrant with no other specialty, they'd probably go for the discharge. The paperwork is a lot easier than trying to explain why the pilot of a chopper full of troops had a cerebral hemorrhage on takeoff. Why, are you looking for a discharge?"

Kevin shook his head. "No, I don't think so. I had planned to go career."

"Well, a few stitches won't hold you up. You'll be here at least another thirty days, then you'll either be returned to duty, or you'll get a drop and they'll send you on to your next assignment. The man who decides that is Colonel Hernandez."

"Who is he?"

"I don't exactly know, to tell you the truth. Admin was never my forte. But they have some kind of special Personnel facility to handle the traffic through here, and he's the Senior Officer. You'll meet him."

The days passed quickly. As he was being wheeled along a wide and airy corridor one afternoon, he encountered Major Frances, who had been the head nurse on his ward during the hellish first two weeks.

"Oh, Kevin, how nice to see you looking so well!" she said with a smile that beamed.

"I'm glad to see you, too," he replied, laughing. "Look, my hair has started to come back in. With my red hair, I'd look like Bozo the Clown if it didn't."

"I've been looking for you. There is another boy here, who says he knows you. I think he was on the same mission with you."

Kevin felt a chill, as though his warm little bubble of convalescent security had developed a sudden leak. "What was his name?" he asked.

"Stevens. Wally Stevens. I think he was a crew chief." She turned to the orderly who was pushing Kevin's wheelchair. "You know Wally, don't you, Songford?"

"Yes, Ma'am. He's out getting some sunshine. If you'd like me to, Mr. Harrey, I can take you to see him in a while."

"Sure," said Kevin. "Why not? I'd like to find out what happened." After his daily schedule of tests and examinations was finished, Songford pushed him out along the sidewalks to a place on the hospital grounds where several other patients sat in wheelchairs enjoying the sun and the cool breeze coming off the sea. Kevin recognized Stevens, a tall, scholarly-looking crew chief from Twitch Miller's slick platoon.

"Gee, you don't remember any of it all?" Stevens marveled,

after they had exchanged greetings and pleasantries. "That was one hell of a mission to forget, Mr. Harrey."

"Just Kevin, OK? Maybe I'm better off not knowing."

"You might be right. Maybe you'd rather not talk about it?"

"I don't know. What happened to you?"

"Took a round in the spine, down low. Can't move a muscle from the waist down. The docs tell me I might get some of it back....but not next week, you know what I mean. I was in the command ship with Captain Miller, and when Mr. Cronin went down in the PZ, we had to go in and make the extraction. We'd never have made it if it wasn't for you guys. We were just coming out of the hole when you got it, so I saw the whole thing, how you got hit, and then put it into the trees. You don't remember any of that?"

"The last thing I remember was the major got fragged, and then I was going to go on a long range recon mission, and I remember going to bed early, and then I woke up here."

Stevens looked at him strangely. "Major Csynes was killed in a rocket attack, a few weeks ago. We went on the LRRP mission and the team got spotted and surrounded. We got the shit shot out of us getting out. You and Captain Randall took a rocket in the cockpit."

"Randall? He's here too?"

"No, Sir. Captain Duke didn't make it back. The other ship that went down was Mr. Padilla and somebody else. They wiped out the main rotor and blew up when they hit the ground."

Kevin sat staring at Stevens. "Padilla?" he said, perplexed. "Eddie wasn't supposed to be on that mission."

"I didn't know that," said Stevens quietly. "You were friends back in The World?" When Kevin nodded, he said, "I lost a close friend, too: Brad Casler."

"I'm afraid I didn't know him."

"He was the gunner on your ship."

"I'm sorry."

Stevens chuckled softly. "That's all right. It's a pretty tight little club, I guess."

"What's that?"

"Gunship pilots."

Kevin stared up at the puffy popcorn-columns of cumulus clouds piling up above the Pali, and his eyes filled with tears. "You know something, Wally? Right now I feel like the last surviving member."

The meeting with Colonel Hernandez came sooner than he had expected. He was instructed to report wearing his khaki uniform, which fit tightly around his bandages. The colonel was a busy man. He sat behind a desk piled with file folders and computer print-out, a dapper little man with curly gray hair, soft blue eyes, and features sculptured in lean Castilian lines. "Please, be at ease, Mr. Harrey," the colonel said as Kevin winced and slowly raised his right hand to salute. "Sit down, if you wish."

"Thank you, Sir, but if it's all right with you, it's a lot more comfortable standing up."

"As you like. Mr. Harrey, I have been going over your file, and you seem to be a very special case. First of all, your medical report indicates that your wounds are healing very nicely. That no doubt should come as good news. Furthermore, all the tests indicate that you have suffered no lasting effect from your concussion, except for headaches and some trouble sleeping."

"Yessir, and the memory loss."

The Colonel nodded patiently. "Well, that is not too infrequent. It will all come back to you gradually. So medically, I think we can give you a clean bill of health very soon. We are going to keep you least another thirty days, and then I expect we will return you to your unit."

"I see, Sir. That's....that's great."

"Good. Now, there is something here I would like to read to you." He opened the file to a letterhead page, and read, "'Warrant Officer Kevin Harrey has consistently distinguished himself as a competent and responsible aircraft commander and fireteam leader, and has earned the respect of his commanders and his juniors. His willingness to endure high risk, to accept discipline, and his constant striving for high professional standards have set him apart from and above his less-dedicated peers. Though it may be fairly said of him that he is headstrong, independent, and dislikes close supervision, it is my opinion that these qualities if exercised with discipline are valuable attributes in a combat commander, the specialty to which he aspires. Therefore, it is with great personal pleasure that I highly recommend that Mr. Harrey be commissioned a First Lieutenant of Infantry upon completion of his present tour of duty.' It is signed, 'Major Jacob Csynes.'

"Your Commanding Officer thought very highly of you, Kevin," the colonel said in a soft grandfatherly way. "I knew Jake Csynes very well, you know, and I was deeply grieved to hear how tragically he had been killed. He was here with us in the burn unit for many months, and I think I have never met another man more completely dedicated to the idea that the life of a professional officer is selfless service. It showed in everything he did — in physical therapy, he endured great pain in order to maintain his flexibility, so he could still fly. He would never stop at nine exercises when he knew he could do ten. When he calls you headstrong and independent as a compliment, he is telling me that he thinks you are very much like himself, and I take that as a high recommendation. Therefore, I have taken some steps available to me, and I am pleased to tell you that your commission is assured — pending medical clearance, of course. So at the risk of being premature, congratulations, Lieutenant."

Kevin sat slack-jawed, emotions tugging at him from several sides. "I...uh....I...thank you, Sir. I don't know what to say."

"Before you say anything, let me tell you the best part. Since you had so little time left on this tour when you were flown out of Vietnam, it is possible you won't have to complete this tour of duty. You will remain here until you receive your medical clearance, then you will be Commissioned, and you will be returned to Vietnam to begin a twelve-month tour in your new capacity. You have a great opportunity, Kevin, to inherit the legacy of Jacob Csynes, and to fulfill what he set out to do."

"That's wonderful, Sir, that's a...a great honor." He hesitated a moment. "Sir, there is one thing. I was looking forward to seeing my family over Christmas, and..."

"You're going to be here another three to five weeks. I see no reason why you couldn't arrange for your wife to spend a week or two here with you. You have spoken with her, of course?"

"No, Sir, actually I haven't. I didn't want to upset her until I knew what I was going to do."

"I see. Well, now you have only good news for her. I suggest you enjoy your stay here, and devote yourself to your health. You ought to take your wife on a flight to see some of the outer Islands. Some folks around here like to say, 'Maui no ka oi.' It means, 'Maui is the best.' Well, I won't keep you here in that uncomfortable uniform any longer. You may go."

"Thank you, Sir," said Kevin. He saluted smartly in spite of the pain, and left the colonel's office.

An hour later he sat in a phone booth, wearing an aloha shirt and a pair of loose drawstring pants he had bought on the way back from the hospital. He stared at the phone, his heart pounding. "I should be looking forward to this," he thought.

He dialed, spoke to the operator, waited, and then heard Carlie's voice, clear, but far away down a long tunnel. "Yes, I'll accept the charges," she said. "Put him on."

"Hi, Honey, it's me. I'm in Hawaii."

"Hi, Sweetheart, yeah, I know," she said casually, "I've been wondering when you were going to call me."

"What? How did you know I was here?" he asked, surprised.

"There was a story about Eddie Padilla in the newspaper in Las Cruces. They made a big thing of it, since his father was just elected to the County Commission. Then Roger Stanton called down here from San Manuel too, to find out if we had heard from you about it. When you still hadn't answered our letters after two weeks, Daddy called the admin office there at Tripler. It was just a hunch, but....well, anyway, we knew where you were, and I'm really glad to hear your voice. How are you feeling?"

"Actually, I'm feeling pretty good. I've got these stitches all over me that hurt like hell, but they're mostly just a nuisance." Kevin closed his eyes and put his finger into his exposed ear to block out the common room, with its babbling TV set and solemn men in pajamas. "I still feel pretty bad about...about Eddie, and the whole Vietnam thing. I don't know, Carlie. My memory has been kind of screwed up, and a lot of things still don't make real clear sense to me. I guess about the only thing I'm sure of is that I love you and George, and you're the only thing that really matters to me."

"Oh, God, Darling, you don't know how much I've wanted to hear you say that," she said, emotion tugging at the corners of her voice. "We miss you so much — and I'm glad you finally decided to call me. I've been just worried sick about you."

"I just wanted to wait until I had a bit better picture of what was happening to me," he said, a bit lamely.

"You could have called me twice, you know. You could have called me every night. But I take it you got some information about what you're going to do?"

"That's what I called to tell you. I'm going to be here another month at least. I got my skin torn up pretty bad — I don't know how much they told you. It's healing up all right, but they want to keep me under observation while I recuperate."

"Oh, Kevin darling, that's wonderful! Well, I mean, it's not wonderful, but it's wonderful I can come to see you, and I've always wanted to see Hawaii. How soon can I come?"

"Soon as you can make the arrangements. We can take a flight out to Maui, stay on the beach a couple of nights, and pretend there's nobody else left in the whole world."

"That sounds just marvelous, Lover, I can hardly wait. But just between you and me, I want to spend my time in one of those beautiful hotels, with room service to bring me buckets of vodka and pineapple juice, and rich tourists running all over the place. Oh, Kevin, I don't care what we do, just so long as we're together every single minute. I do love you so much."

"I love you, too, Carlie, more than anything."

"I'll call the hospital when I get reservations. I guess I better let you go, so you keep your tamale hot just for me, and I'll see you real soon."

"Hey, Hotshot, stitches or no stitches, I'm keeping the whole enchilada hot for you. So, bye bye, now, OK. Love you."

"You too."

She hung up her phone, and he sat for some time holding the receiver to his ear, listening to the empty distance between them. "I love you," he whispered again.

Carlie's flight came in from Los Angeles late at night, so Kevin rented a room in one of the downtown hotels before taking a taxi to pick her up. She ran to him in the airport lobby and hugged him, and he was embarrassed that people stared at him when he cried out in pain. The incident started the visit off on the wrong foot.

They tried to make love, but it was clumsy and strained. She was horrified by his scars, though by then the rows of bristling sutures were gone, and the sepulchral bruises had given way to puffy red welts of new tissue. She tried to assure him that his grotesque disfigurement would never matter to her, and he tried to assure her that he never feared it would. The wounds were still painfully tender, and contact was difficult — even the gentle rhythmic motion of her body kneeling over him set his flesh pulling against the tenuous new bonds in his torn skin.

The experience was far less erotic than it was an act of anxious reassurance. He refused to talk about Vietnam, and insisted that she tell him everything she could remember about little George. She did, and he finally fell into a restless and uncomfortable sleep. They woke early, and lay quietly in bed for a long time, neither wishing to break the silence. They spent late morning shopping for sporting gear, and caught the afternoon flight to Maui.

On the flight over, they met Roz, a young islander who was expecting to meet friends for a weekend of surfing. She was slender, attractive in a homey way, with peeling nose sporting a band of medicated cream, and hair in a shoulder-length blonde frizz. She wore only a knitted halter and a pair of ragged shorts, so full of holes she might as well have been nude, and she carried an Army-green nylon laundry bag as though it contained everything she owned. Though the Harreys were both a bit uncomfortable at first, her freedom from inhibition or exhibitionism soon put them at ease, and they found themselves ignoring the peeking nipples, and instead craning to look down as she described the surf on each beach.

"You two have just got to come with me," she said with matter-of-fact enthusiasm. "Piper, that's my Old Man, and Ken and Britt, who surf with us, have got our tent set up at Honolua. Nothing in the world can improve your outlook faster than learning to surf."

"Do you surf, too?" asked Carlie. "I thought the girls just

stood on the beach and waved."

"I like to catch a small wave once in a while, but mostly, I'm a stand-on-the-beach-and-waver myself." Roz dug into her laundry bag and brought out candied dried papaya, which she passed around. "Britt and the men surf like junkies. She is one of the best surfers in the Islands, and also one of the first women to ever earn a black belt in Shotokan Karate, and maybe, just maybe, the most beautiful body west of Malibu."

Carlie laughed. "Sounds like a woman it would be hard to have fun around."

Roz shrugged. "Depends on what you do for fun."

Roz's friends met them in their rusted-out '58 Olds station wagon, and seemed as delighted as she to invite the two up-tight haoles along on their surfing safari. Britt was about twenty, long and lithe, with full voluptuous curves and smooth, sleek muscles that rolled sensuously when she moved. Her hair and her flawless skin were the same dark honey-gold color, and her eyes were the clearest and palest shade of ice blue. Apparently impervious to sunburn, she wore a bikini and a light coat of oil.

"Sure it's no trouble dragging us along?" Kevin asked as he put the ice chest into the car.

"Ain't no big thing," Britt answered, giving him a casual pat on the behind.

Piper looked like Jesus in cutoff jeans. He was older than the others, perhaps thirty, lean, with powerful shoulders and hard flat-planed calves. "Chopper pilot, huh?" he said with a friendly smile. "I hear you guys play pretty rough."

"Too rough to be fun, that's for sure," Kevin replied.

Ken was smaller, and also in excellent condition. He appeared to be Greek, with dark curly hair and beard, eyes that darted and flashed, and small but full lips smiling impishly.

The six of them jammed themselves into the station wagon, and Piper drove along the winding road which hugged the shoreline and skirted the edge of the towering green crags of the West Maui Mountains. The afternoon was clear except for a few rising columns of clouds crowning the green-shrouded peak of Puu Kukui, which rose from the sea to almost six thousand feet over a distance of only about five miles. In a short time, they arrived at the foot of the beach cliff where they had pitched their tent. Kevin was amused to see that it was a small Army hex-tent, like the one Jake Csynes had lived in. As soon as the car stopped moving, Piper, Britt, and Ken leaped from it and dashed to the tent. Ignoring all else, they grabbed up their surfboards and sprinted toward the water as though expecting it to be gone any minute. "Yeeow! Look at that surf!" howled Piper.

It was impressive, even to a non-surfer like Kevin. The waves rolled in with awesome power, smooth, regular, and impossibly high. They rose up and up, shimmering and changing color from blues to pale green as the afternoon light shone through the clear water. Though he had heard of the phenomenon, Kevin was still surprised to see the crest of a wave curl over to form a rotating tunnel of water. The three surfers hurled themselves into the sea on their boards, and with powerful breast strokes drove through the incoming waves. After a few minutes, they turned toward the shore, paddled furiously a moment, then jumped to their feet. The boards slid down the rising face of the wall of water and sped toward shore so gracefully that the surfers appeared to be flying in front of the wave. When Piper maneuvered himself up the face of the wave and began to work his way back into the whirling funnel of the tubular curl, Kevin found himself involuntarily yelling out with excitement.

"When the old surfers on the beach start calling you 'Kahuna', then you can start thinking about trying that," said Roz, laughing.

Kevin was surprised to see Carlie suddenly run past him, wearing the new bikini swimsuit she had bought in Honolulu. Though her suntan was uneven and she was rounder and softer than the other two women, Carlie still was unusually good looking, and Kevin was pleased to feel himself aroused as he watched her run into the water. She dived head-first into the roiling face of a collapsing wave, then popped up behind it and swam smoothly out to where the others were setting up for their next ride.

The sun felt good on his face, so Kevin took off his shirt and drawstring pants to let the warm rays bathe his tender new skin for a few minutes. Roz gasped in spite of herself when she saw his scars. "Holy shit, what happened?" she asked.

"To tell you the truth, I don't remember," he replied. "They told me I got off easy with just a few scratches."

"Some scratches. Here, I have some aloe vera in my bag. I'll put some of that on them." She peeled the skin from a long green cactus segment which looked like a tentacle, then smeared the goo inside on his scars. "This stuff will fix you right up. It's one of the all-time great healing plants," she assured him.

After a while, Carlie left the water and came up the beach laughing happily. While the surfers continued to worship at their shrine of living jade, Kevin and Carlie set up their small puptent and Roz started a fire in a ring of rocks and cooked chunks of vegetables and pineapple in the hot oil in her wok. When the surfers came to eat, Ken brought some small shellfish he had plucked from the rocks. "Opihi," he said. "Limpets. They're great with a little shoyu." Kevin and Carlie had bought steaks, and they broiled them over the hot coals.

By the time they finished eating, the sky had begun to turn rosy in the west, so Kevin and Carlie walked up a little trail to the top of the beach cliff to watch the sunset. To their left, the Honolua Valley lay already in hazy jungle shade, and across the channel, the island of Molokai wore a crown of flaming cumulus clouds. The sky overhead was clear, but the western horizon was lined with great columns of crimson, thundercells driven up by the tradewinds over Lanai, Kahoolawe, and Molokai. The setting sun reflecting from the bottom surfaces of the clouds cast a warm and intimate light over the cane-covered foothills behind Kevin and Carlie as they stood hand in hand watching the sea turn darker and darker blue.

"Just like home," said Carlie, recalling the way the spectacular sunsets of the New Mexico desert turn the mountains to the east so red at sunset that they bear such names as the Sandias, and the Sangre de Christos, the Spanish words for watermelon and blood. "Oh, Kevin, this is so beautiful, and so romantic. Our friends down there are kind of crazy, but this place is just magic." She stood close to him, took his hand, and reached over to softly stroke his tortured shoulder. "Wouldn't it be wonderful if we could just stay like this from now on?"

He hugged her gently and nodded. "If I could find a way to do it, my sweet Carlie, I would never leave you again," he said, and kissed her tenderly.

After sunset, they sat with the others around the little fire. The surfers had been content to let it die down, but Carlie liked the light, and fed it driftwood sticks to keep it burning. Ken brought an acoustic guitar out of the tent, and sat on an old gnarled log to play and sing as a few joints were handed around.

Carlie asked him if he hoped to make money with his songs, and he scoffed. "I don't have to sell out to the system like that," he said. "I like it better this way."

"You're starting to sound like these hippies we've got back in The States," she said.

"This is The States, love, and I'd be pleased to have it said that I was just a good hippie. The powerful don't like the hippie notion of living without Big Brother because they can't even imagine that much personal freedom. That's why they keep insisting hippies are motivated by the same things which motivate them."

"Which are?" asked Kevin.

"Money, dogmatic ideology to spare them from decisions, bigoted nationalism to assure them they deserve more than all those foreigners, and more and more money. Anyone who can convince them he really doesn't want those things ruling his life, they call an 'anarchist', whatever they think that means."

"So the answer is to become a criminal, and go around breaking the law all the time?" Carlie asked.

"Maybe," Piper interrupted. "I think what you're really asking is why violate the social conventions, not so much the law. I don't break many laws but this one," Piper said, waving the joint he held, "but it is an important case in point. We have made a big issue of marijuana, but what we're really talking about is our belief that the laws should be based on reason and justice, and not just the opinions of the powerful. When the laws are clearly based on ignorance or worse, and the result of trying to enforce them is destructive to society, then it becomes difficult to morally justify obeying the law."

"You have a wonderful way of twisting things around, Piper," said Carlie. "You mean you think it is immoral to obey the law?"

"If the law serves an immoral purpose, where is the righteousness in obeying it? And it isn't just the law. It's other forms of power as well. I used to be an industrial chemist — created new household products. I began to notice some of the products cut costs and pleased the customers, but were hazardous to health. When I pointed this out to management, they told me to mind my own business, and they would use profitable materials until somebody made a law that said they couldn't. And whenever somebody tried to make a law like that, they hired lobbyists, lawyers, maybe even assassins to see to it their stockholders were not betrayed by bleeding-heart busybodies.

"One thing which caught to my attention was tobacco. In America the leading causes of death are heart disease, lung cancer, and emphysema. Old age, murder, and war aren't even in the running. Since those diseases are all associated with cigarettes, the number-one cause of death in our country is tobacco — number O-N-E. Another in the top ten is alcohol. More accidental deaths, violent crimes, and broken homes are associated with alcohol than with any other single factor. The government has been running tests for ten years to try to prove marijuana is harmless, and since they are still testing, that means that they haven't been able to prove it harmful either. Now, let me ask you a question, and let's be fair, OK? Consider this little scenario: Dad gets fired for drinking on the job, and he stops at a bar and spends the rent money consoling himself. He runs over somebody's dog on the way home, where he gets into a fight and beats up Mom. The neighbors call the cops, and when they arrive, they find teenage Junior on the back porch trying to mind his own business listening to some music and smoking a joint. Now, for sixty-four-thousand dollars, who gets arrested? That nasty little degenerate, Junior, that's who!

"Now how do our sane and just leaders handle this tragedy? They impose taxes to subsidize the production of tobacco and alcohol, and they impose more taxes to create an army of narcs — long-haired con-men with badges — to persecute the pot. Next step is giving the cops the right to bust down your door and just come blasting in. Old Dad stands there drinking a beer and waving the red-white-and-blue, and it never occurs to him they have established a precedent that can be used against anybody.

"To protect us from what they alone insist is criminal self-abuse, they take away our privacy, jam our courts and jails with people who have done no harm, create an underworld of big-shot criminals who disrupt the economies of other countries to maintain their market, and they fight that syndicate by hiring more and more secret police to bust the users. We get reduced rights, oppressive government, syndicated crime, increased taxes, lung cancer, alcoholism, and there's even a much worse result."

"What could that be?" asked Carlie.

"The minds of a generation of Americans have been programmed by government violence and injustice to see themselves as outside the law, and their government as an irrational and oppressive force to be hated and feared. Could anything be worse for a nation than that, even, God forbid, a bunch of stoned musicians and gardeners who would rather make love than war?

"The pot issue is just an indicator of the way the people in power these days think. I don't claim to be so smart I can't make a mistake, or so wise I can't do injustice, but the point is I find it pretty hard to let people who think like that make my rules and moral decisions for me. Tell me, Kevin, since you've paid a few dues in this game, can you give me one good reason why a man like you or me should dedicate his life to fulfilling the objectives of any of these political extremist clubs competing for power over the people of the world?"

Kevin stared into the fire and smiled wryly. "To tell you the truth, right now I'm not so sure I can."

"Maybe some clubs live a little bit better than the others," said Carlie.

"Ah, yes," said Piper. "Some of us have more things. That's the other side of the cage, that's all. If you're not shooting somebody to promote your club's right to tell everybody else what to do with their time and their money, you're busting your ass in some sweatshop to buy more things than your neighbor. In America five percent of the world's population consumes forty percent of the resources, and still Americans are out there every day trampling each other down trying to get more. You tell me, Kevin, what makes it so easy for a supposedly free-minded American to agree that he is supposed to spend his one unique human life killing people to promote the careers of a few rich politicians? What keeps all those people living in cold, violent cities struggling at jobs they hate, ready to defend with YOUR life their right to have one more bauble than the next guy. What makes them do it?"

"War is good business," said Ken. "After all, an Isaac or two is small sacrifice, if it means Daddy gets to live in the Garden."

"If you're looking for a reason for the generation gap, that's as good a one as I can think of," said Roz. "It can't make you feel much like one of the family to know that you're being sent away to die so Grandpa and his buddies in the Senate don't get their Social Security payments cut off."

When Ken put down his guitar to listen to Piper, Britt crawled over to the log where he was sitting and wriggled between his knees with her back to him. Without interrupting the conversation, Ken began to massage her shoulders. She leaned back and sighed happily. "The surf is the perfect alternative," she said simply. "We live in the garden already, and we don't have to kill anybody for it."

"Britt, you've got to have some bills," insisted Carlie. "You can only eat so much papaya and...those little oyster things. So how about it? What do you do for money."

Britt laughed — a bit patronizingly, but without malice. "Well, I could always sell dope and turn tricks," she said. Seeing Carlie's face fall, she added, "but I don't. Actually, I own a little cottage on Oahu, which I inherited when my father was killed in Korea, and I earn what money I need by teaching classes to some of the Marines and their wives over at Kaneohe."

"Oh?" asked Kevin. "What kind of classes, Britt?"

"She teaches Japanese Karate," said Ken. "That's how I met her. I went to the Dojo to see if they had a good Tai Chi Chuan instructor. Karate's too yang for me — I prefer the soft forms."

"He's actually pretty good at both," Britt declared. "Well, at least, he will be if he practices a few more years. I was raised with the martial arts. My mother came to the Islands during

World War II — she was a nurse on a Norwegian merchant ship. My father was a Polynesian sailor named Leleo Kahanamoku."

"Gee," said Carlie, "you're half Norwegian and half Hawaiian then?"

"My passport says I'm American, but as far as care, I don't belong to any land. I belong to the sea."

"That's very beautiful," said Carlie, "but what do you think would happen if everybody tried to live like you do?"

Britt shrugged. "I don't believe it makes sense to think about trying to make everybody anything. Besides, it's none of my business. I choose to live free, and if everybody did that, we'd all be free. It's an individual thing, don't you see."

"So all that matters is yourself and surfing?"

"Let me tell you something," put in Roz. "I've got life all figured out, and I've got it reduced down to four simple rules. Want to hear them?"

"This I've got to hear," said Kevin.

"Simple. Rule one is: 'Ain't nothing means shit.' OK? Now, rule two is: 'For a human being to be happy, something has got to mean something to you.' Got it? Rule three says: 'Find something that satisfies rule two without violating rule one', and rule four is: 'Hang onto it, Baby!'"

Kevin laughed. "That's pretty good. Where'd you get it?"

"It's Ecclesiastes, highly condensed."

After a little while Carlie asked, "Can we go to bed pretty soon, Sweetheart? I think I've had all of Paradise I can take for one night." Kevin and Carlie walked in silence back to their little puptent, which they had set up in the hollow between two small grassy dunes, a short way from the surfers' larger tent. After they had crawled inside, she sat beside him and reached over to embrace him gently. "We'll just make our own little tropical Paradise, right here in our own tent," she said. They kissed very slowly and tenderly, and he reached up to stroke her face, and her breasts. "Do you wish I was as pretty as Britt?" she asked him.

"Are you kidding?" he answered, laying her back on the sleeping bag. "If I wanted Johnny Weissmuller with tits, I'd be swinging through the trees, not lying here making love with you."

They lay together quietly for a long time, listening to each other breathe, and enjoying each other's smells. Hers was rich, dark, like the throat-grabbing sweetness of orchid, or daffodil. His musk burst forth in his armpits, and the sharp feral odor cut through the cool salt smell of the sea and hung about them like an enveloping cloak.

"I had a long talk with Colonel Hernandez," he said after a while. "He's the guy who makes the decisions around here....about what happens to guys like me."

"OK," she replied, "what happens to guys like you?"

"There's still a chance I might end up with a medical discharge. Not for these scars, of course. I had a brain concussion, you know, and they still aren't sure just whether or not that did any lasting damage. I don't know. There's still a lot I don't remember."

"Would that keep you out? I mean, if you don't remember?"

"Don't know. I don't think so. I think the chances of my going back to Vietnam in a couple of weeks are pretty good."

"So soon? How much longer will you have to stay?"

"Well, you see, I had so little time left to go, it might be possible they'll just drop the remainder of the tour."

"Then you won't have to go back? Kevin, what are you trying to tell me?"

"You remember I wrote you that I put in for the direct commission to First Lieutenant? Well, it appears there is a very good chance that will come through -- before I leave here."

"Sweetheart, how wonderful! Oh, Darling, congratulations!" She sat up and bounced happily, squeezing herself to keep from hugging him excitedly. Then she saw he was smiling softly and looking off into the night. "Kevin? What is it?" Then her eyes widened. "Oh. Oh, I understand. When you go back, it will be for another year, won't it?" He nodded. "Oh, God. Oh, God, Kevin. I'm so happy for you, but I don't know if I can stand another year away from you." Suddenly, agonizingly, she broke into tears. "I was hoping so much you could get assigned to Panama, like Daddy. It would have been your dream assignment, and we'd have been together, and....and everything."

"They just upped the ante on me," he said, holding her gently.

"I don't know how I can stand it. It's so hard being a single mother, and waiting, and never knowing -- and being alone." She cried on his shoulder, her tears running along the puckered ridges of his scars.

"It will be all right," he said, inanely. "We'll be fine."

She sniffed back her tears, then sat up and held her head erect. "I'm sorry. I'm sorry, I was only thinking of myself. Of course we'll be fine. Oh, Darling, I'm so proud of you. You're so brave, and so good. I wish we could just go away together somewhere forever, and never have to look at another uniform or another helicopter. But don't you worry. I got through the first year with little George being born, and I got through a year of your being in flight school and only getting to come home on weekends, and I got through this year, and I'll goddamn-well get through the next one, too! I don't know what I'm crying about. I knew when we started this, I'd have to make some sacrifices so you can be who you want to. We started this together, and we'll finish it together! All right?"

He nodded. "You bet," he said, quickly taking her into his arms so he could hold her and reassure her without having to look into her eyes.

THIRTEEN

Kevin lay in his room and listened to the screech and chatter of birds. Carlie was three thousand miles away, back in her little apartment in El Paso. She had stayed a week, then left to continue classes she had begun in business skills — keypunch operator training — at El Paso University.

After the night on Honolua Bay, they spent their time in proper haole fashion, seeing the sights and shopping. Carlie was delighted with the picturesque old whaling village of Lahaina, and they spent the night in the old Pioneer Inn. The next day they returned to Oahu to tour historical sites and see the Pageant of the Long Canoes. They enjoyed gorging at a huge luau buffet, and they slept in a room with a waterbed. It was good time. They went, and saw, and did, and ate, and drank, and screwed, and laughed, and forgot. The last thing she said before she left was, "I wish we could have our cake and eat it too, but I'll be brave. I'll do it for us."

He lay in his room in Honolulu, and he remembered clearly what he would have to face when he returned to Vietnam, the fat greasy puffs of flak exploding around him, the Roman-candle comets of fifty-caliber fireballs, and the streaking flamebees of machinegun tracers. He remembered the smells of cordite, and burning oil and shit, and he remembered crouching in a dark wet hole and crying. He remembered what it was like to live in fear, and he didn't want to go back.

The A Lan Valley was once again an American stronghold, and Kevin knew the next step would surely be the invasion of North Vietnamese staging areas in Laos. As a result of his having been assigned to Jake Csynes' unit, he was one of a very small group of pilots who had already been there. And since Death had taken The Major on the slopes overlooking the Promised Land, it was he on whom the mantle had fallen, he who had been chosen to raise his own torn body from its bed and to carry forward the standard in Jake the Snake's name. "Ironic," he thought. "Even dead, the son of a bitch is still likely to get me killed."

Then he remembered that the others he had flown with — the ones who were still alive — would be going home just about the time he got back. He would be working with a new group of men, most of them fresh from flight school. Sometime during the year, they would be equipped with the new Cobra gunships, and he would lead them on the invasion of Laos.

"It will be different this time," he thought. "I've got nothing personal left to prove, and I'm not going to promote some political or moral notion — I'll just have to turn my head and do my job. The sad fact is I'm only doing this for a good life with Carlie and George."

"There's got to be a better way," he said aloud. He rose from the bed and paced the room. Outside, thunder boomed, and the wind made a great rushing in the trees where the birds had chattered. Rain began to fall in great splattering drops. Kevin opened the door and let the cool wet breeze sweep through. He stood feeling the thundershower around him for a time, then went to his suitcase and pulled out a plastic bag containing a generous handful of sticky green buds of Maui Wowie, marijuana which he had bought from Piper before leaving Honolua Bay. He crushed one of the aromatic dried flowertops and rolled a fat joint. He looked out at the sparkling sheets of sunlit rain, and he listened to the distant sounds of the TV set in the common room and someone laughing a few rooms away. "Fuck it," he said. He flicked open his Zippo, lit the joint, and drew a deep toke. "So what are they going to do about it?" he asked himself, "Send me to Vietnam?"

It was only three days later that a knock came on his door. He opened it to a warrant officer and a sergeant wearing military police brassards. "Mr. Harrey, we have come to investigate a report that someone in this room has been smoking marijuana," said the officer, looking most apologetic.

In a few hours, he stood once again before the desk of Colonel Hernandez. "Mr. Harrey, I don't know what to say. I don't believe I have ever misread a man so badly," he said.

Kevin was prepared to stand at attention barking, "Yes, Sir! Yes, Sir!" as he was tongue-lashed and eventually sentenced, but he was astonished to hear the colonel speak with such sincerity. "Sir, with all respect," he said, "what makes you think just because you found out I smoke marijuana, any of those other things you read about me are suddenly not true?"

"Well," replied the colonel, a bit gruffly, "no doubt you really did what you did, but the risk to which you were exposing the other men in your helicopter is inexcusable. Were you high on marijuana when you flew your last mission?"

Kevin hesitated, and looked at the colonel searchingly for a moment, "I don't know. Probably not, to tell you the truth. It is possible, if I was particularly scared about the mission."

"You take the marijuana to escape from the fear?"

"What's wrong with that, Sir? If you had a pill you could prescribe that would take away fear, wouldn't you issue it? Besides, it's not that big a thing. It doesn't turn you into a fearless killing machine, or a mindless idiot. It's more like coffee, only it goes the other way."

The colonel paused a long time, then nodded. "Yes. Just like coffee. I am afraid I cannot share your casual attitude about drug abuse. And in any case, that is not the issue here. You appear to be in violation of the Uniform Code of Military Justice concerning possession of marijuana. It is a serious offense, directly involving your flight status and your security clearance. It becomes very difficult to consider the thought of you leading a flight of aircraft on a sensitive mission."

Kevin felt himself bristling. "Let me get this straight, Sir. After you were going to promote me for flying covert missions into neutral countries, and you awarded me for shooting people who don't want to vote for our candidates in their country, you're going to tell me because I smoke marijuana, you can't trust me to lead in the invasion of Laos? Sir, I just can't understand that kind of thinking."

"It's very simple. If you can't even trust an officer to obey the law, how can you trust him to obey orders?"

"Yes. Yes, Sir, I understand that perfectly. I'm afraid that looks like the bottom line to me too. There is only one crime, and that is not obeying orders. Heil Hitler."

"Just what is that supposed to mean?"

"Sir, there doesn't seem to me to be a significant difference between the legal government of Nazi Germany officially declaring that Jews were the enemies of the state, and therefore every German's right and duty was to exterminate them, and America's declaring the Vietnamese the enemies of the state, and therefore it is every American's right and duty to exterminate them. And all my life I've been hearing about how those German soldiers were morally degenerate because they didn't have the courage to stand up and tell their leaders they refused to do something that was immoral. Then I read in the newspapers that Americans who have stood up and refused to kill Vietnamese on moral grounds are being beaten, arrested, shot at, and run out of the country as amoral cowards. It's really confusing, Sir."

The colonel sat with jaw agape and gazed bleakly at Kevin, confused, defeated, a bit hurt, as though personally betrayed. Kevin was embarrassed, having prepared himself only for anger and abuse. "But how can you not see?" the colonel asked finally, almost pleading. "The difference is that Hitler was wrong."

"Yes, Sir, I see," said Kevin resignedly.

The colonel shook his head. "How a man of your record could possibly...." he began, then stopped. "Mr. Harrey, I guess we have everything we need, so you may return to your quarters until I decide what should be done with you."

The colonel's decision was not long in coming, and Kevin found himself again before the desk. "First of all," Hernandez told him, "your flight status has been indefinitely suspended. You can get it back by standing before a Court Martial and being acquitted. If you are found guilty, you could face imprisonment. On the other hand, you could waive your right to a Court Martial, accept disposition under Article 15 of the UCMJ, in which case the matter will be handled administratively by your Commanding Officer — that would be myself — and no record of the offense will follow you into civilian life. You will be returned immediately to your home of record, and there given a General Discharge on medical grounds."

Kevin's breath caught cold in the back of his throat, and tremendous flush engulfed his body. "Sir, I will be pleased to accept your decision under Article 15," he said immediately.

"I thought you would," said Hernandez grimly. He opened a file which lay at hand and turned it to face Kevin. According to the documents, he was being released as no longer able to perform his duties because combat stress had led to such compulsive behavioral reactions and perceptual irregularities as partial loss of memory, a tendency to escape from reality through abuse of controlled substances, and moral confusion.

"My memory loss was due to getting hit on the head, wasn't it?" he asked.

"Perhaps," Hernandez answered, "but that won't justify giving you a medical discharge."

Kevin bent again to sign the documents, then noticed an item which read "Degree of Disability: 0 %."

"That's right," said the colonel. "You are not qualified to perform as an officer or helicopter pilot, but no disability is evident here to keep you from doing anything else. I hope I never see the day when veterans of this war are paid a disability pension because they fell victim to dope and subversive thought.

"As soon as you have signed these papers, you may return to your quarters to pack your things. You will be outprocessed here this afternoon, and will depart tonight by Military Air Transport to be returned to, uh, Fort Bliss, Texas, I believe."

"That's right, Sir." Kevin quickly signed the papers.

"You know, Harrey, I see boys go home every day with pieces missing, brave boys who gave it all they had, and who have to face the future from a wheelchair, or following a dog. It makes me want to break down and cry...every day. But it's men like you who get to me the worst. To have so much, and to throw it away for weakness of character. That will be all, Mr. Harrey." He answered Kevin's salute with a perfunctory wave and returned his attention to his work.

Seventy-two hours later, more or less, Kevin found himself at a dinner table in the Fort Bliss Officers' Club trying to explain to Carlie and her parents how it was that he had suddenly become a twenty-five-year-old civilian with a GED high school diploma and no employable skills.

"I don't know," he told them. "They said it was because I have loss of memory, and confusion, sometimes. They took a bunch of tests, and decided I can't fly for a living any more. So they just turned me loose."

"Good heavens, man," said Major Gold, "If you had pressed for it, I'm sure we could have convinced them to let you take the Infantry commission. You could step right into any lieutenant slot in the Army, and you could have been right back on the line. You'd have done just fine." Charles Gold looked stiff and vulnerable in the dark gray civilian suit he wore, like a man without his accustomed armor. He spoke too loudly and with too much conviction. "I can't understand why they didn't find some way to keep such a fine officer — especially with a war on."

"Daddy, I'm sure they did everything they could," said Carlie. "You don't have to have a coronary, and it isn't Kevin's fault anyway."

"I'm sorry, you're right, of course," said Gold, blushing. He pulled his neck down into his collar like a turtle. "We're just going to have to get used to the idea that, uh, that Kevin is going to be a civilian from now on."

"Oh, Chuck, don't sound so depressed," said the Golds' close friend and dinner companion, Mabel Bassett. "There are worse things than being a civilian." Like Carlie's mother Alice Gold, Mabel was several years older than the major. She was a civil service administration employee with a twenty-year record of perfect attendance on the job.

Kevin sat subdued at the table, taking what advantage he could of their willingness to permit him to be uncommunicative until he had "adjusted". He found himself feeling as though he were inside some kind of big puppet, peering out through hooded eye holes at strangers. There was Gold, doing his best to make polite conversation, to find something in his manuals for behavior to help him say the right things, and do the right things, so he wouldn't have to live with the fact that his son-in-law was no longer one of the Family In Green. There were Alice and Mabel, two powdered and prissy old birds in beige satin blouses and narrow tweed skirts, clucking with motherly consolation that the system would surely find a place for him. And there was Carlie, made-up and dressed like a debutante. She welcomed him, she made love to him, she fussed-over and served him, but the girl inside the pretty puppet kept her eyes hooded also, and had not spoken to Kevin.

Sucking her third Old Fashioned and peering solicitously over the top of her half-lens reading glasses, Alice asked, "You will be getting a disability pension, won't you, Kevin?"

"Uh, I believe not, Alice," he said. "They told me I got a zero-disability discharge because I wasn't disabled, I just couldn't fly anymore. I really wasn't in a position to argue."

"But surely you will get some income?" Alice persisted.

"I'm afraid not," Kevin said apologetically. "I believe I do get my full VA education benefits, though."

"Oh, then you and Carlie will both be going to school?" asked Mabel.

Kevin laughed with embarrassment and glanced at Carlie, who was paying very close attention to her salad. "We really haven't had time to make many decisions yet. I'd like to just spend some time together through the holiday season, then jump into whatever we're going to do when the spring semester starts."

"That's probably a very good idea, Kevin," said Major Gold. "In the meanwhile, no doubt, you'll be looking for some kind of a job, won't you?"

"Yessir, I guess so."

"Good. Good. I'll tell you one thing for sure, we're going to have to get you to the barber shop. I don't mean to make fun of a man's misfortune, but you do look pretty strange with that red shag rug you've got growing there."

"I've been thinking about just letting it grow," Kevin said.

"I hope not," said Carlie. "I don't know if I could handle your looking like one of those hippies we met on Maui."

"Maybe that's what we ought to do," Kevin said eagerly, "go live on the beach somewhere and be hippies. No, no, sorry, I was just kidding. Speaking of the beach, Chuck, I understand you're being transferred to the Canal Zone?"

"Yes, that's right," said Major Gold. "We'll be leaving immediately after Christmas. It's too bad you couldn't have taken that commission. I'm sure we could have found a way to get you assigned down there with us. You know Carlie and her mother have never really been apart before, and I just don't know what either of them is going to do."

"Oh, Daddy, I'm sure we'll both be fine," said Carlie. "Everybody says the Canal Zone is just one big officers' club, and God knows I'll have enough to do with Georgie, and trying to go to school....part-time, maybe."

Kevin quickly found he was very interested in his own salad, and there was a long moment of silence. Then the major cleared his throat and announced magnanimously, "Well, whatever you kids decide to do, we're with you all the way, and if you get into a bind, be sure to let us know what we can do to help." It was an assurance Kevin heard often over the next few weeks. No particular help was ever proposed. "You just let us know."

Kevin moved into Carlie's one-bedroom apartment, and for the first time in his life found himself living with a little kid. George Harrey was two and a half, and accustomed to his mother's attention. He was a beautiful child, with curly blond hair and wide-set dark eyes, and a big grin like hers. Kevin's heart was moved to see that he looked so much like Carlie, but he was astonished at the extent the little tyrant controlled her. George still slept in a crib in Carlie's bedroom. He woke up when they went to bed, and wanted to jump in to snuggle with his mother, and he sneaked in during the early hours of the morning. Feeling as much in need of her reassurance as he knew little George must, Kevin wanted to snuggle the baby's Mama a bit himself, and found it frustrating that she insisted the "togetherness" was good for the family. He put up with it until the first time Georgie peed the bed, then he felt entitled to demand that huggie-time be huggie-time, and beddie-time be beddie-time, and neither he nor Georgie be given further opportunity to invade each other's beds. Carlie agreed to the demand, but she let the boy slip into the bed in the early hours, and when Kevin ordered him back to his crib, George threw a screaming fit.

"Now look what you've done!" Carlie shrieked. "How do you expect him to like you if all you do is keep him away from me?"

"Look, if you want to sleep with him, do it in his bed!"

"Well, all right, I will! Come here, Georgie." Grabbing up the howling child, she climbed into the crib, which immediately caved in under them and crashed to the floor.

"I just want to know if I still have a bed, that's all," Kevin cried in raging anguish.

"Just what do you expect me to do?" she bawled.

"I don't know. I just feel like a guest you all have to be nice to. I'm sorry I'm not an Army officer any longer, but I keep hoping somebody will be glad I'm here anyway."

With George peering smugly from beneath her arm, she controlled her crying. "I am glad you're back," she said contritely.

"There, you see what I mean?" he pointed out. "You said, 'I'm glad you're back,' and not 'I'm glad you're home.'"

The bed went into the living room, and the bedroom became Georgie's room, and Carlie's dressing room. The nights became more pleasant, but the matter of control was far from resolved. Money was another immediate source of discord. Carlie was accustomed to receiving a regular allotment check. Their savings amounted to about five months at the allotment rate, and the only income source he had to propose was the VA education money, about half of the allotment if he went full-time. "I don't see how I'll manage with you bringing home so much less," she complained.

"That's the first thing," he informed her. "I'll manage. We're going to have to cut back on the expenses, so I'll need to see exactly where it's been going this last year. Get out the checkbook, and the bills for all those credit cards."

"What?" she squawked indignantly. "Those are my accounts. What makes you think you can come in here like some kind of male chauvinist pig and just start running my affairs?"

"They're not your affairs. You act like that was your personal income you've been spending just because the checks came with your name on them. Don't forget I was out there getting shot at about twice a week to earn that money you're so quick to tell me is none of my business." The books revealed quickly where the money had been going. "At least it's pretty clear we'll be able to reduce our expenses very easily. All we have to do is stop having lunch and drinks at the club, and get rid of all these department store credit cards."

"How come you only want to cut out my expenses?" she whined.

"I have no expenses to cut out," he replied. "The only expenses I've ever had are cleaning my uniforms and sending all the rest home to you. I'm just tickled shitless you and Alice have had such a good time spending it, but that's over now."

"I'll still need clothes, and cosmetics and things to wear to school."

"That's another matter, Honey. In order for me to get full VA benefits, I'll have to go to school full time. If you stay in school, we'll have to hire somebody to take care of the baby, not to mention the cost of your tuition and books and things."

"I could take fewer hours."

"Yes, except EPU is on the other side of town. If I'm going full-time, and you're going part-time, who drives the car? You would have to come with me all day, and you would have to pay for babysitting all day, and neither of us would be working."

"You're telling me I have to quit school," she accused.

"I'm not telling you — though you seem to be looking for someone to blame. The situation just is as it is. I'm not trying to make it that way. You've got a baby, and somebody has to take care of him all the time. If I go to school full-time and get a moonlight job too, I can keep us afloat, I'm sure. But that will mean you have to be a full-time mother."

"I'll go crazy! God, I'll turn into one of those baggy frazzled housewives. Kevin, I just couldn't stand that. I'm sorry, I'll do everything I can, but I just won't stay cooped up like that!"

Kevin met with an admissions counselor at the University, and he and Carlie worked out a tentative schedule for the coming semester. He would take a full complement of hours, all in the morning. Leaving George and Carlie at home, he could drive to early classes and return in time for her to drive to an office building where she would work half-time as a keypunch operator. He would stay home while she worked, where he could study, keep an eye on George, and help take care of the apartment.

Neither Charles nor Alice Gold ever set foot inside the apartment, a fact which Kevin noticed with both resentment and gratitude. Alice occasionally took George for a few hours, if he were properly dressed, and delivered to her, and the Golds made a point of inviting the Harreys out to dinner at least once a week at the Club. Kevin found the ritual celebration of Familyness a tedious affair, and it disturbed him to know that he could have run his entire household on the money Gold spent taking them out eating. He also quietly resented knowing Carlie lived for those evenings.

The topic of Vietnam was carefully avoided. Gold had once started into it, asking him, "So what do you think, Harrey? Are the boys about to clean up that Vietnam situation?"

Kevin had taken a long breath, then said, "It will probably be a while before I get it all sorted out, but to tell you the truth, everything I saw over there leads me to conclude that we're being made fools of. The Vietnamese come in two groups: the ones who hate us bad enough to fight us, and the ones who want our money bad enough to sell out their country to get it. Our moral and political position is so weak in the minds of the people that we don't have a chance of winning. We might destroy Ho Chi Minh's people, but we'll never defeat them, because they believe they're right. Sometimes I think maybe they are right."

"Good God, Man, they're Communists!" the major reminded him, looking around horrified to see if someone might have heard the shaggy-headed young man's heresy.

When the haircut was not forthcoming in spite of Gold's offer to pay for it, the family found a restaurant off-post for their evenings together, and the dinner table conversation revolved around Carlie's work, the vacation in the restaurants of Waikiki, and the things Alice and Mabel had read in the Ladies' Home Journal.

One evening about the middle of December, Carlie was late getting home from work. George knew what time it was, and he was anxious. Kevin had gone to extra effort to make the baby and the apartment look good, and he was afraid George would make a mess. Suspecting she had gone off to have coffee somewhere with Alice, he had worked up a good self-righteously-abused pout by the time she finally arrived.

"Well, you finally decided to come home," he mooned.

"Don't talk to me, you asshole!" she snapped, and bursting into tears, she fled to George's bedroom and slammed the door.

Suddenly chilled from scalp to sole, Kevin stared after her in horror. He stepped to the door and knocked on it softly. "Honey? Look, uh....all right, so I'm an asshole. Just what was it I did that...."

"I just found out why you got thrown out of the Army! Mabel ran a query on your file, because Daddy didn't believe they would discharge you without disability. And boy, was he right! Asshole! You've really got your nerve, telling us all it was because you got wounded."

"I did get wounded! That doesn't count any more?"

"Nothing counts any more! Leave me alone!"

Charles Gold told Alice to tell Carlie if he never saw Kevin again, that would still be too soon. "I told you so," he shouted at Alice. "I knew that boy was nothing but a dogface with a slick line the day I met him, and as far as I'm concerned, he has just screwed the pooch!"

A week before Christmas, a delivery truck brought several boxes to the apartment, including two hundred dollars worth of toys and dress-up clothes for George, and a new portable dishwasher. The driver of the truck handed them a card which read, "Merry Christmas to: Carl and Family, Love, Mother and Dad," in an ornate script written by someone at the store. On the 20th of the month, Major and Mrs. Gold left their home in the hands of the movers and departed two weeks early for Panama.

Though disgusted with Kevin, Carlie tried to keep her job and their apartment. Kevin left for school before dawn. Georgie lay quietly in his crib until Daddy left, then ran to jump into bed with Carlie, who began staying there later and later. When he arrived home at midday, she met him at the door smoking impatiently, anxious to depart. Then he took over the house and George, and tried to get some studying done during the afternoon.

Carlie kept the TV set on all the time, and George was furious when Kevin tried to turn it off to study. If he locked the child into his bedroom, he would get into Carlie's make-up, or the toothpaste, and he would have a fight with her when she got home. If he tried to control him, he threw tantrums which were reported to Carlie by the neighbors. Left alone in the yard, he ate dirt and fell down, leaving scrapes and bruises to explain to Mama before dinner. Placed on a leash — a safety line, that was — he almost hanged himself from the kitchen doorknob. He would sit and watch the TV, but the attention-demanding babble kept Kevin from concentrating.

Carlie began to leave more and more of the housework undone. When he found himself having to wash last night's dishes and hers from breakfast to fix lunch for George and himself, he made a fuss, and was sent dodging a hail of dirty cups and bowls.

"You worthless shit!" she howled. "If you don't like washing dishes, just go smoke dope somewhere and forget all about us. We'll get along just fine without you. And now look what you've done. I just spent two hours getting ready for work so we can have a little money around here, and now you've got my makeup running all over my face!"

His attempts to study in the evenings met with frustration also. When Carlie arrived home after work, she did not want to be bothered with a baby who mooned to crawl on her, nor with his hungry Daddy, nor with a hot stove, nor greasy dishwater. She wanted to take a hot bath, be served dinner, and watch TV until time to go to bed. Their sex life dropped off to nothing immediately.

Kevin's grades were not good. He recognized immediately that the syllabus was designed to consume — and thereby control — as much of the students' time as possible. Excess time, however, was not Kevin's problem. With Alice to watch the baby, Charles to take her out to dinner, and Kevin to send her the money, Carlie had been able to treat her studies as a hobby, and her grades had been very good. "I don't see why you're having so much trouble," she harped. "I did it alone, and with an infant. Don't complain to me until you've tried raising an infant while your husband is off someplace."

"Yeah, off someplace sending you a big fat check."

"Now I'm bringing home the check, so don't piss on my leg!"

Kevin didn't like going on the base at Fort Bliss at all, and Carlie had neither the time nor the money to spend with her old friends, the wives and daughters of Army officers. Having concluded that getting involved socially with anyone from the school would be the fastest way to cause more trouble at home, Kevin kept to himself on campus. He avoided the colorful, gregarious, and sappily-earnest young flower children who made up a large part of the student body, and also the stiff-stomping, chaw-chomping, big-hat shit-kickers who made up the rest of it. When he had free time on campus, he sat in the student coffee shop reading his assignments, a scarred, sullen-faced, and shaggy-haired young man wearing an Army field jacket and clutching a cup of coffee, alone.

One afternoon he received a package of mail which had been forwarded to him from Hawaii. It included a letter from Piper and Roz, inviting him and Carlie to come to live with them in a mountain cabin in the hills south of San Francisco. At first the idea thrilled him, and he thought their way out had been revealed to him. Then he considered for a moment how Carlie might really react to his suggesting they do it, and he tossed the letter aside. There were also several envelopes containing fifty-dollar savings bonds made out to him. He laughed, remembering how that lunatic Skip Gilman had put on a combination song-and-dance, revival sanctification, and epileptic fit to get him to buy into the chain-letter which had swept Vietnam briefly while he was there. The letter used the bonds as payoff, and had for that reason been approved by the Judge Advocate General's office. He had several more tucked away uncashed in his old suitcase — his parachute, as he called the stash. The other item in the package was a colorfully emblazoned certificate and a packet of orders awarding him the Air Medal for Valor for his participation in the mission on which he had been shot down. The orders included several other names, including Warrant Officers Harold Gilman, Peter Hawking, Raymond Swomney (post.), and Eduardo Padilla (post.). He put the entire packet beneath his old fatigues in his suitcase, and resolved that he would never show any of it to anyone.

Seeing Eddie's name on the orders brought back a flood of memories. He felt some remorse that he had not been able to bring himself to drive up to Las Cruces to offer his condolences to Eddie's family, but he was unable to confront the notion of sitting with a group of strangers exchanging maudlin platitudes about a boy he had not known, and a man they had not known. He did suggest to Carlie one evening that they put Georgie in the car and drive up to San Manuel to visit Roger Stanton. "We can probably meet a whole new group of people up there, Honey, people who have never even been on an Army base. Maybe we can start learning to put all that behind us."

She immediately shook her head and replied, "Oh, no, no, I really don't want to go up there. You can go if you like, but I just can't handle the guns-and-beer atmosphere."

For a short while they thought they had found friends in Andy and Valerie Delbeni, who introduced them to The Exciting World of Aloe-Magic-21. Valerie picked up Carlie window-shopping at a dress store, and invited her to attend a "shower" at her home for some friends who were launching a new business venture. At the party, Andy got up and delivered the most exciting, inspiring, and enticing presentation Kevin had ever seen. The friends for whom the shower was being held were an older couple who had just invested their savings in Delbeni's amazing new form of business, selling a product of such righteousness that Kevin was moved to rise to his feet.

"Mr. Delbeni, I want to show you something. I'm sitting here listening to you tell about how your cosmetics are made of Aloe Vera, and I've just got to tell you what Aloe Vera did for me." To Carlie's astonishment, he took off his shirt and raised his arms. The dozen or so people in the room gasped to see the pink octopus-print of puckered tissue. "I got hurt, in Vietnam, and these scars had me locked up so I couldn't even move. Then on a beach in Hawaii, a woman I met there put fresh Aloe Vera on all my scars, and now look! See, I've got full movement. I thought nobody else had even heard of Aloe Vera."

Andy Delbeni walked across the room like he had just discovered Cassius Clay in his home. "What is your name?!" he demanded, reverently.

"Uh, I'm Kevin Harrey."

"Kevin, I have been looking for you. I have been praying that I would find you. Now, I don't want to blow your mind....is this your wife? Carlie, isn't it? Well, Carlie I want you to take a deep breath, because I am going to make your husband a very...Rich...MAN!" Delbeni pumped his hand, put his arm around his bare shoulders, and waved to the group for applause.

Carlie was reluctant to commit their savings, but she let herself be persuaded, and they bought their distributorship. She called some of the women she knew at Fort Bliss, and the women with whom she worked, and invited them to showers at Delbeni's fancy house. After a month, they had put four hundred dollars on the credit cards paying for the food, the drinks, and the cosmetic samples consumed at the showers, and no one had shown the least interest in becoming involved. Two of their guests had even made apologies and left during the presentation.

Trusting that he would quickly earn their savings back many fold, and that he would no longer need a college degree to earn a living, Kevin let his studies slide while he cruised coffee shops and department stores looking to strike up a conversation to entice someone to a congratulatory shower for friends. Carlie took her little kit of cosmetic samples, and tried to sell orders. She got a few, but the company was slow in filling them, and the shipping costs consumed most of her profits.

Then an article appeared in the El Paso Times warning its readers of certain high-pressure sales organizations which were operating "pyramid programs" in the city. A week later, Andy and Valerie Delbeni packed their new Fleetwood Brougham, gave Kevin and Carlie a box of samples and an address from which to order product, assured them they would be back in a month, and left town.

"I knew it," said Carlie after Kevin's humiliating first attempt to give the presentation. "So what are you going to do now? If you don't get your grades up, you won't even get your VA check. And what about the credit cards? You have been buying lunch for everybody you could find you thought was a sucker. How are we going to pay for all that?"

"I don't know," he growled, feeling worthless and foolish. "I've never been paid for anything in my life except shooting people who didn't deserve it, but I'll find something."

Then he found among Carlie's cluttered papers a current bill from one of the credit cards he thought she had destroyed. It revealed she had gone several times to the Club and had run up another hundred dollars. When he confronted her, she collapsed in tears and confessed she had been meeting Mabel in the mornings and returning in time for him to get home from class. "I just had to have somebody to talk to," she wailed.

He raged about trust, and about the money, and about the secrecy, and about going to some stuffy old busybody to talk about him, no doubt, and about how he felt betrayed that she would sneak away to take her pleasure in a place she knew he was not welcome.

She took it for a long time, then turned on him in cold fury. "Don't talk to me about betrayal, Kevin. Four years I have paid and paid so we could have something decent. I have lived in crummy Army quarters and lonely little apartments waiting for you to get your shit together. I have sat alone night after night crying because I didn't know if my baby was going to have a father one more day. I put up with all the hardships because I believed in you, that you were going to make something of yourself. I did my part, Kevin! I suffered for you, and all I've got to show for it is a dopehead ex-pilot with no education, no job, no future, and no good goddamn sense! You resent taking care of our child so I can go out and work to pay some of the goddamn bills, and you won't even wash the goddamn dishes! You're flunking out of remedial English, but I have to quit college so you can study business. Then you blow our entire savings on some stupid con-game. I want out, Kevin! Out, out, OUT! I want you out of my life, and I will get along just fine with my baby and my job."

The Golds backed her up. She made a long-distance collect call to Panama, and after thirty dollars worth, made her peace with Alice. They agreed to cover all the costs of the divorce, and to pay for professional day-care for George, so she could work half-time and go back to school half-time. All she had to do was promise never to speak to Kevin Harrey again.

The proceedings were swift. She was awarded the car, the appliances including the new Christmas dishwasher, the furniture, the household goods, the TV set, and George. He was awarded his old suitcase of personal belongings, half of the bills for the credit cards, and an obligation to make child support payments almost as large as his total Veteran's benefits check.

When his next monthly check arrived, he considered his options and concluded if he were to establish a residence near the school, and get a job which would enable him to pay his court-determined obligation to Carlie, he would not be able to carry enough hours of classes to maintain his full-time benefits. The checks were going to be smaller since the divorce, anyway. He cashed the check at the bank and walked back to the apartment, where he began to pack his suitcase. Certain at first that he would be forced to grudgingly leave many of his belongings behind, he was surprised to see how little there was to take or leave. He recognized sadly how little time he and Carlie had ever lived together during the three years they had been married. Her house had never been his home, and with the exception of a few bric-a-brac souvenirs of his first Vietnam tour, there was nothing of him in it. In the back of her closet, he found a suit he had bought in flight school, and in an old trunk under the TV set, he found a box containing his personal archive — class pictures from boot camp, a high school junior class yearbook, a few old letters from Carlie, notes from his correspondence-course studies for his GED, and other little pieces of his past. He stood in the middle of the bedroom and hardly dared touch anything, overwhelmed by the hollow and helpless feeling that he would never know more of his son than an infant he had visited while he was in flight school, and the little kid who had hated him the past few months. On a bedroom shelf, he saw his flight-school graduation picture. He decided to leave it. Perhaps that would be all George would ever remember of him — a picture of a proud-faced boy in an oversized Army hat. She might even tell him his father died in Vietnam.

He left the suit, put the suitcase and the archive box beside the door, and stuffed the pile of savings bonds he had won in the chain letter into his pocket. Then he walked a few blocks to the mile-long stretch of used-car lots which fed on the military population from Fort Bliss, Biggs Air Force Base, and White Sands Missile Range. He shopped for an hour, then bought a battered but sound old Ford van. The interior had been partially paneled, and a foam-padded bench/bed built in the back. The outside still carried the logo of a Mexican food company, a grinning Disney-dog peon wearing a huge sombrero, across the hatband of which was written, "Caribe Pete". Kevin left the motor running as he stepped into the apartment to pick up his belongings. He looked around one last time, opened the refrigerator and decided he deserved at least the luxury of taking Carlie's last Coke, and departed.

Four blocks away, he was confronted with his first decision point. If east, to where? Back to east Texas, to the little family farm, to Bibles, service-station jobs, racists and rednecks, and to another family who wouldn't want to hear how we're losing the war? No. He had joined the Army to escape that world, and he had no desire to return. If west, to where? In his pocket with the two hundred dollars left after buying Caribe Pete he had the letter from Roz and Piper. Somewhere in the hills between San Francisco and Santa Cruz, they had written, they had a mountain cabin with an extra room. That looked like the best shot. He turned toward the entrance to Highway 10W, and resolved that he would not look back until he hit the California border. "Some future," he marveled. "I have two families I don't belong to, a country I can't trust, and which will never again trust me, not one credential or skill I can use legally, and my best shot at basic subsistence is a spare room in some hippie's mountain shack. Welcome home, War Hero."

FOURTEEN

Twenty minutes out of El Paso, Kevin encountered the exit to San Manuel. Across the Mesilla Valley, he could see Roger Stanton's house, the Green Castle. On impulse, he took the exit to the quiet little village. Even with the wires and neon signs, San Manuel looked like a transplant from the previous century. On the back streets — two blocks from the main plaza — the old adobe buildings had settled so far that the window ledges were almost at the level of the dirt streets. Kevin started to take the road to Stanton's home, then decided to stop and call ahead first. He parked behind a hulking Powerwagon painted in camouflage colors, and stepped into Chato's Bar.

He caught the bartender's attention to ask for a phone when he heard Roger Stanton's booming guffaw from the back of the room. He ordered two bottles of Coors and two shots of tequila. "I'll be with Big Rog," he said, handing the plumply attractive young woman a five.

"I'll bring your drinks, Cutie," she said with a big grin.

Kevin walked back into the dark bar and found Roger sitting with two young Mexican women. They were dressed in low-cut secretary costumes, with their hair teased into huge beehives, and their eyes made up like orchid raccoons. Each one was juggling a cigarette, a Margarita glass, and a clutch purse, and doing her best to keep Roger's attention. He sat between them, squeezing and petting. *"Aie, Muchachas, muchichis, muchissimas!"* he said, to their squealing delight.

When Kevin sat down, the three of them looked at him blankly for a moment. They saw a gaunt and solemn-faced young man with shaggy sorrel-red hair, a man still good-looking in spite of the strange band of scar on the right side of his face and the haunted expression in his soft, dark eyes.

"It's Harrey," said Roger. "It's Mr. Kevin fucking-A number-one roto-rooter Harrey!"

"Hiya, Big Rog. How you doing?"

"Well, take a look! I'm doing great. How about you?"

"I'm doing all right. I just got tarred and feathered and run out of town, but I've got a place to go, and a way to get there, so I'm off to California."

Roger unwrapped himself from the two women and leaned across the table. "Jesus, man, I've got to admit it, you look like warmed-over dogshit."

"Thanks. You look like some kind of counter-guerrilla vigilante. I take it that Irwin Rommel Commemorative Powerwagon out there is yours? What the hell are you doing, anyway?"

"I'm starting a survival school," said Roger grandly. He did look like some kind of paramilitary mountain man. In camouflage fatigues and sheepskin vest, he looked healthy and bull-chested as Kevin remembered him, but he was getting a substantial beer gut. He held up his tequila shot. "Remember the greatest four F's?" he asked.

"Yeah, I think so," laughed Kevin. "A good friend, a good fight, a good fuck — 'scuse me, ladies, and, uh, a good future."

"Close. A good fantasy. Well, here's to 'em." They knocked back the shots. "Speaking of a good fantasy, I'm going to call it the Professional American Institute of Survival, PAIS for short. See, I figure the way social change is going these days, the shit could hit the fan around here most any time. So here's the scam. There's a whole class of fat pogeys out there with cushy jobs that keep their asses in soft chairs. They make a lot of dough, and some of them are beginning to figure out that when things get rough, they are going to be the ones who get eaten for lunch. So I figure on setting up this camp, that looks a lot like a Marine Corps bootcamp, right. And I charge these people a ton of money to come out for weekend seminars, or weekly classes, or special projects in learning to get tough and survive. It's good for them, it's good for the society, and it's going to make me a rich son of a bitch." He waved for another pitcher of beer, and two more Margaritas, which the two girls waved to refuse. "Goddamn. I still can't see a Margarita without thinking of Carlie. I just can't believe she walked out on you. Not after all you've been through."

Kevin shrugged. "I guess she was only married to the part I had to leave behind to get home."

"Harrey, to tell you the truth, I've always thought of women like cats. They're lovely creatures, and I like a little pussy around me all the time, but I don't expect any one of them to be around for long." Big Rog chuckled and squeezed the two women.

"Well, at least there's one consolation," said Kevin. "She could have had some Jody motherfucker waiting around the corner all this time, waiting for me to get my ass blown away so he could cash in. Maybe she's got one....I don't know."

"So you could probably fit right in here," said Roger after a moment. "With your background....fuck me to tears, man, I just can't imagine what it must have been like to hang it right in the trees with both of those 7.62-millimeter miniguns spitting hot lead at some slope son-of-a-bitch. And Eddie! Oh, Jesus, man, I just can't believe he's gone. One minute he's right here, you know, tag-along Eddie since we were kids, and the next minute you find out he's a dead combat hero and you're never going to see him again."

Kevin nodded. "That's how it was with me. I didn't find out he was dead until after I woke up in the hospital in Hawaii."

"So how is it going over there, Harrey? You can't believe shit you see in the news. Are we making any progress, or not?"

Kevin snorted derisively and poured himself another glass of beer. "Are you kidding? Ho Chi won."

Roger looked surprised, then shook his head. "Come on, Harrey, just because he has a propaganda victory, that doesn't mean he wins. If the whole bunch of them turn commie, you kill the whole bunch. All they've got to do is get the profiteers and bra-burners out of there, and put the entire Marine Corps on the south end of the country, and you point north and say, 'Kill!' When you get to the DMZ, you keep right on kicking ass and taking names until you start running into Chinese. Then you register the ones left alive to vote in the election, and start getting ready for spring planting."

"That sounds great, Big Rog," said Kevin glumly.

"So what do you think? How do you feel about hanging around here for a while and helping me get the survival school going? Tell you what...what are you driving? We can put a cammo paint job on it!"

Kevin drained his glass. "Well, I appreciate your offer, Big Rog, but I believe I would rather see my van painted any color except camouflage right now. And San Manuel is a nice little town, but it's awfully close to El Paso, if you know what I mean."

"So you're on the road?"

"Soon as the sun sets. How about a plate of *enchiladas* somewhere before I go?"

"No better place in the world than right here," said Roger. "My treat."

After dinner, Kevin gave Roger the address Roz had sent him from California. "Roger, don't give that address to anyone. You're the only person in the world who has it. But forward stuff to me, will you."

"You'd better get rolling," said Roger. "It's getting to be about time for me to shift into whiskey gear." As Kevin rose to leave, Roger reached into a pocket. "Here," he said, handing him two white pills. "Trucker's bennies. Those ought to get you to Phoenix."

Kevin popped the pills with a last half-glass of beer, then flashed Roger a comradely salute, and left. He cranked up Caribe Pete and drove back to the highway.

In April 1979, ten years later almost to the day, Kevin next heard from Roger Stanton. Mail had been forwarded, and Christmas cards exchanged, but they had made no other contact. For three years, Kevin had lived in Clarkwood, Arizona, a little town south of Flagstaff. He had taken work at the tiny local airport, at first employed only to work on the line, and to help with the paperwork. He had soon discovered he could easily transition to the fixed-wing aircraft, and he set out to get his license. He found his veteran's benefits could be used to obtain flight training, and with the help of his employers, he eventually became a Certified Flight Instructor. The CFI earned him almost nothing in the tiny town, but it did give him the opportunity to fly once in a while. By working at the airfield, and selling a little pot to friends, he made enough money to rent the small trailer where he lived alone. He had girl friends in the nearby ghost city of Jerome who were always glad to see him, but he had made no lasting relationships with any of them. With his Food Stamps and his TV set, he could hang out there indefinitely, he was convinced.

He came into the operations office of the little flight school one afternoon to find a message written on the chalkboard: "Big Rog says to be home at 21:00." He was followed by his sweaty and shaken-looking student, a rancher who drove in once a week from the hills to fly. He spent half an hour debriefing the flight, then walked out to make sure the airplane had been properly tied down. He took off his Chinese-commie soft cap and shook the sorrel-red curls which hung halfway to his shoulders, then put it back on and turned up the fur collar of the leather Navy flight jacket he had picked up in a shop in San Francisco. "Roger Stanton," he thought. "What could that crazy bastard want?"

On the way back to his trailer, he took his liquid estate out of the left front pocket of his dusty brown slacks and ran a quick audit to see if he could afford a pint of Southern Comfort. He couldn't, but he bought it anyway. When he got home, he poured a snifter of the poor man's Gran Marnier, rolled a couple of fat joints, put a can of beef stew on the stove, and sat down to wait for Roger's call. Just before nine o'clock, it came.

"Harrey? Big Rog. Listen, I've got a proposition for you." Kevin was amused that Roger still sounded like a big eager kid, though his voice was deeper, and gravelly. "I need a pilot," he declared.

"Smuggling dope?" asked Kevin innocently.

Roger laughed. "Naw, this is strictly test pilot work. I do smoke a little of that shit now and then though. I got tired of watching all my friends get up and go outside like they were going to take a pee together or something, then come back looking like they all just got fucked. You know what, though? That shit doesn't do a goddamn thing for me. You're still flying, right?"

"Yeah, I am. So what is this test pilot business?"

"I'm starting an airplane factory. Yep, that's what I said, an airplane factory. One year from now we are going to be marketing the Harlequin Flying Cycle."

"Holy shit, Rog! Are you serious? How did that come down?"

"Well, Harrey, my folks died a few years back — yeah, both of them, my mom in '72 and my dad of cancer in '75. So I've got the business now, and I think I can get the jump on a whole new market for aviation recreation vehicles. That's where you come in. See, I need somebody with a lot more experience in certain areas, and you're the best qualified I can think of."

"Really? Just what is it you need me to do? You're still a pilot, aren't you?"

"I can't get past the medical examiner these days — one look and they've got me pegged for the alky ward."

"You gotta be kidding. Can't you just dry out for a week and then go take the physical?"

"Last time I dried out for a week was at the Fort Bayard Turkey Farm — alcoholic rehab center. That was two years ago. It was terrible — took me two weeks of hard drinking to recover. But that's not the point. I need you for a lot of other things too. Like some administration, somebody to run the front office, you know. You'll go on the payroll as an independent consultant, and we'll make some airplanes, OK?"

"Well, Jesus, Roger, I don't know...."

"You've got a place to live here at the house. Hey, look, I know this must sound kind of crazy, but it's on the level. Otto Stanton was a squirrel, you remember? He put away all kinds of little piles of nuts, and I need to put them into something before I drink them all up, so I'm going to invest the bucks in this project, and go for it. I'm going to pay somebody One Big G every month to be my design consultant, admin officer, and chief test pilot. I want to find out if that's you, or not."

"A thousand bucks and a place to live? Starting when?"

"I put a check in the mail yesterday for one thousand dollars. That's to cover your travel expenses. You go on the payroll the day you get here. If you decide not to take the job, just send me back the check. That's a Rog?"

"Uh, yeah, Roger that."

"Big Rog, out." The line clicked dead, and Kevin sat with the receiver to his ear. Like a ghost from the long-dead past, the call brought back a flood of memories. All that was so long ago, before Arizona, before the whole crazy world of California, hippies, and cocaine, back in the lifetime of that other Kevin. And could he really live in the same house with that goofy big-mouthed fuckhead Roger Stanton, even for a grand a month?

The check was the clincher, as Roger had correctly surmised. Kevin packed his belongings into the Fury, told his employer he would have to take over his two flight students himself, and left town without looking back.

Early afternoon, he took the San Manuel exit from Interstate 10, and found himself once again on the little plaza. The sense of timelessness gave him an eerie feeling. There were two cars parked beneath the tiny red-and-white neon "Bar CHATO'S Coors" sign, and so little had changed that he halfway expected to see the camouflage Powerwagon. He drove out to the Green Castle, parked beside a big battered green Chevy crewcab pickup truck and walked up to the front door of the house. There was a strange silence about the place, and the soft sepia light coming through the thin cloud cover cast no shadows. Seeing an open wrought-iron gate, Kevin walked through to the big low-walled patio which extended around behind the house, and which faced like a stage out to the valley below. The sliding glass doors which led into the living room of the house were open about a foot. The glass was dusty, and had greasy handprints on it. "Hey," he said, stepping inside a foot. "Yo, Stanton. Big Rog? Hey, boy!" Getting no answer, he walked on around the building to a sidewalk which led back beneath some low overhanging purple-leafed plum trees. He heard a muttering, and saw a screen door hanging open.

It was a small single-room apartment, with a half-wall divider down the middle to separate it into a bedroom area and a kitchen area. The walls of the room were marked with patches of bare plaster and old paint, sanded smooth, and newspapers covered the floor. On the room divider, a portable radio babbled and hissed, the surf-like surging gabble of two overlapping stations poorly tuned, and far away.

Roger Stanton lay sprawled across a fold-down couch, snoring with his arm across his face. His grubby jeans were pulled halfway down his hips, and his little toes showed through holes in the sides of his ragged old boots. His great hairy belly hung to one side like an enormous tit, and it quivered when he snored. The flesh was doughy, and mottled with little purple veins. On the couch beside his hand was a cigarette butt, resting in a circle the size of a quarter charred in the upholstery. The wastebasket in the corner of the room had several beer bottles and a six-pack carrier spilling from it, and a quart bottle of vodka with four fingers left in it stood beside the wall. Roger had one arm across his eyes, and the other was protectively cradling a green plastic 2-liter lemon-lime soda bottle.

"Incoming!" said Kevin loudly, and he kicked the couch.

Roger jerked in surprise, tried to sit up, and spilled the soda down his belly. "Fuck! Oh, it's you. You no-good egg-sucking peckerwood little bastard! You scared the fuck out of me." He sat up and rubbed his eyes with the back of his hand, then grimaced at the spilled soda. "Fuck me to tears," he muttered. He took a drink, washed it around in his mouth, and swallowed it. Then he picked up the vodka, poured about half of it into the soda, and tasted the mixture again. "S'better," he said, and drank about a pint. He offered the bottle to Kevin.

"No thanks," said Kevin. "I just had lunch in Deming."

Roger lit a cigarette, stood up, and headed for the bathroom. About halfway, he stopped and began to cough mightily. "I was hoping you'd get in last night so we could get this room painted," he wheezed. "I've been working for weeks so you'd have this place when you got here."

Roger stumbled into the bathroom, leaned against the wall and pissed copiously. "Come on," he said, tugging at his zipper. "I'll show you the house — oh, you've been here before, though, haven't you?"

"Yeah, a couple of times, back in '65, then '67, I guess — right after flight school. I was just here for a couple of parties, though. I never got to see much of the house."

Roger led him back to the sliding glass doors, through the big living room with the stone fireplace, and down a hall to a large bedroom. The room was dominated by a large waterbed frame, a heavy chest of drawers, and a roll-top desk. Everything was piled two feet deep with magazines, boxes, bottles, camping equipment, tools and pieces of machinery, hunks of styrofoam, blankets, and dirty clothes. Ash trays spilling butts sat on the desk and on both ends of the headboard of the bed. A wastebasket full of bottles and fast-food packages sat beside the desk. Leaving him to explore the room on his own, Roger stepped into the bathroom nearby and peeled off his clothes, then turned on the shower. Glancing in after him, Kevin could see that the sink was blackened with grime, and splotched with gobs of soap and toothpaste.

When Roger stepped out of the bathroom and walked naked into the bedroom, Kevin was surprised to see how old he looked. He walked flatfooted and stiff-kneed, carrying his beer gut like an old woman pregnant with a hundred-pound blob of oatmeal. His legs were thin, and the cheeks of his ass sunken and flaccid. He scrubbed with a towel at his scraggly shoulder-length hair, and peered out from underneath it through baggy red-rimmed eyes. "That's better," he said after a minute or two. He raked back his hair with his fingers. "I was feeling like two hundred and forty pounds of unamalgamated bat guano. I think I'll survive if I can get to a taco joint soon enough. Speaking of joints, there's a dope tray in that sliding shelf in the headboard, if you want some."

"Thanks," said Kevin, locating the stash. He crushed one of the dried lumps on the tray and rolled it up while Roger got dressed. He had just finished smoking it when Roger came out of the bathroom, shaved and looking pretty good in spite of the pale yellow cast of his skin and eyes.

"I guess it's been months since I've been upstairs," said Roger, indicating a carpeted stairwell leading to a pair of closed French doors. "That was my mother's territory. She spent the last ten years of her life up there, locked away in her rooms living on chocolates and chicken soup and watching an old black-and-white TV set she got back in the fifties. It's pretty weird. I don't think there's a thing up there except for the TV that was made since 1939. Let's see what's in the kitchen. I thought I'd left one in there on the counter the other day."

The sink was filled with dishes, trash, and garbage in six inches of sludge. The crusted maw of the oven hung open to reveal a broiler pan of charred drippings and hard white grease. The floor stuck to Kevin's feet as he walked, and he had to step through several overflowing sacks of trash to get into the room.

"Ah, there it is," said Roger. He waded through the trash and snatched a vodka bottle from among a group of others. "Great," he said triumphantly. "Half full. We can moon the tacos off until after Chato opens up, so we don't have to go to town. Come on, I'll show you where it all really happens."

The shop building was almost as cluttered and dirty as the house, but it was still impressive. Along each side of the big metal warehouse were fine machine tools bolted to the floor, and workbenches with rows of cabinets and drawers. Boxes, pieces of motorcycles and automobiles, rolls of this, and bundles of that lay in disorder all around.

"Didn't you tell me your father was into old farm machinery? I keep expecting a plow on a pedestal, or something," said Kevin.

"Yeah, he did that. The collection was the one part of his estate I didn't get. He gave thirty-seven major pieces and a whole bunch of little stuff to some museum in Kansas City. When he found he had cancer, he sold most of his stock and bought every good piece he could find. At collectors' prices, it was worth easy a quarter of a million bucks. You know, Harrey, the strangest thing about that was that he had another collection of historically-valuable pieces that he just considered a scrap pile. I've watched him root through a box and pull out an experimental gimbal ring he'd made for an early Viking rocket, and just cut it right down to fix somebody's irrigation pump. He thought an early McCormick was a piece of history worth preserving, but an early Otto Stanton he couldn't see as anything but scrap metal. So I went through his stuff and gave a good-sized truckload of authentic space-age memorabilia to the Space Hall of Fame over in Alamogordo. Then I sold the rest of the stock and put the money into the Harlequin."

The center of the room was dominated by two long tables. On

the first lay a styrofoam and fiberglass airfoil section about twelve feet long, and on the second sat a peculiar assembly of tubes and panels resembling a heavy-metal dogsled.

"That's part of it?" asked Kevin.

"Take a good look. What you see there is going to be one hell of an airplane. We are going to take that to the airshows and when everybody gets over being pissed off because some hotshot came in and got into a hassle with everybody he could jump, and they look at the fact that he beat everybody who was crazy enough to go up and dogfight with him, then suddenly we've got a marketable airplane on our hands. You follow that?"

"Weeell, yeah, I guess so. You expect to fly into airshows like some kind of black knight, get the guys in the Pitts Specials to dogfight with you, then blow everybody's doors off so bad you get national attention. Right?"

"Wrong. I expect you to go to the airshows and blow everybody's doors off. What I've got is the design concept and enough shit left lying around here to finance putting the prototype together."

"Who's going to do that? No, don't tell me. You're going to sell the antiques on the top floor, and the two of us are going to build the airplane."

"You got it. That refrigerator over in the corner there has cold beer in it, by the way, if you want one."

"No, thanks. How about a coffee maker?"

"I think there's one in the kitchen somewhere. Here, let me show you some pictures of the Harlequin." Roger picked up a roll of paper and spread it out on the resin surface of the composite airfoil structure. "That's our Harley," he said.

It was a beautiful airplane, Kevin had to admit, like nothing he had ever seen before, a sleek swept-wing canard sailplane with a pusher prop. In the artist's rendition, the pilot was sitting astride the fuselage just forward of the wing, which stretched twelve feet on each side from his shoulders. With the little canard stabilizer on a long narrow boom in front, and the pilot grasping a pair of handlebars, the effect was much like a long-forked motorcycle with wings.

"It flies like something out of Star Wars," said Roger. "That's a Cuyuna 430D experimental aircraft engine on the back there, and it will push this bird to about 95 in level flight."

Kevin had his doubts about the dogfighting competitions, and he certainly had his doubts about Roger, but something about the design of the little sport airplane struck him as profoundly right. "You know what, Stanton? I've got a strange feeling you might really be onto something here," he said.

Roger guffawed heartily and broke down coughing. He bent over retching and hacking, came up red-faced and pop-veined, glurbed up a blob and spat it into a barrel of trash, and kept laughing, banging on the bench with the palm of his hand. "I think I'm gonna die of oxygen poisoning," he croaked, when his spasm of hilarity had passed, "but you think you see what the old Big Rog has got going up here, do you?" He took another big slug from the bottle, then lit a fresh cigarette. "It's a market concept, designed to appeal to a special kind of person. Think about it. It's basically an aerobatic powered sailplane. If you were to use your engine only to maneuver yourself into good soaring conditions, and carry a camping pack, you could get across country on a Harlequin faster, cheaper, and with more privacy than by any other means. Everything else that flies these days is built for all these Howard-Johnson-Mickey-Mouse people, these nice little beavers with lifetime jobs and Sunday School classes. Their thinking is all based on cars, because that's what they drive, and their airplanes are like cars. But there's a whole class of people who would rather ride for their thrills on motorcycles, and my airplanes are designed for them. I want to build an airplane the bad boys can appreciate, one they can't break in the air, an airplane for people who don't like airports and don't file flight plans — for guys like us, you know, the Vietnam-era guys."

Kevin nodded. "An airplane for Namvets — pretty weird, Big Rog. But it looks to me like you're right on the money. That thing really looks bad!"

"Then I take it you're ready to get started?"

Kevin laughed. "You say that like we were going to have the whole plant humming in time for dinner. Speaking of food, I don't think I want to start drinking lunch — it's a habit that leads to drinking dinner. And speaking as your new Aviation and Administration Consultant, I recommend we hit town for a chicken-fried steak, then do some grocery shopping. Then we've got to come back here and hose this house out, and then I've got to get my one trunkload of shit out of my car and into that little room downstairs — and I don't give a fuck if we paint it or not."

"We'll paint it, all right!" said Roger. "No half-done projects. It's the same with the airplane — if the workmanship isn't just exactly right, you stall, spin, crash, burn, and die. So we'll paint it, and you can stock the refrigerator with any thing you want. We'll go get you a chicken-fried, and I can pick up a fresh bottle."

"Sounds good to me, if you mean we start with the steak, and along about now. So how much of that stuff does it take to keep you supplied these days?"

Roger shrugged and took a long pull from his green plastic jug. "I was hitting it pretty hard there for a while when I was on the Bourbon, but lately I've been on maintenance, not really drinking. I can stay just fine on a maintenance level of about twelve ounces a day, more or less. It's just I was born with an alcoholic metabolism and that much just keeps me stabilized."

"So you're drinking about a fifth of vodka a day?"

"Well, I usually buy quarts or half-gallons, but, yeah, I think that's about right. I cut it pretty heavily with the soda, and the sugar helps a lot. So whadd'ya say? You want to cruise down to old El Pisshole? How about a couple of shots in the U-Boat, just for old times sake?"

"Jesus, Roger. I don't think there's anything in El Paso or Juarez I ever need to see again. How about the truck stop?"

"Can't handle Juarez, huh? Roger that."

Thirty minutes later, Kevin put two packs of sugar into his coffee and dug into a chicken-fried steak at The Marshal's Truck Stop. "Nothing like real American food," he said.

"You got that right," said Roger, taking on a big green chile enchilada. "Like this stuff. Don't tell the Viva-Chicano *pendejos*, but the best of all this so-called Mexican food is totally unknown in Mexico. You go down by Mexico City and ask for *enchiladas verdes* and they think you're having trouble with the language. The best chile dishes in the world were created right here in the Mesilla Valley."

"Some town," said Kevin, waving to the waitress for more coffee, "the birthplace of the space age and the green enchilada. Here, let me have a bite of that. Yum. Outstanding!"

"So, tell me, Harrey, what the hell have you been doing all these years?" asked Roger after they had eaten a while.

Kevin finished off his last biscuit, and leaned back in the big leather booth. "California. It's like a different lifetime — six years, I was out there. I tried all kinds of shit, Rog, trying to find some sense of direction, some sense of identity. I finally came to the conclusion I was failing at something very important — though I was never sure what. When I left El Paso, I went to hang out with Piper and Roz, some people I met on Maui. Yeah, they sent me a card, so I went to live with them. Thinking like a hippie already, right? They lived up in a redwood grove out of Santa Cruz, and they told me I could just set up in the basement and hang out for a while to get my head together. They looked to me just like hippies, but they liked to eat out in fancy little restaurants, and there was always a cabinet full of booze, and a cookie jar with about a quarter pound of pot in it."

Roger laughed around a mouthful of chile. "Sounds like the only thing missing was the cocaine."

"I was just getting to that. I went upstairs one afternoon to meet these friends of Piper's who had come down from the city. I walked into the room, and there was this big pile of sparkly stuff on the table about a two feet wide and six inches high."

"You're talking a hundred G's worth of toot!" said Roger.

"I think it was closer to forty, at those days' prices, but it was still a ton of bucks. Hell, I'd never seen the stuff, but I developed a liking for it in about two toots. You put a little of that shit in your nose, and instantly, a big voice in your head starts yelling, 'More cocaine!' The guys who brought it were hotshot jet-set kids from some place down in South America, and Piper was their broker. I have no idea how much money they were making, or what they did with it. I didn't have any, so I wasn't in on the deals. I was just the broke hippie in the basement, but I covered my right to stick my nose in the bowl by being the security officer."

"Nothing like having some basic skills to fall back on," agreed Roger.

"Yeah, I was the guy in the shadows with the machinegun. It was really a pretty secure situation. Piper only dealt with people who would drive up to our place in the woods alone. I had a beautiful old folding-stock paratrooper M-1 Carbine — Piper's, natch — to keep the peace with."

"Did you ever get to use it?"

"No, but I got too close too many times. I mean, when you put fifty grand worth of uncut flake and fifty grand in small bills in the same room without the protection of the law, it's likely to draw some flies. I'd had enough of being shot at in Nam, so I had to get out of that situation.

"I was in and out of different job things over the years, and I spent some time just hitch-hiking around, then ended up in Clarkwood. Now here I am back in San Manuel, with a run-out old Plymouth and what's left of the bonus you sent me. Ten years running in a circle, and all I've got to show for it is older. What's worse, I keep reading everywhere that the reason for that is that I'm a Vietnam veteran. It's not something that was wrong with the situation, they keep trying to tell me — it's something that's wrong with me. You can't imagine how it feels to consider that they might be right."

Roger had grown quite solemn, and he sat staring at his empty plate. "I need a drink," he said. "Let's get the fuck out of here."

As soon as they were back on the road in Kevin's old Fury, Roger chugged about two inches from his big green plastic bottle. "I think I've found the perfect mixture of vodka and soda," he said with a self-indulgent grin, "one to one." He patted his distended belly and breathed in shallow snuffling huffs, eyes heavy-lidded, red-rimmed, and pale gold. He dug into his pocket and pulled out a crumpled pack of cigarettes and an old-fashioned Zippo lighter. He lit the tobacco with the greasy black-edged orange flame of the lighter, sucked half an inch off the end of the cigarette, and immediately began to cough rackingly, his tongue protruding through flubbering lips.

"What the hell do you put in that thing, Stanton?"

232

Roger rolled down the window, spat a glob into the wind, and reached for his bottle again. "Aw, come on, don't tell me you guys didn't put jet fuel in your lighters."

"Yeah, until they invented butane. And that shit you're using isn't JP-5 anyway."

"It's kerosene — just about the same stuff."

Kevin shook his head. "Roger, I think sometimes you take this Vietnam-veteran thing too seriously."

"Hey, gimme a break. I used to fly jets a little myself, you know."

"Oh, yeah, that's right. Eddie told me about that."

"Eddie told you? What did he say? Maybe you better not tell me -- I was telling people all sorts of things back then."

"So what's the truth?" Kevin asked.

Roger laughed. "Fucking gunship drivers — gotta cut right through the bullshit. Well, the truth is I got to drinking and fucking and showing the Brothers I had the right stuff until too late one night, and I missed a step in the landing pattern and got an instructor pilot killed."

Kevin nodded.

"It was the booze, pure and simple. I've been through every program there is, Kevin, and it's just a fact of life that I was born an alcoholic. This stuff is going to kill me, you know."

"Yeah, I'd sort of figured that out. How long do you think it's going to take?"

"A few months, a few years — shit, it could happen any time. I know the signs — I've seen a lot of old alkies die."

"So what's this airplane thing all about?" Kevin asked. "And why the hell did you bring me back here?"

Roger took another drink, and lit another cigarette with the butt of the first. "You want to know? Listen, everybody keeps trying to find some way to save me, and nobody can. But there is one thing that just might give me something I'd be willing to put myself on minimum maintenance for, and that is to put Big Rog in the saddle of that Harlequin one time and go out there and say 'Good morning' to a big hawk just as I come over the top of a loop and start down the back side. I might just keep right on going straight down, but it's going to be worth all the hell of detox again just to be there one more time."

Kevin started to say, "There are easier ways than building an airplane company," but he checked himself, and then he knew why the project had consumed so much time and money, and why it would never be completed, and he understood for the first time what it was Roger really expected him to do. "You know what we ought to do, Rog," he said, "is build two prototypes from the get-go. You're an old fighter pilot. You know that flying an airplane is great, but when you get two of you up there, then you find out what that environment is all about."

"Roger that!" agreed Big Rog earnestly, sitting up straighter and pounding Kevin heartily on the shoulder. "That's the greatest idea you've had since you got here. In fact, that's worth the whole grand I sent you."

Kevin glanced over at him, and for an instant he saw again the bright-eyed and cocky burrhead kid he had met in Juarez, who had been looking forward so eagerly to his future. "Well, all right. What do you say we go back to the Castle and start getting that shop cleaned out?"

"Yeah, that sounds great. We can have those birds in the air by the end of this summer for sure, don't you think? Oh, by the way, we need to hit a package store on the way back so I can get a fresh bottle. If we're going to be doing a lot of burro work, I'm sure I'm going to need it. Besides, I'm out of soda."

"Can't have that," agreed Kevin sympathetically. "So tell me, whatever happened to your survival school project?"

"Haw, haw, haw! That's right, I was into that last time you saw me. Well, to make a long story short: nothing. That's right. I did make a pile of money, though, setting up vehicles for desert and mountain survival and selling them. I built about eight or ten of those crazy things, starting out with that big old Powerwagon. I was still making a pretty good lick with my camera, too, but the thing that really put an end to all that was when my Dad died. I didn't need to make money any more, and I didn't really want to see a lot of people, so I just kind of stayed home for a while. It was pretty rough, Harrey, watching Otto shrivel up and die over about six months. Neither of us had ever got over Mom's dying two years before, to begin with. In the end he just shit and puked his guts out, and I had to shoot him up with morphine every few hours. He wouldn't go to the hospital — he wanted to die in his own bed, at least. I'll never let those fucking ghouls get their hands on me, either. They'd have run up a bill for fifty grand watching him spend a week dying on their intensive care machines. And he was the last one, the last of the Stantons, except for me. Since he died, I've been living up there by myself in that huge old house full of ghosts — four years now."

Kevin drove in silence a moment or two, cruising north toward Las Cruces to find Roger a package store. "You know what surprises me most?" he said after a time. "It's that you never got landed and domesticated by some predatory mama cat."

"Yeah," Roger laughed, "that always surprised me, too. Fact is, I like pussy too much to get married." He chuckled to himself, and took a long drink from his nearly-empty bottle. "I did almost get married to one woman," he said. "She never knew about it, though. Far as she knew, she was just poontang to me."

"So how come you didn't marry her?"

"Oh....too much water under the bridge, I guess. You know how it goes."

"Yeah, I guess I do," affirmed Kevin.

The job of cleaning out the house took the better part of three months — that is, without getting into the top floor at all. Roger was usually good for about four hours per day of productive activity, and the rest was devoted to sleeping, eating, and sitting around the house or at his favorite table at Chato's drinking. Every room had a trashpile, and a dozen opportunities to stop to have a drink and tell a story about some object found in the mess.

They often spent the evenings sprawled on the floor in front of the TV set, or before a projection screen looking at the hundreds of slides which Roger had taken of his early development of the Harlequin. He had spent thousands of dollars on books, magazine subscriptions, filmstrips, long phone conversations recorded on tape, consultant services, membership in organizations, invention promotion studies, fancy professional letterhead, and even an early model small business computer he had never learned to use.

One evening toward the end of summer, Roger fell asleep on

the living room floor, and Kevin went down to Chato's alone. He ordered a bottle of Coors and stepped around the bar to the back of the room where the tables and the jukebox were set up. He fed the box a quarter, punched up a couple of songs, and sat down by himself to listen to the music and to watch the people.

There weren't many to watch. Three older people sat at the bar together, speaking quietly in Spanish. A long-haired young Hispanic wearing the patched jeans and leathers of a biker sat alone, watching a group of three people sitting across the room. Two of them were together, a gringo couple about thirty. He was tall and very thin, with wavy hair and an earnest but strangely sad and penetrating gaze, and she was round and friendly, with short red hair, and a delightfully wicked laugh. Kevin had seen them before, and he knew they were friends of Rogers, but he did nothing to catch their attention. Their companion was a younger woman — early twenties, Kevin guessed — Spanish, and quite dark. She was short, broad across the ass, and she wore her hair straight down her back like an Indian. Her features were strong, with the high-bridged nose and deep dark eyes of the lost Aztlanic culture. There was something about her that nagged at Kevin's memory, as though he had known her somewhere before.

As he watched, the gringo couple finished their drinks and left her by herself. At the bar, the biker began to twitch nervously, watching her closely for a signal. After a minute, he put his cigarettes into the pocket of his tattered denim vest, apparently ready to make his move. Just anticipating him, she picked up her drink and walked to Kevin's table.

"Hi," she said. "Would you mind if I joined you?"

"No," Kevin replied, surprised. "Please sit down."

"Thanks. My name is Cecilia. What's yours?"

"Kevin. Nice to meet you, Cecilia."

She sat down beside him, smiled warmly, and looked into his eyes. "So what brings you to San Manuel, Kevin?" she asked.

"I live here. Well, I have since April, anyway. I live in the big green house on the mesa."

"You live with Roger Stanton, then?"

"Yeah. You know Roger?"

"I grew up in Las Cruces. I've known Big Rog a long time. So where is he tonight?"

Kevin shrugged. "He fell out early."

"So he's still drinking really heavy, huh? Tch. I wish there was a way to make him stop. Last time I saw him, his eyes were all yellow, and he could hardly get out of his truck. It's really too bad. When I was in junior high, I remember having a crush on him because he was so big and strong and fun to be around. Can I buy you another drink, Kevin, another Coors?"

"Uh, sure, thanks. Actually, I'd rather have some Southern Comfort in a wineglass."

"You've got it. Don't run off, OK? I really appreciate your company."

"I'll be right here."

After an hour, and he had bought the second round of drinks, she reached over and put her hand on his. "You know, Kevin, I really enjoy sitting here talking with you, but it would sure be nicer somewhere we don't have to be so formal."

"Want to go up to the Castle?"

"I thought you'd never ask."

They left the bar, and she drove her little white Rabbit and followed him up to the house on the mesa. He led her around to the back of the house to his room. He had painted it, brought furniture from other rooms, and stocked his refrigerator, and the place was beginning to feel quite cozy. He snapped on the overhead light, and she snapped it back off as she followed him into the room. "Got a candle?" she asked.

"I just happen to," he said, flicking his lighter on and lighting a restaurant jar-candle which sat on the room divider. In the soft light, they embraced, kissed, and slowly undressed. In bed he found her warm and pliant, and it pleased him to stretch out the foreplay to bring her to a panting and trembling state.

"Have you got a joint?" she asked later, after they lay quietly together for a time. He nodded and reached under the bed for his rolling tray. She watched him roll one, then took a long toke. "Mmm. Thanks....for everything. You were fantastic — but I knew you would be. I know who you are, you know."

"What do you mean, you know who I am?"

"You flew in Vietnam, with Eddie Padilla."

Kevin looked at her in surprise. "How did you know that?"

"He used to write home about you. He really worshiped you, did you know that? I still have some of his letters, telling about how you did one heroic thing or another, or told some officer to go fuck himself."

He gaped in astonishment. "Then you're...."

"Cecilia Padilla. When I was younger they called me Ceci."

"...Eddie's little sister. I remember he used to show me your letters, but gee, Ceci, you were just a little kid."

"I was thirteen when Eddie was killed. That was ten years ago, Kevin."

Kevin looked at her searchingly for a long moment, surprised that he had not noticed how much she looked like his long-dead friend, Bullseye Padilla. "I guess life goes on, huh?" he said.

"Yes, for some of us, anyway. My mother has never been the same. She still acts like it was just yesterday. It was kind of hard to live with for a long time. See, she has this place in her bedroom set up like kind of a shrine. There's a picture of Our Lady of Guadalupe, and a picture of Jesus, and a picture of Eddie when he graduated from flight school....and his medals. She goes in there every day to burn candles and cry, and to pray to the Virgin Mary to help her endure the suffering, and she always wears black to Mass now. You know something, Kevin, I've always had a funny feeling that's what she really wanted — to lose a son so she could suffer like Mary."

Kevin nodded solemnly. "I think Eddie knew that, deep down inside. I remember always laughing at him when he said what he wanted from the war was to be a hero for his mother."

Ceci nodded and snuggled close to him, her smooth dark skin cool against him in the warm summer night air. "So she got what she wanted, I guess. My father has made a big thing of it politically. He's a State Senator now, did you know that? Most of the Mexicans in this state's politics are Democrats, but the money is with the big ranchers and the military contractors, who are mostly Republicans. They like Mundo Padilla because he's so pro-military. He's active in the VFW, and has made a big thing out of getting special honors for Hispanic Vietnam Vets."

"Oh, that's peachy. What kind of honors?"

"All kinds of things. Grants, scholarships, special help in getting certain government jobs, that kind of thing. And of course, you've seen the Boulevard."

Kevin nodded. "Eduardo Padilla Memorial Boulevard. Ten blocks of concentrated banks, real estate companies, and lawyers' offices."

"When Papa bought that land twenty years ago, it was just open desert east of town, but the Boulevard has made him a millionaire. I guess war is good business, huh?"

"I guess. It sure leaves me feeling empty. Like an old looney I met up in the Arizona mountains told me one time, 'We have nothing to fear but irony itself.' The politicians make out, the bomb-builders make out, and as usual the banks make out. Even Jody makes out. All it costs is a little blood."

"Who's Jody?"

"Jody is a demon who haunts the soldier. He's the guy who stays home and fucks your old lady while you're out getting shot at. Like nightmares and jungle-rot on your balls, he comes with the territory."

"Did that happen to you?"

"I don't know. Probably. Truth is, I never really knew that woman very well — my wife, I mean. We were married four years, and I don't think we actually lived together more than six months total out of that time."

"Where is she now?"

"Carlic? Still down in El Paso, I think. I haven't heard from her in several years....got no reason to go looking for her, that's for sure. When I got back, I wasn't what she wanted, and it's not very likely I'm what she wants now, whatever that may be. I guess that's the hardest part about being a Vietnam veteran. You have to pretend that a lot of what's inside you just doesn't exist. There's no way to explain to people what it feels like, because they would have to put aside too much they hold to be unquestionable. How can you tell that to somebody like your father?"

"Nobody can tell my father anything," said Ceci. "He just waves his VFW magazine and yells, 'Don't tell me I don't know about Vietnam. I lost a son in Vietnam.'"

They lay together quietly for a time, and she tenderly stroked and kissed the wrinkled white network of old scars which marred his shoulder, belly, and thighs. "Lie still," she said. "This time I get to make love to you. And then I'm going home. I like to wake up in my own bed in the morning....but I'll be back, if that's OK with you."

"I'll say it's OK," he purred as she found reason to stop talking. "Ooo, that feels wonderful, Ceci."

FIFTEEN

By mid-October, Roger was a staggering hulk. He was no longer able to drive his truck to town without running into things, and no longer able to pee in the night without splattering thick orange urine on the floor and walls. When Kevin drove him down the hill to Chato's, he was loud, and pressed maudlin comraderie on everyone. It was difficult for him to get in and out of the old-fashioned bathtubs Otto had preferred, so he seldom bathed, and his hair and beard had grown long and matted. His voice had degenerated to a gravelly baritone rattle with a wheezy whining overtone. His old drinking buddies began to avoid him, and one night even old Chato asked him if there wasn't someplace he could go to get dried out. "I've been in this business a long time, Roger," he told him, "and I can see what's happening to you. Isn't there anything somebody could do to help you stop?"

Roger put his hand on the old man's shoulder and stood up straight and looked him right in the eye, and said, "No, Elfego my old friend, I don't think there is." Shortly thereafter he stopped going.

Kevin concluded there was no point in adding himself to the list of those trying unsuccessfully to save Roger, and he resolved that he would simply be the one who walked the last mile with him. Once a day he helped Roger put on his heavy Marine Corps overcoat and climb into the truck for the ride into Mesilla to buy a fresh half-gallon of vodka, and sometimes a carton of cigarettes, or the latest edition of a Las Cruces newspaper.

One Sunday morning he fixed himself a cup of coffee with Roger's microwave oven and sat down in the kitchen with the newspaper to read what was important in the world. Shaking his head sadly at the news of America's continued meddling and bungling in Central America, Kevin scanned through the Arts and Entertainment section looking for interesting TV shows.

Suddenly his jaw dropped in amazement. In the supplement magazine, he found an article about an artist, a sculptor. "Hey, Big Rog, look at this," he called. "Look here. You see this? I knew this guy. 'Walter "Buddy" Nichols, a disabled Vietnam veteran and former Army photojournalist,' it says."

There was a picture — which Kevin did not recognize at all — of a man with curly hair and a full beard, wearing heavy-rimmed dark glasses. Beside him were several busts he had sculpted. Kevin stared at the bizarre pieces. They were of vaguely Oriental-appearing old people and children, and of young Caucasian men with helmets and bandages, and all were wearing the tortured expressions of long suffering. The style was fluid, as though the faces had been melted, drawn out, and polished by some flame swirling around them. According to the article, Nichols had developed a rare eye disease and had gone totally and permanently blind. He had been a photographer making a living with a small gallery in Taos, the off-Santa-Fe art colony, and in a moment of inspiration and genius, he had switched to sculpture in clay. Now available in a limited number of bronze castings, his tactile creations were drawing top prices.

"This guy used to fly with us," Kevin told Roger. "He was crazy as we were, hanging out the side of a gunship with a 16mm movie camera taking pictures of the gooks shooting at us. And now he's gone blind. Jesus."

"Yeah, listen to this," said Roger, reading from the article. "Nichols, who claims that his blindness is his Karma, says, 'I never killed anyone myself, but I was there, and I didn't do anything to stop it, and I saw it. I can't ever forget what I saw. It's all I'll ever see.'"

"He went blind for guilt, so everybody ought to run out and buy one of his little painful reminders, huh? I think that's taking the Little-Matchgirl sales technique a bit too far," said Kevin, dropping ashes from his joint onto Nichols' picture.

"This guy flew with you on hot missions taking movies?"

"That's right."

"Well, hey, look, Harrey, baby, doesn't it occur to you that he might still have some of those films? He might have movies of you in combat sitting in a box right here in New Mexico."

Kevin felt a cold rush, and he stepped to a chair and sat down. "Holy shit," he said.

"What is it?"

"I just had this incredible feeling, like I was going to have a heart attack or something, and I flashed cold, and...oh, shit, I just got this picture, looking up a rope at Buddy Nichols leaning out of a slick taking movies of me hanging on below. It was the last mission, Roger, and he was there. I got pulled out of the jungle on a rope — a McGuire rig — and he was taking pictures of me. It's the first time I've remembered it!"

"Maybe he still has them. Even if he doesn't, he'll remember that mission, for sure. Let's call him!"

"Call him?"

"Sure. What the fuck, why not? He's got a phone, doesn't he? Come on." Roger gallumphed into the living room and picked up the telephone. He went round and round with the information operator, but finally located the number, and in a few minutes, they heard Nichols voice from Roger's tabletop speaker phone.

"Nichols."

"Buddy, this is Roger Stanton, down in San Manuel. My friends just call me Big Rog, OK. Look, I have a friend of yours sitting here, from a long time ago. Buddy, say hello to Kevin Harrey."

"Who?"

"Harrey, Kevin Harrey, of the 17th Assault."

"The 17th....oh, the 17th Assault Helicopter Company. Yeah, yeah, I remember those guys. What did you say the name was?"

"Harrey," said Kevin, "Warrant Officer. I was one of Duke Randall's gunship drivers. You probably remember him."

"Duke? I sure as hell do. He was one of the best officers I ever met — him and Jake Csynes, old Major Jake the Snake. God, what a tragedy those two men didn't get to come home."

"Yeah, I'll say. I was the other pilot flying with Randall on the mission he was killed on."

"Oh, yeah? You were the guy on the rope! Well, far out, I'm sure glad to hear you survived. I tell you, I thought you were dead for sure. Fifty clicks back to the nearest field hospital, and you were trailing a stream of blood all the way. Far out. Well, uh, what's happening with you?"

"Oh, not much. I'm living down here in San Manuel with my partner Roger Stanton here, and we've got an airplane factory going. Yeah, we're going to build some very unusual new sport aircraft. But look, the reason we called — besides just wanting to say hello, and congratulations on being one of the survivors — was that we were wondering if you happened to have any film left from any of those missions, like that particular one, for example?"

"Film? Hah!" Nichols scoffed bitterly. "I got some incredible footage of that mission, and a bunch of other missions, too, and I thought I had really accomplished something with all the crazy risks I took, but you know what happened?"

"They burned all your film before you left Vietnam?"

"No shit!! We were out of country on that trip, so they took every foot of film that didn't have immediate intelligence value to them, and burned it. And they burned every foot I took of the Vietnamese people, too. They said that wasn't part of my job. That was my first big revelation that I'd been taken for a chump. So, hey, sorry to disappoint you, but no home movies. Here's wishing you the best on your airplane venture, though. And it's sure good to hear from you, Harrey. I haven't heard from any of the guys since before they shut down Fort Wolters."

"They did what?" asked Kevin, surprised.

"Yeah, industry moved into some of the buildings, but mostly, it's abandoned."

"Where's that?" asked Roger.

"Fort Wolters, Texas, at Mineral Wells. It was the primary training base where I went through flight school," said Kevin. "Closed. I guess I've imagined it going right along, with the WOC's having Grundy Day every class and pooping around in the Mattel Messerschmidts — TH-55's, that is. Well, look, Buddy, congratulations on your work — wish you the best of success."

"Thanks, Harrey. Hang in there, and you too, uh..."

"Big Rog."

"Yeah, you too, Big Rog. So long, now."

Kevin stared at the phone speaker a long time before moving. "That was weird," he said finally. "That's the first time I've remembered any of that -- except maybe in dreams. I've had nightmares...I guess they're nightmares, since I keep waking up feeling in terror and can't remember what I was dreaming about. And it's so strange to hear Fort Wolters is closed, like learning a friend has been dead for a long time. Weird."

"Hey, Harrey, I tell you what let's do." Roger stepped close to Kevin and looked into his face, something he rarely did, and it seemed to Kevin the big man was just that moment the most completely lucid he had ever seen him. "Let's make a pilgrimage to Fort Wolters. Now. Let's just go get into the Chevy and go, and we can light a few candles on an old shrine. Whadd'ya say, Babycakes?"

"Babycakes? How the hell did you know about that?"

"You've been a legend in my life a long time, Harrey. I probably know more about you than you do. So what do you say?"

"Big Rog, old buddy, I think you're onto something. Let's roll a couple of doobies for the road, and hit it."

Half an hour later they climbed into the big '66 crewcab, drove through San Manuel to the Interstate, and turned toward El Paso on the first leg of the 600-mile trip. Roger had a fresh half-gallon of vodka and a big bottle of soda, and Kevin lit the first of a pocketful of joints he had rolled.

"I remember one afternoon, the craziest thing happened," Kevin told Roger as they settled into the ride. "We had just pulled this LRRP team out of the jungle, and we were all sitting around The Blade and Spade, having a few drinks. The leader was this wacko Green Beret sergeant, and he was sitting there looking bored, and he picked up a light bulb and he said he was going to eat it. He put up some money, and some bets got placed, and then he broke the bulb and took a bite of it. That was enough for me — he could take my five hundred P — but he just crunched up the whole thing and washed it down with beer."

"Now that's one I'd like to have seen," laughed Roger. "I'd probably have tried it."

"That was only half the show. His PFC sidekick only had

245

four days to go in-country, and we'd just pulled him out of the jungle under fire. Well, he'd caught a frog somewhere, and he was fucking around with it, dunking it in his beer. When the sergeant finished his light bulb trick, this kid said he was going to eat the frog alive. We were all loose enough by then we didn't give a shit, so somebody got a camera and everybody was having a hell of a good time, and he crunched down the frog, kicking and squirming. It was pretty funny, except that he must have missed one of his Ranger survival classes, because about ten minutes later, he fell off the barstool, dead as shit. Seems he ate the wrong frog."

As Kevin drove past the signs indicating the road to White Sands Missile Range, Roger took a big chug of his vodka and soda, and chuckled with nostalgia. "You know what gets me, Harrey?" he asked. "I get to thinking about what I would be doing right now if I hadn't screwed the pooch that morning in jet school. I'd be a major now, maybe one of the pilots training to fly the Space Shuttle in 1982 or 1983. Pretty strange how fate goes, huh?"

"Yeah," Kevin agreed, laughing. "I can remember when I was a hard-corps lifer of 20, figuring I could retire comfortably in 1983 and settle down to an old-age hobby business. Now the '70's are over, and I still feel like a kid who hasn't decided what he wants to do when he grows up. If I'd stayed in the Army — and hadn't got my ass blown away in Laos — I'd be a major, too. No Space Shuttle jockey, though, I'm sure. I'd probably be a hard-ass old burrhead, battle-scarred and too gung-ho for my own good, stuck away with a company of old helicopters somewhere trying to stay sane for just four more years — or else I'd be right in the middle of Iran and all that shit. It gives me chills. I keep remembering an officer I knew like that. The weirdest thing is he might have been fragged by one of our own guys."

"You mean murdered?"

"Murder? The word is a legal distinction, a footnote after the fact. It's pretty hard to tell what's murder and what's not in those circumstances. The fact is for one reason or another, I was persuaded to kill a bunch of people, and so were some other people, he was just one of the ones somebody killed. Let me tell you something, Roger. I understand exactly where Charlie Manson was coming from when he sent his troops into that neighborhood to blow those people away. I'm in exactly the same position as his lieutenant Tex Watson. For one reason or another, I decided to believe that some person had the right, or the wisdom, or the spiritual insight to make my moral decisions for me, and I let that person send me with a machinegun into the neighborhood of some strangers, and I killed them. My government's reason for sending me was to use homicidal violence to make a statement about things they did not like about the victim's social structure. Manson and his followers enacted precisely the same scene, for precisely the same reason, but without the covering blanket of the government's supposed right to sanction the act. Mom and Pop America look at that one small raiding-party sortie in Bel Air and put Manson on the shelf with Adolf Hitler and Attila the Hun. But there are a lot of men in this country who know exactly what it feels like to be in the position of Manson's team, and to go blasting into somebody's dinner party and kill them all, just because somebody told you it was all right, and ordered you to do it. And as for being a mass murderer, hey, I was a gunship driver, remember. Charlie Manson and Bill Calley and Richard Speck together don't add up to one good month back when I was killing people for fun. I became a murderer the first time I recognized the Vietnamese deserved better, but kept shooting because it was my job. Compared to me, that Tex Watson is a choir boy, but history calls him a psycho and me a hero for doing the same thing. It's not what you do that gets you hailed righteous or evil by the world, but whose permission you have."

"Could you still do it, if you had a reason?" Roger asked.

"You mean deliberately kill people? You're damn right I can. It means a lot to me to know that I can still be a warrior if the chips are down. I don't happen to have a reason right at the moment to go out and kill someone, but I still really believe in those ideals and principles they told me I was fighting for, and I still believe they are worth fighting for. Unfortunately, I'm afraid if I ever get pressed far enough to take up arms again for those principles, it will probably be my own government I've got to resist to protect them. And that's a pretty scary idea. One thing's for damn sure, though. I'll never kill for the Empire again."

"You didn't like flying for Darth Vader, huh?"

"You've got that right. You want to know the truth, Roger? You want to know what the whole crazy-Namvet syndrome thing is really all about? It's the one thing folks back home will never be able to understand and accept. You know, the World War II vet listens to everybody making such a big thing about the terrible violence the poor Namvet had to witness, and how seeing a buddy get blown away is what has fucked him up so bad. Well, to a guy who watched five thousand Marines reduced to beach pollution in a couple of days, or who spent six months in London under the V-2's and the Luftwaffe, that makes the Namvet sound like a gutless pussy. The truth is that nothing in Vietnam could come close to the hamburger horror of Iwo Jima or Bastogne. But it isn't the physical violence that fucked up the Namvet, it's the discovery that we were the big bad guy who got his ass kicked by the little peckerwood standing up for his rights — while we soldiers really believed in our hearts we were the good guys. You know how I see that fight? Joe Palooka, a fat and complacent showbiz Champ at forty, against Bruce Lee, an eighty-year-old coolie who just refused to roll over to the syndicate.

"I'm the most un-Communist guy you know — I'm so down on collective-owner living I think condos should be outlawed, but the 1770's American in me insists that the Vietnamese had the right to their self-determination when they kicked out the French in 1954, and when we came running in there to pick up the puppet strings, that made us the Redcoats. It's just too damned clear no government which has to defend itself from its constituency with a foreign army has the right to call itself a democracy. The thing that drives guys crazy is having evidence shoved up your nose that your country has behaved as a world-class bully and a stupid self-righteous hypocrite, and got exactly what it deserved. Then you have to come home where that's the one thing you just must not believe, if you intend to become a part of the fabric of the society again. If that weren't enough, you have to put up with your own people blaming you for losing the war, since their alternative is to recognize their idols in Washington, and on Wall Street, have feet of clay."

"So what the fuck do we do about it?"

"I don't know. I haven't figured out yet how to do much about anything. Coming up with reasonable ideas seems easy enough, but the thing is not a reasonable beast, and it doesn't seem to have a seat of control."

They stopped in Hobbs for box chicken shortly after sundown, and bought another half-gallon of vodka so Roger would not have to worry about running out during the night. They began to encounter fog on the highway, and occasional drizzle, so Kevin kept the speed down, smoked his dope, and enjoyed the cruise.

Roger slept for an hour or two, then woke up suddenly, looked around to see where he was, took a big drink, and quickly smoked a cigarette, sucking on it to pump up an inch-long coal. "I can't figure it out," he said, his voice deep and scratchy. "Why do I get dreams about combat, and I come up swinging, ready to fight, like I was some kind of crazy Namvet myself? I can't figure out where I get that."

"You mean how come you act the same as the guys with Namvet stress disorder? You tell me. It's an interesting image they're pushing these days — the stereotype Vietnam Veteran — I don't think it's much good for the vet, but what else is new, huh?"

"Well, I was supposed to be a Vietnam veteran, and in the end I guess I've learned to think like one...I just didn't get to go to the party, that's all," Roger whined.

"Maybe you ought to stick around. You could end up a veteran yet...from Nicaragua, El Salvador, Libya, Lebanon, not to mention Poland, and Pakistan. You know what frightens me, Roger? It's not that somebody is going to start World War III. Nah. It's that the old generals and jingoists are going to try to finish World War II."

"Right on. Those old boys are still running on the Nip-and-Hun propaganda they were fed in the Army Air Corps." Roger chuckled and took a long pull on his bottle. "Except now they drive their Toyotas down to Fort Bliss to teach the Luftwaffe how to use guided missiles, and yell about hating Russians."

After a while, Roger asked, "Did you know that more Vietnam veterans have committed suicide since the war than died in it?"

"I didn't know that," said Kevin. "Because of guilt for losing the war, no doubt, according to the official version."

"No doubt."

"You see what I mean about that image not being good for the Namvet — crazed with guilt and gory nightmares, suicidal or homicidal, and bad with banners if you corner him."

"Right," said Roger, lighting another smoke. "The Namvet looks like a hippie in an Army coat, but he's really a deadly weapon with a hair trigger, just waiting to explode."

"Yeah, but you can tell them apart from the hippies because Namvets don't get into lines and carry stupid signs. But you see what I mean. This character keeps showing up in the movies, and in the newspapers. You know, 'Vietnam Veteran Axes Grandmother While Sleepwalking', and they've got a picture of this long-haired wacko in a field jacket. Never mind he was a blind paraplegic illegitimate son of the former Prime Minister of Putzenberg and she used to run a Nazi concentration camp — he swung the axe, he's a Vietnam veteran. They're saying, 'It's not his fault he's crazy, but then, it wasn't Old Yeller's fault he got rabies, either. We're very sorry, but the Vietnam veteran is mentally disturbed, anti-social, about half-brainwashed, and extremely dangerous. Don't listen to a word he says, and help him get to a government therapist as quickly as possible.'

"That's the part that scares me the worst. Those government people really are very sorry we got mental rabies, and they aren't going to feel good about themselves until they have some way of saying, 'Look how much we're doing for the poor looney Namvet.' Unfortunately, the only trick they can think of these days is give-away minoritism, and that shit is crippling."

"What do you mean by that?" asked Roger, pouring the last of the first bottle of vodka into his soda bottle.

"Minoritism, the idiot backlash of the '70's. What we've got now is more and more groups who band together for superficial reasons and use their collective political power to squeeze the government for special favors for their particular group. And the whole bunch are competing to prove which of them is most shit-on, and least competent, and so most deserving of being first in line at the government trough. The result is a generation of people who think the road to success is to prove to the government that you're a failure because everybody hates you for being a speckled morphodite.

"The first thing they have to do to make a minority-program out of Vietnam veterans is to get everybody agreeing that the Namvet is an unfortunate victim who needs help. And if a Vietnam veteran expects to get anything from them, he must first be convinced that his reactions to what he experienced are insane, his conclusions wrong, and his only shot at returning to American sanity is to submit to a group of state-licensed mind-fixers. Then they get him to believe that when they get his head straightened out, he will be happy and able to get a good lifetime job in a respectable company. Until then, of course, he can't survive in a decent lifestyle without the assistance of the IRS and the welfare department. A lot of guys are being tempted by that federal molasses and cornbread to declare themselves unable to survive without the government, and they are being led into re-programming centers and taught to think like the other minorities, to demand their rights — that is, to demand that the government take more control over everybody else's lives and resources, and to put them on some kind of freebie program that nobody else gets. Minoritism."

Roger nodded sagely. "And what the government hears is all of them yelling, 'We can't survive if you don't take more control.'"

"Right," said Kevin. "So we get more people becoming less able to take care of themselves, and submitting to more and more control. That is not the way to preserve freedom and democracy. If we don't have the strength of character to handle being free, the government will take over, and give us a work schedule and a bowl with a number on it, and that's life on the turkey farm, kids. You remember the communes? They didn't work for exactly that reason — it just isn't true that if you get enough people who can't take care of themselves to band together, they can create a society which can take care of all of them. Well, it may be true, but it wouldn't be a democratic nation of free citizens, that's for sure."

"You don't think there should be programs for stuff like Agent Orange, or radiation damage?" Roger asked.

"Agent Orange will blow over. The potential client group is too large for them to ever permit a blanket settlement for much, just like that bunch of guys they staked out on the atom bomb test ranges of Nevada in the '50's. There should be medical treatment available for anything they can cure, of course, but punitive damages in the form of deficit-dollar disability pay? Nah, bullshit. Don't waste your time looking for ways to prove you're disabled — sooner or later you're going to start believing it.

"Big Rog, the best advice I can give the other Namvets is to stay the hell away from people trying to sell us a solution to our problem. First they've got to convince us that we have a problem, and the fact is that we're not part of the problem, we're part of the solution, if we will be. The kids who stayed home while we fought that war learned that ten thousand people standing in a line carrying signs that said, 'Somebody Do Something' still did not constitute anybody doing anything, even if they did call themselves activists. But ten thousand people who have a clear view of what it means to live free who are each taking care of his own little piece of the action, and looking for ways to make something around him work just a little bit better, or look a little bit better, or feel a little better — now they're a real and active force. Ho Chi Minh's teacher Mao Tse Tung said if he had five percent of the people in a country where fifty percent were apathetic, he could take over anywhere. I think Namvets are about eight percent of the population of the United States. If instead of crying about how Vietnam fucked us up, and somebody owes us lunch, we would recognize that we're right, and start helping to promote the kind of street-level self-sufficiency that has enabled us to survive all this time as outcasts and hermits, but on a much wider scale, we can be the group in the best position to identify and take the prudent middle ground between the minoritist socializers and the militarist empire-builders."

"Commies on the one side, Fascists on the other. Sounds good to me," chuckled Roger. "To quote Chesty Puller, 'Now we can attack in all directions.'"

"A Marine to the end, huh, Big Rog?" Kevin laughed. "But it means we've got to come out of hiding, not waving a white flag, or the Stars and Stripes, but just taking what influence we can and making things go right."

"Oh, yeah? I thought the big myth was to score land down in Costa Rica or New Zealand, and set up a survival farm to weather out the holocaust. Whatever happened to that idea?"

"It's still a nice way to live, but there is no longer any place to hide. Even if there were, I don't think I'd like to go to my grave knowing that I set my son up to be the first caveman in the next attempt at world civilization. No matter how far we turn our heads, the forces that created the war in Vietnam are still with us, and they are still the problem....our personal problem, like it or not."

"So what are you talking about getting into, Kevin? Business? Politics? Maybe industrial sabotage, or something like that?" asked Roger. "Is there anyone you think is so individually evil that it would be righteous to go hunt him down and kill him? I mean, is there really a Darth Vader?"

"I don't think so. Individual violence looks like a quick fix, but I don't think it ever changes the system for the better — it just puts it on a more severe defensive posture, and who needs that? They're right about one thing — we Namvets do have the knowledge and the objectivity to do that sort of thing, but I don't think you'll see many of us doing it. It's not practical. I personally think the answers to the real problems do not lie in forcibly stopping the old ways, but in just bypassing the system. Everybody just does whatever he can do in a productive way. It doesn't call for an organization. It's an attitude, that's all."

Roger laughed. "Harrey, why do I get the feeling this is a very new idea with you?"

Kevin blushed. "OK, I haven't exactly been leaving a trail of tended fields behind me, have I? You're right, it is a new idea, and it's the best-feeling idea I've had in ten years."

"So what changed your mind?"

Kevin drove silently for a moment, staring ahead into the drizzling haze of the night. "Oh, a lot of things, I guess. Like the nuclear arms race, and knowing we've got to stop it, and like turning 35 on Food Stamps." He paused. "You want the truth? The truth is I got to looking at that airplane out there in the back, and how sad it is that you won't be around to see it fly, and something deep down inside me, something I haven't been able to ignore since, said, 'What the hell are you going to do about it?' I start hearing that voice yelling that at me every time I go downtown or pick up a newspaper. It's not like dinner table rhetoric either, an invitation to speculate over the prawns why we ought to change the status quo. It's more like, 'Given a human life, freedom of choice, and the alternative of sitting on my ass until it ossifies, what can I actually do to fix the things I can see are wrong with the world, my world, my personal big, wide, heavily-populated blue planet?' Well, I don't know what the hell I'm going to do about a lot of things, but I'm going to start by making that airplane fly."

About two o'clock in the morning, they pulled into Mineral Wells, and Kevin suddenly recognized the two brick pylons which had framed the main gate to the school he attended twelve years before. The two helicopters which had been mounted there were gone, and a sign announced the place as an industrial park. "Welcome to Fort Wolters," he said.

"This is it?" asked Roger blearily, leaning over the seat. He had turned up the heat and crawled into the back seat, where he had sprawled dozing for a couple of hours.

"Yep." Kevin drove slowly, looking for something familiar. Then he recognized the long low building to which he had first reported in the fall of 1966 with the men who were to become his classmates. "Yeah, I remember that place," he said. "Gee, it looks so forlorn." He followed the road on around, and past some other buildings he did not remember, and then started up the long climbing curve toward the high ground where the Warrant Officer Candidate residence buildings stood, rows of gaunt three-story barracks, their windows and weathered walls bleak and colorless. Bare streetlamps on two corners glowed dully on the overhanging mists, creating an enclosed ambiance, as though the buildings were in a vaulted chamber, poorly lighted. The sharp lines of leafless branches of rows of trees were softened by the haze of silent drizzle, creating an effect like old cobwebs in the vault.

"There," he said to Roger, pointing to a building on which was painted the emblem of a tiger's face on a winged shield, "that was my barracks." Kevin pulled over and turned off the engine.

Roger opened the back door, tried to get out of the truck, and fell to the ground, clawing at the side of the vehicle. "God damn it! I just can't keep my feet under my ass any more."

Kevin helped him get to his feet, find the sleeves in his overcoat, and to put on his crushed and grimy old straw hat. "Oh, hold it," said Roger. "I want to get my bottle." He opened the door, snatched up his big green plastic bottle, and shuffled to keep up with Kevin. "There. Can't toast old times with an empty glass, can you?"

"I reckon not," said Kevin. He shrugged his shoulders to pull the fur collar of his old flight jacket up around his neck, and strolled slowly down the middle of the street.

"Which room was yours?" asked Roger.

Kevin pointed. "Up there, top floor, second from the end. I used to stand right here, every morning in formation, rain or shine. Bizarre, huh?"

"Yeah." Roger turned and looked all around at the high empty windows, then he yelled out in a rasped and cracking voice, "Company....FALL IN!"

Kevin laughed. "Company B-2, all present or accounted for, Sir!" he hooted. For a moment, they listened breathlessly, as though expecting to hear the report continue, and the sounds of troops marching. Their voices reverberated from the blank walls, muffled by the drizzling cloud.

Roger grinned, and banged his heels together clumsily. "Leof.... FEESE!" he barked. "Forkward.... HUT!"

Enjoying Roger's boozy good humor, Kevin began goose-stepping in time to his lumbering big friend's cadence.

"Yo' Leop, yo' leop, yo' Lep ear Lope," chanted Roger.

"What the hell kind of cadence is that?" asked Kevin.

"I guess you never heard a Marine DI sing cadence, huh?" said Roger. "They all got their own personal cadence, right. Here, lemme show you one." Kevin fell into step, and they marched down the street. Roger's voice cracked and screeched, and he had to stop to cough often, but he sang the cadence.

"Eh, ho, he-ey, aie-do LEP, yo he-ey, aie-do LEP, yer LOPE! Yo LEOP! Yo LEOP! Yo Lep ear Lope!"

Kevin laughed. "That's pretty neat. Fucking leathernecks have a sense of showmanship. All I ever heard in the Army was the Jody calls. It's always that fucking Jody. You can't get away from him. Try this one:

One, toop, threep, ho! Sergeant, Sergeant, I've been told,"
Roger responded, ("Sergeant, Sergeant, I've been told,").
"Beatin' your drum gets mighty old. ("Beatin' your drum gets mighty old.")
Ain't no use in going home; ("Ain't no use in going home;")
Jody's got your girl and gone. ("Jody's got your girl and gone.")
Am I right or wrong? ("You're right!")
Am I right or wrong? ("You're right!")
Sound off! ("One, two.")
Sound off! ("Three, four.")
Sound off! ("One, two, three, four, One, two.....THREE-FOUR!")"

Marching side by side, but half-stepping so Roger could keep up, the two men cried out their nostalgic chant.

"Sergeant, Sergeant, I hear tell, ("Sergeant, Sergeant, I hear tell,")
Green Berets are tough as hell. ("Green Berets are tough as hell.")
Ain't no use in feeling down; ("Ain't no use in feelin' down;")
Kick Jody's ass when you're in town! ("Kick Jody's ass....uh-haugh, cough!")
Am I right or wrong?" ("Cough! Uuuuggh.")

Roger fell out of the formation, staggered to the side of the street, and leaned against a boulder which sat in front of one of the buildings. He coughed and retched, and spit a big bloody gob on the side of the stone.

"Am I right or wrong?" sang Kevin.

"You're right," croaked Roger. He sat down and leaned against the wet boulder, wheezing and shaking.

Kevin walked over to stand beside him. "Well, I'll be damned," he said in surprise. "I remember this. This is the WOC Rock." The boulder was about fifteen feet long and five feet high, and had been painted with the winged insignia of the Army Aviator. Kevin smiled and reached to tear off a piece of the peeling paint. It was a dozen coats of paint thick, and lay heavy in his hand like a silver dollar. He put it into the pocket of his flight jacket. "It was a trophy. The best WOC battalion got to keep it in front of their building. It was a good hoot to win — the winners had to go over to the losers' barracks and carry it home. I forget how many tons it weighs, but you can see it's a pretty big hunk of rock."

Roger struggled to his feet and stepped into the street to view the painting on the WOC Rock, leaving his hat on the ground behind him. He stood for a long moment, staring at the emblem. His boots were torn on the sides and broken down in the heels, and his muddy coat hung from his sagging shoulders. His eyes were swollen, and his mouth hung open. Abruptly he broke into tears and stood weeping helplessly, hands dangling at his sides and spittle drooling from his chin.

Kevin stood beside the rock and watched him. "What the fuck, Big Rog?" he asked, finally.

"Aw, never mind me," blubbered the broken big man, "I was just wishing...wishing that Eddie could be here to share this with us."

Kevin nodded silently. "Me too," he said at last, very softly. "Hey, come on. I'm going to find a way to break into that barracks. I want to see my old room again."

"I'll never make it to the top floor," groaned Roger.

"Well, all right, then, we'll find a room on the bottom floor. Come on." Kevin walked around the base of his old barracks building, and soon found a window that had been broken out and patched with fiberboard. "Watch this," he said. He took aim and fired a shoulder-high side kick at the middle of the board. It broke inward, and fell to the floor of the room. "Now we can see if there are any ghosts in here," he said, crawling through the window into the room.

Roger poked his head through the window, grunted and struggled, and eventually tumbled to the floor, and for a moment they were silent, listening to the greater silence of the old building. Kevin flicked his lighter to life, and then shielded the flame with the other hand and peered into the darkness. "It feels like what I'd expect a of sunken ship," said Roger. "I keep expecting to see an octopus clutching some dead sailor."

"There was the TAC's office," said Kevin, peering into a room. "He was a crazy fucker — used to write messages to us on the floors with shaving cream if we left our lockers open. When we graduated, we gave him a beautifully-engraved brick."

"A brick? What did it say?" asked Roger.

"It said, 'For Suppository Use Only'.

They stepped into one of the rooms, and Kevin held the lighter over his head. The built-in wall-lockers gaped open, and the room was completely bare. "We used to hand-polish these fucking floors," said Kevin. "That's how they made trained killers out of us." He stepped to the side of the room and sat down on the cold floor. "How about that toast?" he asked, fishing a joint from his pocket.

"You got it," said Roger, flopping down heavily beside him. He tugged his bottle from the deep side pocket of the overcoat and twisted off the cap. "Here's to Eddie Padilla," he said.

"I'll torch up to that," agreed Kevin, putting the lighter to his joint. Roger drank deeply from the jug, and they sat quietly together for a few minutes in the semi-darkness.

"I keep remembering the first time we met," said Roger.

Kevin laughed. "Yeah, a hot night in old Juazoo. We really tore that bunch of jerks in the U-Boat a new asshole, didn't we. It's funny, but I remember you two guys sitting there before the fight, and I can remember — just like I was there right now — seeing Eddie's face when you called them out. He was just plain astonished."

Roger shook his head solemnly. "I guess I had a bad habit of getting Eddie into fights, huh? I wish I'd always been around to pull him out." He sighed, drank again. "I remember seeing you in the bar before the fight, too. My first impression of you didn't change much for a long time."

"Oh, yeah? What was that?"

"I thought you were a smug little prick. I kept thinking that for a long time, but you know what bothered me the most? You always had the stuff to back it up. I was even glad for a while that the world kind of shit on your head back a few years ago, but you've even managed to come through that — and come through stronger than you were then. Guess I've got to hand it to you in the end, goddamnit."

"Well, thanks for saying so, even though the truth is you were right from the beginning." Kevin took a long toke on his joint. "I always thought you were a clumsy buffoon, Stumbo The Giant Clown. You know what always bothered me the most?"

"No. What?"

"You always had such a good time, and other people could relax around you. You always made people feel good, Big Rog. You were a good friend to a lot of people. I envied you that."

Roger coughed up a glob and spat it across the room. "That's funny. I always felt so lonely, and I always felt like I had to do something or people wouldn't like me, like buy them a drink, you know. And then there was Eddie. Aaaaw, God, it tears me up. 'Cause you know, Eddie was a real friend, he...he really loved me. He followed me around like a goddamn dog, and I was so busy using him to reassure myself that somebody liked me, I...I never knew how much I loved that little guy until he was gone." The big man slumped forward and wept, blubbering onto the floor between his feet.

"It's all right, Roger," said Kevin. "It was his own life, and his own destiny. It isn't your fault."

"I'm so shamed," cried Roger. "I am put to shame by Eduardo Santiago Padilla. When the chickens all came home to roost, he was the one who proved he really had all the things I kept telling him I had — and a whole lot more. Now every time I go to sleep I'm haunted by his ghost, and it's always little Eddie, the little kid I first met, and he's always wearing this bloody oversize flight suit, and calling out to me, asking me, 'Did I do good enough, Big Rog? Did I have the balls?' Oh, God, ooooh!"

Kevin turned to Roger, trying to remain the calm comforter, but his memory suddenly flooded upon him like a burst dam, and he remembered Eddie. His words caught in the back of his throat, and he put his hands over his face and cried out. Hot tears rushed down his cheeks. "Oh, Eddie, no," he sobbed. "Why did you have to....why couldn't you just....oh, God."

"You knew him," said Roger, pointing an accusing finger. "You knew the man, Harrey, the real Eddie Padilla. And you saw him die! You saw it!"

Kevin slumped against the wall. "Oh, Roger, I am so shamed. I am so shamed." The words began to flood from him, and with them came the memories he had so long denied. He leaned his cheek against the cold wall of the room and stared vacantly into the darkness, seeing again the inside of the tent at Bao Trang, seeing Eddie sitting on his bunk, rubbing his ankle and keeping his eyes lowered as Duke Randall named him Eddie's replacement on the LRRP mission scheduled for the dawn. "I'm going to tell you what happened, and I am going to remember it all. I owe that much to both of you. He really was a hero, Roger. Heart, mind, and soul, he was a hero, and I tried to talk him out of it. I taught him to cheat the system, because I was trying to find a way to get him home alive. I taught him to put the other guy's life on the line to save his own, just the way I had. I just didn't teach him good enough."

SIXTEEN

The sky was just beginning to show the first gray light as the Dagger crews lugged their gear to the flight line. Without anyone having suggested that they would need extra equipment, almost everyone carried a few additional things — a couple of candy bars, extra pistol ammunition, or flare pens. The ghostly pre-dawn light made fuzzy silhouettes of the ships, and as Kevin walked past the row of helicopters, even the murky yellow pools of light from the crews' flashlights seemed cold and alien. He tossed his chicken plate and helmet into the left seat of the minigun ship he would fly with Captain Duke Randall, and began his pre-flight inspection of the bird.

Half an hour later, the fireteam climbed out into the dawn following the slicks toward fire support base Fort Tularosa, where they were to meet and pick up the LRRP troops. Kevin sat hunched in his seat, wishing the sun were up so the cockpit would get warm. The sky had begun to get light, so the mountains to the west made a dark, jagged, and uncertain skyline, a setting for a horror movie. Duke appeared to be relaxed and looking forward to the mission. He hummed and whistled to himself, and holding the cyclic gently with only the tips of his fingers, he flew with the precision of a skater, without a wasted motion.

"Say," he said, "did you hear about the Mig?"

"No. What happened?"

"I was talking to Ritchey — the Lurp patrol commander — last night at the Division Intelligence briefing. He said one of the Cav units flying for them on these things over the border had a fireteam of the new Cobras in there get jumped by a Mig-21."

"Holy shit. What did they do?"

"One of the gunships dived for the deck, caught a treelimb with a skid, and wiped out. The other Cobra cranked it around head-on with the jet and let loose with full frog-pods — thirty eight rockets in a neat fan pattern. Nailed him solid."

"He got the Mig?"

"Big as a bear."

"Damn! Did you get the pilot's name?"

"Snead, maybe. Ritchey wasn't sure."

"I expect they'll make a big deal about it in the news. In this game, that ought to qualify for Ace."

Duke shrugged. "Naw, nobody will ever hear about it. He was out of the country."

Kevin shook his head. "What a rip-off," he said.

Duke seemed to Kevin to grow larger the farther west they flew. "I've got to admit he has class," thought Kevin. "Getting Captain Pan in supply to scrounge fire sirens to put on the gunships was real showmanship."

As they approached the firebase, Randall dropped to a hover, then set the gunship down gently behind the slicks. "Go ahead and shut her down, Harrey," he said, unbuckling his safety harness. "I'll meet you inside."

Kevin allowed the engine to run at idle for a minute or so to cool the tailpipe, then touched the idle-stop button and rolled the throttle off. He got out of the bird, checked it over again, then stood waiting for Skip and Hawking to shut down.

"You don't look happy at all," said Hawking as he strolled over to join Kevin. "Afraid Duke is going to go berserk again?"

"I hope not. When he gets ballsy and talking about Jesus, I get shook up just getting in the bird with him."

"So he likes contact sports — give him a break," said Skip. "Come on, let's go get this briefing."

"And some hot coffee to go with it, I hope," added Hawking. They walked to a low sandbagged structure about fifty meters from the aircraft, half dug into the ground, and covered logs cut from the local timber.

"OK, that's all of us," said Duke Randall as the three gunship pilots walked into the low-ceilinged room. "Let's get everybody introduced. This is Mr. Cronin, who will be flying the primary insertion and extraction ship. Captain Miller, air mission commander, will be calling the shots from the number-two slick, and he will be primary rescue ship if anybody goes down. Mr.

Ramsey is flying the back-up ship. The co-pilots are Hoyt, Pulver, and Betts. I'm Captain Randall, the fire team leader. Mr. Gilman will be on my wing, and Hawking and Harrey there will be on the blooper and the miniguns. This gentleman is Captain Fry, who will be flying the Air Force FAC. His call sign is Pride. Now I'll turn the briefing over to Lt. Ritchey."

The patrol unit leader took the floor. He pointed to six men in camouflage fatigues and greasepaint sitting along a wall sipping coffee and smoking a last cigarette. "The team's call sign is Sweetheart. This is team leader Sergeant Kelly, that's Rose, Garza, and three ARVN Rangers. We will be inserting them into a suspected base camp area for a battalion of North Vietnamese regulars." He pulled down a map showing a section of the western border of Vietnam. "Along here," he said, "runs the A Lan valley, a primary corridor on the Ho Chi Minh Trail. Notice the valley runs right along the border, and these mountains on the west side are out of Vietnam. The North Vietnamese have gun positions along these mountains, and since the Tet Offensive, they have been massing divisions of troops over there. To control that valley, we must know what is waiting for us on the other side. Our insertion site this morning is here, just about thirty clicks past A Lan airfield." The lieutenant pointed toward the map, then moved his hand to the left, and further to the left, and yet further.

Kevin's lower guts twisted, and the hair rose on his neck. "The Graveyard...then twenty miles west."

"As you might expect," Ritchey went on, "the area is well defended. We've been in there before, and we've lost a couple of helicopters. We ran a people-sniffer a few days ago with some guys from the 101st Division and took fire from here..." He pointed to a line of red pins on his map. "...and here, and here. The pilot said it was mostly small automatic weapons fire, with some scattered fifty-cal stuff, but the Russians have given these bozos a bunch of 37mm anti-aircraft cannons. They're good equipment, hydraulic operated and radar controlled." There was a murmur of voices. "That's right, real flak, designed to knock out low-flying jets."

"Actually, men, the flak is not that big a thing," put in Duke

Randall, "because it's not designed with us in mind. If we stay on the treetops, the 37mm rounds don't have time to arm themselves. What we've got to watch out for are the fifties, and I don't have to tell any of you how to cope with them."

"Get the hell out of there, and call the gunships," said Captain Jack Miller.

"Right," said Duke.

"Captain Miller, how about describing the actual insertion for us," asked Ritchey.

"Uh, right, thanks." Miller took the floor, looking thin and nervous. "All right, gentlemen, this mission will use three slicks, one fire team, and Pride, who has a pair of Phantom jets parked up in a high orbit. When we get to the insertion site, the slicks will be fifteen seconds apart in trail on the treetops. The last click or so, I will climb up two hundred feet to call directions. When I tell him to flare, Mr. Cronin will stand his ship on her tail and drop right into the hole. Then I will fly directly over the LZ, followed by Mr. Ramsey. When both have passed overhead, Cronin will pull out and take the trail position. In this way we can conceal the location of the insertion point from almost all observers.

"The extraction will be the same drill. If the LZ is cold, Checker Cab will drop in, take up trail position on the way out, and off we go. If it's hot, well, we fight our way in, and we fight our way out. Everybody straight on the flight part of the mission? Oh, yes, Captain Fry. Go ahead, please."

The Air Force pilot stood, looking strange in his blue flight suit. "Thanks. I'll be flying an O-2. I think most of you know the bird, the Cessna pusher-puller. I will have a two-plane section of F4C's loaded with 750-pound bombs and 20mm cannon orbiting over the area before we get there. If it turns out to be too hot for us to operate in there, we'll call in the jets to give us some heavy covering fire so we can get the hell out. And when we leave, we'll let them dump whatever they have left to keep Charlie busy until the B-52's get there."

"Thank you, Captain," said Ritchey. "Kelly?"

The stocky team leader took the floor and described the patrol team's part of the operation. He covered the nature of the terrain, the intelligence reports on what they could expect to find in the base camp, the times they would try to make routine calls, and what they would expect from the air cover. "The insertion LZ is about two-and-a-half clicks from the base camp. If everything goes well, we plan to move in quietly, take a look around, plant a few goodie-pops — boobytraps — and then get back out if possible without being seen at all. If we're spotted, we'll call you immediately so we can try to get out before they get a chance to set up gun positions around us. We'll try not to get caught."

"Anything else?" asked Captain Miller. "Oh, yeah, Buddy Nichols, the hotshot with the camera there in the back of the room, is going along with us. He'll be in Checker Three to get some good pictures for the folks back home, so you all remember to keep smiling. OK, gentlemen, if there is nothing else anybody just has to say, let's get some air under these bitches!"

The ships were loaded, cranked, and airborne in minutes, and then shortly, with the sun behind them, the flight cleared the last ridge and dropped down into the A Lan valley. Kevin pulled out the pistol-grip sight to his minigun and checked for a good light reticle.

"You're likely to see all kinds of things to shoot at," said Duke, "but save every round you can. If we run into something hot, you'll need them all."

"Right, Sir."

"There's the Graveyard — A Lan airfield," said the big pilot, pointing ahead toward the khaki scar in the greenery of the valley floor. "We'll go low level right over it. Well, the slicks will be low-level — we'll be up a couple hundred, right in the old Suicide Zone."

"Better view. Wouldn't want to miss anything, would we?"

"Attaboy. We'll make a proper gunnie out of you yet, Harrey, if you don't get hit by a taxi somewhere on R-and-R."

The flight moved quickly across the valley and headed up a narrow jungle-choked gorge. Captain Miller zoom-climbed two hundred feet and called directions to the lead slick. "Checker Cab, your LZ is dead ahead, just where the canyon forks, about thirty seconds away." Miller's voice was squeaky with excitement, but his commands were strong and sure. "Five hundred meters — two degrees left — two hundred meters — dead ahead — OK, start your flare — fifty meters — you're right on top of the LZ. You've got it."

"Tight!" came Cronin's terse reply. His helicopter dropped into the tiny hole in the jungle and held a low hover while the six men of the patrol team jumped out. When Mike Ramsey's trail ship crossed them fifty feet overhead, Cronin pulled smoothly out of the LZ and accelerated through the treetops. The five Hueys hurdled a ridge and dropped into the adjoining gorge to sprint back toward the valley.

Kevin saw the tracers before Miller got off the call, "Receiving fire!" Two probing streams of golfball-sized red comets singled out the first ship in the flight, firing down on it from the ridgeline above. A jolt of adrenaline charged him as he realized that he would be running that gauntlet line himself in a few seconds. His horror was doubled when he saw Duke react instantly to the tracers by pulling in full power and climbing up the slope to attack the fifty-cal position.

"On HOT!" he yelled into the mike, sweeping the arming switches with his palm. He heard Duke chuckle, and he felt a terrible urge to wet his pants. Duke drove the gunship up the side of the ridge clipping treetops, prancing and weaving like a fast running back to deny the heavy machineguns a clear shot at him.

"We get one pass," called Duke on the gunships tactical FM channel, "that is, if nobody goes down. Ready with those miniguns," he added, to Kevin. "Here goes." He popped up suddenly to a hundred fifty feet. Kevin's guns snarled and sprayed the ridgeline below with sweep fire to keep the enemy's heads down. The helicopter seemed to hang still in the air for a second before Duke tipped the nose down and began to pickle off his rockets. The stream of fireballs reached out at them, and the cockpit was suddenly filled with acrid smoke as the chin-bubble windshields at the pilots' feet shattered. In that second, Kevin spotted the pile of logs and shrubbery that served to camouflage and protect the gun position. He held the ring of light in his sight on the spot and kept mashing the trigger switch to keep the guns spitting. Duke used four pairs, then broke off his attack at treetop level. Kevin watched the explosions chew into the pile of logs as the ship banked steeply and dived down the slope.

Skip Gilman was close behind, and as soon as the lead gunship banked away from the gun position, he fired three salvos of rockets. On the 40mm grenade launcher, Hawking lobbed his shots, watching each round arc out toward the target, and applying loft and english by eye.

"Lead, Checker Three," called Ramsey. "I think we're clear...not taking fire."

"Break off, Daggers," called Randall immediately. The flight dashed across the valley clipping buffalo grass. As they passed the bomb-scarred Graveyard, Duke turned to Kevin and grinned. "Bet you never thought you'd feel safer getting back here, did you?"

Kevin looked through the shattered chin bubble to see the burned hulk of an old crash. "Sure didn't."

When the flight cleared the ridge and began to drop down toward firebase Fort Tularosa, Duke contacted the Operations office at the base and requested that they make a landline call back to Bao Trang. "Request you call Black Sabre and tell them if they have another gunship in flying status to send it up here immediately. Our lead gunship has taken some fifty-caliber fire, and we're not sure of the status of that aircraft. Over."

"Roger, you request they scramble one Dagger."

"That's affirm, thank you." He turned to Kevin. "OK, that takes care of the easy part. They know we've got a team in there, so we'll just have to wait for them to move, then we'll rip 'em a new one, right?"

"Right," said Kevin, pawing his pocket for a smoke.

They landed at Fort Tularosa and sat down beside the birds to wait for the extraction. Kevin inspected his gunship closely, and found that the two slugs which had shattered his chin bubbles had passed out through the bottom of the airframe, doing little damage. However, a third slug had struck the rotor blade and chewed out a fist-sized piece of the aluminum honeycomb. It was technically a good reason for grounding the aircraft. The tear might have no effect, or it could suddenly begin to peel the surface of the blade away, and the rotor could shake itself apart

— an uncommon, but spectacularly fatal occurrence. Kevin hoped Duke would ground the bird, but he knew as long as the team was in the field, and no replacement had yet arrived, they would risk destruction and fly if the team got into trouble.

"We've got to be crazy," he said to the other pilots.

Skip laughed sympathetically. "Yeah. But what about those lunatics we leave on the ground out there!"

The nearest friendly unit was twenty-five miles away, a lonely ridgetop observation post, and the only contact Sergeant Kelly and his team had with the rest of the world was the FM radio set carried by his good buddy and assistant team leader, Mel Rose. They had spent the time since their insertion moving toward the suspected base camp that had been located by the chemical corps' people-sniffer.

The team stopped to rest a few minutes, sitting in a rough circle facing outwards to watch their respective sectors. Nobody spoke. The jungle was hot and the air was thick with the heavy, fetid mists rising from the rainsodden floor of the triple-canopy forest. They had found plenty of evidence that Charlie was in the area in large numbers, but had not made contact with them, so the tension was beginning to become numbing instead of alerting. Out of long habit, they checked equipment and weapons again as they lay listening to the jungle.

A few meters to the side of them ran the trail they were following. Though it was too far beneath the interlocking tops of the trees to be seen from the air, the trail was well maintained and wide enough for two men. Somewhere hidden in the trees along it was the base camp they had come to locate.

Catching the eye of Mel Rose, Kelly signaled the big black man to form up the team and get moving again. Mel hefted the PRC-25 radio set he carried and signaled to the Vietnamese Ranger beside him. They all stood quietly, and prepared to move out. Then as one, all six of the recon troops froze. "There, again," silently indicated one of the Rangers, pointing to his ear at the sound, a sound that did not belong to the jungle.

Kelly nodded, hearing the soft rattle, the splattering. "Bicycle," he whispered. With crisp and decisive hand signals,

Kelly ordered his team to take up an ambush position on the narrow trail, using only silent weapons. Moving like cats, they chose their places quickly. The rider was one man, middle-aged, wearing a light shirt and short pants. Carrying an AK-47 rifle and a message pouch, he was enjoying a pleasant ride through a secure area. He was taken completely by surprise when a Vietnamese in camouflage fatigues stepped into the center of the trail, pointed a rifle at him, and said, "Stop." Before he could utter a sound, he was jerked from the bicycle by his neck.

Holding the man's head against the back of his heavily-muscled arm with his guitar-string garotte, Mel dragged him a few meters into the jungle. "No noise," he whispered in Vietnamese into his terrified captive's ear. Then he and the senior of the three Vietnamese Rangers crouched over the messenger and bound him, while Kelly moved the bicycle away from the trail. "Put a boobytrap on that," Kelly told one of the troops. He motioned to Garza to keep a good lookout, then he moved to join Mel and the Ranger with the captive. The man was bound face down with his elbows pulled together behind his back. He was not gagged, but Mel kept the garotte around his neck just tightly enough that he could breathe occasionally, but could not cry out. The Ranger began to question him, leaning over his shoulder to speak softly into his ear. The man said nothing, but began to tremble and weep. When the Ranger began to probe at his anus with the point of his bayonet, he bit through his lower lip. The knife slid deeper and the body bucked uncontrollably, but it was obvious the man was resolved to die and would not speak. The Ranger put away his bayonet and began to examine the contents of the man's kit. Mel tightened the garotte until blood welled out of the crease in the neck. The body shook, the bowels suddenly let loose their burden of shit and blood, and the messenger died.

"Number One," said the Ranger to Kelly, holding papers from the pouch. "Very important, Kelly."

"Right. Let's round 'em up and move on."

As Kelly turned to signal to Garza and the others, Mel drew his bayonet and pried open the jaw of the dead messenger. "There's some shine," he muttered, peering inside. Placing the point of the heavy knife against the root of a molar, he smacked the heel with his palm sharply to knock the tooth free. He wiped it against his sleeve, clucked in satisfaction at the size of the gold inlay, then dropped it into the small leather pouch he carried around his neck.

"Let's go," said Kelly as Mel joined him. "We've been here too long." He gave Mel a friendly pat on the shoulder, waved to the four other men to move into their advancement positions, and raised his hand to signal the team to move out. Then, to their right and ahead of them, something in the jungle moved.

They froze. For a second the jungle was strangely silent, then they heard the soft but unmistakable sound of someone moving slowly through underbrush. Kelly quickly made his decision. The drill was routine. They would lie low listening until they knew how many there were and in which direction they were moving. Then he would decide whether to follow them or to bypass them. Kelly took a compass reading, checked his map, and frowned. Something wasn't right. When he glanced up he saw Mel looking at him with a worried expression, and he nodded. Mel leaned toward him and muttered almost silently, "I don't like it. Dey makin too much noise," Kelly chewed his lower lip. Maybe that was it. Following his ear and his compass readings, Kelly was certain that the enemy were not walking on the trail, but were moving parallel to it about twenty meters to the side. If the enemy felt secure enough to make so much noise, why weren't they moving down the cleared trail?

The answer came in a second. On the opposite side of the trail, somebody snapped a stick. "That ties it," thought Kelly. "They know we're here, and they want us to think they don't." He motioned to Mel. "We're moving out. They've got us pegged and they're trying to get us to follow them. We'll call for a quick extraction before they can get their perimeter set up around us."

Mel nodded agreement and reached for the Prick-25 to scramble the extraction team. Kelly stopped him and fumbled for his map. He knew within minutes after the call, the choppers would be flying, and within the hour — if everything went right — they would be back at Fort Tularosa for dinner. But one detail still kept Kelly from feeling the situation was in hand. The

Vietnamese had long-since proved to him they were nobody's fools, and these were well-trained NVA regulars, not a bunch of VC kids. If Charlie had reached the point in his game where he was revealing himself to the team but trying not to spook them, it was likely he had set up an ambush at the PZ. If an unwary helicopter could be lured in, a couple of claymore mines or a rocket-propelled grenade could easily claim the costly prize.

"Here," he said, pointing to the map. "We'll use that clearing we passed, half a click from the PZ. I figure the PZ will be hot since they know we're here. If we call the birds now, we'll have just enough time to get to this spot. Maybe we can catch them sleeping."

Mel called for immediate extraction, giving coordinates for locating the tiny clearing. "On the way," he said, giving the thumbs-up.

"Let's get it on," said Kelly. They moved out, and when they neared the clearing, changed direction and skirted around it about fifteen meters out into the brush. When they were on the opposite side, they closed into a wedge and moved in. The enemy wasn't there.

"Where the hell are those choppers," Mel muttered as the team dropped into a defensive circle to wait.

Eddie Padilla lay on his bunk, staring up at the dusty tent roof above him. He was glad he was not along on the mission, and that fact was very disturbing to him. The notion of riding through the crowds of Las Cruces in a hero's parade suddenly seemed strangely real — not romantic, a rapture of triumph, but a simpleminded ceremony like a Sunday School pageant, a ritual enacted not to his glory, but for their comfort and reassurance. How ironic, he thought, that they could never know how much more a hero, and how much less a hero he was than the symbol they made of him.

He tried not to worry about the mission, tried not to picture Kevin sitting in the place that had been meant for him. Perhaps, he thought, Kevin would only be getting what he had coming to him. After all, if he had sent Kevin to take the bullet that was meant for him, had he not merely followed Kevin's advice? But then had he not proved the bottom line in his own personal book of rules was, "Dog Eat Dog"? Tears welled to his eyes, and he swore he would tell Kevin how wrong he was the next time he saw him. "You're right, Babycakes," he would tell him, "there is no righteousness in waging this war, or any war, and most who fall in combat die in vain. But without sacrifice, life is hollow, because a man who has nothing to die for has nothing to live for."

Eddie prayed that Kevin would be safe, and he swore he would be the hero his mother hoped he would be.

His thoughts were interrupted by the runner from Operations, who came to the tent to notify Bergin and Swomney they were to scramble the reserve gunship.

"What's up?" asked Bergin, jumping to pick up his flight gear.

"I dunno, Mr. Bergin. We got a call that the lead ship on the Lurp mission got shot up by fifty-cal fire, and you need to get to Fort Tularosa ASAP."

Eddie flashed cold sweat. He sat and watched in silent horror as the two pilots ran from the tent and jumped into the back of the three-quarter. As the vehicle drove out of sight, Eddie suddenly leaped into motion, grabbed his own flight gear, and ran toward the Operations building. He tossed his gear into the Admin Officer's jeep, then stepped inside to the key locker. "Scramble team forgot a helmet," he said to the clerk on duty. He leaped into the front seat of the jeep and drove speedily to the flight line. Bergin was just beginning to run up the engine when Eddie ran to the cockpit door, flight gear in hand.

"Round John, there's been a change of assignment," Eddie told him. "I'm going to take this one. Operations sent me down here to stop you."

Bergin and Swomney looked at Eddie's face and knew why he had come. They could see too clearly the terrible need in his eyes, and were shaken by the recognition that he feared something much more than dying, and that something was on the line.

"I'll straighten it out with Cap'n Duke when we get back," Eddie pleaded, "but you've got to let me go."

From the left seat, Swomney held his breath and watched helplessly. He was sure his doom was sealed when Bergin released his lap belt and opened the cabin door. "OK, Eddie, they'll probably start a new Shitbird List for us, but you've got it." He stepped down out of the helicopter and closed the door behind Eddie when he had climbed in. The two gunners glanced at each other and cast worried eyes to heaven. Swomney sat motionless watching Eddie go through the checklist, a forlorn and vacant gaze on his face, like that of a man peering through the peephole of a prison door. "Do what you have to," said Bergin, "but try to get all four of you buttholes home in one piece, OK?"

"Thanks, Johnny," yelled Eddie over the rising whine of his turbine, "that's one I owe you."

Captain Jack Miller stepped into the LRRP briefing room and waved at the crewmen. "The team has been spotted," he said. "We're going to pull them out. This is a scramble. Let's go!"

With the others Kevin leaped to his feet and grabbed his gear. The crew chief ran to release the rotor tie-down, and people yelled last-minute instructions back and forth. While Duke Randall was cranking up the turbine, Kevin watched Buddy Nichols and Lt. Ritchey run from the building carrying flak jackets and steel helmets, and jump aboard the trail ship enthusiastically. "Good grief," thought Kevin, "why would anyone go out of his way to bum a ride on a trip like this?"

In seconds, Duke was pulling pitch to launch the gunship forward. "Daggers are up, Checker Lead," he reported. Then he yelled, loud enough to be heard in the aircraft without the intercom, "Yeeehah!" He snapped the switch to the fire siren mounted on the helicopter's skid. Banshee-wailing, nose low for speed, they took off into the glaring mid-day sun.

"Checker Lead, Pride," came Captain Fry's call from the FAC spotter plane. "Your jets have bounced, and they'll be over the site about the same time we are."

"Roger the jets, brother. We're probably going to need them," replied Miller earnestly.

"You tell 'em, Twitch," Kevin muttered, grinning.

The flight topped the last ridge of B-52 scarred hills, dropped into the valley, and sped past A Lan airfield. "This place is getting to be just like home," Kevin declared, squeezing the switch to transmit.

In minutes they were on the treetops making their way up the narrow gorge, and a voice came up on the FM tactical freq used by the team. "Checker, this is Sweetheart. We've got you coming up the canyon east of us. We're know we have enemy within seventy-five meters, but so far nobody has opened fire. Over."

"We're about a minute out, so pop your smoke," Miller instructed the team. From the lead gunship, Kevin scanned the ground intently to pick out the clearing. Duke allowed the ship to climb another fifty feet above the treetops to extend his view, flying above and to the side of the Checker Cab. Kevin noted with dismay that it was also a particularly vulnerable position — he pictured the target they presented to the enemy as an elephant with a rotor-beanie.

"Smoke is out," came the reply. The recon troops had waited to throw the smoke grenade until the last minute since it marked their position for the enemy as well as for the helicopters. The plume rose quickly and Kevin spotted it, closer than he had expected.

"I've got lemon smoke at eleven o'clock," called Duke. He pulled his gunship into a steep zoom-climb to four hundred feet and tipped the nose over, hanging almost motionless in the air above the tiny pickup zone. With Miller calling the shot again, Cronin settled toward the narrow space where the team crouched. Kevin marveled at the size of the confined area Cronin was carefully slipping his ship down into. The tightest ones used in school were airfields by comparison. While he sprayed the trees and underbrush with minigun fire to keep heads down, he saw the recon team clambering aboard, using the rope ladders and the skids to climb aboard the low hovering slick.

"Looks like we're going to get away with it," Kevin thought. Then a burst of automatic weapon fire slashed up from a position close to the insertion site. From the nearest ridge came another spray of tracers as the enemy opened fire, caught out of position but not surprised.

Duke carried his attack almost to the treetops before banking the helicopter steeply and climbing back up the side of the gorge for another pass. The door gunners kept their M-60's blazing to cover the breakaway, but still Kevin could hear the crackle of enemy fire coming from the trees only a hundred feet below. Then he heard the tinny thunk of rounds striking the helicopter. One round punched through the ship's skin above his door, leaving a dime-sized rose with aluminum petals.

"We're taking hits, One-three," called Duke calmly. "There's quite a bit of fire down there, Skip."

"No shit!" replied Skip, diving into the tracerfire with all guns spitting.

Below, the six men of the team had scrambled up the rope ladders. Rose, the last man to climb aboard, waved an OK to the crew chief as soon as he could stand on the skid. The crewman slapped Betts, the copilot, on the shoulder and shouted, "We got 'em all. Let's go."

"Coming out," called Cronin. The doorgunners chopped into the brush with their machineguns, and a string of bursts from Hawking's grenade launcher ripped the jungle. The helicopter had just begun its motion upward and forward to make good the surprise pickup when the front windshield suddenly erupted in a shower of splintered plexiglas. From somewhere only a few scant meters in front of the extraction slick, one of the NVA troops disregarded the deadly gunships, and fired a thirty-round full-magazine burst from his AK-47 toward the rising helicopter.

Rounds smacked against the rear bulkhead of the cabin, and in an instant Kelly heard a change, an unwinding, in the engine's turbine howl. He saw the gunner sitting beside him take a bullet in the shoulder, shattering his collarbone and splattering meat. He saw the pilot turn and try to speak with a crimson pencil-hole an inch below his right eye, and he knew that the aircraft had been fatally struck. Looking for a soft place to land, trying not to think of the whirling blade and the loaded tanks of gasoline, Kelly leaped clear of the ship.

The big delta-model slick slid forward as it settled, and when the rotor struck a tree trunk, the helicopter wrenched over sideways and slammed against the ground. Ripped free of its mounts, the engine screamed to a stop, and pieces of the rotor flew in all directions.

Though the PZ was filled with sound, it seemed to Kelly that a sudden terrible silence had settled around him. He looked up to see one of the gunships breaking off, tracers streaking both from it and toward it as the door gunners battled the hidden NVA soldiers. Small arms fire crackled all around him, and the PZ stank of the sweet sickening odors of cordite explosives, shattered earth, and spilled fuel. A Vietnamese rose from the brush only a few feet from him, and the recon soldier almost shot him before recognizing him as one of the Rangers of his team. A high nasal voice yelled something in Vietnamese, and a burst of fire chopped the side of the helicopter above them. They could hear the enemy troops hacking and crashing through the jungle, trying to get close enough to the stricken team that the gunships couldn't get their fire on them. His own fluency with the language was minimal, but he had a good repertoire of curses and insults. Yelling to inform the attacking troops that they had no genitals, and that he would pee on the graves of their mothers, he worked his way around to the other side of the wreck. He found a pair of legs sticking out from beneath the crumpled metal, oozing blood. The body had been crushed a foot into the soft soil. "Rose?" he shouted.

"Gimme a hand," came the urgent reply from inside the ship. At once Kelly jumped up onto the hulk to a place where he could look down into the cabin. An easy but defiant target for the enemy snipers, he stood exposed and sprayed the jungle around him with fire from his stubby commando-model M-16. Mel was standing on the torn shrubbery under the open side door, trying to help the wounded gunner climb to escape. At his feet, the shoulders and head of the crushed Ranger stiffly stuck face-up from the dirt beneath the wreck, the face a mask of pop-eyed horror, with streams of blood oozing from mouth and ears. Kelly grabbed the staggering gunner by the back of his blood-soaked flak jacket, and using strength he could not normally have called upon, he jerked the man halfway out. Conscious, but in shock and confusion, the gunner fell to the ground and clawed for cover.

"That pilot's dead," said Mel to Betts and the crew chief, who were trying to free Cronin's body from its armored seat. "Let's get out of here before they shoot something heavy at us." He grabbed a handhold and pulled himself to the top of the wreck with Kelly, then jumped down to make room for the other two men. Halfway out of the ship, Betts took a round in the leg and stumbled back. The crew chief clutched at him, pushed him the rest of the way out, then jumped down after him and helped him move back toward the center of the PZ away from the downed helicopter.

"Watch your ammo," called Kelly. "Let the gunships do the shooting unless you've got meat in your sights." The team and the flight crewmen returned the enemy's fire, slapping fresh magazines into their M-16's and lashing the jungle with the tiny high-powered bullets. A gunship dived toward them, miniguns spitting crimson streams of tracers, and making a sound like a huge sheet of canvas being ripped. He was amazed to hear another sound, which set his scalp prickling until he recognized it as the demonic howl of a fire siren.

"Down!" yelled Mel, and the men hugged depressions in the ground as the chopper's tubes began to slam four-foot rockets into the enemy's position. SSSSHHHOOOORRHAK! RRHAK! RRHAK! The rounds struck beyond the wreck, about forty meters away, and the team could clearly hear the enemy troops screaming in pain, and shouting orders as the deadly gunships pounded the jungle around them. Grabbing his PRC-25, Mel yelled, "Beautiful! Move that shit closer about halfway." That was calling for unusual accuracy, Mel knew, as the bursting radius of the rocket warheads was about fifteen meters. But the enemy were that close, and if the gunship drivers weren't that good, well, so long LRRPS. "There's eight of us alive, some wounded, and we're taking heavy fire," he called. "Is there any way you can get in to get us out?"

There was a moment of silence, then the voice of Captain Jack Miller came up on the FM freq, high and cracking with fear. "Sweetheart, Checker Lead. Get to the center of that hole and pop another smoke. I'm going to try to get you out."

Then another voice cut in, "Checker Lead, this is Dagger One-five, with another gunship about zero-three out. Hang in there, and you'll have a heavy fire team."

"Glad to have you with us, Bullseye," said Duke Randall. "Get behind the Frog and join the party."

"Roger. Glad to see you, too," replied Eddie eagerly. "I heard you'd gone down. Goddamn, it looks hot in there. You're taking fire all over the place."

Kevin squeezed his trigger again and again, awed even in the heat of the action that he could see streams of tracers coming back up at him as the NVA held their ground and fired back into the face of the terrible miniguns. As the gunship made its pass, he saw the incoming fire from several places, and he felt as though he were on some kind of macabre carnival wheel.

"OK, Checker Lead," called Duke as he rolled off his attack and climbed up for another. "We're down to fifty percent. It's got to be all or nothing on this one. Get under me on this pass, and I'll follow you down."

From the third slick, Ramsey called, "Lead, suggest I make a pass in front of you to draw fire and keep some heads down. I've got Ritchey aboard with his M-79."

"Can you get in front of me?"

"Let's go, Checkers! We can't sustain this rate of fire much longer."

"I can get there, Lead. Let's go."

"Roger. Receiving....oh, shit!"

"Checker, this is Pride. You're drawing fifty-cal fire from the ridge. I'm going to put the jets on it."

The FAC dived almost vertically, fired two phosphorous spotting rockets from his wing to mark the position of the enemy guns, then zoomed steeply away with tracers flashing after him. As the first of the big Phantom jets swooped down to blast the ridgeline with its 20mm cannons, Duke rolled in to begin his gun run covering Jack Miller. Ahead, Checker Three dived to a position in front of Miller's ship and drove toward the tiny pickup zone with both doorguns spitting rounds, and with Ritchey hanging out of the side door plunking grenades from his M-79 into the trees ahead.

Duke made his pass much slower than usual, decelerating with the slicks and hanging in the air above them, a fine platform from which to provide covering fire, but a most vulnerable one. Twice Kevin felt the subtle but unmistakable thunk of bullets striking the rotor blade, and he remembered how badly damaged it had been already. Duke ignored the hits and continued down, carefully placing rockets one at a time around the PZ. Then Kevin heard a shattering, a ringing blow, and saw Duke knocked back into his seat. He felt a jerk as the big pilot clutched at the controls, and he flashed a glance over to see that the front of Duke's plastic sunvisor had been shattered, and there was a line of blood running down the side of his nose.

"My God, he's been shot," thought Kevin. He quickly took the controls, made a rapid adjustment in the collective lever setting, then tightened the friction ring to hold it in place, freeing his left hand. Flying with his right hand, he held the pistol-grip in his left and kept the deadly shower of bullets raining down on the enemy below. Beside him, Duke jerked off his helmet, revealing a gash on his face where the shattered plastic had been forced through the skin. He grabbed the broken visor, wrenched it out and threw it aside, then shoved the helmet back onto his head.

"I've got it," he yelled. Almost on the treetops, he tipped the gunship on its side and broke off his run, siren screaming in defiance. "Took a round in the rocket sight. Damn thing hit me in the face." Kevin saw in front of Duke the ruined rocket sight, its heavy glass plate knocked from the mounting by the bullet and hurled into the pilot's face.

As Checker Lead settled into the smoke-filled hole in the jungle, Miller squeezed his mike trigger to broadcast and began to stutter through teeth obviously chattering, "Keep that stuff coming, Daggers, we've gotta get out of here this time. We only got one chance. Ok, let's go, let's go out there!"

Mel was the first to get to the ship, and would be the last man aboard. He looked up and saw Captain Miller's face, white, knotted with fear, and even over the roar of the rotor and the howl of the turbine he could hear the pilot shouting, "Let's go! Let's go out there! Move your asses!"

The first man up the ladder was Garza, followed by one of the Rangers of the team, and the wounded crew of the downed helicopter. Fifteen feet away, Kelly crouched and fired his M-16 to provide covering fire. He darted toward the open door of the helicopter, then something struck him like a huge fist, knocking him off his feet. Stunned, he lay groping for consciousness, his hands clawing for his weapon. Then a pair of hands grabbed him by the straps of his pack and hoisted him toward the open door of the chopper.

Miller flashed a look back to see what was holding up the team, and he saw that Kelly couldn't get up the ladder, but was pulling gamely at the ropes, blood streaming down his face. He looked around the aircraft quickly and allowed it to settle another few feet into the brush. As the rotor chopped into the vegetation, it made a sound like a string of firecrackers exploding. The tiny limbs and branches were cutting gashes and dents into the skin of the rotor, rips which could catch the air as the blade whipped around, and peel the skin. Miller bit his lip and fought to hold back the urge to scream.

Overhead the gunships were still blasting away, but the ammunition was clearly beginning to run short. Miller held his ground as Mel hefted Kelly high enough that the others could grab him, then he stepped up onto the ladder. As soon as Mel was off the ground, the crew chief slapped Miller on the back to let him know they all were aboard. Keeping one eye on the trees and the other on his torque meter, Miller applied full power to the rotor. The ship rose up sharply, then turned with nose low to sprint back across the A Lan valley. Mel was clambering up the rope ladder as the slick cleared the treetops, and was just inside the cabin when the men again heard the tinny plinking of rounds hitting the ship. With a look of surprise, Mel suddenly sagged to the floor. Kelly tried to sit up, fighting the roaring pain in his head, and he saw the familiar slick stain spreading darkly around the hole in Mel's shirt.

Spec-4 Stevens, Miller's crew chief, had also been hit, somewhere in his lower back. He was not losing much blood, but he sat on his bench looking stunned, and pensive. He carefully pulled his lap belt tight and held onto his M-60, watching as one of his limp and unfeeling legs flopped out to swing in the wind.

Mel's shirt was soaked with blood, and as they turned him over, the shirt moved wrong, as though he had something alive under it, a rat or a snake. His eyes, glassy and quivering, focused for an instant, and just before he died, he said, "My God, my fucking guts."

As Captain Jack Miller pulled up out of the hole, Duke Randall made a final pass to cover the slick. He was out of rockets, and Kevin was down to his last few minigun rounds. As he fired the guns, Kevin saw a soldier in pajama fatigues step out from behind a tree and carefully take aim at him with an RPG, a bazooka-like Russian-made rocket propelled grenade. He held the ring of light on the man, concentrating the fiery streams from his miniguns, but still the Vietnamese infantryman held his aim, ignoring the rounds splashing the bark from the trees beside him. Kevin's jaw dropped in amazement as the soldier stood his ground and launched his weapon. The rocket streaked directly toward the gunship, and Kevin was horribly certain it would strike them right in the middle of the windshield. Then it flashed beside the ship and struck the door post at Duke Randall's side.

The explosion rocked the helicopter violently, and pieces of shrapnel tore through the cockpit. Kevin took a terrible ringing blow on the head, as though someone had clubbed him with a bat. The world went glassy, and rang with a sound that squeezed him with tremendous pressure. Like stop-motion, he watched pieces of Duke Randall's legs fly up against the instrument panel. The ship shuddered and slewed around sideways, and Kevin watched his own foot slide forward to make an automatic correction in the pedal setting. Tossing the pistol-grip aside, he took the controls, noting the peculiar burning sensations in his arms and legs. The aircraft shuddered and lurched as the rotor began to shed its skin. Nose-high and settling fast, the helicopter hung on its fluttering rotor, and when Kevin pulled pitch just before impact, the top surface of the damaged blade tore away and chunks of the honeycomb inside flew out. The rotor folded and splintered an instant before the tail struck the underbrush. The body of the helicopter wedged itself between the limbs of a great gnarled tree, and came to rest.

Captain Duke Randall slumped in his harness, with half his face blown away, and the gunner behind him dangled across the minigun pylon. Kevin opened his lap belt and cabin door and jumped down to the jungle floor. Apparently unhurt, the crew chief took one look at Kevin, and moved quickly to help him. Kevin motioned him away, in his shock completely unaware that his own clothes and his skin were hanging in tatters, and that he still wore on his head a steel, ceramic, and anti-ballistic-fiberglass helmet from which the top four inches had been ripped, exposing the bloody pulp of his scalp.

They had flown far enough away from the PZ to escape the ground troops for the time being, and they had gone down in an area open enough that they could be seen from the air, and so that a rope could be dropped to them from a helicopter in a high hover. Almost immediately, Checker Three was over them, and the crew chief waved to Lt. Ritchey, who threw out the long rope with the loop of nylon webbing which the Green Berets called a McGuire Rig. Kevin looked up and waved at Buddy Nichols, who took pictures as the crew chief struggled to get the wounded and shock-disoriented pilot to sit in the loop of nylon webbing. He put Kevin in the loop, then sat straddling him so he could put his arms around him to grasp the straps and hold both of them in the simple sling. Just as the helicopter began to lift them from the trees, a stream of fifty-caliber fire began to lash at it. Kevin looked up to see a gunship bearing down to cover the slick, miniguns flashing, and he watched as the heavy fire switched to the gunship, and hit it.

Eddie could clearly hear the jarring thunk of rounds hitting his ship as the enemy gunner found his range. Someone, it might have been him, was yelling, "Taking hits, Holy Shit, we're getting..." He pulled in power until the rotor began to lose RPM, and the strident tone of the warning horn cut through his earphones. He heard a scream which had not come over the intercom, and he looked over and saw Swomney clutching at his minigun sight, fear sharpening the lines in his face.

"I'm hit...I'm bleeding...ooh," somebody croaked on the intercom. The ship shuddered and lurched, diving out of the path of the deadly fire. For a second, Eddie felt a wave of relief. Then he knew something was wrong. The nose of the ship began to come up quickly. He shoved the cyclic forward slightly, then more as the helicopter failed to respond to his control movements. In sudden horror Eddie moved the stick wildly in all directions, but still the nose came up steadily. The airspeed began to fall off and the rotor began to wap, biting the air as the bird slowed.

"Take the controls!" he shouted to Swomney. "My controls are out!" Swomney grabbed the controls and grimly moved them in all directions. He dropped the collective, hoping that would halt the rising of the nose. By then it had risen over halfway to vertical, higher than Eddie had ever raised it himself.

Hanging fifty feet below the accelerating slick, Kevin watched in awe as the gunship climbed into the noonday sun, tilting toward that point from which a helicopter cannot recover. "The other minigun ship — that's the Bullseye. He's dead on the stick, or else...no...he's had his control mixing bellcrank shot out!" In fascination, he watched Eddie's gunship run out of speed and began to tip over onto its back. It jerked suddenly as the rotor blade slammed into the tail boom, knocking chunks flying. The blade began to disintegrate and the ship tumbled wildly. From one side of the aircraft the crew chief spilled like a rag doll. He flapped there for a few seconds on the end of his monkey strap as the wind and the gyrations of the ship beat him against the weapons pylon. Then a strip from the rotor struck him, cutting him loose to spin toward the ground.

As the nose of the ship pointed to the sky, Eddie knew the cold finality of certain death. He tried to cry out, and a wave of nausea swept him. Then as the rotor blade struck the tail boom and the ship began to tumble, a strange calm flowed over him. Swomney slammed the cyclic back and forth with mad force, and Eddie saw him push it forward until it began to bend. Eddie didn't notice the grinding of metal as the blade splintered and the transmission tore itself free of its mounts. He gripped the sides of his seat to keep from being flung around, and he gave himself up to helplessness.

A curious realization came upon him. "Why, I've always

been falling like this," he thought. Free at last of all hope, he looked upon his life as past, as though to take final reckoning. Like a child awakening from a bad dream, he discovered with delight that he could almost recall something so wonderful, so important he knew he could never really have forgotten it. He looked around himself a last instant, saw high overhead an eastbound jet liner cut a contrail of icy lace across the crystal blue sky, and saw below him the tracers streak after the fast-departing slick with the rescued men dangling on the long rope beneath it. Then as the jungle swallowed his broken body of metal and flesh, he laughed, a bright unechoed note.

SEVENTEEN

After the trip to Fort Wolters, Roger's condition went
downhill pretty fast. He slept most of the day, rising occasionally
to drink, or to stagger to the bathroom. In the afternoons, Kevin
put firewood into the big stone-faced fireplace and turned on the
television set, and Roger would come dragging himself out of his
bedroom. Often as not he was nude, and mumbling apologies
about how pleasant it was to be among people who didn't care
about such minor niceties. Kevin tried to maintain a
nonchalance, but he was appalled by the destruction Roger's
habits had caused. Though the big man still weighed close to
three hundred pounds, his legs were almost as thin as Kevin's
own — and he was a wiry one-forty-five. The cheeks of his ass
were sunken and flaccid, and only a wrinkle of his foreskin
protruded, dripping ochre. His shoulders had become bony, with
skin stretched thin and ash-gray. His hands and feet were clumsy
swollen appendages, and his hands were stained with tobacco
smoke and scarred with burn sores between the fingers. As
though embracing him with arms of fat around his kidneys, the
gross distended bag of his guts hung on him like a corpulent
parasite sucking the life from the shriveling body of its host. His
face sagged, a half-melted mask of horror, the greasy purple-
green of the undead. His nose bled often, and his scraggly
moustache was crusted with blood and snot. His lips were
swollen and burned, and when he coughed, his tongue protruded,
looking like raw pork frosted with patching plaster and lard. His
eyes were almost mustard yellow, and gazed sorrowfully out
from beneath heavy lids.

"Jesus, look at the size of my liver," he groaned. "I think this
is the night, Harrey. You've got to promise me in writing, no
matter what happens, I don't want to get taken to any doctor or
hospital. Don't let them get me in there with their tubes up my
ass and their hands in my pockets. I want to be here at home,

like my Dad." When Kevin assured him he wouldn't take him to the hospital, Roger patted him on the shoulder. "Good. I appreciate that, you know. I wish everybody else could just come over and party and have a good time like nothing was happening."

Kevin stayed in the Castle with him, resolved to see it through. Once a day he made a drive into town to the package store, and to Roger's favorite taco joint. Assuring Kevin that his health was on the upswing, and that he would soon be flying airplanes again if he just made sure to eat properly, he would order a double basket of tacos with green chile. An hour later he would be leaning on the back of the toilet tank, retching up the spicy food. Then he would wash his mouth out with vodka and soda, smoke a cigarette, and settle down with his bottle to watch movies and drink until late at night. When the programs were bad, they talked about flying jets, and sky diving.

A few days before Christmas, Kevin sat in the living room by the fireplace and listened to Roger snore in his room. After a while he stood up and walked down the hall, and ignoring the stench of vomit and piss which pervaded the dark and fetid bedroom, he leaned against the doorjamb and watched. Lying on his back, Roger snuffled and gasped, his chest heaving even in sleep as his body tried to breathe in enough oxygen with ruined lungs and polluted blood. Again Kevin considered the idea of just ending Roger's misery. It would be simple, painless, and would leave no trace whatsoever. All he had to do was go into the kitchen and get two feet of plastic refrigerator wrap, and carefully wrap it around the sleeping man's face. More cling — no leak — and Roger would be gone in two minutes without a struggle. Again he decided it was not his place, even if it was motivated only by a desire to end the man's suffering. It was Roger's suffering after all, and in any case, it would not be long.

Christmas came and passed unnoticed except for the holiday's intrusion into the regular programming of the television stations. On the morning of the day after Christmas, Roger shuffled down the hall, through the living room, and around to the side of the house to pound on Kevin's door. "Harrey! Goddamnit, Harrey, you've got to let me in!" It was the first time in several days that

Roger had walked that far, so Kevin was sure there must be some emergency. He jumped out of bed, birdwalked shuddering across the cold floor, and opened the door. Roger stood groggily leaning against the wall, wearing only his Marine overcoat. His yellow eyes glowed and protruded with horror. "Harrey, you've got to get up and go into town. You've got to."

"What is it? What the fuck do you need in town?"

"You've got to get me some cigarettes. I can't even find a decent butt. If I can just get a cigarette, I'll be all right." He began to blubber and weep, standing in the doorway so Kevin could not close it to keep out the freezing winter air.

"Cigarettes! Roger, dear boy, you try my patience. Haul your slimy ass out of here, and go back and put your pants on. Go on, you walked out here, you can walk back. I'll be in there in just a few minutes." Kevin shut the door behind him and returned to his bed, grumbling curses. He started to get into it, then put on his pants instead. A few minutes later he went into the living room, where he found Roger standing by the fireplace trying to put on his pants. Holding the jeans with both hands, he stood wobbling back and forth, trying to get one foot or the other to come up off the floor.

"OK, Big Rog, here's the deal. We're going to find out if you still have anything left to live for. If you really have to have that cigarette, then you and I are going to walk down the road to Anaya's service station and buy some. It's just about one last mile down there and back. We walk it together, or we die here for lack of tobacco. What's it going to be?"

Roger wept and complained, swore his stomach was too upset, his liver too inflamed, his feet too swollen, and his heart too broken to walk. Kevin held his ground, and shortly the two left the house and walked beside the bare chile fields in the crystal cold clarity of a bright winter morning. Wearing his overcoat, boots, and a knit stockingcap, Roger shuffled slowly along like an animated corpse from a voodoo movie. When they got to the old plastered-adobe station, Roger told Kevin to get some bouillon cubes and a carton of cigarettes. Kevin started to tell him the salt probably wouldn't be good for his already-overloaded kidneys, then he nodded. "Bouillon. Good thinking," he said.

Kevin left Roger standing outside, and stepped into the little store. When he came back out, Roger had found a bench, and had slumped onto it. "How about leaving me a pack of those cigarettes and bringing the truck back here to get me?" he suggested, whining.

"On your feet, Jarhead," Kevin snapped. "You've got one more hill to take." They lit cigarettes, shuffled in silence, stopping from time to time for Roger to cough and wheeze. Then, as they walked along the road through the bare fields, Roger began to chuckle.

"What the hell, Big Rog?" Kevin asked.

"Look at us," said Roger. "We look just like those two guys in 'Of Mice and Men'. You remember, the little guy and the big guy who got his brains kicked out? Hey, listen to this: 'Duhh, tell me about the airplanes, George. Tell me about the airplanes.' Haw, haw, haw."

Kevin put his arm around the big man's slumped shoulders and laughed too, tears springing to his eyes. "God, Big Rog. What a life, huh?"

"Yep. This is it."

A few days later, on New Year's Eve, Roger called Kevin back into the bedroom where he had stayed since the day they had walked into town for the cigarettes. The bed was a tangle of stained sheets and an old Army sleeping bag, and it was pocked with the black marks of many cigarette burns. Beside the bed sat the bottom five inches of a plastic soda bottle which Roger had hacked off to use for his ash tray and spittoon. He had filled it with filter butts and spit into it until it overflowed, and the spittle and blood had soaked the butts to a soggy mass which flowed down the sides of the plastic and formed a glistening scarlet-and-black pool of clotting slime on the carpet. "That," Kevin concluded silently, "is the single most horrid and revolting thing I have ever seen."

Roger raised an arm weakly and pointed toward his closet. "Top shelf," he said. Kevin looked, and saw a metal filing box about a foot on a side. Roger nodded, and motioned for Kevin to bring him the box. He fumbled with the lock, then opened it and pawed among the few papers it contained. He took out a sealed envelope — marked with dirty fingerprints — and tucked it under his pillow. "For later," he said. Kevin nodded. Roger hesitated a long time, then sighed with a deep shudder and handed Kevin an 8-by-10 glossy print of a photograph.

The picture had been taken from almost exactly the same place where Kevin stood, at the foot of Roger's bed. A Navajo Indian blanket had been spread across it, and on it sat a young woman, nude. Kevin's guts knotted, and his ears rang. It was Carlie, young and very beautiful. She sat with the soles of her feet together, and she was leaning back against the pillow and seductively holding her labia open with both hands. She wore a vacant, self-indulgent, freshly-fucked expression, and her long hair tumbled to her shoulders. He stared for a long moment struggling with his churning emotions until the significance of that long hair suddenly struck him. When he had returned from Vietnam the first time, he had found his young wife a serious mother with an infant and a new short-shag haircut. The girl in the picture had not yet come to him pregnant, and had not yet married him on the eve of his departure to war.

Suddenly oblivious to the filth, Kevin sat down on the end of the bed. "Why didn't you marry her, Roger?" he asked.

His face streaked with tears, Roger shrugged. "You know why. When you came through here back in 1969, I ran for the phone the minute you were out the door. But I never made the call. I couldn't do it, Harrey, I just couldn't face it. I couldn't call Eddie a hero and then shit on you at the same time. And I didn't have the guts to stand up for you then....because I still wanted her."

"What about George?" Kevin asked.

Roger shrugged again. "He looks like her," he said simply. They sat there for a long moment, staring at the picture lying on the bed, then Roger handed Kevin an opened envelope and put the file box onto the floor beside the bed. He rolled to his side and lay sobbing softly into his pillow. "Fucking Jody," he blubbered. "Fucking Jody."

The envelope contained a letter from Carlie, dated in late October, and addressed to him in care of Roger Stanton. "Dear

Kevin," she wrote, "I heard on the jungle drums that you are in San Manuel with Roger. So many times I have wished that we could sit down and talk again. I have been through so many things since I last saw you, and I know you have too, and it seems like all of the things that meant so much to me back then don't mean anything at all now. I try to remember who we really were back then, and it's all pretty unclear. I guess the truth is that we never really had time to get acquainted during all those years, and I often wish I had known you better. George is going to be fourteen next Valentine's Day, and he is getting to look more and more like you. He is the best disco dancer in his school, and makes straight A's (almost). If you can forgive me for being young and stupid, and you would like to get together again sometime, just to see....my phone is listed under C.G. Harrey."

He looked up to speak to Roger, but the big man had fallen asleep. He nodded, left the picture lying on the bed, and went back to the fireplace.

Two days later, Kevin returned to Roger's bedroom in the morning to check on him, and found him dead. He went back to his room, rolled himself a joint, lit it, then went to the kitchen and fixed himself a cup of instant coffee in the microwave. Then after a while, he went back into the bedroom and pulled the envelope from beneath Roger's pillow. It contained a single page, a hand-scrawled, but still quite clear Last Will and Testament which Roger had made up and dated a few days after the Fort Wolters trip. It had not been notarized, but it bore Roger's fingerprints in blood. It was simple. It stipulated that half of his estate, whatever that should be, was to be given to Kevin Harrey, and the other half was to be given to Carlie.

Kevin stood beside the bed and cried, and for the first time since he had understood what Roger had wanted of him, he wished truly that he had known some way to save the man. "You didn't have to do it, Big Rog," he said softly. "Not because of Vietnam, and not because of Carlie. It's just not that big a thing."

In the first week of 1980, Kevin Harrey stood on the mesa west of the Mesilla Valley and looked down upon the little town of San Manuel. He marveled at how little it had changed in the years since he first saw it. He shuddered, not with the evening chill, but as his mind rushed back over all he had been through those years, and he wondered if he had really changed at all.

He turned to face the Green Castle, then walked quickly inside and found a number in the El Paso telephone book. In a few seconds, he heard Carlie's voice. He hesitated, his words catching in his throat. "Carlie? It's me, Kevin. I'm up at the Green Castle."

"Oh! Oh, hi! Kevin, I'm delighted. I was afraid you had decided never to call me."

Tears flushed Kevin's eyes as he heard the earnestness in her voice. "I just got your letter today. It was with the will. Carlie, Roger Stanton is dead."

She was silent for a long time, then she sighed. "I'll miss him," she said.

"You're in his will — for half the estate."

"I see. And the other half?"

"It's mine."

"Well, that wily bastard," she said, finally. "So we either make up or fight over it, huh? Can I come up there, now?"

"You can, but you don't want to. Give me a day to get the body handled and the place cleaned out a bit, OK?"

"OK. Tomorrow night, after work? I'm running a weight-loss clinic, making a bunch of money, but it really demands that I be there all the time."

"Fine. Sounds like you're doing great. Carlie?"

"Yes?"

"You can't imagine how much I want to see you."

"Me too. Oh, do you want to talk to George?"

"George? Uh...yeah."

She took the phone from her face and said something, then he heard the boy take the receiver. "Hey, what's happening?" said a youthful voice.

"Hi. Uh...is this George?" he asked hesitantly.

"Yeah. It's me, George. So you're my Dad, huh? Hey, is it all right if I call you Kevin?"

"Sure. Sure, that's fine with me."

"Hey, wow, I'm really looking forward to meeting you," said

the boy eagerly. "Mom says you were one hell of a war hero — uh, sorry, Mom. So tell me, Kevin, is it true? Were you really the hottest gunship pilot in Vietnam?"

Kevin tipped back his head and laughed tearfully, joyfully, and silently, then struggled to answer him. "You're damn right I was, Son," he said with pride choking his voice, "and I'm looking forward to telling you all about it."

THE END

American Honor Books

BLOOD OF MONTENEGRO, with Bajram Angelo Koljenovic
 -- an epic three-generation family historical novel.
FORGOTTEN SOLDIERS, Bajram Angelo Koljenovic
 -- the tragedy of Bosnia.

www.americanhonorbooks.com

The Scribes Of Osiris

SEDONA ESOTERICA -- Dowsing / IChing / Candles
 -- about psychometry, magic, and divination.
THE STONE VESSEL OF SAQQARA, by Anne Forrest
 -- a tale of the Old Kingdom, of Pharoahs and scribes.

www.thescribesofosiris.org

NewPulp Publishing

THE SAM COHEN CASE ADVENTURES, with Shelly Waxman.
 -- hardcorps action with a tough maverick Chicago lawyer.

www.postpubco.com/newpulp.htm

Postscript Publishing Company

LOST ILLUSIONS
 -- a counter-culture novel of the seductive 1970's.
THREE TALES IN LASTIMA
 -- romantic action comedy in 1850's old New Mexico.
KING'S KNIGHT, A Science-Fiction Anthology
 -- still-prophetic 1970's SF aboutliving in virtual reality.
THE ANTI-CYCLOPS PAPERS
 -- the collected cage-rattling column essays.

www.postpubco.com

About The Author

James was born Aquarius 1943, raised near White Sands, New Mexico, son of a rocket radio engineer and an artist. In high school a science-fair winner, thespian, and president of Chess and Writing clubs, he wrote his first novel (utterly non-publishable) and lost the only copy. A better athlete than his slender build and techno-geek ways led folks to suspect, he was a winning swimmer, gymnast, and wrestler in college. Seeking to enhance his peer status, he resolved to get tough. After two years at remote New Mexico Tech studying geophysics, James dropped out in 1963 to enter Marine Corps jet pilot training. Though fully trained, unfortunate circumstances kept him from serving in the jets. Not to be denied his desire to fly combat aircraft, he retrained and served as an Army helicopter gunship pilot with the 101st Airborne in Vietnam, 1968. He was decorated for valor, including the Distinguished Flying Cross, but drummed out of service for smoking marijuana. He became a flight instructor and Forest Service helicopter pilot briefly, then seeking to put youthful dreams behind, he resolved to get free and discover truth. There is a seeker born (again) every minute. After going from the DMZ to Woodstock in 1969, James tuned in, turned on, and dropped out. Sex, drugs, rock'n'roll, and religion. Psychedelics, Scientology, Wicca, Tao, and Jesus. Three quick divorces. Folk music composer, stage and film actor, singer, playwright, TV show host, and occult publisher's editorial assistant. Ordained a non-denominational minister, and founder of The Scribes Of Osiris. Resolving to select a workable truth and settle down, in 1980 he returned to his home town Las Cruces to raise a family. They went to high school in Las Vegas NV, where James enjoyed being a professional sports book player. He now lives in Albuquerque, and continues to write and perform, and produces a public-access TV series, The Fringe Element.

33332336R00163

Made in the USA
Columbia, SC
09 November 2018